DEVILFISH

OCTOPIAN SHIFTERS BOOK 1

ANNA KENSING

Cover photo: Period Images

Cover design: Anna Kensing

Editing: Laura Blackwell

ISBN: 978-1-7342344-0-4 (paperback)

ISBN: 978-1-7342344-1-1 (ebook)

CHAPTER 1

*A*t the sound of breaking glass, Elliot Bishop closed the book he was reading. He hadn't put the latch on the front door for the night because he often received late messengers from one of his warehouses. Besides, burglary was uncommon in uptown Port Townsend, unlike the petty thievery and debauchery that occurred every day and all night downtown. He listened hard. It had been blustery all day; if someone had left a window open somewhere, perhaps the wind had simply blown something over.

The floorboards outside his study creaked, and Elliot set his book aside and got up. Grabbing a poker from the fireplace, he crept to the half-closed door to the study. He pressed against the wall behind the door and waited. The door slowly opened further, and Elliot tightened his grip on the iron shaft.

The shadowy figure moved into the room and Elliot rushed from behind the door, poker lifted in both hands to smash down on the intruder's head. A gloved hand stretched up and caught it before it made impact. Elliot kept hold of the poker in his left hand and drove his right fist into the intruder's side. The man twisted under Elliot's arm, tearing the poker from him and tossing it onto the carpet behind him.

The only sources of light in the room were the fire and the small oil lamp Elliot had been reading by, so it was too dark to see the intruder clearly. Elliot blocked the man's left hook but flinched at a right jab into his ribs. They fought for a few furious minutes until the man hooked his leg behind Elliot's and jerked his feet out from under him. He fell on top of Elliot and drove the breath from Elliot's chest.

Elliot scrabbled a hand on the floor, feeling for the poker, a chair leg, anything to smash into the man's head. And then the man chuckled next to his ear, a sound he'd know anywhere. He froze so that he didn't arc up against the now-familiar weight pressing down on him.

"Declan? What the hell are you doing here?"

Declan chuckled again, his breath raising the fine hairs on Elliot's neck. "You're a little rusty, aren't you? Gotten a little soft with all your fine living?"

Enough of this. Elliot hooked his leg around Declan's, pushed his left hand into Declan's shoulder, and leveraged his right elbow to flip them over, pinning Declan beneath him.

Declan grunted. "Not that rusty after all, eh?" His breath smelled like whiskey, and Elliot couldn't stop a shiver of pleasure at being this close to Declan after all these years.

Declan tapped him on the shoulder twice. "Let me up, you big oaf."

Elliot got up before he could do anything he'd regret, like crush his lips to Declan's or bury his face in the man's neck. He reached a hand down to pull Declan up, then took a few steps back toward the fire and the armchair he'd been sitting in.

"What the hell are you doing here?" he repeated.

Declan's eyes roamed around the room and caught sight of the half-empty tumbler on the table near Elliot's chair.

"Well, I was looking for a glass of quality whiskey." He headed straight for the sideboard, pulled his gloves off, and poured himself three fingers from the decanter. He saluted Elliot with the glass and took a long swallow.

"Ah," Declan sighed. Elliot shivered again, remembering the last time he'd heard Declan make sounds of pleasure like that. Declan winked at Elliot. "Much better than the swill they serve at the Delmonico." A soft smile lifted his full lips and crinkled his green eyes. "It's good to see you again, man," he said. The firelight gleamed on his disheveled hair, turning it chestnut and gold.

Before Elliot could respond, he heard another noise outside the study and tensed. It was only Celeste, hovering tentatively in the doorway, clutching a pale blue dressing gown around her.

"Elliot?"

Declan's head turned at the sound of her voice, tracking her movements as Elliot held his arm out and drew her into the room. Celeste tucked her hand under his elbow and looked curiously from Elliot to Declan.

Elliot sighed internally. It would have been easier if she'd stayed upstairs in the guest wing while he dealt with Declan, but he couldn't very well refuse to introduce her now.

"Celeste, allow me to introduce Mr. Declan Fitzgerald. Declan, this is Celeste Brady, my fiancée."

Declan glanced at Elliot, a startled look on his face. "Your fiancée?" Then Declan stepped forward and bent over Celeste's outstretched hand.

"Captain Fitzgerald," he corrected. "But please call me Declan. After all, we're about to be family. I'm Elliot's brother."

"Stepbrother." Elliot's turn to correct Declan. "Declan's father married my mother when I was an infant." He flushed at Declan's knowing glance. Why did he feel the need to clarify that they weren't blood relations?

"Wait…Captain?" he asked, turning to Declan. "Your father let you get your master's certificate?"

Declan still held Celeste's hand and bent over it, brushing his lips across her fingers. Ignoring Elliot, he said, "It's an honor to meet you—Celeste, was it? I can't imagine what my stepbrother did to convince any woman to marry him, much less a woman as beautiful as you."

Celeste blushed prettily and pulled her hand from Declan's— reluctantly, it seemed to Elliot—and dropped a small curtsy. "The honor is mine, Captain. It's a shame you missed our dinner party this evening."

Declan picked up his glass and leaned against the sideboard as Elliot tugged Celeste an appropriate distance from him. "And when is the happy event to take place?" he asked, eyes flicking between Elliot and Celeste over the rim of his glass as he sipped from it.

"Tuesday," Celeste answered, before Elliot could. "I do hope you're staying for a few days, Captain, and will stand up for Elliot at the wedding. I hope we get to know each other, as well. Elliot hardly talks about his family."

Declan gave Celeste the full, slightly crooked smile that Elliot had seen charm every woman he came across, ladies and parlor-maids alike. He lifted his half-empty whiskey glass to them and drained it.

"It would be my pleasure to get to know you, my dear. You must tell me how you managed to entice my brother into matrimony." He glanced sideways at Elliot. "Not a state I'd ever expected him to embrace."

Elliot squelched a flash of irritation. Of all the times for Declan to stroll back into his life. Elliot had spent the last five years building a safe, comfortable life and in only a few days, he'd be married. Why now, after all these years?

As if on cue, Declan bowed slightly to Celeste and said, "My apologies for getting you out of bed at such a late hour, my dear. Your intended and I have some family business to discuss. You surely have a hundred things to do before your big day. Please don't let us keep you up any longer."

Celeste looked at Elliot as if deciding whether she wanted to insist on staying. He smiled and gently steered her toward the door. "It's nothing you need to concern yourself with, darling. I'll see you in the morning."

He kissed her on the cheek, and she smiled back at him. "I was just checking to see if I left my reading glasses down here." Elliot found them on the corner of his desk and handed them over. Celeste drifted out of the room with a last curious glance at Declan.

Declan sat down in Elliot's chair near the fireplace and stretched his long legs out with a sigh. When he closed his eyes and turned his face to the fire, Elliot gave in and let his eyes travel the length of Declan's body. His black coat was tailored to fit his broad shoulders, and his white lawn shirt gleamed crisply in the firelight. His vest was black too, or maybe dark blue. Silk, Elliot thought, with leaves and vines embroidered in silver thread. Black trousers hugged his hips and strong thighs, ending over a pair of short black boots, recently shined.

"Captain, eh?" Elliot asked. "Looks like you've done well for yourself."

Declan shrugged. "Thought it was time to start dressing the part." He winked at Elliot. "Couldn't very well show up at my brother's wedding dressed like a common seaman, now could I?"

Elliot didn't point out that Elliot hadn't known where to send news of his engagement to Declan. Then Declan ran his fingers through his hair, brushing it out of his face and tugging it free of the leather thong that held the unfashionably long strands at the nape of his neck. His thick, glossy hair fell nearly to his shoulders, and Elliot snorted. It was reassuring that Declan seemed to be the same near-pirate as ever underneath his fine clothes.

He crossed to sit in the other chair in front of the fire. "Why are you here, Declan?" he asked quietly.

Declan sighed and looked directly at Elliot, his green eyes boring into him. "Father's missing. I need your help to find him."

"I'm sure he's fine. You know half the time his voyages take longer than he expects."

Declan shook his head. "This is different. We were supposed to meet at the usual place in Friday Harbor. I waited there for a week, but he never made it. The lighthouse keeper at Cape Flattery hasn't gotten any messages from him, and neither have any of the usual message drops. I've spent the last several months sailing up and down from San Francisco to Nootka Sound, and no one's seen or heard from him."

"That doesn't mean he's missing. Maybe he's just laying low, or looking for other buyers to avoid paying duties on his most recent cargo."

"If that were it, he'd have found some way to leave a message for me."

Elliot shrugged. "Well, what do you want from me?"

Declan looked at him like he'd suddenly sprouted tentacles. "I want you to help me find him. He's the closest thing you have to a father, and he's missing. Not to mention he's your primary source of those fancy goods you sell in your fancy uptown shops." Declan paused and took another sip of whiskey.

"I think he was close to finding out what happened to your mother when she disappeared. If only for that reason, I thought you'd want to come with me."

Elliot ignored the cold shiver that came over him every time he thought about his mother and her disappearance. "He always thinks he's close to finding out what happened to her. And yet he's never found any real answers. What makes this time any different?"

Declan pulled a folded square of paper from his inside coat pocket. He opened it and spread it across his knees, angling it toward the lamplight. The paper was soft and grubby from passing through who knows how many hands. The top right corner had been torn away, leaving a jagged, curved edge.

"Father left this for me in Friday Harbor."

Elliot leaned forward and examined the faint drawings and intersecting lines scattered over the paper. "It's a chart."

"Of course it's a chart. Look, here's Vancouver Island." Declan pointed to an elongated shape on the map. "And these are meant to be the Queen Charlotte Islands, I suppose," he jabbed his finger at a smaller triangular shape above Vancouver Island. "But this spot here," he traced lightly around a small dot marked farther west of the other islands on the chart, in what looked to Elliot like the middle of the Pacific Ocean, "is on none of the charts I'm familiar with."

Declan sat back in his chair and looked expectantly at Elliot like all this was supposed to mean something to him. Elliot scrubbed his hands over his face. The adrenaline from Declan's unexpected arrival was wearing off, and he'd already had a long day. He was tired, and thinking about the night his mother disappeared always made him feel ill. "So, the Captain sent you an old, inaccurate chart. I still don't see what this has to do with me."

Now Declan sighed, like Elliot's tutor used to when he caught Elliot daydreaming instead of conjugating Latin verbs. "Elliot, this is a chart showing an island more or less due west of here that no one's ever charted before. And it came from *Father*. He left it for me for a reason. I think it's the best clue he's found about where she went."

Elliot launched himself from his chair to stand before the fire, holding his hands out to it against the sudden chill in the room. He'd been a boy of eight when his mother had drowned in Port Townsend Bay. At least, that's what his stepfather had told everyone in town. Except Declan.

Declan spoke softly from his chair behind Elliot. "Don't you want to know? Find out for sure what happened to your mother?"

Elliot turned back to Declan, the fire barely warming him. "My mother drowned, Declan. In a storm that flooded half of downtown. I miss her every day, but drownings aren't that unusual here. I know the Captain thinks she was spirited away against her will or something, but there's no reason to think she's still alive."

Or that she wants to come back if she was, Elliot thought but didn't say out loud. The Captain had married his mother when Elliot was six months old, and since she had never given Elliot his name, most of the town gossips assumed she'd finally run off with whoever Elliot's real father was. And yet, the Captain had convinced himself the truth was far more complicated than simple infidelity.

Before Declan could say anything more, Elliot dropped back into his chair and held up a hand. "I'm tired, Declan. Can we talk about this in the morning, please?"

Declan drained the last of his whiskey and stood up. "Fine." Two long steps forward and he was crowding against Elliot, hands braced on the chair arms. He bent his head, and Elliot was suddenly sure Declan was going to kiss him. He couldn't decide whether to push him away or grab the back of his head and pull him the rest of the way down.

Declan's eyes narrowed as he looked Elliot over. "Tired, eh? Already experiencing wedded bliss with your fiancée? Does she like it when you—"

Elliot shoved Declan backwards, cutting off the rest of his sentence. "No! Damn it, Declan, shut your filthy mouth. I won't have you talking about her like that. She's properly chaperoned by her maid and staying in the guest wing. And she's about to be my wife. If you can't show her some respect, you can get the hell out of my house."

Declan shrugged and held his arms out in surrender. "Sorry, little brother. I'll be on my best behavior, I promise. I'm just a little surprised to find you engaged, that's all. Especially after…" He looked Elliot up and down with a lewd expression, and Elliot blushed.

"That was a long time ago, Declan, and we were just boys. It's time for me to grow up and settle down. Past time for you to consider the same."

Declan winked at him as he took a few steps back. "Never, Ellie, my lad. You know I'm not cut out for that. Too many places to see and people to do." Smiling in spite of himself, Elliot stood up and let Declan clap him on the shoulder and steer him toward the study door.

Declan slid a hand down Elliot's hip. "Once more before your wedding, for old time's sake?"

Elliot shoved him again, but playfully this time. "Not a chance, Declan. Your old room is still at the end of the hall. And don't make me lock my door against you."

Declan looked wounded. "I never go where I'm not wanted." Elliot snorted but wrapped an arm around Declan's shoulders as they went up the stairs together. God, it was good to have him back, whatever his reason for coming home. At the top of the stairs, Declan turned right willingly enough and Elliot called softly after him. "Good night, Declan. I'm glad you're home."

Declan threw a blinding smile over his shoulder. "Me too, man. I'll see you in the morning."

Elliot reached his bedroom and closed the door, hand hovering over the lock. He doubted that Declan would sneak into his room, but he knew he wouldn't be able to resist him if he did. Locking his door would send the right message: that he was serious about putting their past behind him and committing to his marriage to Celeste. Which he was, of course. He'd introduce Celeste properly to Declan tomorrow. Once Declan saw how happy she made Elliot, they could settle back into a normal, brotherly relationship. With a firm twist, he locked the door and got ready for bed.

CHAPTER 2

*E*ven with his late night, Declan's habit of rising with the sun meant he was the first up the next morning. Not much had changed in the Bishop house in the years he'd been away. The upstairs hall was quiet, bedroom doors closed, but he could hear faint stirrings in the kitchen downstairs. Sally Jenkins, housekeeper and cook for the Bishop household since before his father had married Elliot's mother, rose even earlier and would already have coffee brewing. He'd get some breakfast and catch up with Sally before discussing with Elliot what he knew about his father's most recent voyage.

Declan passed Elliot's bedroom and heard a soft groan from the other side. He paused. He'd only been teasing Elliot last night about taking up where they'd left off, but he wondered how much Elliot thought about those days. Another low moan, and Declan shook his head but kept walking. It wouldn't do to be caught listening outside his stepbrother's bedroom door while Elliot pleasured himself. He made a mental note to tease Elliot about investing in some thick curtains to muffle the sounds from his marital bed. For the servants' sake, at least.

He jogged down a few steps, then heard a louder groan, and

something that sounded like a drawn-out protest. That didn't sound like pleasure. He went back up the stairs and pressed his ear to the door. Elliot was breathing heavily, harsh pants that sounded like he was running hard, away from something.

Declan tapped lightly on the door and called Elliot's name softly. Elliot had been plagued by night terrors as a boy, ever since his mother disappeared. He used to crawl into Declan's bed in the middle of the night for comfort, which was how things started between them, after Elliot got old enough to crawl into Declan's bed for a different sort of comfort.

The nightmares happened less and less as Elliot got older, but Declan had never left Elliot to wake up from one on his own. He couldn't just walk away from him now. He knocked again, a little louder, then looked over his shoulder at the other doors along the hall. Elliot surely wouldn't appreciate him calling the whole house's attention to his nightmares. But the noises he was making were louder now, so it was just a matter of time before someone else heard. Declan turned the knob on the door. Locked. Damn it.

Declan tapped his thumb against his bottom lip, thinking. It stung a little that Elliot had followed through on his threat to lock his door last night. He'd never made uninvited advances to anyone, male or female, and had plenty of other sources for companionship these days. But Elliot wasn't waking up on his own, and he sounded truly frightened now. Declan would slip in quietly and shake Elliot awake, that's all.

The lock was easy to jimmy with his pocket knife, and Declan eased the door open and slipped into the same room Elliot had slept in since childhood. The same four-poster bed, same bed curtains that kept winter drafts at bay, tied back at the posts despite the damp early spring chill. Declan focused on the figure thrashing under the twisted bedclothes. The air was close and musty, with the sharp smell of Elliot's fear-sweat. Heavy, dark curtains were closed against the early spring air, and the coal in the fireplace had long burned down to cold ash.

Declan approached the bed and reached for Elliot's shoulder. Elliot slipped from his grasp as he rolled onto his side on the far edge of the bed. He wasn't wearing a nightshirt and when he turned over, he pulled the bedclothes with him, balling them up against his chest, exposing his back to the cool air. Declan couldn't help gazing at the smooth expanse of muscle and the narrow channel of his spine. He pulled his gaze away from where the curve of Elliot's ass disappeared under the bedclothes. Elliot was whimpering quietly now. It was past time to wake him up.

He had to kneel up on the bed to reach Elliot's shoulder, hot and damp under his hand. "Ellie," he whispered, squeezing firmly and shaking him a little. "Time to wake up, lad."

Elliot flopped over onto his back but didn't wake up. He'd stopped whimpering, at least. Declan shifted position to lie on his side along Elliot, propping his head up on his right hand and stroking his left over Elliot's sweaty forehead. He pushed the damp strands of hair off Elliot's face and murmured, "Come on, man. Wake up now." He hummed soothingly, a wordless lullaby he'd used on nights like these when Elliot was a boy.

Elliot's face relaxed, and his hands loosened the grip he had on the bedclothes. His eyes moved under his lids but didn't open. Declan kept stroking his forehead, smoothing his hair back and still humming. Elliot's body gradually relaxed, and his breathing changed from the harsh pants to soft sighs that suggested he was falling back into regular sleep. Declan debated waking him all the way up, but decided it would be better if he left before Elliot knew he was there. He stroked a hand down Elliot's stubbled jaw, over his collarbone, and down a firmly muscled arm just once. Then he pressed a light kiss to Elliot's forehead and shifted to get off the bed.

"Declan?" Elliot murmured. His eyes were still closed and he rolled onto his side again, this time right up against Declan. The warmth of his damp skin seeped through Declan's shirtfront, and he slung his arm over Declan's waist. "You came back," he whispered into Declan's shoulder.

Declan's heart ached. He hadn't wanted to leave in the first place. Declan didn't want to think about how he'd woken up after a night of carousing in Delmonico Saloon to find himself aboard the *Argonauta*, sick as a dog, with his father standing over him, a thunderous expression on his face. Not while he held Elliot's sleep-heavy body in his arms this morning.

"I came back," he agreed. Only to find that Elliot had gotten over him and decided to marry. He supposed it was no more than he deserved. Probably the right choice for Elliot—a normal life with a proper wife and helpmeet to support his position as a prosperous uptown merchant. Not the sometime paramour of a smuggler and sailor like Declan, away at sea as often as he was in the various ports he called in to on his voyages. He had his crew to take care of, anyway. He lifted Elliot's arm and tried again to slide out of his bed, but Elliot rolled on top of him.

Fuck, this was exactly how things had started between them. Declan had woken one late night to Elliot's mouth on his cock, Declan's hands fisted in the bedclothes, ready to burst as soon as Elliot moved his tongue the slightest bit. While he was away, he'd tried very hard not to think about the number of times that happened, but that familiar desire for Elliot had never really gone away, and Elliot's hard length pressed against his thigh made it difficult to concentrate on anything else now. Declan's own prick was rapidly filling, and he couldn't stop himself from pushing up, seeking friction through the layers of cloth separating them.

Elliot ground his hips against Declan's. He started panting again, his breath warm against Declan's shoulder, humping faster and faster until, with a low groan, he shuddered and slumped bonelessly against him. Declan couldn't keep himself from wrapping his arms around Elliot and holding him close. Until Elliot jerked his head up.

"Declan?" Elliot stared down at him. His hazel eyes were wide awake now and flickered from Declan's face to Declan's clothed body and his own half-naked one sprawled on top. "Oh, God," he said hoarsely. He rolled immediately off Declan and plucked the damp sheets away from his skin. Covering his face, he demanded, "What the hell are you doing in here, Declan?"

Declan rolled off the bed, stood, and adjusted himself. He'd been desperate for his own release but that was fading in the face of Elliot's reaction. He crossed the room to the tall casement windows and pulled the drapes open. The gray morning light brightened the dim room.

"You were having a nightmare," Declan said, still looking out the window. The Bishop house was built on a bluff overlooking the harbor, the bay shimmering silver in the haze. White plumes of fog rolled across the bay, obscuring and then revealing the greenery on the small island across the bay. The rooftops of downtown businesses were just visible on Water Street when he pushed the windows open and leaned out a little. A pair of gulls circled overhead, shrieking at each other, and the cool, damp February air blew in, clearing Declan's head and freshening the stuffy room.

Declan heard the bedclothes rustle as Elliot rose and poured water from the pitcher on the washstand into the bowl. "So, you broke into my room to wake me up?" His voice was muffled as he splashed water over his face. "I'm perfectly capable of taking care of myself, Declan."

Declan turned around and glanced deliberately at the sheet Elliot had wrapped around his hips. "Yes, I see how good you are at taking care of yourself."

Elliot flushed red, water droplets still dripping off his chin. He scrubbed at his face with a towel, then tossed it on the wash-stand, and ran his fingers through his hair. "You shouldn't have come in here, Declan."

There was a perfunctory knock on the door and the clang of a coal bucket set down outside. "Morning, Mr. Elliot," a young feminine voice called out. Declan raised an eyebrow at Elliot as her footsteps clomped along the hall.

Elliot sighed. "One of Sally's girls. They work as housemaids. They just leave the coal and hot water outside my door."

Declan couldn't resist a small chuckle. "Like Sally used to, when we were boys? Guess it's a good thing she taught them about privacy in this house."

Elliot glared at him. "I don't need that kind of privacy any more, Declan, because the things that used to happen between us are not happening again."

Declan glared back at him. He kept his voice low as the housemaid clomped past Elliot's room again and started down the stairs. "You tell yourself that, Elliot, but I didn't start anything here. You were making enough noise I could hear it from the stairs. I came in to wake you before you woke the whole house. What the hell kind of dream were you having anyway, that sounded like a nightmare and ended with you rubbing off on me?"

Elliot drew himself up to his full height and crossed his arms over his chest. He wasn't the lanky seventeen-year-old boy Declan had known anymore. His shoulders were broad, his chest filled out with strong pecs and defined abs. He shook his head as Declan's eyes flicked down to where a thin line of hair disappeared under the sheet wrapped around his hips.

"My dreams are none of your damned business anymore, Declan. And none of that would have happened if you'd respected my privacy the way everyone else in this house does. Next time you hear any noises from my room, do us both a favor and stay the hell out."

No matter what Elliot said now, Declan knew he hadn't misheard the sleepy happiness in Elliot's voice when he rolled into Declan's arms. He held Elliot's gaze until Elliot flushed again and turned back to the washstand. He wanted to demand that

Elliot face up to what just happened, but Declan knew he'd lost his place as first in Elliot's affections when he'd left five years ago. The rest of the house was stirring anyway and it wouldn't do to be caught here, so he left Elliot's room and softly closed the door.

"Another nightmare?"

Declan jumped. Elliot's fiancée, Celeste, stood a few steps down the stairs, looking back up at him as he came out of Elliot's bedroom. He sighed to himself. So much for keeping that a secret.

"Good morning, Miss Brady."

She nodded at him and then at Elliot's door. "I've heard him, you know. These last couple of nights. I asked Sally about it. She says he has nightmares every now and again?"

"Now and again," Declan acknowledged. Once a month, more or less, when Declan was living here, but he didn't know how much Elliot had confided in the girl. If she had to ask Sally questions about her fiancé, Declan would guess not much. He doubted that Sally told her much more than absolutely necessary, either. He almost pitied the girl for marrying a man with so many secrets.

She was reasonably pretty, he supposed. Tall for a woman, maybe four or five inches shorter than his own six feet, and slight, with dark hair pinned up in a practical chignon. A few escaping tendrils curled around her ears and at the nape of her neck, and a short curled fringe framed her pale face.

"I'm glad you woke him from it," she said, looking up at Declan. Her eyes were large, round, and the color of amber, the pupils wide in the dim light. "Sally said not to let it bother me, but it seemed like someone should do something to wake him up." She lowered her eyes, then glanced up again at Declan. "It's not as if I could. At least not yet."

Declan tried not to imagine this girl sharing Elliot's bedroom after they wed. He came down a few steps, planning to pass her and head for the breakfast room. She was dressed in a loose smock with long, wide sleeves and had a covered basket over her arm. "A bit early for shopping, isn't it?" he asked, largely to distract her from further questions about Elliot's nightmares.

She smiled and her eyes crinkled, her slightly stern features transformed into real beauty. "I'm off to the shore. It's time to feed my cephalopods."

Declan stared at her, not familiar with that word. "Beg pardon?" Before she could answer, Elliot's door opened and he appeared, washed and fully dressed, his damp hair slicked back from his face, dark brown ends curling around his ears.

"She has some sort of contraption that traps sea creatures in the water down past the end of Water Street. Goes out every morning and evening to observe them."

Celeste smiled a good morning at Elliot and he smiled back, his eyes still shadowed and his face pinched, but clearly making an effort for his fiancée.

"I'm about to submit my most recent observations to the *Magazine of Natural History* and I just need to verify a few details," she said. She shifted her attention to Declan. "Would you like to see them?"

Startled, Declan looked from Celeste to Elliot. Elliot shrugged. "She asks everyone, but so far, not many have taken her up on the offer. Go on, if you want. I'll catch up with you later."

Declan was suddenly curious about this girl Elliot planned to marry. He offered an arm to escort her down the stairs. "Why not? Let's get a bite of breakfast, and you can show me your cephalopods."

CHAPTER 3

*E*lliot had his usual breakfast, served quietly by one of Sally's girls. Eugenia, he assumed, based on the green ribbon in her hair, though Clarice liked to trick him into confusing her with her twin. He smiled his thanks when she brought him the morning paper, but found it hard to concentrate on the day's news. He usually relished this quiet calm in the mornings, before his day started with the constant questions and demands made on him. The background sounds of Sally whistling and clanging pots around in the kitchen seemed louder than usual today, and Elliot massaged his temples against the headache that always accompanied his nightmares.

At least he'd woken up before the point in the nightmare when he started to drown. Or, been woken up. Elliot felt hot shame wash over him at how he'd woken up rubbing off on Declan. Five years since Declan left, and still Elliot threw himself at Declan like nothing at all had changed, despite last night's resolve. How desperate Declan must think him.

And yet, Elliot remembered the feel of Declan's arms around him as he surfaced from the nightmare. That feeling of safety, a bulwark against the terrors in the night, Declan's low rough

voice in his ear, telling him that he was all right, Declan had him,
would never let anything happen to him. Declan had made him
feel safe and loved ever since he was a small boy, even if the
depth and intensity of the feelings Elliot still had for Declan
terrified him.

Elliot glanced out the breakfast room windows. The fog had
lifted a little, and he wondered what Declan thought of Celeste's
tanks and sea creatures. Eugenia and Clarice whispered fantas-
tical tales to each other about Celeste's devilfish. Celeste had
tried more than once to explain that they were harmless, but
Elliot usually avoided thinking about Celeste's work as much as
he could.

He wasn't sure he wanted Celeste to spend very much
unchaperoned time with Declan. It wasn't gossip or her reputation Elliot was worried about. Well, not really. Declan had a
reputation as a rake when he lived in town, but no more so
than the usual sailor. Only Elliot knew that he was as likely to
pay one of the town's prostitutes with whom he was friendly
just to give her a night off as he was to take advantage of her
services.

He was more worried about what Declan might tell Celeste
about their past than about Declan making any inappropriate
advances. Celeste had a way of getting information out of people
without them realizing she was angling for it. There were plenty
of things she didn't need to know about Elliot.

Elliot pushed back from his chair and got to his feet. He'd join
Declan and Celeste down at her waterfront tanks, be there while
his stepbrother and fiancée got to know each other. Not to
compare them, of course. But if Declan was planning to spend
more time in Port Townsend, it might be nice to try being a
family together.

The cool briny breeze off the bay eased Elliot's headache a
little, and he whistled as he jogged down the steep steps to the
lower part of town. He imagined Declan bringing presents from

his voyages for Elliot's children, who would scramble all over their uncle Declan, while Celeste looked on indulgently.

Elliot waved at Henry Landes, one of the trustees of the Port Townsend Southern Railroad, as he picked his way along the construction at the end of Water Street. Landes lifted a hand in response, but kept his head bent toward the foreman supervising the extension of the seawall west from Tyler Street. Once the railroad between Port Townsend and Portland was finished, Elliot might consider expanding Bishop Mercantile and opening an outpost near the train depot. In the meantime, this end of Water Street was marshy where the bay waters rushed in and crashed against the bluffs.

Declan and Celeste were perched on a jumble of rocks at the water's edge, Celeste pointing and gesturing, pale hands flashing in the thin sun. Declan stripped his coat off and rolled his shirt-sleeves to his elbows while Celeste sank gracefully down on a flat rock next to a small pool, tucking her skirts under her. Declan crouched next to her and pointed at something. From Elliot's vantage point slightly above them, he could hear only snatches of their conversation.

Celeste's cheeks were pink and her eyes bright, the way she looked when talking about her work. She pointed at something and gestured with her other hand, explaining something to Declan. Declan nodded, and asked a question Elliot couldn't hear. When Declan looked up, he caught sight of Elliot and waved him down. Elliot picked his way down the slippery rocks.

"Celeste's showing me her little collection of devilfish," Declan explained. "Seems like an odd place for them to settle, with all the activity along the docks." Declan gestured to the bustling hive of men loading and unloading the ships at the nearby Tyler Street docks and Union Wharf. "But she says she found them in these pools here and she's got some wooden barriers set up so they don't escape."

Elliot navigated to the other side of the pool and crouched

down next to Declan. Celeste was leaning over it, cooing at something barely visible underneath the surface.

"Hello, my beauty. You've some special visitors, so come on out and show us how pretty you are, won't you?" The pool was a couple feet deep, strewn with rocks of different sizes. Eelgrass and kelp clung in waving tufts to the rocks, and anemones waved spiny fingers in the gentle flow of water. A large, leathery, ochre starfish was plastered to the side of a large rock and a small mound of rocks were piled against a pair of larger boulders, clamshells strewn around it.

"That's a den, you see," Celeste pointed at the rock mound. "She's hiding right now, but she usually comes out when I feed her." Celeste reached into the bucket she'd brought with her and tossed a handful of clams in. Before the first clam drifted to the bottom of the pool, a thin, pale pink tentacle flashed out from behind the rock mound and grabbed it. Elliot jerked back.

"What the hell is that?" he asked.

"The arm of an *octopus punctatus*, a ruby octopus," Celeste replied. "She's a little shy, but give her a minute and you'll get a good look at her."

Elliot wasn't sure he wanted any look at the creature. Neither Celeste nor Declan seemed to notice his hesitation. Declan was gazing into the pool like he'd never seen something so interesting. Celeste grabbed a couple more clams from the bucket and dropped them in at the other end of the pool from the octopus's den.

A second tentacle unfurled from behind the rocks, questing along the sand for the clams. When it extended to its full length but couldn't reach them, both tentacles withdrew behind the rocks. Then a misshapen, mottled red head squeezed through a tiny opening in the rock den, and the devilfish slowly unfurled. It splayed eight pale pink limbs out from a web under its head, as if stretching awake after a nap.

"There you are, Eleanor," Celeste murmured. She turned to

Declan, her eyes shining. "Watch how she uses some of her arms to walk across the sand at the same time these front two arms are reaching for the food."

The octopus grabbed a clam in each of its front two arms. Elliot watched in uneasy fascination as the clams traveled up the octopus's arms, sucker by sucker, and disappeared under the web where all the arms joined the rest of the creature's body. The creature's head turned a dark gray color as it curled its web around the clams tucked under it.

There was a faint crack, and the empty clam shells drifted to the sandy floor. "She's got teeth under there?" Declan asked. Celeste shook her head.

"Not teeth, exactly. More like the beak of a parrot. She's never let me get close enough to see it, but I've seen some excellent illustrations of *cephalopoda* beaks drawn by Mr. William Evans Hoyle in some detail."

When it was done chewing its food, the octopus rose in a sinuous motion so it was standing on the tips of its tentacles, its bulbous head pulsing a little as it wandered closer to the edge of the pool. Celeste unbuttoned her cuffs and rolled her dress sleeves and the wide sleeves of her smock up to her shoulders, exposing both arms. When she shifted position and leaned forward, Elliot realized what she was planning to do.

He took a step forward and grabbed her left arm just as she thrust her right arm into the pool. There was a flurry of motion under the water, and Elliot was suddenly doused with cold seawater. Celeste yanked out of his grip, unbalancing him. Declan lurched forward and grabbed Elliot's arm to keep him from falling in the pool.

Elliot sputtered and blinked the water from his eyes. By the time he could see again, the octopus was half out of the pool, a pair of tentacles wrapped around each of Celeste's wrists as she leaned over the edge, the rest of its tentacles splayed against the rocks, head lolling half under the waterline. Celeste was making those same cooing noises.

"Did he scare you, Eleanor? I'm sure he didn't mean to." She looked over her shoulder at Elliot. "She uses her siphon to shoot water. It's how she propels herself along the ocean floor, you see. But she sometimes also shoots water as a playful warning, like that."

As she talked, the creature's tentacles undulated up her forearms, extending and flexing, creeping slowly along her skin. "I have other cephalopods I observe, but Eleanor's the most friendly. At least with me. Hardly anyone else comes to see her, much less interacts with her."

Declan leaned forward. "I've seen plenty of devilfish in the ocean. They trail along the ship sometimes. And I've eaten octopus before, of course, but I've never looked at one so close."

"Devilfish" was an excellent name for a creature that didn't look either friendly or playful to Elliot. Its skin color had deepened to an angry red, pimpled with raised white spots. Its head was about the size of Elliot's outstretched hand, with protruding orange eyes that had horizontal black pupils. The devilfish's eyes rolled around, taking in its surroundings, then fixed on Elliot, unblinking and eerie.

The devilfish inched a third tentacle up the rocks, then another, reaching for Celeste. She shifted her arms and gathered the creature into them. Water streamed down the front of her smock as she allowed the beast to rest its head on her bosom.

"See?" she grinned at Declan. "I told you she was friendly. You can touch her, if you like." The devilfish slid a pair of tentacles over her shoulder, up either side of her neck, and twined around her ears into her hair.

Declan reached a hand out and stroked his fingertips gently over the creature's skin. "She's so soft," he murmured. He picked up the end of a dangling tentacle and stroked up from the tip, then turned it over and passed his fingers lightly over two rows of suckers lining the underside. He pressed one finger into the center of a sucker, then pulled back against the creature's grip. "Look, Elliot," he beckoned with his other hand to Elliot. "Touch her, see how strong she is."

Elliot stayed away. "I'll pass, thank you." The tips of Celeste's fingers were turning white, and patches of skin bloomed red from the strong grip of the creature's suckers. He wanted to rip it off her and throw it back into the ocean. He'd known Celeste spent most of her days studying these creatures but seeing it crawl all over her was deeply disturbing.

"Put it back," he ordered. "Before it strangles you."

Celeste ignored his demand. "She's not hurting me, just exploring. She's probably as interested in studying me as I am in studying her."

Declan cupped a hand under the creature's misshapen head and stroked the fingers of his other hand gently around its eyes and down the tentacles draped over Celeste's arm. He and Celeste shared a smile over the ugly creature, like a pair of proud parents.

"What made you think of studying them?" Declan asked.

Celeste bent over the pool and dipped her laden arms under the water. It seemed like the creature gave one last squeeze with all its tentacles before it slid back into the water, withdrawing each tentacle from Celeste's skin so agonizingly slowly that Elliot wanted to tear them from her. Celeste gave a fond smile to the beast as she pulled her wet smock over her head and fetched a towel from her basket.

"For the sake of knowledge, I suppose. There's so much we don't know about these creatures. They're so very different from us, but there are surely things we can learn from them."

Elliot couldn't imagine what useful things she was expecting to learn from devilfish. When they married, he'd try talking her into leaving the creepy things alone. Surely there were other things she could study. Birds, maybe, or plants. Something that didn't stare at Elliot like it knew all his deepest secrets and was just waiting for him to recognize them too.

Celeste rubbed at the sides of her neck with the towel. The skin just above the collar of her dress was reddened, and her arms were a patchy red and white where the creature's suckers had attached. She noticed Elliot staring and rolled her sleeves down to her wrists.

"The marks go away after a while. At least she didn't shoot her ink at you when she sprayed you. That would have been messy." She glanced at Elliot's water-spotted vest and jacket. "Well, messier," she conceded.

Declan grinned at her, then smacked Elliot's arm when he didn't respond. "What's the matter with you, Elliot? Your fiancée's the most interesting woman I've ever met. And I've known some interesting women," he winked at Celeste, then turned back to Elliot. "Smart, interesting, beautiful—what more could you want in a wife?"

It's you that I want. The thought came before Elliot could control himself. That may have been true before Declan went away, but now what Elliot wanted was a quiet, respectable life in town. More than one of his business acquaintances had expressed surprise when Elliot had started stepping out with Celeste, telling him that most of their wives thought she was an odd duck. But they suited each other, and Elliot knew he could make her happy. She might share a little of Declan's penchant for defying society's expectations, but at least she wouldn't leave Elliot the way Declan had. They'd be happy together, Elliot was sure.

"Of course, I think she's smart and beautiful," Elliot replied, half-bowing to Celeste. "But we should be getting along, Declan. We need to discuss some business." He kissed Celeste on the cheek. "I'm sure you can occupy yourself with your notes and things, my dear."

Celeste smiled at Elliot. "Of course," she replied. "I have plenty of observations to record." She turned to Declan and held out her hand. "Thank you for allowing me to show Eleanor to you."

Declan shook her hand. "It was my pleasure. I'll never look at an octopus the same way again, I can tell you that."

Elliot tugged Declan away from her and led him along the shore back toward Water Street and the edge of town. When he looked back, Celeste had a notebook open on her lap, pen dangling from one hand, and was gazing out over the water.

CHAPTER 4

*A*s they neared the construction at the edge of Water Street, Declan veered away to keep walking along the beach. Elliot followed him, their boots crunching in step as they walked along the pebbled shore. Declan looked sideways at Elliot several times, like he wanted to say something, but didn't speak. Telling Celeste that he had business to discuss with Declan had been mostly an excuse to get away from her devilfish, but if Declan wanted to show him something, Elliot could spare the time to follow along.

He could wish Declan had chosen a different spot than this particular stretch of beach, but squelched such a childish reaction. Declan surely had no reason to remember why this beach was a place he didn't much like to linger on. Before he could ask where they were headed, Declan cleared his throat and spoke.

"What was that all about, man?"

"What was what about?" Elliot asked. The wind off the bay was a biting cold, but that didn't slow the bustle of activity on the wharves jutting out into the bay ahead of them. He shoved his hands into the pockets of his greatcoat and hunched against a matching chill in his bones.

"Your hostility to Celeste's scientific studies. Don't tell me you're one of those men who think women shouldn't exercise their minds?"

"Of course not," Elliot said, startled from the memories he was trying to keep away. He glanced at Declan and quirked the corner of his mouth up in a small smile. "Though Mrs. Rothschild and Mrs. Plummer have both informed me that their daughters are quite docile and compliant, for when I come to my senses in choosing a bride."

Declan snorted. "I've had more intelligent conversation with Mrs. Viola and her girls at the Green Light than with either Mrs. Rothschild or Mrs. Plummer, so I can just imagine what their daughters are like." He glanced sideways at Elliot again. "I gather Celeste doesn't quite fit in with uptown society?"

Elliot shrugged. "She's the Reverend Brady's only child, and they say he spoiled her a little. He had an extensive library and let her read anything she was interested in. I think she got her interest in the natural sciences from him. When she was young, he'd take her on long walks and encourage her to write down her observations of the plants and animals they'd see along the way. As he got older, he couldn't walk as far with her, and that's when she started studying marine plants and creatures. So he could sit on the beach and keep her company while she observed things and collected specimens."

The Reverend's heart had given out the week after Elliot had asked him for Celeste's hand, and he knew she still missed him. They'd postponed the wedding for Celeste's mourning period, and Elliot himself had only recently stopped wearing a black armband in honor of the man who'd been almost a second father to him.

"Before he died, the Reverend made me promise I'd support Celeste's work after we married. I would have anyway, but his will stipulates that the small amount of money he left Celeste is hers alone to use for her research. He was very kind to me and he loved Celeste very much. It's no hardship for me to comply with his wishes."

Declan pulled his coat tighter around him. The wind had picked up off the bay and clouds were scudding across the leaden sky. "Then why were you behaving so oddly before?" Declan asked, ducking his head against a gust of wind. "Celeste showed me some of her notes. I didn't understand all of it, but it seems like she's spent a lot of time observing several kinds of devilfish. I had no idea they were so fascinating."

Elliot shuddered. "I don't think 'fascinating' is the right word for them."

"There you go again," Declan said. "What's your problem with her studies? Her devilfish scare you or something?"

Of course the damned things scared him. He cast a sideways look at Declan. "You don't remember?"

"Remember what?"

Elliot stared out at the bay. "I saw something the day before Mother disappeared. I didn't know then what it was, but when Celeste started showing me illustrations from her scientific journals…I realize now it was probably some kind of cephalopod." He huffed a mirthless laugh. "That's the scientific name for them, she says. Your name for them seems more…apt, I suppose."

Declan shrugged. "I don't deny they're very strange creatures. And sailors are a superstitious lot. But the sea is full of strange creatures, some even stranger than your fiancée's pets."

Elliot turned away from the water, but Declan stopped him with a hand on Elliot's arm, and Elliot saw the understanding cross his face. "Your nightmares. They started after your mother disappeared." He squeezed gently and tugged Elliot to a large driftwood log. Elliot sighed as they settled on it, side by side. How pathetic, to still be so frightened about something that had happened so long ago.

"What did you see that day, Elliot?" Declan asked softly. He was facing forward, looking at the bay instead of directly at

Elliot. It helped a little, not having to face him while he explained his childhood terrors.

"We were walking along the shore, here," Elliot said, gesturing to the tracks they'd made along the pebbled beach. "I was throwing rocks and sticks in the water." He remembered asking his mother dozens of questions about the ships tied up at Union Wharf and anchored out in the bay. His mother pointed out the Captain's ship, which had come in a few days earlier. The Captain had brought his mother a bolt of sapphire-blue silk, which nearly matched the color of her eyes, from Shanghai. He'd brought Elliot and Declan presents, too, small trinkets Elliot still had, tucked away at the back of a desk drawer in his study.

"It started off a nice day," Elliot recalled. "But you know how the weather can change suddenly sometimes here. The skies darkened and the wind picked up and then suddenly, it was raining and I was soaked to the skin." He glanced at the sky. Today's weather seemed ominously like that day and he shivered, pulling his coat closer around him. A few fat raindrops fell, making dark splotches on the bleached driftwood log.

"I tugged on Mother's hand. I was wet and cold and couldn't understand why she wasn't already hurrying us back home. Instead, she squeezed my hand so hard it hurt and pulled me toward the water, murmuring something to herself I couldn't hear." Elliot stared out across the bay, remembering how the wind whipped the water into churning waves, whitecaps forming and breaking over the rocky beach, swirling around his mother's skirts.

"I could see Union Wharf from where we were and there were men rushing all around, tightening the lines tying the boats to the dock, packing up things that could blow away, tying down everything else. No one noticed us, especially when a small scow bashed against the dock and broke up into pieces."

"I remember that storm," Declan said quietly. "I was hanging around the Bishop warehouse, running messages for Father, when we heard the shouting from the wharf."

"Mother was splashing back and forth just at the edge of the water line. Like she was looking for something in the water, something she'd lost and had to retrieve before we could go home. The waves were getting bigger and her skirts were soaked to her waist, but she still wouldn't come away."

Elliot had looked frantically around for someone to help him, but the beach was empty and every man on the wharf was racing for higher ground. The larger ships anchored farther out in the bay listed crazily as the waves pummeled them.

"I remember thinking to myself that no one was coming to help us. That I'd have to be a man and save her myself." He rubbed at his burning eyes and then blinked the film of tears away. "I couldn't, though," he said. "I was too small."

Declan gripped his upper arm and angled into Elliot's field of view. "Of course you couldn't," he said. "You were eight years old, Elliot." He shook Elliot's arm. "And she was saved, remember? Once Father realized the two of you were down there, he grabbed me and we came running."

Elliot remembered the Captain picking him up and tearing up the beach before thrusting him at Declan. The sharp note of command in the Captain's voice when he shouted, "Take him back to the house and keep him there until I come back. Go, Declan, now!" How Declan's arms tightened around him when he struggled to get free and run back to his mother.

Over Declan's shoulder, he saw his mother chest-deep in the water, swimming out after something. Then Declan hoisted him more securely in his arms and carried him home. He got Elliot into dry clothes, tucked him into bed, and held him while Elliot cried himself to sleep.

"Whatever your mother was doing on the shore that day, it's not your fault, Elliot." Declan got off the log and crouched in the sand in front of him. He rested one hand on Elliot's knee and curled the other around the back of Elliot's neck. Elliot wondered in the back of his mind whether anyone could see them like this. He didn't really care when the broad bulk of Declan's body blocked the wind off the bay and the warmth of Declan's hand on his neck anchored him against the terror of what he'd seen that day.

He shook his head slightly, then rested his forehead against Declan's and closed his eyes. "It was, though," he whispered. "My fault. She told me when we set out that day that she had something to show me, something beautiful that she could show only me, not you or the Captain." He lifted his head and looked at Declan through tears that filmed his vision.

"And I wanted to see it," he confessed. "Mother used to tell me when she tucked me in at night that I was special, that someday she'd tell me who my real father was, and that I shouldn't listen to the other boys at school who said I was just a bastard and my mother a whore who your father had only married for her money."

Declan stared back at him. "You never told me people said that." His hand on the back of Elliot's neck tightened, then relaxed when Elliot winced. He shifted back onto his heels and ran that hand through his hair, mouth pressed into a thin line, a muscle jumping in his jaw. "You should have told me. I'd have kicked those snotty prats' asses off the bluffs."

Elliot smiled slightly at Declan's predictable protective reaction. "It doesn't matter now," he said. "What mattered then was that I thought Mother would finally tell me who he was, when she said she wanted to show me a secret on the beach."

He looked past Declan's shoulder, out into the bay again. "She didn't tell me, though. And I still don't know what she meant to show me, but I definitely saw something in the water."

He couldn't tell what it was at first, only catching glimpses of a dark shape floating within the waves that steadily rolled up the beach. The water was as warm as it ever got that early September day, but still chilled his toes as it spilled over the tops of his shoes. His mother didn't seem to notice the cold, her skirt belling out around her just before the next wave brought the creature closer to her.

"It was a devilfish ten times bigger than the one Celeste showed you. I felt a slimy arm brush against me as it grabbed Mother and pulled her into the water." He didn't mention how the creature lifted its bulbous head and stared at Elliot, nor the shock of recognition he'd felt when he'd looked into those huge, alien eyes. The creature had reached for Elliot too, and Elliot faintly heard a deep humming that made him want to swim out toward the thing.

He swallowed thickly, his skin prickling at the recollection of how the beast had felt brushing up against him. "You know the rest. The Captain grabbed me, you took me home and put me to bed. He found Mother and brought her home too, but the next morning, she was gone and I never saw her again."

He sniffled and tried to pull himself together. Declan resettled himself on the log next to Elliot. He nudged Elliot's shoulder with his own. "So, that's why you don't spend a lot of time with Celeste's octopuses. Have you told her what you saw with your mother?"

"Of course not," Elliot said. "And you are not to tell her. There's no reason to dredge all that up again. She's young enough that she doesn't remember the scandal when Mother disappeared, and no one even talks about it anymore. Not to my face, anyway."

Declan was quiet for a moment. "Keeping secrets from your bride doesn't seem like a recipe for a happy marriage," he finally said. His tone was mild, but the last thing Elliot wanted was marital advice from Declan, of all people.

"What do you know about happy marriages?" he said without thinking. When Declan put on a wounded look, Elliot's heart gave a lurch. If Declan was about to tell him that he'd married,

Elliot would—well, he wasn't sure what he'd do. But then Declan shook his head.

Declan looked out at the ships in the harbor, then back at Elliot. "Might be that she'd understand, though. And she'll eventually find out about your nightmares, unless you're planning to sleep in separate rooms."

Which was exactly what Elliot was planning, though he hadn't broached the subject with Celeste yet. He knew he'd have to perform his marital duties, but Declan didn't need to know how hard it had been for Elliot to move on after he'd left. He stood up and brushed the sand from the seat of his trousers.

"I'm not discussing my relationship with Celeste with you, Declan. Celeste and I understand each other. I'll be a good husband to her, and she's free to continue her work. I don't need to know very much about it."

Declan looked up at him skeptically and drummed his fingers against one thigh briefly, but thankfully dropped whatever else he wanted to say. Elliot looked at the black clouds rolling in from across the bay, then caught sight of a familiar shape in the forest of rigging floating out there. "Is that the *Black Dove*?"

Declan flashed a smile at Elliot and stood, brushing his shoulder against Elliot's. "Bought her off Father when he bought a larger windjammer for his Far East voyages."

Elliot stole a glance at Declan's face. "She's beautiful," he said.

Declan looked pleased at Elliot's reaction. "Isn't she?" he said. "She's faster now, too, after making some changes to her rigging. Easier to outrun the revenue cutters."

"What's her crew?" Elliot asked.

"A handful of men I've sailed with on Father's ship. A stowaway I gained while staying with Nance Carrigan, who's turned out to be an excellent first mate. Couple more I picked up while wintering in the Caribbean. And Thomas, of course." said Declan.

Thomas. Of course. Elliot knew about Thomas, the young cook the Captain had picked up somewhere along the Mexican coast, just before Declan started joining him on shorter voyages. Declan's early letters to Elliot mentioned Thomas as being about Declan's age and a good friend. Elliot wasn't sure how he came to know that Declan and Thomas were sleeping together, since Declan had never confirmed it to Elliot and Elliot had never asked.

Elliot could hardly expect Declan to stay faithful to him, especially since he was about to get married. But he'd never been able to stop himself from feeling a little jealous every time Thomas's name was mentioned. Thomas got to have Declan these last five years, while Elliot had been left behind. He wondered who Declan would choose if he ever had to—Elliot? Or Thomas?

He shook his head and pushed the thought away. Declan would never have to choose between him and Thomas because Declan would never stay on shore long enough to choose Elliot. After a few more moments idly watching the activity in the harbor, Elliot took a deep breath.

"Why did you come back now, Declan?"

Declan glanced at him, then back at the *Black Dove*. "I told you, Father's missing. I wanted you to come with me to find him."

Elliot shook his head, and Declan sighed. "Of course. Can't leave a new bride during your honeymoon. I'll stand up for you at the wedding and leave Wednesday morning."

Elliot nodded and didn't trust himself to speak. He'd had five years to get used to Declan's absence but just these few minutes sitting next to Declan, and suddenly he had no idea how he'd survive the next time Declan left him.

"Storm coming looks like a bad one," Declan commented, as he stood up and dusted the seat of his trousers off. "Come on, I'll buy you a drink at the Belmont Saloon, and we'll toast your wedded life."

CHAPTER 5

*W*hen Declan and Elliot returned uptown that evening, the kitchen and dining room were bustling with dinner preparations, but Celeste wasn't overseeing them. Declan privately wondered how Sally would adapt to a new mistress after being in charge of the household since his stepmother had disappeared, but knew better than to ask. For one, it probably hadn't occurred to Elliot there might be a conflict between his new wife and his old housekeeper. From his observations of Elliot today, Declan could tell that he was more comfortable dealing with inventory and figures than people. Declan guessed that as long as his needs were met, Elliot would be more than happy to let Sally and Celeste navigate their respective roles in the domestic arrangements of the Bishop household.

Celeste hadn't struck Declan as particularly domestic herself, though. She'd let Sally pack a hearty breakfast for them this morning, but was antsy to get out to the shore and her octopuses. Declan raised an eyebrow at Elliot, silently asking where his fiancée was. Elliot smiled slightly and tipped his head at the half-open door to his study. Declan caught a glimpse of Celeste, engrossed in a pile of papers and books spread open across Elliot's desk.

Declan ducked into the kitchen to say hello to Sally while Elliot went upstairs to wash up. He kissed her cheek and she grinned back at him, but she was elbow-deep in pastry dough and snapping at her girls to pull the roast out of the oven before it burned and to add more butter to the mashed potatoes, so he got out of her way and wandered back to the front hall.

Celeste was still seated at Elliot's desk, a finger holding her place in one periodical while she flipped through the papers in a stack to her left. She lifted her head, and he caught sight of a pair of wire-rimmed spectacles perched on her nose and a smear of ink above one eyebrow. He smiled at her but she didn't react, so he took the few steps toward the room and pushed the door further open.

Celeste's eyes focused on him. "Oh, hello," she said. "I didn't see you there."

"You were staring directly at me," Declan said.

"Hmm?" Celeste asked vaguely, glancing back down at the papers on the desk and flipping back to the page her finger had been marking.

"You—Never mind," Declan said, coming farther into the room. Celeste picked up a pen and scribbled a few words on the paper in front of her. "Work going well?" he asked.

Celeste scribbled a few more words, then set the pen down and looked at Declan. It felt like she was finally seeing him, her eyes focused on him this time, instead of just trained in his direction.

"Yes, I think I have everything I need now. I'll need to copy it over, of course, before submitting it." She stacked several pieces of papers together and tapped the stack on the desk's surface to align them. "But I can do that tomorrow and then mail it off to the magazine."

She glanced at the clock on the mantel. "Goodness, is it

dinnertime already? I feel as though I just sat down." She tidied the books and pamphlets into a pile on the edge of Elliot's desk and rose to cross the room. Declan offered her his arm.

"Roast beef and mashed potatoes. And, if I'm not mistaken, Sally's famous huckleberry pie. Which I've dreamed about many a night while at sea, I can tell you."

Celeste smiled at Declan and tucked her small hand under his elbow. "That sounds wonderful. Sally's an excellent cook, and I'm very grateful she's agreed to stay on after Elliot and I marry."

Maybe Sally and Celeste would get along just fine after all. He motioned to her forehead, then rubbed his own fingers across his. "You've got some ink on your face, there." Celeste rubbed her fingers on her forehead but only smeared more ink around her hairline. She caught him smothering a smile and grinned back. "I should wash my face, shouldn't I?" She glanced down at her ink-stained hands and pulled back from Declan. "And my hands, too. My apologies if I've gotten ink on your jacket."

Declan shrugged. "I've had worse," he said. He watched her climb the stairs to the second floor as Elliot came down from his room. They paused in the middle of the staircase and exchanged a quiet word but neither of them reached out to touch the other. For a couple about to marry, they seemed oddly indifferent to each other.

Dinner was delicious, as Sally's dinners invariably were, but filled with awkward silences. Elliot related a few tales of their day to Celeste, and she feigned interest but mostly seemed distracted. Declan tried asking her about her work, and she answered his direct questions about the scientific journal she planned to submit her paper to, but each time she got into specifics about her octopus observations, Elliot unsubtly changed the subject to something else. Declan couldn't help but wonder how a life that barely overlapped would satisfy either of them.

It wasn't as though he had anything different, he supposed. He'd found companionship with Thomas when he first started sailing with Father—and they still occasionally met each other's physical needs—but Declan couldn't let any special feelings for him interfere with his responsibility to the rest of the crew. Declan chewed a bite of Sally's succulent roast beef, sipped the excellent French wine his father brought to sell in the Bishop Mercantile, and wondered what it would be like to have a partner in life as well as in bed.

As they finished eating, Celeste got quieter. Declan didn't notice at first, since he and Elliot were engrossed in a discussion about whether Mr. Brooks, the customs collector, would ever be indicted for embezzlement. When Celeste rose from the table, Declan had barely half-risen before she waved a hand at both of them.

"Please, there's no need for you to get up," she smiled. "I think I'll get some air, but you stay and finish your conversation."

Elliot glanced out the window, where it was full dark. Declan could hear the steady rain drumming against the side of the house. He exchanged a look with Elliot.

Elliot stepped around the table toward Celeste, already halfway across the room. "Why would you want to go out in this weather?" he asked.

"I need to check on Eleanor and Stella."

"Your octopuses?" Declan asked. "They live in the ocean; surely the rain can hardly affect how wet they are."

Celeste shook her head, that same distracted look on her face she'd been wearing since Declan saw her in Elliot's study. "I just need to—" she started and trailed off as she cocked her head, as if listening to something she could barely hear.

The only things Declan could hear were rain pattering against the windows in a gust of wind, and the muted sounds of Sally and her girls washing the dinner dishes and setting the kitchen to rights before breakfast. Elliot took two long strides and reached Celeste before she made it to the doorway. He took her hand gently in his.

"Come, darling, let's go into the parlor. There's no need to go out tonight. Your creatures will still be there tomorrow morning, like they always are." He looked over his shoulder at Declan as he steered Celeste across the hall to the parlor. Declan followed, wondering what on Earth was going on with her.

In the parlor, Elliot tucked Celeste into a big horsehair wing-back chair and slid an ottoman with embroidered vines and flowers under her feet. He stoked the fire in the fireplace and added a shovelful of coal to warm the room. Declan watched him bustle around the room, trying to make Celeste comfortable, to keep her settled. Every time Celeste shifted position, Elliot was at her side, bringing her a glass of sherry, tucking a lap robe more securely around her, offering to have Sally bring her a cup of tea.

When she rejected his fourth offer, of something to read this time, and irritably pushed away both the blue cloth-bound copy of *Molly Bawn*, a novel by someone named The Duchess, in one hand and the scientific periodical in his other hand, Elliot leaned back on his heels and sighed.

"How about a game?" Declan suggested. Elliot looked gratefully at him.

"Yes, a game," Elliot agreed instantly, rising to his feet and replacing the book and periodical in their respective places on the bookshelf. He patted Celeste's shoulder as he returned to the sofa and sat next to Declan. "Charades?"

Celeste, hemmed in by a tiny tea table with her sherry perched on it at her side and nearly mummified with the lap robe tucked around her, gave in. "Fine," she sighed, staring over their shoulders at the rain-lashed windows.

"Great," Elliot said, a note of relief in his voice. "I'll start."

He jumped up and stood before the fireplace. Declan fetched a glass of whiskey while Elliot thought about his charade, then resettled himself on the sofa at the end closest to Celeste's chair. She'd at least stopped trying to convince them she needed to go to her creatures, but she looked like she was only biding her time until they relaxed their vigilance.

"All right, I've got one," Elliot said. He held up one finger, then cocked his head and furrowed his brow. He closed his hand into a loose fist and held up two fingers.

"Two words?" Declan guessed. Elliot gave an exaggerated shrug and held up only one finger.

"One word," Celeste said in a bored tone.

Elliot nodded his head, then shook it and held up two fingers again.

"Something that could be described with either one or two words," Declan concluded, and Elliot tapped his nose and pointed at Declan with a smile. Declan smiled back. It had been a long time since he'd played this silly game. At least it gave him an excuse to stare at Elliot.

Elliot squared his shoulders and turned a little toward the fireplace behind him, angling so he faced the open space between Declan's end of the sofa and Celeste's chair. He held both arms straight out, then stacked them on top of each other, about a foot in between his hands. He closed each hand into a circle, fingers touching his thumbs.

"Wave," Celeste guessed. Elliot rolled his eyes and shook his head again.

Elliot lifted one leg and swung it over something imaginary, planting it again on the ground with plenty of space between both feet. He crouched a little and hunched forward and Declan let his eyes roam down the long line of Elliot's back and over the curve of his ass and down his legs.

"Horse," Celeste suggested. Elliot nodded and shook his head, then rolled his hands to suggest she should keep going.

"Horse something? Something horse?" Declan put in, and Elliot nodded and smiled at him. He was pretty sure he knew what it was by now. But as Elliot resumed his hunched and squatting position, extending his arms straight out in front of him and sticking his ass out, Declan decided he'd let the game go on a little longer.

"Hippocampus!" Celeste crowed, sounding certain. Elliot dropped his hands and stood up, looking confused. Declan turned toward her too, no idea what she just said. "The Latin name for seahorse," she explained, as if both of them should have already known that.

"Huh," Declan said. Elliot's face cleared, but he shook his head and got back into position. He kept one arm where it was and lifted the other a little higher. Opening his hand, he moved it up and down in the air, as if petting something with his hand flat.

Before Celeste gave another strange guess, Declan gave in. "Hobby horse," he said with a smug smile at Elliot.

"Yes!" Elliot dropped his pose and flopped down on the sofa next to Declan. "You remember that hobby horse I had when I was a boy?"

"Of course," Declan responded. "Father brought it back for you on one of his voyages. You took that thing everywhere. I couldn't get you to leave it in the house, even when we went to the beach. You even named it. What did you call it?"

Elliot ducked his head. "Maisie," he said. "It was a she."

Declan chuckled. "Right. Maisie. Don't know where you got that name from but you loved that thing. I think you slept with it for an entire year." When Elliot had nightmares, he'd drag the hobby horse to Declan's room and crawl into Declan's bed, curling up against Declan, the damned horse clutched in one hand. He shook his head at the memory of the number of times he'd woken up with Maisie's glass eye staring blankly at him and the broomstick end of her jabbing him in the stomach.

Celeste pushed the lap robe off and got to her feet. "I think I'll go to bed."

Elliot colored and dropped his eyes from Declan, like he'd been reliving the same memory. He stood too and stretched a hand out to Celeste. "No, darling, I'm sorry. Declan only guessed right because I made it too easy for him." He glanced at Declan, then back at Celeste. "Why don't you go next? Declan and I used to play this game all the time when we were younger, but I promise you, I'm much better at guessing than he is."

"Don't listen to him, Celeste. I'm the one who taught him everything he knows," Declan responded without thinking. Elliot colored again and turned his back to Celeste to give Declan a warning look. Declan leaned back against the sofa and spread his arms across the back of it. If Elliot was going to get competitive at a game of Charades, two could play at that game.

Celeste looked for a moment like she wanted to refuse, but allowed Elliot to position her in front of the fireplace. Elliot sat in her wingback chair instead of returning to the sofa next to Declan and kept his face turned toward Celeste when Declan tried to catch his eye. All right then, the game was on.

Celeste lifted both arms in front of her and waved them up and down, then repeated the motion with her arms stretched out on either side. The cream-colored lace sleeves of her tea gown fluttered as she moved, falling back to expose her pale forearms, then drifting over her wrists again. She spun around to face the fireplace, her pink embroidered skirt swaying as she turned, and did it again, flapping her arms up and down, then at her sides. She turned around and faced Declan and Elliot expectantly.

"Um, dancing?" Declan guessed, having no idea what she was miming. Celeste shook her head and looked at Elliot, who shrugged.

She rolled her eyes at them both and tried again, waving both arms up and down in slow, fluid motions, turning slowly in place.

"Swimming?" Elliot guessed, and Celeste smiled but shook her head no. She stopped and dropped her arms, thinking a minute. Then her face brightened like she'd had an epiphany. She grabbed her forearm with her other hand just under the elbow and gave it a sharp tug, like she was tearing her own arm off. She mimed handing it off to an imaginary person next to her, then moved away, pushing the air away with both arms and circling them around in front of her. She really looked like she was swimming now, but she'd already said that wasn't the word.

Celeste glided over to the window, still swimming her arms through the air. "I thought you boys were good at this game," she taunted.

Declan looked at Elliot and shrugged. "She's your fiancée, man. Shouldn't you know her well enough to guess?" Declan knew Elliot well enough to guess his charade.

"Come give us another hint, darling," Elliot called. Celeste was still at the window, staring out into the still-driving rain. "Celeste?" Elliot called again.

"Hmm?" Celeste finally turned around and smiled vaguely at Elliot. Declan was inclined to just give up guessing and ask Celeste to reveal the word she'd chosen, but Elliot crossed the room and tried to draw her back into the game. She shook her head at whatever he murmured to her. "I'm tired of this game. I believe I will go to bed after all."

She resisted Elliot's attempts to convince her to stay but offered her cheek for his kiss. Declan stood and gave her a slight bow as she left the room. He poured himself another whiskey while Elliot followed Celeste out of the room and saw her upstairs. When Elliot returned, he stood in the middle of the parlor floor like he wasn't sure where to sit or what to do.

"You're sure you wouldn't rather marry one of the Rothschild or Plummer girls after all?" Declan meant it as a joke, but Elliot looked annoyed.

"It was unfair of us, talking about things she couldn't participate in. Besides, you liked her well enough this morning, remember?"

"I did. I do, but you have to admit her guesses were pretty strange. I mean, how hard is it to play Charades? And what the devil was she miming there during her turn?" He sipped his whiskey and looked at Elliot over the rim of the glass.

Elliot shrugged. "She lives in her head most of the time, thinking about what she's studying or reading. And yes, sometimes she's not exactly like the other girls in town. But she suits me, and I care for her. Besides, everything is settled for the wedding tomorrow."

"You care for her?" Declan sighed. "Elliot, is that all you want in a wife? Someone you care for? What about love?"

Elliot shook his head. "Of course, I meant that I love her. We'll have a good marriage, Declan. There's no reason for you to worry about me."

Declan poured Elliot a glass and brought it over to him, mostly as an excuse to be closer. He ducked his head to look into Elliot's face. "I'll always worry about you, little brother."

Elliot lifted his head and looked directly at Declan for the first time since Celeste left the room. There was something sad in his hazel eyes, something that made Declan's heart ache. Declan stretched his arm past Elliot to set his own glass on the mantel, close enough that his sleeve brushed Elliot's. When Elliot didn't move away, he let go of the glass and rested his hand on Elliot's shoulder.

"I just want you to be happy, Elliot. Are you sure you will be with her?"

Elliot swallowed and Declan watched his Adam's apple bob in his throat. He slid his hand across Elliot's collarbone and curled it around Elliot's neck. His thumb stroked the skin under Elliot's jaw, catching lightly on a bit of stubble. He waited for Elliot to do something, move toward him, pull away, say something, anything. Some clue as to what Elliot was feeling, because Declan was damned if he could figure that out.

"Declan," Elliot whispered. "Please."

"Please what?" Declan slid his fingers into the soft hair at the base of Elliot's skull. "Tell me what you want, Elliot. Is it really her? Or something else?" This morning, it was clear that Elliot still wanted him, and Declan had never stopped wanting Elliot.

He'd spent the last five years drowning his guilt about leaving in work and whiskey, fucking dozens of others, men and women both, as if any of them could come close to what he really wanted. Two days in Elliot's presence, and it was like he'd never left.

He stroked Elliot's throat with his thumb, slipping his fingers through his soft hair, waiting for Elliot to decide what to do next. Elliot closed his eyes and swayed forward just a little. It was enough to brush his forehead against Declan's and bump their noses together. Declan stood firm, neither leaning forward nor pulling back. Elliot's lips parted, and his warm breath drifted over Declan's face.

"I want—" Elliot started, then licked his lips and swallowed again. He opened his eyes, and Declan smiled encouragingly at him. Elliot rested a hand against Declan's chest. The warmth of it sunk through Declan's vest and shirt. But then he pushed against Declan and said, "I want you to stop tempting me, Declan. I've made my choice and I'm not changing my mind."

Declan's hand stilled. He let go of Elliot and stepped back. "Fine." He left his whiskey glass on the mantel and pivoted on his heel. He wasn't surprised as much as disappointed. But if Elliot wanted to deny what he really wanted, then he was welcome to a woman who didn't seem to want him either. Declan grabbed his jacket off the arm of the sofa and shrugged into it.

"Declan. I'm sorry, I didn't mean to—"

Declan kept his face schooled in a pleasant expression. "There's nothing to apologize for, Elliot. You should get a good night's sleep before your wedding. I'll find my own entertainment."

He tossed a smile over his shoulder and left the house. There was plenty of companionship to be found downtown, where at least he knew he'd be wanted.

CHAPTER 6

*T*he next morning, Declan leaned his aching head against the red double front doors to the Bishop house while he fumbled with his keys. He'd dragged himself back from the Green Light brothel through the damp early morning fog, grateful that no one was about to see him pause halfway up the rickety Adams Street stairs while his heart pounded and his head swam. He'd definitely drunk too much last night.

Mrs. Viola gave a man his money's worth in liquor, that was certain. It was his liquor anyway, good Canadian whiskey he'd smuggled in on his arrival in Port Townsend two nights ago, slipping the *Black Dove* past the revenue cutters under cover of darkness. Joey and Luca made the deliveries to the Delmonico and Pacific saloons, but Declan had brought Mrs. Viola her share himself the night he arrived and stayed to catch up on the town news. She was the one who'd told him that Elliot was engaged to the Brady girl, though he hadn't believed it until he'd arrived at the Bishop house and met Celeste.

After the charade that was their little game of Charades last night, Declan returned to the Green Light. He wasn't sure whether it was comfort or oblivion he'd sought, but Viola did her level best to provide both at once. She'd kept his glass topped up, and sent two of her best girls to flirt with and tease him until she was done taking care of her other business and ready to retire. Declan paid well for the privilege of her company after hours, whether he took advantage of her personal services or not.

Just as he found the correct key and shoved it into the lock, the door opened, and Declan nearly crashed into the solid mass behind it. Large, firm hands gripped his upper arms and pushed him upright.

"Declan?" Elliot's voice boomed in Declan's ear and he winced, yanking an arm free to cover the ear closest to the source of the noise.

"Who else?" he muttered as Elliot pushed past him onto the front porch. Declan took a careful couple of steps inside the house and leaned against the wall, trying to stay upright until he could reach his bed and fall into it. Never again that much whiskey, he promised himself. At least not in such quick succession. How many had it been? He'd lost track after the fifth or sixth, he thought, and the Green Light's shot glasses were more like tumblers to begin with.

"Is she with you?" Elliot asked, glancing over his shoulder at Declan but turning immediately to scan the walkway leading to the house.

"Why would I bring her back here?" Declan asked. Viola wasn't welcome uptown any more than Declan himself was. Not for the first time, Declan wondered whether he should have just sailed back out on the Strait of Juan de Fuca after making his deliveries and left Elliot to his carefully planned life.

"So, she's still out there, then?" Elliot asked, returning inside. He gripped the doorknob in one fist and braced the other hand on the doorjamb, as if he wasn't sure whether to close the door or step outside again.

Declan pushed off the wall, then reconsidered and braced himself up with one hand against the flocked wallpaper. His eyes were burning and his mouth cotton-dry, and he was in no mood for whatever bee Elliot had in his bonnet at this ungodly hour.

"Out where? What the hell are you talking about, Elliot?"

"Celeste! Who do you think I'm talking about?" Elliot snapped, then stooped to get a good look at Declan's face. He looked Declan up and down. "Wait, have you been out all night?"

Declan brushed his hands down his wrinkled shirt and tugged the unbuttoned edges of his vest together. "What of it? It's none of your business what I do at night, remember?"

Elliot closed the door and sagged against it. "So, you weren't out with Celeste this morning?"

Declan squeezed the bridge of his nose, trying to stop the railroad spike being pounded into his skull. "Elliot. Quit with the Twenty Questions, please. I haven't seen Celeste this morning and right now, I'd rather not see you until I've had some coffee and a bit of a lie-down. I'll meet you at your office later." He pushed off the wall that was supporting him and took a stumbling step forward.

Elliot's strong hand caught him under his elbow. Declan threw him off and kept walking to the staircase. "Declan, please. Celeste is missing." The fear and anxiety in his voice finally penetrated the fog in Declan's head. He stopped at the base of the stairs, though kept his back to Elliot because if he turned around too fast, he might fall down.

"What do you mean, missing?"

"She's not here. Eugenia says her bed doesn't look like anyone slept in it, and the basket she always takes with her is still by the kitchen door. Declan, I'm worried something's happened to her."

Declan turned slowly around to look at Elliot. His face was pale and his eyes worried. He was fully dressed for his wedding day, but he looked beseechingly at Declan now. As if Declan could ever resist Elliot when he needed help. He scrubbed his hands briskly over his face to wake himself up.

"Coffee. A shave. And breakfast. In that order," he said. "Then we'll figure it out."

When Declan felt human again after breakfast and a quick wash and shave, he pushed back from the table. "All right. Tell me why you think something's happened to Celeste."

Elliot, who had been pacing between the windows in the breakfast room while Declan chowed down the plate of eggs Sally whipped up for him, took Declan's coffee cup and refilled it. He pulled the chair across from Declan out, turned it around and sat down, crossing his forearms on the high wooden ladder back and resting his chin on his arms.

"I went to bed shortly after you left last night," he started. He looked like a small boy pressing his face against a shop window, and Declan's heart clenched.

Elliot dropped his eyes and said, "I didn't sleep well," which Declan took to mean he had another nightmare, "and gave up trying just before dawn. I thought I'd have breakfast with Celeste before she went down to the shore and waited for her to come downstairs. She's usually up at dawn anyway, but Sally said she hadn't seen her yet. I figured maybe she'd slept in after not feeling well last night, so I had some breakfast and read the paper and waited for her."

Declan sipped his coffee and nodded at Elliot to go on.

"Eugenia came down from cleaning the upstairs rooms and said that Celeste's bed was still made. I don't know where she went or when she left, but you and I were the last ones who saw her last night. When I saw you coming up the walk, I assumed you must have gone out early with her to see her devilfish. You're sure you didn't see her? On your way home this morning from…" he dropped his eyes again, the lashes dark spikes against his pale cheeks, "wherever you were last night?"

Declan shook his head. "I came up the Adams Street steps, from the Green Light." Screw Elliot if he didn't want to hear where Declan spent the night. He said he didn't want to be in Declan's bed, so he could just deal with whoever else Declan chose to be in it. Something eased in Elliot's expression, though. As if he'd been expecting Declan to have been somewhere else, and the Green Light was better than the alternative in his mind.

"Did you go anywhere else last night?" Elliot asked hesitantly.

Declan took another gulp of coffee. He'd taken the Taylor Street steps down last night, probably faster than he should have in the dark and driving rain, but he was annoyed at Elliot's mixed messages and trying to outrun the hard-on he'd gotten when Elliot had nearly kissed him. "I stopped at the Pacific Saloon at the top of Union Wharf to say hello to Pat Lennan. Shared a few rounds with a couple sailors who knew Father, then hoofed it over to the Green Light when Pat closed down the Pacific."

And then he remembered.

"Wait," he said. "Pat noticed something last night. I didn't pay it any mind, but he mentioned something about a new ship in the bay. Said it hadn't been there before sundown."

"Really? How could he tell, in the dark?"

"Full moon last night," Declan replied. "The rain stopped just before I got to the Pacific and when the clouds cleared the moon was huge, the kind of supermoon that brings the spring tides. The whole wharf was lit up like it was almost daylight."

Elliot tapped a finger against his lips. "So, Pat says he saw a ship that came in after sundown? What does that have to do with Celeste?"

"I don't know that it does." Except that he had a terrible suspicion that it did. And Pat wouldn't have mentioned the ship to Declan if there hadn't been something unusual about it. A strange ship appearing last night—and now Celeste missing—had obvious parallels to the ship that appeared the night before Elliot's mother disappeared.

Declan shook his head, which was a mistake, and he slid his coffee cup to Elliot for a refill. With Elliot's back to him, he let his head fall into his hands. If Elliot hadn't made that connection yet, Declan wasn't going to point it out. Celeste had probably gone down to the beach early this morning. There was no reason to jump to any conclusions.

He lifted his head and nodded thanks when Elliot slid his coffee cup back in front of him. Father had told him a lot more about the day Elliot's mother disappeared and why he thought something had taken her, but neither of them had ever wanted to tell Elliot the whole story. Elliot could tell he was holding something back, though.

"What is it, Declan? This is the woman I'm supposed to be marrying today. If you know where she might have gone, you need to tell me."

Declan swigged the rest of his coffee and wiped his mouth with his napkin. He was only marginally recovered from last night, and his brain wasn't thinking clearly. There had to be a logical explanation for a connection between two sightings of a mysterious ship and the disappearance of two women from Port Townsend. Assuming those things were connected at all.

Speaking of logical connections, they'd best start with ruling out the ones they could think of. Maybe movement would help his hangover too. "Let's go downtown and look for her. We'll talk to Pat first, see if he saw her last night or this morning."

CHAPTER 7

*T*he ship Pat Lennan had seen the night before was gone by the time Elliot and Declan reached the wharf after breakfast. Elliot sat at the end of the bar in the Pacific Saloon, nursing an unwanted beer Declan had ordered for him, watching Declan make small talk with Pat.

Elliot itched with impatience while Declan meandered the conversation around to the ship. Pat shook his head.

"Didn't see her leave, neither. Might've moved farther out and anchored in deeper water. Or maybe she sailed on out the Strait."

"And you have no idea what she was doing here?" Elliot put in. "Did she unload any goods? Take on any passengers?"

Pat shrugged. "Low tide was 'specially low last night. She'd'a run aground had she tried getting much closer to the dock overnight. Didn't seem to have no business to conduct here, but I don't keep track of all the smaller boats ferrying things 'tween the big ships and the docks."

Declan dug his hand into the bowl of boiled, salted peanuts on the bar in front of him and popped a few into his mouth. "I know that ain't true, Pat. Ain't nothing goes on at these docks you haven't either seen or heard about." His voice had lost the cultured tone Elliot was familiar with, sounding more like an ordinary seaman than the son of Captain Jack Fitzgerald and stepbrother to the owner of the Bishop Mercantile.

He leaned forward over the bar and lowered his voice. "You know I know better'n most how them customs bastards try to take all a man's profits. I ain't looking to interfere with a fellow skipper's business. I'm just wondering if maybe you saw anyone go out to that ship and not come back. Don't care about nothing else she might've brought off or taken on."

Pat flicked his eyes from Declan to Elliot and back, as if trying to decide whether to say anything. Declan wiped his hand carelessly on his trousers, then dipped into his vest pocket. He laid his half-closed fist on the bar, a silver coin glinting between his fingers in the low light from the lamp hanging over the bar. Pat looked at Declan's hand, then at Elliot, and tucked the towel he'd been using to wipe down the bar into the apron strings wrapped around his ample middle.

"Speakin' of business, I got a crate of whiskey just delivered in the back room. You wanna come help me shift it, Captain? Tell me whether it's worth the price I paid for it?"

Elliot opened his mouth to demand that Pat answer Declan's question when Declan kicked him in the ankle. He shut his mouth again while Declan hoisted himself off the barstool.

"Sure thing, Pat," Declan said cheerfully and pushed the bowl of peanuts toward Elliot. "Finish your beer, Elliot. It'll put hair on your chest."

Elliot shot Declan a dirty look as Pat lumbered toward the back room. Declan gave a slight shake of his head and Elliot sighed. Fine. He'd stay here and let Declan pretend to slum it with a saloon owner who probably hadn't seen anything anyway. It would serve Declan right if Pat robbed him of all the money he had on him in the back room. Unless Pat wanted something else from Declan besides money.

Elliot buried his face in his hands, elbows propped on the bar.

Jesus Christ, he was sitting in a dockside saloon at eleven in the morning, waiting for his stepbrother to bribe a man for information about his missing fiancée and quibbling with himself over whether he'd prefer Declan to bribe the man with money or his cock. What kind of man was he?

There were a smattering of other patrons in the bar, men with tired eyes and grubby clothes, taking advantage of Pat's free hot lunch with the purchase of two beers. A few of them cast suspicious looks at Elliot while they served themselves from the buffet along the wall opposite the bar. Elliot kept his eyes on his beer until he felt Declan slide back onto the bar stool next to him.

"Pat says he saw a woman walking along the beach last night after he closed up. Says he couldn't tell who she was, but I think he knows it was Celeste." His voice was low, head bent toward Elliot's ear so his words didn't carry beyond them.

Elliot picked his head up and looked at Pat, industriously wiping down the other end of the bar. "Well, if he saw her, why didn't he say so in front of me? Why the ruse about the back room? And what did you pay him, anyway? Can you even trust what he told you if he won't give us any information without being bribed?"

Declan nudged Elliot. "Keep your voice down. Your fiancée's considered a strange one down here, you know."

"And that's a reason to keep information about her from me?" Elliot didn't see any reason to keep his voice down. What did he care what Pat Lennan thought of him or Celeste? "Did he talk to her? Try to find out what she was doing? A woman walking alone on the beach in the middle of the night and he just what? Goes to bed like it's none of his business?"

"It *ain't* any of my business," Pat snapped, still at the far end of the bar. Elliot's voice had risen without him quite being aware of it. "It ain't my business that you let your woman wander around downtown alone. You can't keep a closer eye on her, it's your own fault what happens to her."

Elliot launched himself off his stool, nearly unseating Declan in his haste to get at Pat. "And what the hell happened to her?" he demanded. "If you know so damned much about her, why can't you just tell me where she is? Did she leave on that ship? Did something else happen to her? Did she—?"

Declan grabbed Elliot's arm and yanked him down onto the nearest stool. "This isn't helping," he hissed at Elliot. A few men set their beers down and stood up, like they were about to come to Pat's rescue. Declan waved them off and one by one, they slowly took their seats, still eyeing Elliot suspiciously. Elliot took a deep breath and cleared the lump from his throat. "Did she drown?"

Pat crossed his beefy arms over his chest. "I told you, ain't none of my business what happened to her. If you'd been paying attention to what she was doing, you wouldn't have no need to be asking me where she is now."

Elliot turned to Declan, who smacked a hand against Elliot's chest and rolled his eyes toward the patrons still watching the Elliot's standoff with Pat. "Let's go," he said firmly. He tossed a handful of banknotes on the bar. "Thanks, Pat," he called as he steered Elliot toward the door.

"Thanks?" Elliot scoffed when they were outside on the boardwalk. "What did he do to deserve any thanks? Unless he gave you something more than information in that back room?"

Declan grabbed Elliot's upper arm in an iron grip and marched him to the end of the boardwalk and along the beach. "Shut it, Elliot," he snapped. "He was very helpful, despite your hostility, but there's no way he was going to tell us what he saw in front of a bar full of superstitious sailors." He let go of Elliot's arm and pushed him none too gently to keep walking.

Elliot kicked at a piece of driftwood but kept pace with Declan stalking along the beach. After a short silence, he asked in a calmer voice than the one he'd used on Pat, "What did he tell you, then?"

"In a minute," Declan said. He stalked along the beach like a man on a mission, Elliot trailing behind him.

"Where are we going?"

"To Celeste's observation pools."

"Why?"

"That's where she usually goes in the mornings, right? And in the evenings, before dinner?"

"Yes, but she always comes back long before now. You think she's still there? Why wouldn't she have come home by now?"

"I think we should retrace her steps from yesterday. She said she wanted to go check on her creatures last night. Let's just take this one step at a time, okay?"

Elliot couldn't bring himself to ask Declan the question he really wanted to ask. But if Celeste had drowned and Pat knew that she had, why would he tell Declan and not Elliot? And what would he have told Declan that he didn't want to say in front of the other bar patrons? Declan's face was shuttered and his eyes on the pebbled beach in front of him. Elliot couldn't tell what he was thinking.

In a little while, they reached the rocky section where Celeste kept her observation pools. Elliot surveyed the beach and saw no sign of Celeste. Declan removed his coat and squatted at the pool where Celeste kept the one she'd named Eleanor. He rolled his shirtsleeve to the elbow and swished a hand in the water, fingers brushing through the eelgrass and kelp strands. Elliot tensed as he gently turned over the rocks that made up the creature's den, expecting the thing to shoot out and spray water at him like it had done yesterday morning.

Nothing happened, though, and after Declan had turned over every rock in the pool, he sat back on his heels, water dripping from his fingertips onto the slippery rocks lining the edge of the pool.

"She's gone." Declan pointed at two large boulders leaning against each other closer to the water's edge. "And the barrier

Celeste set up to keep her in this pool is gone too. She must have come down last night and freed her."

He stood and glanced out at the water in the bay and then down at the pool at his feet, as if measuring the distance between the pool and some point offshore. "Or something did," he murmured. Elliot felt a stab of fear on top of his anxiety about Celeste.

Declan gazed across the rocky shore, pieces of netting, broken-up bits of wood, and piles of eelgrass scattered all around. "I'd guess she freed all the creatures she's been studying, but it doesn't really matter now."

Elliot shivered in the cold breeze off the water. Dark clouds were coming in from the bay. More rain on the way. "Why not? Declan, for Christ's sake, stop being so mysterious and tell me what you think."

Declan sighed and nudged a pile of empty mussel shells with the toe of his boot. "I really don't know, Elliot. It seems impossible, but I can't think of any other explanation."

"What seems impossible?" Elliot grabbed Declan's arm and shook him. "Just tell me whatever you're thinking."

"Pat says he saw a ship out on the bay last night. Far out, far enough that it was hard to see any distinguishing features on her, much less her name. But there's one thing you can tell about a vessel even out in the middle of the bay, right?" He paused, like he was expecting Elliot to answer. When Elliot just looked at him, he sighed again.

"Her masts. Even with her sails furled, you can count how many masts she has. And if you can tell whether she's square-rigged or fore-and-aft, that narrows down your options, see? Gives you more information to identify what type of vessel she is, and maybe the company that built her."

"So?" Elliot didn't need a lesson in ship identification. He needed to know what happened to his fiancée—and if Declan didn't get to the point soon, he might punch him in the face.

"Pat said it was an eight-masted schooner," Declan said.

"Eight?" Elliot had never heard of a schooner with eight masts. "That can't be right. He must have miscounted in the dark."

Declan shook his head. "He was dead certain about it. Counted them five times, he said, to be sure. It's why he didn't want to say anything in front of the other men in the saloon— didn't want them laughing at him for seeing things."

Elliot thought for a minute. "I heard that the Hall brothers on Bainbridge Island are building schooners with five masts, and Mr. Kruse down in Oregon is talking about building one with six, but I haven't heard of anyone who's tried building one with eight."

"She'd have to be huge," Declan agreed. "Can't even think why you'd need that much sail. The *Black Dove*'s plenty fast and she only has two masts. Father's barquentine, the *Argonauta*, has three, and that's good for the long-haul trips to the Far East like he does, but why anyone would want eight is beyond me." He paused for a minute and glanced sidelong at Elliot. "Only…"

"Only what?"

"The ship that showed up the night before your mother disappeared had eight masts too."

"It did?" Elliot thought back to the little he'd overheard the Captain telling people what happened that day. "I didn't know that."

"That's part of why your mother's disappearance was so strange. A few days before she disappeared, some folks saw a big ship in the bay. It came and went, was there one morning and gone in the afternoon, then back again in the evening. I didn't pay much attention at the time, but Father told me later that folks argued over what it looked like. No one ever talked to anyone who'd come ashore off it or gone out aboard."

Declan paused a minute, looking out across the choppy waves rolling up onto the beach. "Half of downtown had flooded in that storm that came up while you and your mama were on the beach. Father tore what remained of the town apart the next day, searching for her."

He shook his head and winced, putting a hand to his temple and pressing hard. "Most people were picking through their own property, salvaging what they could, and hadn't seen Marie since before the storm. Someone finally mentioned that he'd seen a woman walking along the same beach late that night. When Father asked Mr. Garfield at the customs house for the records of all the ships that had come and gone that day, Mr. Garfield said a big schooner had been spotted far out in the bay but had never checked in with him. It was gone that morning, though, and no one knew where it had come from or where it went."

"So, you think Celeste went away on the same ship that your father thinks took my mother?" Elliot tried to sound matter-of-fact. Like he didn't care that anyone he'd ever loved eventually left him. First his mother, then Declan, and now Celeste. What was it about him that made everyone leave?

Declan looked at him, his green eyes filled with sad kindness, like he understood what Elliot wasn't saying. He stepped forward and squeezed Elliot's shoulder. "I don't know, Elliot, but I think it's a distinct possibility. There's more, though."

Elliot blinked a film of tears from his eyes and swiped his sleeve across his dripping nose. "What else?" he asked, trying not to imagine what could draw both his mother and fiancée away from him, on a ship that was too impossible to even exist.

"Father sailed as soon as he could, and he asked about that schooner at every port he put in to. Turns out it's been seen before, off and on, for decades, and wherever it shows up, a few days later, at least one woman in the town disappears."

Declan squeezed his shoulder again and sighed. "We should check to see if anyone else in town saw her, and start a diving search in case she drowned, but I think you'll have to call the wedding off today."

Elliot nodded, his throat tight. Declan pulled him into a strong embrace. Elliot dropped his head onto Declan's shoulder but kept his arms loose at his sides. The rough wool of Declan's coat prickled against his forehead, and he breathed in a whiff of pipe smoke and Declan's skin.

With another firm squeeze, Declan let go. Elliot lifted his head and surveyed the forest of ships clustered around Union Wharf over Declan's shoulder, counting their masts in the half hope that the schooner Pat had seen was still there and he could get some answers. When Declan turned away to head back to town, Elliot followed.

CHAPTER 8

*E*lliot spent the next few days going through the motions. When he and Declan left the spot where Celeste had kept her devilfish, they tromped along the beach from Union Wharf to the marshes around the sawmill at Point Hudson, then doubled back along Water Street. They canvassed everyone they saw on the docks and asked in at all the shops Celeste might have gone into. No one had seen Celeste since the day before.

Divers searched all the places Celeste's body might have drifted with the tides, and several men and boys from both uptown and downtown spread out to search. Pretending to keep up hope during those two days of searching was excruciating, since Declan was convinced Celeste wouldn't be found, and Elliot had no hope to cling to.

Even worse was having to explain to Mrs. Brady that the volunteers were calling off the search and her only daughter was gone. "Gone" was the only word he could give Mrs. Brady as an explanation when he sat across from her in the front parlor where he'd spent the last few months courting Celeste. That one word raised more questions from her than Elliot was able to answer.

"What do you mean, gone?" Mrs. Brady asked, her voice quivering and her brown eyes brimming with tears. "Where could she have gone? She was so excited about getting married."

She looked up at Declan, standing behind Elliot's shoulder. "They're still looking for her, right?" she asked him.

"I'm sorry. She's gone," Elliot repeated, swallowing around the lump in his throat. "The divers found no trace of her and they don't think there's any point in continuing to look for her."

"But she's a good swimmer, you know she is," Mrs. Brady said, bewildered. "Maybe she just swam out farther than she ever had and came out on a beach somewhere and got lost on her way back. Please," she begged, sinking to her knees at Elliot's feet and clasping his hand in hers. She pulled Elliot's hands against her bodice.

"You can't just give up on her. We need to keep looking for her. She's still out there somewhere, I know she is." Celeste's mother broke down completely, tears streaming down her face. Elliot closed his eyes and let the sound of her crying fade into the background of his mind. It was Declan's suggestion to let everyone believe Celeste had drowned, the same as everyone believed his mother had. It made little difference anyway. Even if both of the women who'd claimed to love him had left alive on that ship, his mother had never come back, so what reason did he have to think Celeste would?

Mrs. Brady's tears dripped on his icy hands, but he had no comfort to give her. After a few moments, Declan stepped out from behind him.

"Mrs. Brady, I'm terribly sorry. We've been searching for her for two days, and there's nowhere left to look." Declan tucked his hand underneath her elbow and lifted her to her feet. "Come," he said. "Let's get you to your room. There's nothing you can do for Celeste now." He led the sobbing woman to the doorway and turned her over to a maid hovering just outside the door. He said a few quiet words to the girl and then came back into the parlor and sat down on the sofa where Mrs. Brady had just been sitting.

"We should go home, Elliot," Declan said softly. "There's nothing you can do for Mrs. Brady."

Elliot nodded dully. He let Declan help him up and walk him back home. It had been raining ever since Celeste disappeared, icy sheets of water beating down on the searchers' heads, slipping under coat collars and soaking everyone to the bone. It made the search even harder, and part of Elliot was grateful when they called it off.

Still, the rain continued relentlessly all week, through Celeste's funeral service on Saturday morning. It was as if the heavens themselves were mourning Celeste. He was conscious of Declan's solid form beside him at the church, accepting condolences on his behalf, making small talk Elliot couldn't bear to take part in. At least there wasn't a graveside service too. No body to bury, after all.

When it was finally over, Declan insisted Elliot try to get some sleep. He steered Elliot up the stairs to his bedroom and kept one hand on Elliot's back, gently stroking up and down. Just like on the day his mother disappeared when he was a boy, Declan helped him change out of his wet clothes, pulled back the covers, and settled him underneath.

Elliot turned over onto his side and closed his eyes. Declan rubbed small circles on his back, the way he used to when Elliot had a nightmare. "What can I do, Elliot?" Declan asked softly. "Tell me what I can do to make it better."

"There's nothing you can do to make it better, Declan," Elliot replied, refusing to look at him. "Just go away. Please just go away."

Declan's hand on his back stilled, then pulled away. He felt the weight of Declan's body lift from the bed, then the soft snick of the door closing, leaving Elliot alone.

He fell into a fitful sleep, flashes of Celeste drifting through his dreams. He saw her skirts fluttering in the breeze as she walked along the beach next to him. The two of them sitting in the Reverend's library the day he first thought of marrying her, sunlight shining on the smooth coil of her dark hair as she bent over one of her biology periodicals. In the dream, same as on that day, she looked up and caught him staring at her, then pulled her eyes and mouth into a grimace that made him laugh out loud. He remembered the soft click in his heart he'd felt that day, as he realized that he could build a life with her on the strength of their friendship.

Elliot turned over in his half-sleep, and the dream images shifted. Celeste floating under water, in a yellow dress, water-logged and swirling through murky water, her eyes open and staring accusingly at him. She was wearing the same open-mouthed grimace, but this time it was terrifying instead of amusing.

The dream images shifted back and forth. A fond memory of Celeste, some particular expression or mannerism so familiar to him, echoed grotesquely with her floating under water. Elliot tried to push away the images and wake up, but the dream held him fast.

He turned over again and this time, Celeste was surrounded by her devilfish, tentacles wrapped around her arms and waist, tendrils of her hair drifting around her head, like an underwater Medusa. Her eyes were open, still staring at Elliot, mouth gaping and gasping. Her yellow skirts belled around her, puffing out until they strained at the seams and then tore into vertical strips, dangling limply below her waist.

Elliot tried to swim toward her, but something came from underneath and held him fast. He struggled against it, but it wrapped around his legs and squeezed until he couldn't feel anything below his hips. He stretched his hands out toward Celeste, and she reached out for him, but they were too far apart to touch.

The yellow strips of Celeste's dress undulated in the water, then firmed into long, round, muscled limbs. They were thicker at her waist where they met and tapered to delicate, thin tentacles with rounded ends. Elliot counted six of them, as Celeste stretched and flexed, testing her new limbs. She was no longer reaching for him. Instead, she was petting the devilfish swimming around her, playfully twining her tentacles around theirs and letting them crawl all over her new body.

When she finally noticed Elliot struggling to get free, she tucked all six limbs tightly under her and shot them together behind her, propelling her through the water toward him. She swam up his body, pressing her still-womanly bosom against his chest and wrapping her new lower limbs around Elliot's legs. The creature behind him let go of his arms, and Elliot tried to swim away, back to the surface, to wake up, but she held him fast.

Celeste closed her eyes briefly and when she opened them, they were different. Still the same amber-colored irises, but her pupils were thin rectangles spanning the width of each eye. She opened and closed these uncanny eyes, blinking as if trying to convey a message. He couldn't speak and she didn't either, just smiled slightly, kissed his mouth with closed lips, and pushed off him with her tentacles.

She floated before him, beckoning with her still human arms, her lower limbs drifting in the water, the tips curling and uncurling gently as if encouraging him to come closer. Elliot, who could barely look at her transformed body, shook his head. The creature behind him was no longer keeping him still, just supporting him in the water as Celeste swam lazy circles around them. Elliot flinched every time she came close to him but couldn't just leave her here in this horrifying new form. The water pressed against his eardrums, and he struggled to wake up.

Finally, Celeste swam around him one more time, dragging her tentacles across his skin as he recoiled. She brushed her hand against his cheek, smiled sadly, and let him go. She turned away from him, zipped through the water with amazing speed, and disappeared into the gloom of the water, her small devilfish trailing just behind her. The tentacles that had been holding Elliot let go as suddenly as they'd arrived, and Elliot woke with his heart hammering in his throat, gasping for air.

He threw the covers off and lurched out of bed to the wash-stand. He clenched the cool porcelain of the wash bowl and bent his head, breathing shallowly through his mouth. He waited through waves of nausea, but nothing came up. After a few minutes, he poured some water from the pitcher into the bowl and splashed a handful over his face.

He needed to get out of his room and away from the night-mare, but couldn't bear the thought of going downstairs and speaking to anyone.

The upstairs hall was deserted, all the bedroom doors in this wing closed except one. The door to Celeste's room was ajar, a shaft of late afternoon light shining through the crack onto the polished hall floorboards.

He pushed the door open. The room was cold and damp, wind and rain beating steadily against the windows. The cold sweat of Elliot's nightmare had dried, but he still felt waterlogged and chilled to the bone.

He glanced over his shoulder at the still-empty hall and stepped into the room, pushing the door nearly closed behind him. The room was filled with trunks and boxes—Celeste's things stored here temporarily until she settled in after the wedding. A feminine drift of fabric and lace lay across the reading chair in the corner by the window. He grazed his finger-tips over the pale blue silk dress on top, recognizing it as from a bolt of fabric the Captain had brought back from China and which Elliot had given Celeste as a wedding gift. He caught sight of the scattered pearls embroidered on the bodice and wondered whether this was the dress she'd planned to wear to their wedding. He turned away, blinking tears back.

He couldn't tell for sure, but it didn't look like Celeste had taken anything with her, if indeed she'd left on the strange ship that Pat saw. He recalled Sally marveling that Celeste had arrived last week with two steamer trunks and eight hatboxes. He counted the same number of hatboxes piled on top of one trunk. The other trunk was half-open at the end of her bed.

A small writing desk under the window was piled with untidy stacks of books and paper. Celeste had the most logical and organized mind he'd ever known in a woman, but tidiness in the physical realm was not her strong suit. She'd insisted Eugenia and Clarice not touch the desk when they cleaned her room, claiming that she had a system and if they moved her books and papers around, she'd never be able to find what she wanted.

Elliot idly sifted through the stacks. A couple of scientific periodicals on biology, one open to an article on the taxonomy of marine invertebrates, the other closed around a half-finished letter marking a page discussing the discovery of a possible new species of cephalopod. The first page of the letter was carefully copied in a small, neat script. Celeste had a habit of scrawling out first drafts in her journal while she organized her thoughts, then copying out a final draft to be readable by someone less familiar with her idiosyncratic handwriting.

This letter seemed to be in response to the article about the new cephalopod species. Elliot's eyes drifted over the letter, not really reading the unfamiliar scientific terms, until he caught the gist. The article claimed the new species was a type of squid, but Celeste's letter argued that it was more likely some sort of hybrid octopus because it had eight limbs, even though two were situated closer to the creature's head than the other six. Celeste also argued that these new octopuses were not solitary, as the author of the article claimed, but lived in large groups near a particular Pacific island, though the letter ended before she identified the island or how she knew about them.

Underneath the letter, the periodical had an illustration on the page facing the article Celeste had marked of a creature that looked very like the devilfish from Elliot's childhood nightmare, with a longer body and smaller head than the small octopus in Celeste's tank, and a pair of tentacles growing out from its sides, almost like human arms.

Elliot stared at the illustration for a few moments, fragments of his dream tugging at his mind, then pulled Celeste's journal from under the stack of papers, sat cautiously on the delicate chair in front of the desk, and began to read.

CHAPTER 9

*A*fter convincing Elliot to get some sleep, Declan paced back and forth from the parlor to the kitchen. The house was still, and his footsteps echoed dully on the polished wood floors. Sally's girls scuttled out of his way each time he passed them, and Sally finally shooed him out of their way so they could finish cleaning and get a head start on dinner preparations. He settled on the front porch in a wicker chair, pipe in hand, tobacco pouch on a small table next to him.

The sky was still gray, clouds scudding over the sliver of the bay visible from the porch. At least the rain had stopped. He breathed in the fresh scent of new wet leaves and other budding things. The cool breeze was refreshing after he'd been cooped up in the house and church all morning. He dipped into the pouch for a large pinch of tobacco and shaved a tiny piece off a small block of hashish, crumbled it into the tobacco, and packed the bowl tightly.

After lighting the pipe, he took a couple of short draws and stretched his legs out as the smoke drifted over his head. He kept off the opium he smuggled from British Columbia into various ports in the Pacific Northwest and California, but a bit of hash mixed with his tobacco was relaxing after a day like today. The service at Saint Paul's had been stifling. All of uptown society and a fair handful of downtown denizens had crowded into the narrow pews, filling the close air with their sighs and sniffles.

Most of them had come out of respect for Celeste's father, Declan gathered, who had been the rector of Saint Paul's for fifteen years before he died and was still remembered fondly. Declan had grabbed Mrs. Brady's arm to steady her as she stumbled from the front pew after the service and somehow ended up between her and Elliot in the receiving line after the service, the clutch of her gloved hand under his elbow tightening as the line of neighbors and gossips murmuring condolences seemed never to end.

Elliot was pale but calm, in the detached way that meant he was barely present. Declan brushed the back of his hand casually along Elliot's hip a few times. He couldn't do anything more, in public like that, to remind Elliot he was there, but each time, the tension in Elliot's jaw eased a bit more, and he shifted a little closer to Declan.

These last few days had been hard on Elliot. Declan didn't think he'd slept more than a couple of hours since Celeste disappeared. It was easier to go along with the notion that she'd drowned, rather than keep the town on edge about whether she might be alive. Especially considering that Elliot, Declan, and maybe Pat Lennan were the only ones who knew about the strange circumstances under which she'd disappeared. But Declan had heard snatches of gossip after the service that suggested some townsfolk still remembered how Elliot's mother had disappeared fifteen years ago.

"So strange," an older woman Declan hadn't recognized murmured to her companion in a ridiculous tall felt hat. "Just like his mother, you know. Remember how she disappeared one night? They said she drowned too, but I think that was just a story to hide that she sailed away with her lover."

The woman in the felt hat gasped obligingly, and the older woman continued. "Oh yes, my dear, you know young Elliot was six months old when Marie Bishop convinced Captain Fitzgerald to marry her. I suppose youth and beauty hide a multitude of sins, and the Captain had been looking for new business opportunities. Well, he got more than he bargained for with that girl, that's for certain. Why, she'd never even let young Elliot take the Captain's last name."

Declan had caught the eye of the felt-hatted woman, who tugged her friend away with a shame-faced glance over her shoulder at him. At least that gossiping shrew hadn't offered her fake condolences to Celeste's mother and Elliot. Declan's forbidding glare caused her to step out of the line with whispered apologies about needing some air. He was sure she wasn't the only one who remembered the scandal of Elliot's conception, though.

As far as Declan knew, Marie had never confessed who Elliot's father was. He knew it couldn't have been the Captain, since he'd been en route from Shanghai when she must have gotten in the family way. It was a whirlwind courtship, his stepmother had told him later. Father had sailed into town, met Marie when he was negotiating new business with her father, and asked for her hand only a few days afterward. Mr. Bishop agreed; Father sent for Declan, who was being cared for by a maternal aunt he barely remembered now; and Marie became the only mother Declan had ever known.

Declan shifted position, the wicker chair creaking underneath him. He repacked his pipe and let the hash relax his irritation at the narrow-minded gossips in town. It did nothing to ease his foreboding about whatever had been stalking his family for two generations now. The reappearance of the schooner his father had been chasing for fifteen years, at the same time the Captain himself disappeared, couldn't possibly be a coincidence. And the second woman in Elliot's life to go missing suggested that Elliot was somehow at the center of it all.

Declan closed his eyes and turned it all over in his mind, until a high, sweet whistle interrupted his thoughts. He cracked an eye open. Joey Carrigan was crunching up the gravel path to the house, wrapped in a giant waxed cotton overcoat and floppy-brimmed hat, dodging the muddy puddles still dotting the walkway. Declan set his pipe on the table next to his chair and stood to greet him.

"Afternoon, Captain."

"Joey." Declan returned Joey's handshake, his first mate's small hand nearly lost in his own, but Joey's grip was firm and his hand callused from years at sea. Declan gestured to the matching wicker chair on the other side of the small table and took a step toward the door. "Have a seat. I'll have Sally bring some coffee."

Joey waved his hand at him. "No need, sir, but thanks." He perched on the edge of the chair, and Declan returned to his own. Declan busied himself with his pipe while Joey surveyed the well-tended garden laid out between the house and Jefferson Street.

"Never been this far uptown. Nice here," Joey commented. Declan made a noncommittal sound as he drew on his pipe. He figured he knew what Joey had come to speak to him about but would let him say it in his own time.

They sat in comfortable silence for a few minutes, Declan blowing smoke rings that drifted over the rhododendron bushes planted along the front edge of the porch. Joey took a deep breath.

"I heard about Miss Celeste, Captain, and I'm that sorry to disturb you today. But we've been in port longer than usual, and the men are getting antsy."

Declan sighed. "I know. It's not as if I'd planned to stick around this long."

"Of course, Captain. It's just that…" Joey trailed off.

"Another few days won't matter much, Joey. Nance'll understand."

"She ain't exactly the understanding type, Captain." Joey's tone held only a trace of bitterness.

Declan gave him a small smile. "She'll come around eventually, Jo-Jo. She loves you, even if she has a hard time showing it."

Joey snorted and gazed across the well-tended herb patch just visible on the side of the house. His fine blond hair flopped across his forehead, and he pushed it absently behind his ear. "Anyways, we got a schedule to keep, Captain, if you'll pardon my saying so."

"The new cargo's loaded?"

Joey nodded. "She's filled to bursting with everything you wanted. Should fetch some good prices when we get there."

Declan couldn't tell whether Joey was looking forward to or dreading the *Black Dove*'s annual trip to his mother's compound on the west coast of Vancouver Island. Nance ran a major trading hub that served ships traveling between the U.S. and British Columbia and didn't ask questions about where the goods came from or whether the excise taxes had been paid.

Declan was reasonably certain the cargo he'd chosen would placate Nance for taking her only child away with him two years ago. He hoped. It wasn't like it was Declan's fault that Joey had stowed away and only revealed himself when they were halfway to San Francisco. They both knew why Joey had picked Declan's ship to run away on, and Declan knew Nance still blamed him for it.

"Plus, we still got stops to make along the way. And the sooner we get underway, the less trouble the crew'll get into downtown."

Declan raised an eyebrow. "Someone's causing a ruckus? I don't pay them well enough to behave in town?"

Joey grinned. "Everything was fine until Mr. Levy's man came round the Pacific Saloon looking for a new crew for one of his ships."

Declan straightened up in his chair, shaking the effects of the hash off. "Levy? He's sneaking around, trying to poach my crew?" Damn the man. Max Levy owned a boardinghouse for sailors and was a notorious crimp. He rustled up crews for several masters of the Pacific-crossing windjammers, in exchange for a cut of each sailor's advance money, plus a fee per man, and he wasn't particular about the sailors' willingness or sea experience.

Joey chuckled. "Reg sorted him. He offered to rustle up half a dozen crew for the man, for pay, of course. Levy's man Sonderson refuses at first, says Levy is paying him for exactly that, and he ain't sharing with nobody what he can earn for himself. Reg shrugs and offers to buy him a beer. Sonderson hesitates but says sure, and Reg went to fetch him a pint from Pat."

Joey leaned back in his chair, his lips twitching. Joey's smooth, beardless cheeks made him look younger than he was, and there was a dark smudge on his jaw. Declan resisted the urge to wet a thumb and wipe it off. He narrowed his eyes at Joey.

"Well?"

Joey tried to look innocent and failed spectacularly. Declan kicked the front leg of Joey's chair. "What the hell happened?"

Joey broke down in giggles. "Reg dumped enough laudanum in his beer to fell an ox. When he passed out, we dragged him down to the *Queen Elizabeth* and heaved him into a hammock. By the time he wakes up, he'll be halfway to Cape Horn."

Declan stared at him until the light dawned. "You shanghaied Levy's own man? The one he's been paying to drug and abduct sailors onto long-haul voyages?" He felt the first smile in days lift the corners of his mouth. When Joey's giggles grew to a full belly-laugh, Declan let go and laughed along with him.

After a few cathartic moments, Declan wiped his eyes with the back of his sleeve. "That's the best thing I've heard in days," he said. He knew well enough what it was like to wake up on a ship bound for China with no warning or opportunity for goodbyes. Declan had never viewed the crimps as a necessary evil like some ships' masters did, and Sonderson deserved a taste of his own medicine.

Joey snickered a few more times and gingerly wiped a hand down the side of his face with the smudge. Declan leaned forward to get a better look at his jaw. "Is that a bruise? You're not brawling downtown, are you, Jo-Jo?" he asked, gesturing at the smudge.

Joey pulled back from Declan's hand. "It's fine. Caught the bastard's elbow when we tossed him on deck, that's all. And quit calling me that, you know I hate it." He glanced quickly at Declan. "Sir."

Declan settled back in his chair and repacked his pipe instead of fussing more. Joey was as close to a son as Declan would probably ever have, but he knew one of the reasons Joey had run away from home was because of his mother's refusal to let him be the kind of man he wanted to be. Joey was young for being a first mate and even though Reg and the other crew had no trouble taking orders from him aboard, they looked out for him in port, since his baby face and small size made him an easy target for other sailors who didn't know who they were dealing with.

In any event, it sounded like Reg had handled the situation with Sonderson more creatively than Declan himself would have. And as long as his crew was safe and still loyal, Declan couldn't ask for much more.

Joey slapped his hands on his thighs and stood up. "I gotta get back, Captain. The men are gonna ask me when we sail. What do you want me to tell them?"

Declan sighed. "Monday, I suppose. Assuming you can find an available pilot tug. Check with Captain Libby about his schedule. He brought us in on the *Pioneer*, and his fee covers the round trip."

Joey nodded. "Give my condolences to your stepbrother."

Declan stood and briefly clapped Joey on the shoulder. "I will, Jo. I'll see you day after tomorrow."

Joey jogged down the steps from the porch and disappeared past the Douglas firs and madrona trees that shielded the Bishop house from prying eyes along Jefferson Street. Declan watched him go, leaning against the wooden railing along the edge of the front porch. He gripped the top rail with both hands. He was more than ready to be back on deck on the *Black Dove*, the wheel in his hands, wind in his face, underway on the home he'd made for himself, with the men who trusted him to look after their interests.

The door behind him creaked open, and the scent of apples and cinnamon wafted past. "Leaving him again, are you?" Sally asked. Declan turned and leaned against the rail. Sally's arms were crossed over her ample bosom, her mouth a thin stern line.

"It's happening again, and you just going to leave him to pick up the pieces?"

Declan met her brown eyes, which gazed steadily back at him. He always suspected Sally knew more about what happened in this house than she let on. He motioned toward the wicker chair Joey had just vacated, but Sally shook her head.

"What do you know about all this, Sal?" As far as Declan was aware, Sally rarely ventured downtown. She did the marketing at the uptown shops, attended services at Saint Paul's, and visited with the Rothschild's housekeeper on her days off.

Sally shrugged. "I heard the Captain and the missus talking about that ship. Couple days before she disappeared. She asked him about it one morning at breakfast, but he just dismissed her as seeing things. She stopped talking about it then but she spent more time away from the house over the next few days. I asked her what she did all day, but she just said she was out walking along the shore. Stopped doing the marketing, stopped going to the Mercantile, just spent all her days outside and came back with her dress all soaked in seawater.

"Then when the Captain brought her home, wet and shivering, she kept saying that she needed to go out to it, begged him to take her out to meet it."

Just like Celeste had insisted she needed to go out in the rain to check on her devilfish the night before she disappeared.

Sally sighed and pleated her apron between her fingers. "She finally fell asleep, and the Captain slept in his study so he wouldn't disturb her. The next morning, I went to wake her for breakfast, and she was gone."

"And when Father learned about the ship, he believed someone had taken Marie and she hadn't just drowned."

Sally nodded. "Someone, maybe. Or some*thing*. The more your father talked to other people who knew about the ship, the more he started thinking whatever took her wasn't human."

Declan stared at her. "Not human? What are you talking about?"

Sally shrugged. "Everyone knows there are monsters in the ocean. You've surely seen some. Stands to reason some would want to take people from shore for their own reasons."

Declan turned and looked out at the bay. It looked calm from this distance, the sun finally peeking out from the ribbons of clouds drifting apart, glinting like diamonds on the surface.

"Every sailor's seen things out there that he can't explain. But that's out in the middle of the ocean, not here in Port Townsend."

Except that Elliot had seen a huge devilfish try to drag his mother into the water the morning before she disappeared. But surely that was just a coincidence. It's not like devilfish need a ship to get around in the ocean. And what would they want with human women anyway?

Sally leveled a look at Declan. "You ever known your father to be fanciful?"

Declan shook his head. Captain Jack Fitzgerald was not a man of great imagination. Except for his insistence in the face of all logic that his wife had been taken somewhere and had not drowned. And his unrelenting search for the ship that had taken her. Declan put his hand in his coat pocket and fingered the note Father had left him with the chart. The cryptic warning he'd written in it was making more sense now.

He stepped forward and took one of Sally's capable, broad hands in his own. She let him squeeze her hand briefly, then pulled back.

"I need you to look after him, Sal." Declan said. He hated to leave Elliot again, especially now, but there was one thing he could do for Elliot at sea that he couldn't do in town. "I'll find her. I'll find Celeste and Father and bring them both home."

Sally nodded once, then turned to go back into the house.

"Do it soon, then," she said over her shoulder. "Before it's too late."

CHAPTER 10

*D*eclan appeared in the study's doorway as Elliot turned to a fresh sheet of paper, listing the supplies they'd need.

"How many casks of fresh water does the *Black Dove* already have aboard?" he asked immediately, to stop Declan from asking yet again how Elliot was doing. "I assume the crew's been eating and drinking in town, so how long will it take to provision the ship? Does Thomas keep a list of things he likes to have on hand?"

Elliot didn't even feel the usual stab of jealousy at the thought of Thomas's place on Declan's ship, and in his life. He was too busy sifting through the dry scientific hypotheses he'd read in Celeste's scientific publications and the vision of Celeste swimming away from him, half-changed into a creature illustrated in one of her journal articles, turning over what it all meant.

"You want to help me provision the *Black Dove*?" Declan asked, stepping into the study. He placed his hands on the back of the chair facing Elliot's desk. "Why?"

Elliot kept his eyes on the page as he wrote "bacon, potatoes, lard, flour, salt," then tapped his pen against his bottom lip in thought and added "limes." Focusing on the mundane task of making lists kept some of his incredulous panic at bay.

"You asked me to go with you to find the Captain. Fine, I'll go. We can look for him too while we're searching for Celeste. I can have everything we need in a day or two. Whatever the Mercantile doesn't have, I can get from Zee Tai's. The ship doesn't need any repairs before we set sail, does she?"

Declan was silent for a minute before replying, "No. She's ready to sail."

He sat down in the chair and tried to catch Elliot's eyes. "Elliot, are you all right?"

"I'm fine," Elliot said sharply. He squeezed his eyes shut. If he let Declan comfort him like he had after all his boyhood nightmares, the fear and panic and grief would overwhelm him. The urgent need to move, set sail, find the ship before it disappeared in the vast Pacific was tugging at him. He needed to do something, take some kind of action. Planning for the voyage was something he could do now, until the ship was ready and they could leave.

Elliot opened his eyes and pushed the lists aside, ignoring the splotches smearing the ink on the page. Declan folded his hands on the desk's surface and looked at Elliot with soft eyes.

"Elliot, I appreciate the offer, but I've already taken care of everything. I came in to tell you I'm leaving Monday. I have a full cargo hold and a schedule to keep. I'm already planning to check in at every port on either side of the Georgia Strait and try to track where the ship has gone. But I think you should stay here."

Elliot stared at Declan. Declan unclasped his hands and turned one palm up, extending it across the desk, like he wanted Elliot to put his hand in it. "Ellie. You need time to grieve. Bury yourself in the business if you need to. Until the pain of losing her gets better."

"No." Elliot glared at Declan. "I don't have time to grieve. And the damned business can shift for itself. I need to find the ship that took Celeste and get her back before..." He stopped and swallowed hard.

Declan looked just as hard back at him. "Before what?"

"Before something terrible happens to her." Elliot leaned forward, although he didn't come close to touching Declan. "She's still alive, Declan, I know she is."

Declan leaned back in his chair and sighed. "How do you know she's still alive? Just because we didn't find her body doesn't mean she didn't drown."

Elliot shook his head. "I cannot believe you, Declan. Your father spent my entire childhood chasing after a ghost ship that he claimed took my mother, and now you think Celeste drowned? You know Pat Lennan saw the ship. If it's the same one that took my mother fifteen years ago, then what the hell are we waiting for?"

He let a long sigh escape and dropped his shoulders, some of his anger burning off. "Look, you wanted me to help you find the Captain, who's already on the trail of this thing, so what's your problem?"

Declan leaned forward again, then sat back and rubbed his hand absently down his thigh. "That was before—" He closed his mouth, those full lips thinning as he pressed them together, then started again. "The *Black Dove*'s a small ship, Elliot. She's not built for passengers, and I keep the crew at the bare minimum necessary to handle her. I don't have an extra cabin for you."

Elliot shrugged. "I'll bunk with the crew. If there's not enough room to squeeze in an extra hammock, I'll work opposite shifts with someone. I'm not looking for special treatment here, Declan. And I'm not expecting White Star Line luxury accommodations."

Declan scrubbed his hands over his face and ran them through his hair. Then he said, "I don't think this is a good idea."

Elliot threw his pen down on the desk and crossed his arms over his chest. "Why the hell not?"

"I think this thing is connected to your nightmares, Elliot, and I don't want you anywhere near it."

Elliot couldn't stop the short bark of laughter but then bit his tongue, fearing if he let go, he'd drown in a wave of hysteria. Of course it was connected to his nightmares. First his mother disappeared, and he started having nightmares about that terrible creature that tried to drag him and his mother into the sea. The nightmares had faded as he grew older, and he'd convinced Declan and Sally, if not himself, that they were merely echoes of that early traumatic memory. But now he knew they were more than that. The fact that they'd started up again a week ago, even before Celeste disappeared, couldn't be a coincidence.

He had a terrible sense that he knew what Celeste wanted from him in his most recent dream. That her turning into a version of the devilfish from his nightmares was just the beginning of other changes in store for him. He had no intention of telling Declan all the details about his most recent dream, though.

"You're trying to protect me? Still? Declan, my fiancée disappeared under the same circumstances as my mother. The time for protecting me from whatever took them is long past."

Declan opened his mouth to say something, but Elliot barreled over him.

"What was your plan for finding the Captain, then?" Elliot demanded. "I haven't seen you in five years, I haven't been on a ship in twice as long, but you couldn't find your father without me along? You've crisscrossed the Pacific since you were a boy. You show up at my door in the middle of the night, the great smuggler and explorer Declan Fitzgerald, claiming to need my help to find your father, but now that there's someone missing who I care about, you think I should stay home where it's safe?"

Elliot stacked his lists up into an untidy pile and pushed back from his desk. "Fuck you, Declan." He kept his voice low so the Sally and the girls wouldn't hear. "I don't need your protection or your ship. I'll hire another ship and find them without you."

He shoved his chair back and got up from the desk. He needed to pack and send a message downtown. Captain Tibbals would know of any ships available for sale or rent. As he stalked around the desk's corner, Declan grabbed his arm.

"Elliot, wait."

Elliot jerked his arm away, but Declan's grip was too firm. He looked down at Declan's upturned face.

"You're right," Declan said, softly. Those eyelashes, even longer than Celeste's, swept down, shadowing his stubbled cheeks. Then Declan turned the full force of his green eyes on Elliot.

"Of course you want to find Celeste." He swallowed, and Elliot's eyes tracked the movements of his throat without even wanting to.

"And I promise I'll do everything I can to find her. But you don't even know where to start looking."

Elliot scoffed and swept his other arm over the surface of his desk. "I know how to read a chart, Declan. The one you got from your father doesn't have a scale on it, but it wasn't that hard to figure out more or less where that island is. I'm sure you can plot a course there."

Declan surged to his feet, crowding into Elliot's space. He let go of Elliot's arm and planted both hands on the desk. He pushed Elliot's lists aside and stared down at the grubby old chart lying on top of the large blue-backed Imray and Son chart of the North Pacific Ocean Elliot had pulled from the top shelf of the bookcase across the room.

"You took this from my room? So, privacy is something only you're entitled to?"

Elliot stepped back from the desk, confused by the sharpness in Declan's voice.

"What does it matter?" he asked. "You showed me this chart the night you arrived. You told me you wanted me to come with you. Why the sudden change of heart, now that I've agreed to come?"

Declan pinched the bridge of his nose and took a few deep breaths. When he lifted his head, Elliot couldn't read his expression at all. He picked up the chart and ran his thumb along the jagged curve of the bottom right corner.

"There's more to finding this island than just the distance. This section had writing on it. Not latitude or longitude but other clues about how to find it. Father had it translated and wrote me that you're the key, Elliot. I came to see you, because according to Father, you're the key to reaching this island."

Elliot stared at him. "All right then. I'm going. So, what's your problem?"

Declan sighed. "Don't you see, Elliot? I did want you to come with me. I've missed you, Elliot. I wanted—" He shrugged and shook his head slightly. "Well, that doesn't matter now. But I came here and found out you were getting married, Elliot."

He smiled sadly. "I couldn't drag you away just when you were about to start a life with Celeste. And now that she's disappeared, it's clear that whatever took your mother is active again. I don't think it was a coincidence that it took a second woman from you. We've no idea why they were taken or even if they're still alive. Father was obsessed with finding your mother, but if you're at the center of all of this, Elliot, then I'm not risking your life or safety on a voyage to who the hell knows where to find a ship we know nothing about or whether we'll find at all!"

His voice had risen, and he was shouting in Elliot's face now. His eyes were hard and his cheeks flushed, chest heaving. He crumpled the map into his fist, then tossed it on the desk. Elliot stared him down and waited until Declan calmed down a little.

"There's nothing left for me here, Declan," he said flatly. "This town wasn't safe for my mother or Celeste. And if your father is right and I am to blame for all of this, then there's no reason to think I'll be safe here."

Declan blinked. "I didn't say you were to blame, Elliot." His voice had lost some of the hard edge, but he still looked ready to argue against Elliot's coming along. "Why would you think that?"

Elliot shrugged and turned away. He'd always known deep down it was his fault his mother had disappeared and if he'd somehow warned Celeste, kept her from the shore and her damned devilfish, maybe she'd still be here too.

Declan sighed. "All right. We'll go together." He held a finger up in Elliot's face. "But I'm the master, Elliot, aboard ship and off, and you'll do everything I say. If I tell you to stay below decks, or hang back when we get there, or any other command I give you, you'll goddamn well do it, exactly as I say. Understood?"

Elliot took a deep breath, the fear and anxiety driving him to go after Celeste lessening a little. "Understood," he said. Then he glanced at Declan with a tiny smirk and said, "Captain."

Declan snorted and pushed him away. "Go on," he said. "Get packed. We'll leave with the morning tide on Monday."

Elliot set about tidying the study and gathering the few things he planned to take with him while Declan bent over the charts on his desk.

"What language was it written in?" he asked as he shelved the books Celeste had left strewn around various surfaces.

"Hmm?" Declan had a pair of dividers in his hand, one tip resting on a point on the Imray and Son chart. He walked the dividers to another point across the chart and made a small notation in pencil on the chart.

"The part torn off the chart, that you said the Captain had it translated. Translated from what?"

Declan walked the dividers across the Captain's map too and made another note on it with his pencil. A lock of hair fell across his face, and he tucked it behind his ear as he looked up at Elliot.

"Oh, Latin," he said. "Something about the son being the key and the key opens the way."

Elliot thought back to his Latin studies. *"Clavis aperit viam?*

That would be the literal translation of 'the key opens the way.' I suppose '*filius est clavis*' would translate into 'the son is the key', although *clavis* is technically a feminine noun."

Declan looked up. "How much Latin do you remember?"

Elliot shrugged. "A fair bit. Probably enough to translate whatever was on that bit of the chart, if you still had it. Roughly, anyway."

Declan tapped the dividers against his lips. "There were a few words Father couldn't figure out. Any idea what *iactura* means?"

Elliot crossed the study to pull his battered copy of Riddle's Latin-English dictionary off the shelf and blew the dust from it. He sneezed twice and flipped through the pages. "Well, it depends on the context, of course, but it could mean damage, loss, cost, sacrifice. Idiomatically, it's typically used in relation to throwing something overboard."

Declan looked sharply at him. "A sacrifice that's thrown overboard?" He sighed. "Elliot."

Elliot closed the dictionary with a snap. "Don't, Declan. You can't keep me here based on the figurative translation of one word out of context. Show me the original and I can check the Captain's translation, but either way, I'm coming." He tucked the dictionary under his arm and grabbed his coat off the back of his desk chair. "I'll start packing."

He left before Declan could say anything in response and ignored the troubled look in his green eyes.

CHAPTER 11

a week later, they were out on the Georgia Strait. They'd put in at Declan's usual stops in the San Juan Islands, trading silk and tobacco for smoked salmon, wool, and the first berries of the season. These he'd take to Nance Carrigan in trade for the opium and whiskey that were his primary source of income in trade between British Columbian and American port towns. Declan knew Elliot chafed at the time it was taking to find Celeste. They'd asked in every port and coastal town on either side of Haro Strait, between Vancouver Island and San Juan, about the ship Pat Lennan had told them about, but found few leads.

Only a few people they spoke with knew of the mysterious ship, and none had seen it recently. In Victoria, it had last been sighted in 1880, but reports from other settlements were varied and conflicting. No one admitted to seeing it so far this year.

The weather hadn't helped, either. Fog blanketed the straits most days, with sudden squalls blowing up almost every day since they left Port Townsend, tossing the ship about. Declan's crew struggled to keep her from drifting too close to the dozens of tiny islands and rocks that made up the San Juan archipelago.

They spent an extra night in Victoria waiting for a southwestern gale to blow over. Elliot chafed at the delay, but Declan knew of too many ships that had been stranded along the Vancouver Island shore to risk running the straits in those conditions.

Today, the storms were finally over and the cloudless sky was a clear blue. The air was cool and the wind was blowing from the southeast, strong enough to fill the topsail and t'gallant. As worried as he was about Elliot and his father, Declan was glad to be back on the water, the soothing motion of his ship rocking beneath him as he stood on the quarterdeck, legs braced wide for stability.

Declan knew Elliot was glad to be underway too. Every port they checked with no leads wound Elliot tighter and tighter. Declan ached to find something to distract him from the anxiety he could see was eating away at him. Elliot stuck to their agreement about submitting to Declan's authority as Captain. He bunked with the crew, took his meals with them, and threw himself into learning the ropes, above and below decks. Declan saw him only during the occasional evenings he wasn't on watch, when he'd spend a few minutes reading at the mess table, lamp light softening the deep lines between his brows and shining on his dark brown hair.

Declan sighed. He wasn't sure how he would survive this voyage with Elliot so close in physical proximity but so far away in spirit. He rested one hand on the ship's wheel, keeping his ship steady on the course through Boundary Pass and into Georgia Strait. Zig-zagging between the British Columbia mainland and the eastern towns on Vancouver Island would make what should have been a week's voyage from Port Townsend to Nance's compound into a tedious month-long sojourn. But Elliot refused to leave any stone unturned.

His bosun's dismayed shout pulled his attention down to the main deck. It had been years since Elliot had worked aboard the *Black Dove* and he'd forgotten nearly everything the Captain taught him. Reginald was an excellent bosun, but not a very patient teacher. And while Declan and Reginald had kept the foremast's square rigging, they'd changed the mainmast to the fore-and-aft rigging of a schooner and adapted a system of rings to haul the mainsail up the mainmast. It made the *Black Dove* more maneuverable with a smaller crew, but it meant that Elliot was starting from scratch in learning the names and purpose of the ship's lines.

Right now, Reginald was yelling at Elliot for mistaking the fore t'gallant buntline for the clewline and for failing to properly coil the fore halyard. Declan couldn't hear all his words, but he knew Reg had a general disdain for gentlemen and was likely doing his level best to scandalize Elliot with his seaman's language. Declan chuckled under his breath. He'd taught Elliot all the curse words he knew when they were boys, including several choice words he'd learned from Reg. Elliot didn't react to Reginald's language, and Declan had to respect his dogged determination to learn everything he could from the salty old man. At least the work gave Elliot something else to focus on besides his missing fiancée.

Thomas's dark head appeared as he came up the steps leading to the quarterdeck. He handed Declan a pewter mug with a hinged lid. The mug was warm, and Declan wrapped the chilled hand that had been on the wheel around it. Opening the lid with his thumb, he breathed in the spices Thomas put in the hot rum and took a deep sip. A few more sips, and Declan set the mug on a shelf next to the binnacle in front of the wheel. He nodded thanks to Thomas, the rum warming him from the inside.

Thomas stood next to Declan at the wheel, facing forward, the wind blowing his disheveled black curls across his face. This late afternoon visit before Thomas went back to the galley to finish preparing dinner had become a ritual of sorts over the last few years. Normally, Declan appreciated Thomas's thoughtfulness of bringing him a hot or cool drink, depending on the weather. They'd chat for a few minutes, and Thomas would keep Declan apprised of the news, gossip, or petty squabbles among the men. They were a tight-knit crew and got along well enough, but eight men could hardly serve aboard a ship as small as the *Black Dove* for months on end without occasionally erupting into arguments or minor fisticuffs. Thomas was usually privy to all sides of any conflict.

Today, Declan wasn't sure he wanted to hear Thomas's gossip. He was pretty sure it would be about Elliot, even though Thomas and Elliot had barely spoken three words since they set sail. It was odd, since Thomas was a man everyone got along with and the unofficial mediator among the crew. But Thomas and Elliot had taken an almost instant dislike to each other, and Declan had a feeling he knew why. It was damned annoying to watch two grown men—one who knew he didn't have a permanent claim on Declan and one who claimed he didn't want one—circle each other like marriage-minded maidens at a church social.

"Your brother isn't much of a sailor," Thomas said, looking forward. Elliot was re-coiling the fore halyard, properly this time, and nodding occasionally as Reginald launched into his next set of instructions.

"He'll pick it up," Declan said mildly. He hadn't interfered in the crew's good-natured tests of Elliot's mettle, mostly small pranks and minor altercations. But there was no moment on his ship when Declan didn't know exactly where Elliot was, what he was doing, and who was with him.

"I suppose your brother has other talents on land," Thomas said, still gazing forward. Declan hadn't missed the emphasis on the word "brother" the first time Thomas said it, but the repetition was really too much.

"You have something to say to me, Thomas?" he asked, injecting a note of command in his voice that he rarely had to use with anyone on his crew.

Thomas glanced sideways at him and back forward. "No, Captain," he said.

"Then I'm sure you have work in the galley you should be getting back to." The last thing he needed was to deal with a jealous Thomas on top of a grieving and obstinate Elliot.

"Aye, Captain," Thomas said. He took a few steps forward, then paused. "It's only," he said, glancing back at Declan.

"What is it?"

"He's not sleeping." Thomas jerked his chin at Elliot, who'd finally done something to Reginald's approval, apparently, since Reg was slapping him on the back and Elliot was grinning like a schoolboy.

"What do you mean?" Declan asked.

"He has nightmares," Thomas started, and Declan grunted in acknowledgment. Thomas continued. "He wakes the men up with them. And last night, Joey was on watch and he says your broth—" he stopped and glanced at Declan's frown, "he says Mr. Bishop was standing at the rail in his shirt, looking down at the water. He didn't respond when Joey called to him, and when Luca came and touched his arm, he started like he'd just been woken up."

Declan kept his eyes on the horizon. "They're just nightmares. He's had them off and on ever since he was a boy." Declan had no intention of telling Thomas what Elliot's nightmares were about. As far as the crew knew, this voyage was to introduce Elliot to Declan's regular trading posts and explore potential new ports. He told Joey they were also searching for news of his father, but otherwise, there was no need for the men to know what they were really looking for.

"I'll talk to him," he said to Thomas.

Thomas looked like he wanted to say something else.

Declan sighed. "What is it?"

"After Elliot went below, Luca thought he saw something too. He couldn't see it clearly, but it was big, he said. A giant devilfish swimming alongside the ship. It disappeared for a while, then reappeared on the other side of the ship. Luca said it kept up with us all night, though no one else saw anything unusual after dawn."

Declan smiled at Thomas to cover his sudden apprehension. "We've all seen devilfish before. Probably just curious about us, like the dolphins and sharks that trail behind the ship sometimes."

Thomas looked unconvinced. "Luca said it was the biggest one he'd ever seen. Much bigger than usual. And there was a strange sound, too. Like some kind of singing he could barely hear. Sounded a little like the sound Elliot makes when he's having nightmares, before the screaming starts."

Declan kept his face calm and broadened his smile a little. "Well, you know how the ocean at night can play tricks on your mind. It probably just looked bigger than usual because we're near the new moon and there's no light from it." He took another sip from the mug and set it back on the shelf.

Dammit. Declan couldn't afford sleep-deprived men seeing strange visions in the water. And if Elliot really was sleepwalking, Declan would need to keep a closer eye on him. He knew Elliot would protest the only solution he could think of, but maybe it would give them a chance to spend time together again. More than almost anything else, Declan missed the easy companionship they'd once shared.

"Anything else going on?" he asked Thomas.

Thomas grinned at him. "Luca and Seamus are at it again. They think they're being discreet this time."

Declan couldn't resist smiling back. Luca and Seamus fought and fucked like cats but were the best sailors he had, after Reginald and Joey. Only Thomas could keep track of which they were doing at any given time.

He finished his rum and handed the mug back to Thomas. "Send Mr. Bishop up when you go down, will you?" Thomas nodded shortly, clearly not pleased to have to speak to Elliot. Declan sighed. In for a penny, he supposed. He put a hand on Thomas's arm and squeezed gently. "Probably not for a while, Tom. I am sorry about that."

Thomas's eyes searched his face, and Declan knew he was only confirming Thomas's suspicions about his relationship with Elliot. He'd surely miss the man's mouth, not to mention his sizable cock. But taking care of Elliot was his first priority, even if it meant denying himself the full extent of his cook's talents. He only hoped this wouldn't affect the quality of his meals.

Declan watched Thomas head down the few steps to the main deck, snag one of the crew and point to Elliot before disappearing down the hatch to the galley. Declan rolled his eyes. Elliot was only a few feet forward of the main hatch, but Thomas still went out of his way to avoid speaking directly to him. He checked the horizon and waited patiently for Elliot to finish his work on the deck and come to him. He'd leave Thomas and Elliot to work out their issues themselves, if they ever did.

Elliot jogged up the steps to the quarterdeck, and Declan couldn't resist a broad smile. The wind and Elliot's exertions had flushed his cheeks a deep pink, which only made him more handsome than usual. His hands were reddened too, chapped from the cold and blistered from the lines, but Declan didn't fuss over him.

"You wanted to see me, *Captain*?" Elliot smirked as he put a cheeky emphasis on the title. Dammit, now Declan couldn't help thinking about hearing that from those lips in an entirely different setting. He cleared his throat and adjusted his stance, trying to ignore the twitch his cock gave at the thought.

"I hear you were sleepwalking last night." Might as well get straight into it. The smirk left Elliot's face, and his lips pinched closed. He didn't say anything.

"You'll sleep in my cabin until we can figure out how to stop your nightmares."

"Absolutely not," Elliot snapped.

"Elliot," Declan started.

"I'll tie myself to my hammock, if I need to."

"That's not enough and you know it, Elliot," Declan snapped back. "Your nightmares are disturbing the crew."

"I don't want any special treatment, *Captain*," Elliot replied, putting a hostile emphasis on the title this time. "I told you that. Besides, isn't your cabin usually full enough?"

Declan raised an eyebrow at him, surprised Elliot would make even a veiled reference to his relationship with Thomas.

"If you're looking for the kind of special treatment given a seaman who defies his captain's orders, that can be arranged." Thomas's jealousy was understandable, but Elliot was the one who said he didn't want Declan anymore.

Elliot turned to face Declan and crossed his arms over his chest. He'd left his pea jacket somewhere while working on deck, and standing here on the quarterdeck where the wind was stronger, he looked chilled in only his shirt and vest. Declan squelched the urge to offer Elliot his own coat.

"I'll share Joey's cabin, then."

"No," Declan replied. He was the goddamned captain of this ship. "Joey's cabin is half the size, and it's his right as first mate not to share it. Do you really want him to hear your nightmares?"

Declan lowered his voice, keeping his frustration and worry in check. "Elliot. I brought you along in exchange for your agreement to do exactly as I say. Remember that?"

Elliot's shoulders dropped. "Fine," he sighed, not looking at Declan. "Permission to return to work, Captain?"

Declan gazed at him for a long moment, but Elliot refused to meet his eyes. Finally, he nodded. "You're dismissed." Elliot returned to the main deck without another word. Declan focused back on the sea ahead and tried not to think too much about Elliot in his cabin that night. In solving one problem, that of keeping Elliot from disturbing the crew, he'd just made his other problem that much worse.

CHAPTER 12

*E*lliot stumbled against the wall of the passageway between the mess and the aft section of the ship. Reginald had organized a round of toasts to celebrate Elliot finally learning the names and functions of all the ship's lines, and he'd drunk more than he realized.

"Fore topsail clewline, fore topsail inner buntline, fore topsail outer buntline, fore t'gallant clewline, fore t'gallant buntline, fore t'gallant leechline," he murmured to himself, leaning his head on the wall to rest a minute. He'd always been good at memorization and just like reciting Latin verb forms worked when he was a boy, the same technique worked to memorize the ship's lines now. The ship groaned beneath his cheek, an omnipresent sound Elliot had only gotten used to after several days aboard.

Being belowdecks still made him a bit queasy, and the rum sloshing around in his stomach wasn't helping. The mild seasickness was part of why he'd volunteered as a deckhand. He felt better on deck, moving with the motion of the ship, having tasks to focus on, rather than sitting on his ass belowdecks, wallowing in his anxiety for Celeste.

It helped him feel less indebted to Declan too. Every other

man on the ship worked, and worked hard. Their respect for Declan was obvious. Each man spoke about their captain with something close to worship. Watching Declan interact with his crew, Elliot could see why. He was firm and decisive but always ready with a ribald joke to lighten a tense moment. He ate meals with the men and matched them drink for drink but never seemed inebriated. Not like Elliot, whose prior drinking experience was limited to a glass or two of wine at dinner and a small sherry before bed. But the rum also muted the nightmares, at least sometimes, and that was a plus. Mostly.

He reached Declan's cabin and paused outside the door. He didn't know how he'd survive spending an entire night in Declan's cabin. He'd only spent years fantasizing about being in this very place.

Declan was sitting at his desk, writing. Today's entry in the ship's log, Elliot supposed. He wondered if Declan wrote anything about him in it, or how. *Blackmailed my stepbrother into sleeping with me by trading on unfair knowledge about something that's none of my business.*

Elliot sighed. That was unfair. It wasn't Declan's fault that Elliot's nightmares and sleepwalking were disturbing the crew. But Elliot had been simmering with anger since they left Port Townsend. At Celeste, for disappearing and causing him to be on this ship in the first place. At Declan for making the obvious suggestion that Elliot should sleep in a cabin with a stout door so he didn't disturb the crew with his dreams or accidentally sleepwalk over the rail of the ship into the ocean. At the crew for the range of looks from barely hidden disdain to bemused concern he got when he woke them with his screams. But mostly at himself, for whatever was so wrong with him that not even working himself to exhaustion or drinking until he couldn't stand kept the dreams at bay for very long.

"Stop hovering," Declan said without looking up. His desk was centered toward the back wall of the cabin, under a line of portholes in the ship's stern. "Come in and sit down before you fall down."

Elliot stumbled in a few steps and collapsed into the only other chair in the cabin, in front of Declan's desk. He let himself sprawl against the padded back, resting his arms on the carved wooden arms of the chair and stretching his legs out. It felt good to take up the full space his body occupied. Everything on the *Black Dove* was compact and coiled, folded, or tucked into its proper place. Elliot had spent the first couple days aboard learning how to stay out of the way unless needed and how to accomplish the tasks Reginald gave while taking up as little space as possible. At over six feet tall and after a lifetime of better food than most of the crew had grown up with, Elliot was by far the largest man on the ship.

He shifted restlessly. The chair was comfortable, but Declan's silence wasn't doing anything to alleviate the anxiety churning under his skin. He gazed around the cabin to avoid looking directly at Declan.

The cabin took up two-thirds the width and length under the quarterdeck, the rest being Joey's cabin. Declan had told him the *Black Dove* didn't take on passengers, and there wouldn't have been any room for them, since the captain's and first mate's cabins were the only truly private spaces on board the ship.

A glass-fronted bookcase on the interior wall separating Declan's cabin from Joey's held books and charts and a few other items. He stood and took the few steps from his chair to examine them so he'd have something to do while Declan ignored him. Also, so he wouldn't have to look at the wide bed that took up most of the rest of the cabin's space.

He ran his fingers lightly over the assortment of things Declan had collected on his travels. A small bowl with bits of blue and green sea glass, a starfish bigger than the width of Elliot's hand propped next to a large conch shell, small mementos from trips he must have taken with his father to China and Polynesia.

Declan finally put his pen down and capped the ink bottle. "Drink?" he offered Elliot, reaching for the whiskey bottle on the corner of his desk.

"God, no," Elliot groaned. "I've had more than enough as it is." He paced the few steps between the desk and the bed, still trying not to look at it. It was far bigger than the hammock he'd been using in the crew quarters but not so large that he'd be able to avoid touching Declan while they slept.

Declan poured himself a sizable amount, judging by the glug of liquid into his glass. "It didn't used to be so terrible," he said.

Elliot turned around. "What didn't?"

Declan gestured with his glass at the bed. "Sharing a bed with me." He took a long sip, and Elliot watched his throat move as he swallowed. Damn Declan for being so irresistible.

"Is there anyone who considers sharing your bed to be terrible?"

Declan's jaw tightened and he slowly set his glass down. "I am trying to help. The crew thinks your nightmares are bad luck and they're superstitious enough about this voyage. Not to mention, the last thing we need is you sleepwalking off the goddamned ship in the middle of the night. Unless that's your plan—to join your fiancée in the deepest part of the straits. In which case, I'll be damned if I let you kill yourself for her."

Elliot knew Declan was trying to help. The problem was that he didn't want to need Declan's help. He wanted the nightmares to stop, but there was little Declan could do about that. Except that his nightmares had always been less frequent when Declan was around. These dreams were different, though: Celeste calling for him, just outside his reach, but calling him to find something he didn't much want to find. But Declan's overprotectiveness always made Elliot feel like he was a terrified child again. Except when Declan made him feel other things, which didn't help Elliot's situation either.

"Well, I doubt Thomas is very grateful for how much you're

helping me. Are you sure you wouldn't rather be *helping* him instead of me?"

Declan's temper, which Elliot knew was never long to begin with, snapped. He pushed his chair back from his desk with a harsh scrape and with two long steps, was around the desk and pushed Elliot hard against the back of the cabin door.

Declan was a couple of inches shorter than Elliot but broader in the shoulders after his years at sea. His hand gripped Elliot's shoulder hard, shirtsleeves rolled up to the elbow, the muscles in his forearm shifting as he pressed Elliot against the door.

"Thomas is none of your concern," Declan said, in a low, hard voice. He'd never admitted to Elliot that Thomas was anything other than his ship's cook. But ever since Elliot came aboard, he'd been watching Thomas look at Declan the same way Elliot was afraid he looked at Declan when no one was else was watching.

He shouldn't blame Declan for finding someone when Elliot had Celeste. But damn it, he didn't want Declan to have anyone other than him. And tonight, Elliot was spoiling for a fight. He'd lost track of whether it was from jealousy over Thomas or anger at Declan's overprotectiveness. Or the constant state of semi-arousal he'd been swimming in since Declan came back into his life. Regardless, he'd drunk enough to not give a damn what came out of his mouth.

Speaking of mouths, Declan's was only a few inches away. Elliot watched the tip of Declan's tongue pass across his bottom lip. Declan dropped his eyes from Elliot's to his hand clenched in Elliot's shirt. He opened his hand and smoothed the fabric.

"You should go to sleep," Declan finally said in an even tone. "You have the early watch."

Elliot said nothing. But when Declan stepped back and turned away, he grabbed Declan's shoulder and swung him around. He shoved Declan back across the room until he backed up against the edge of his desk and had his tongue in Declan's mouth before Declan could say anything.

He tasted like whiskey and felt exactly like Elliot remembered. He didn't kiss Elliot back at first, but when Elliot pushed his full length up against Declan's body, Declan groaned and slid his arms up around Elliot's shoulders. Elliot shrugged his arms off and pushed his hands away.

"Be still," he growled in Declan's ear. He didn't want gentleness or comfort. He just wanted…God, he just wanted something *real* after the dreams he'd been having. He pressed harder against Declan's body, until Declan had to brace his hands on the edge of the desk to stay upright. Elliot twisted one hand in Declan's hair at the nape of his neck and thrust his tongue in Declan's mouth. Declan thrust back, their mouths open and panting, teeth clacking, tongues twining and jostling. As long as Elliot kept Declan's mouth occupied, Declan wouldn't be able to ask Elliot if he was sure he wanted to do this.

He didn't want to think about what he was doing, or why now. He just wanted what he'd been missing for so long. He pulled his hips back just enough to get his other hand in between their bodies. Declan's cock was straining against his trousers, just like Elliot's. He kept his hands braced on the desk but thrust his hips forward as Elliot's hand grazed over his fly.

Fumbling at the buttons, Elliot got first Declan's trousers open, then his own. He groaned into Declan's mouth as he finally touched the hard silk of Declan's cock. Declan groaned too, as Elliot slid his hand over the already-wet tip and down his shaft. He braced his feet on either side of Declan's, slotted his cock next to the one in his hand, and wrapped both hands around them together.

It didn't take long. Three or four firm strokes and Declan spilled into his hands, head tipped back, a low groan escaping his parted lips. Elliot came just after, the warm wetness slicking his last couple of strokes, and slumped against the bulwark of Declan's body. He dropped his head on Declan's shoulder and briefly turned his forehead into Declan's neck. He breathed in Declan's scent as his heart rate returned to normal.

Then Declan shifted position, letting go of the desk edge and lifting his arms, but Elliot pulled away. He wasn't angry anymore, at least not at Declan. More ashamed of himself, for betraying Celeste and using Declan without regard to whether Declan would consider it a betrayal of Thomas. He pulled the rest of his shirt from his waistband and wiped his hands on the tail, not caring about the mess. As he fastened the buttons of his trousers, he could feel Declan stirring behind him.

"I'm sorry," he said, without turning around. "I shouldn't have done that."

"Elliot," Declan started. He didn't sound angry, but Elliot couldn't stay in the cabin a moment longer.

"I'll swap the night watch with Joey," Elliot said, and left the cabin before Declan could say anything else.

CHAPTER 13

The cold air on deck blew some of the muzziness from Elliot's head. Joey was lounging on the quarterdeck in the helm's chair, scanning the sea ahead and humming snatches of the song they'd been singing after dinner. Elliot didn't call attention to himself just yet. He liked Joey, but he so rarely had time to himself on the ship that he wanted to savor these few minutes unnoticed. In the dark, tucked in the shadow of the ladder to the quarterdeck, Elliot was just out of sight unless Joey looked directly down at him.

He hummed along with Joey under his breath until he realized that it wasn't Joey singing on the quarterdeck above him. The low humming was coming from below, off the ship. Elliot leaned over the rail, listening harder. Tiny waves rippled outward from the ship, their crests sparkling in the starlight. The water still slapped against the sides of the ship, and the lines still creaked, but Elliot felt the humming even more than he heard it. Like the clanging of a giant bell, the sound thrummed through his whole body. He leaned farther over the rail, straining to discern where the sound was coming from and what the message was.

Something stirred just under the water. A pale tendril winked above the surface, then disappeared. Then another rolled over with a tiny ripple, gleaming wetly in the moonlight, and a third unfurled a long length on the water's surface. Elliot could sense rather than see a large body under the black water, floating alongside the ship, beckoning to him. He let himself lean farther and farther over the railing. If he could just get close enough to it, he'd be able to hear the music, match the thrumming under his own skin to whatever was making that irresistible sound. It was like something was calling to Elliot. Something that needed him as much as maybe Elliot needed it.

Elliot sidled along the side to the main starboard shroud. After a quick glance at Joey, still idly sprawled in the helm's chair, gazing at something off to port, he swung a leg over the railing and hung from the lines connecting the shroud to the hull. He dropped into the water with barely a splash. The frigid water soaked immediately through his clothes into his bones, but the sound was louder and deeper underwater. It resonated in his body, thrumming along his blood, washing over him like the ocean's gentle waves.

Elliot kicked back to the surface and turned over to float on his back. His limbs were heavy, his clothes and boots weighing him down, but something rose underneath him, supporting his back and head. He relaxed into its firm cradle, the humming louder now, in his ears, echoing in his bones, radiating along all his nerves.

Something long and muscular snaked up from underneath him, wrapping over his thigh and twining around his leg all the way to his ankle. Elliot kicked lazily with his other leg, but a second limb twined around it, dragging his hips under the surface and spreading his legs apart. Soft suckers on the under-side of each tentacle wrapped around his legs grasped and flexed against his legs, briefly warming him before the pressure numbed him from toes to mid-thigh.

The humming inside his head dulled his thoughts, and Elliot relaxed against the creature cradling him. His face was enough above the water to breathe, and he stared up at the star-spangled sky, not caring about the flurry of activity aboard the ship he was slowly floating away from. Another creature slithered up the front of his body, sandwiching him between it and the one he was lying against. He closed his eyes as something warm and firm nudged over his groin, and his hips thrust forward even as a part of his mind tried to wake up and fight back. He pulled half-heartedly against the tentacles wrapped around his legs, to see if he could wriggle out of the beast's hold. It merely tightened its arms around his legs and wound two more tentacles around his arms, immobilizing him.

The humming increased, not louder, precisely, but deeper, echoed by the sound waves rippling under his skin and along his nerves, flowing through him and relaxing him, as the limbs wrapped around his arms and legs squeezed tighter. The creature on top molded itself closer, enveloping him as his hips thrust against it. With his eyes closed, he could just concentrate on the creatures slithering and squeezing against him. The less he struggled, the better they felt against every inch of him, even through his sodden clothes.

Elliot vaguely heard shouting above him and then a sharp crack followed by a splash. The creature on top of Elliot jerked and rolled over, Elliot still clutched in its grasp. Elliot's eyes opened underwater, face to face with a bulbous head and glowing orange alien eyes. A second crack, the sound muffled through the water this time, and all the limbs that were holding him suddenly released. Elliot sank down amidst a cloud of swirling black ink and a confusion of flashing and rippling tentacles.

He kicked up through the churning water as the creatures shot away in separate directions and gasped a mouth full of water as his head broke the surface. Treading water, he sputtered and coughed, then looked around for the *Black Dove*. She was several feet to his left, what looked like half the crew leaning over the sides, yelling and waving.

A life ring splashed into the water, and Elliot swam for it. His legs were dead weight but he dog-paddled to the ring and clung to the outside edge of it, threading his hands through the rope. He rested one cheek on the top and let the crew haul the ring and him to the side of the ship.

Somehow, Joey got him up the ladder and back on deck of the ship. "Don't tell Declan," Elliot whispered, teeth chattering, as Joey scrubbed roughly at his head with a towel.

"The fuck I will," Joey retorted, snapping his fingers at Seamus, who was hustling forward with a steaming mug. Joey wrapped two heavy wool blankets around Elliot's shoulders and shoved the mug into his shaking hand. "You'll tell him your goddamned self and you'll make sure he understands none of us even knew you was up here. We ain't taking the Captain's punishment for your damn fool antics."

Elliot sipped at the hot rum and wrapped both his chilled hands around the mug's warmth. "Declan wouldn't punish you," he assured Joey. "And he really doesn't have to know about this. It will never happen again, I promise."

Joey tossed the damp towel aside and squatted in front of Elliot to work at the waterlogged knots of his bootlaces. "You don't know a goddamned thing about the Captain if you think he don't know every fucking thing happens on his ship. Or that he wouldn't blame us if anything happens to you, you reckless eejit." He glanced up at Elliot, his thick-lashed blue eyes flashing. "And you tell him what you went in after, or so help me, I'll make you wish you had."

Elliot swallowed more of his rum and nodded. He outweighed Joey by fifty pounds, at least, but something about Joey's quiet ferocity convinced Elliot not to test him on this. He'd already noticed that everyone on the crew deferred to Joey and he knew Declan trusted Joey more than he did most people.

Maybe more than Declan trusted Elliot right now. Joey was right anyway. It wasn't fair to ask the crew to keep this from Declan. "I'll tell him," he sighed. He stood up and slung his waterlogged boots over his shoulder. "Guess I better get it over with."

Declan was already halfway up the companionway ladder when Elliot slipped through the hatch opening. He stopped at the sight of Elliot, flicked his eyes up and down Elliot's body as if checking for injury, and glanced pointedly at the water dripping off Elliot's clothes to splash on the steps. He didn't say anything, just went back down the ladder, pushed the door to his cabin open, and followed Elliot in. He didn't even slam the door closed, though his fist clenched against the wood briefly, and then opened and dropped to his side.

He returned to his desk and leaned against its edge, arms crossed over his chest. "What happened?" he asked. A muscle clenched in his jaw but his voice was mild, the same voice Elliot had heard him use before to get information before deciding what action to take.

Elliot dropped his boots near the door and stood dripping on Declan's oriental carpet, trying to think how to explain what happened. "I went overboard," he started.

"I see that," Declan replied, his eyes traveling from Elliot's wet hair to his bare cold feet, and back up his body, as if the first assessment he'd done couldn't be trusted and he needed further reassurance that Elliot wasn't injured. "Why?"

Elliot shrugged. "I thought I heard something." Declan raised an eyebrow and waited. "In the water." Elliot swiped the back of his hand over his forehead and pushed his wet hair back away from his face. "I don't know how to explain it."

Declan waited a moment, then said, "What will Joey tell me if I ask him?"

Elliot huffed a mirthless laugh. This, at least, he could answer. "That I'm a, what was it he called me? A reckless eejit."

Declan's lips twitched slightly. "Sounds like Joey. Don't know that I'd disagree with him. What else would he tell me?"

Elliot sighed. There was no way to get out of telling Declan what happened. Thinking about how to tell it from Joey's perspective actually helped. He wondered how often Declan used this trick to get one of his crew to confess something. "He'd say there were at least two giant devilfish in the water, maybe more, and I was floating in the water, and they were wrapped all around me."

He risked a glance at Declan's face. "I wasn't in any danger of drowning," he assured him. "One was underneath me, supporting me, and my face was above the water the whole time. It wasn't until Joey shot at them that they swam off and I went under."

He couldn't tell Declan what else the devilfish did to him. He shivered hard, water dripping down his neck, under his collar, echoing how the creature's slippery skin felt sliding along his body. Declan pushed himself off his desk and went to the trunk at the end of his bed. He returned with a wool blanket spread in his hands and flapped the ends at Elliot.

"Come on, you need to get out of those wet clothes."

Elliot fumbled with the buttons of his soaked shirt. His cold fingers were stiff and uncooperative. He got half the buttons undone, each one taking longer than it should. He shuddered again and reached for the blanket. If he could just get warm, he could feel his fingers and finish the buttons. Declan wrapped the blanket around him and rubbed briskly up and down his arms.

Declan pulled away and tossed a shovel of coal into the belly of the small stove in the corner of the cabin. When he came back to Elliot, he reached under the blanket and finished unbuttoning Elliot's shirt.

"Come on, man," he soothed, as he slid Elliot's arms from the sleeves and drew the shirt off, tossing it on the floor near the door. "You'll feel better when you're dry." Elliot swayed on his feet, hardly noticing Declan's fingers unbuttoning his fly. Declan crouched at his feet and Elliot leaned against his shoulder while Declan pulled one leg, then the other, from his sodden trousers. The trousers joined the shirt with a wet squelch, and Declan rose and tugged Elliot to the bed.

"I'm fine," Elliot said irritably, trying to bat Declan away without exposing his arm from under the blanket. The wool was scratchy but thick, and Elliot already felt a little warmer, but he couldn't stop the fine shivers running through his body.

Declan ignored his feeble struggles and pulled him stumbling to the bed. He grabbed a towel from the washstand tucked in the corner near the bed and rubbed Elliot's legs dry. A gentle push, and Elliot was sitting on the edge of the bed. Declan lifted the covers and nudged Elliot's legs. Elliot obediently swiveled them under the covers. He kept the blanket wrapped around his shoulders and fell back against the pillows.

Declan drew the covers up over his shoulders and sat on the bed next to his hip. Elliot turned on his side away from Declan and closed his eyes. He curled as tight as he could, still shivering under the layers of wool and linen.

Declan rubbed soothing circles on his back, and Elliot gradually warmed enough to stop shaking. Exhausted, he let his mind drift. He was half-asleep when he heard Declan ask in a quiet neutral voice, "Why did you go into the water, Elliot?"

There was a reason Elliot shouldn't tell Declan the truth but at the moment, he couldn't remember it. "They were calling to me. They said they'd take me home," he heard himself say from a distance. Then Elliot let himself tip softly into sleep.

CHAPTER 14

$\mathcal{A}$ full week passed without Elliot having a nightmare, and Declan was relieved that he seemed to be sleeping better. He no longer had the violet shadows under his eyes Declan had noticed the morning after he'd arrived in Port Townsend, and the pinched look to his face had eased. The last few days of sun and warmer weather had even put some color in his cheeks. Declan let his eyes linger on Elliot's broad, sunburned back, muscles rippling as he hauled the fore sail's port clewline to furl the sail as they pulled closer to the wharf at New Westminster, up the Fraser River in British Columbia.

Sharing his cabin with Elliot was both harder and better than Declan had expected. When Declan asked the morning after Elliot went overboard what he'd meant with that cryptic comment about the devilfish taking him home, Elliot pretended he didn't know what Declan was talking about. But Declan caught him staring into the water so frequently over the next several days that he flatly refused Elliot's suggestion of taking the first or middle watches. There was no way Declan was risking Elliot being lured overboard in the middle of the night again.

Instead, Elliot worked harder than ever during the day on

deck and spent his evenings chatting with Joey or Luca or reading at the mess table until well past midnight. The fact that he chose to spend his evenings in closer proximity to Thomas than Declan wasn't lost on Declan, but he held back from saying anything to Elliot.

Because when Elliot finally came to the cabin after he thought Declan was asleep, Elliot would crawl into bed and stretch alongside Declan, his chest against Declan's back and his knees tucked behind Declan's. Each night, Declan waited until he was sure Elliot was completely out before tugging Elliot's arm around Declan's chest. Each night, Elliot relaxed a little more against Declan's body. Declan didn't take any further advantage beyond lacing their fingers together and kissing the back of Elliot's hand. In the mornings, Elliot disentangled himself and got up before Declan woke, but falling asleep against Elliot's warmth, his soft snores rumbling in his ear, was more than Declan had expected, if less than he wanted.

Elliot had finally stopped complaining about their glacial pace. He'd even stopped insisting on accompanying Declan in his inquiries about his father and the eight-masted schooner. After some trial and error, they'd discovered that Declan tended to get more information from the dock workers and harbormasters on his own. He'd been in most of the towns along both sides of the Georgia Strait at least once and was less of a stranger than Elliot.

Still, Elliot had a knack for developing new trade with town shop owners. Declan dispatched him, accompanied by Joey, to negotiate new deals for goods they didn't know they needed that Elliot could provide from the Mercantile or Declan could bring the next time he sailed through. He'd already increased Declan's profits on this trip and had a handshake arrangement with several new establishments Declan hadn't considered developing.

Declan stepped off the *Black Dove* onto the wharf and headed for the harbormaster's office. New Westminster was a thriving town with warehouses, storefronts, and houses lined the riverbank, sloping uphill and petering out before a forest of red cedar and Douglas fir trees began.

The harbormaster, Kenneth McKenzie, shook Declan's hand and said no unusual ships had put in at New Westminster, which didn't surprise Declan, but mentioned that Captain Jack Fitzgerald had, which did.

"My father was here? When?"

McKenzie thumbed through a stack of papers. "'Bout three months ago. Asked a bunch of questions about ships sailing in and out of here." McKenzie looked at Declan over the tops of his wire-rimmed spectacles. "Near run out of town with a couple black eyes and a split lip after asking too many questions about some of the town's womenfolk. You want to leave town with your nose in the same spot it is now, I suggest you don't go around asking the same questions."

Declan held his hands up. "I'm not here to cause any trouble. Just trying to track the old man down." He cast a sideways glance at McKenzie. "Even if he is a nosy bastard."

McKenzie's mouth quirked in a small smile. Declan knew him to be an unrepentant gossip who'd probably pointed Father in the direction of who to talk to, then sat back and watched the resulting brawl for his own amusement. "You happen to remember who he spoke with?" Declan asked, feigning idle curiosity.

McKenzie winked. "No one who'd answer his questions, I can tell you that. Except old Charlie Lauder. Folks say he's a little touched," McKenzie tapped a couple fingers against his temple. "He spends all his days watching ships coming in and out. Waiting for his daughter to come back, they say."

"His daughter?" Declan asked.

McKenzie shook his head. "Poor man lost his youngest daughter in '72. Left the house late one night, must have fallen off the wharf and drowned. Least, that's what everyone but Charlie Lauder believes."

"And Charlie?" Declan asked.

"Charlie swears she left on a big schooner no one else saw and that she might come back next time the ship comes in. He's been waiting near on sixteen years now."

Almost as long as Declan's father had been looking for his stepmother. Declan asked McKenzie where he could find Charlie Lauder.

"Down by the Fraser saloon. There's a little porch outside that looks out on the harbor. He's there most days when the weather's nice. Quiet old man, don't bother no one. Just sits there, waiting."

Declan thanked McKenzie for his help and headed for the saloon. This was the first solid lead he had since they left Port Townsend. He stopped inside the saloon and bought two beers, then carried them out to the dockside porch.

A man with a frowsy gray beard and a faded black-brimmed cap was sitting on a wooden ladder back chair, tipped onto its back legs and leaned against the saloon's wall. His eyes were hooded under the cap's brim. Declan let his boots thump on the planks of the porch in case the man was dozing and hooked another chair a couple of inches closer to Lauder with his foot before settling into it.

He set one beer on the floor next to Lauder's chair, then stretched his legs out and took a long sip from his own glass. The day was cloudy but warm, and a soft breeze wafted the scent of red cedar from the old sawmill a few hundred yards along the waterfront.

"She yours?" Lauder asked, jerking his stubbled chin to where the *Black Dove* floated at the end of the wharf.

"Yep," Declan replied.

"Got nice lines." He sounded grudging, like it pained him to admit it.

"She's a good ship."

"She fast?"

"Fast enough. Gets me where I want to go."

"Where you coming from?" The old man's eyes were closed again and his voice indifferent, but something about his placid willingness to talk to Declan fanned a tiny spark of excitement that maybe he would finally learn something useful.

"Port Townsend, Washington." He waited a beat, then introduced himself. "Captain Declan Fitzgerald. I understand my father Jack passed through here a few months ago and talked to you."

Lauder cracked an eye open and looked sideways at Declan. Declan leaned forward, picked up the beer he'd brought, and offered it to Lauder. The old man hesitated, then the front legs of his chair thumped down and he took the offered glass.

"You must not take after your daddy much," Lauder said, lifting the glass in a half-salute.

Declan chuckled. "I take after my mother." He didn't know if that was true, but distinguishing himself from his father in this town couldn't hurt. They sipped their beers together in silence for a few moments.

"Mr. Lauder, I'm looking for the same ship he was looking for. I hear you've seen it. A Pacific Coast-built schooner." He took a deep breath. "Eight masts."

Lauder drained the rest of his beer, then swiped the back of his hand across his mouth. He set the glass down on the porch next to his chair. "Ain't many folks around here call me Mr. Lauder. Crazy Charlie's what they call me. Everyone knows there ain't no such thing as a schooner with eight masts. You think you've seen one, maybe you're as crazy as I am."

"I haven't seen it myself," Declan admitted. "But I believe that it exists. Will you tell me what you know about it?"

Lauder leaned his chair back against the wall again and closed his eyes. Declan waited long enough that it seemed like maybe the old man had fallen asleep and cursed himself for not pushing him a little more. Just as he was about to shake his shoulder, Lauder spoke.

"Folks like to say I'm the crazy one, but knowing a thing happened and just going on pretending like it didn't—don't that seem crazy too?" Lauder asked. Declan wasn't sure if he was really seeking an answer, since he'd tugged his cap back down over his eyes, but nodded anyway.

"What happened?" he asked quietly.

"Ship like that came and took my daughter, Eva, away one night in July. 1872 that was, on a warm night with a big full moon." Lauder spoke like he didn't care whether Declan believed him or not, like he'd told this story so many times it no longer had the power to hurt him.

Declan waited for a moment, gazing out on the wharf. Elliot and Joey were returning to the *Black Dove* from town. Elliot was talking to Joey, his hands gesturing animatedly, until they reached the *Black Dove*. Joey disappeared aboard, but Elliot gazed up the wharf for a long moment, his hand shading his eyes. Declan resisted waving at him.

"I'm very sorry for your loss, Mr. Lauder. If you don't mind my asking, how do you know it took your daughter?"

"Damned thing's been taking young women from coastal towns around here long as I can remember. First time I heard about that was in October '65. Big schooner appeared near Victoria one night, some girl gone missing next morning. I was living there then, working in one of the shipyards. Moved up to Nanaimo for a time—showed up there in '69. Early spring, that was, and another girl gone."

Declan knew it had shown up in Victoria again in 1870 and '80, though he hadn't been able to confirm whether young women disappeared both those years or just in '80.

Lauder continued recounting dates, an oddly specific thing to have kept in his memory all these years. He supposed since Lauder had lost his girl to the schooner, he had as much reason to keep track of the dates as Declan did.

"I been here in New Westminster since 1870. Brought my

wife and Eva over from Victoria after it showed up there in April. But then it came here, in June of '71, and again in July '72. When it took my Eva."

"Did you see it each time, sir?" Declan asked softly. "I've tracked the appearances in Victoria and some other towns in Washington, but there aren't many people who've seen it. Or who'll admit to seeing it."

Lauder nodded. "I don't sleep much," he said with a shrug. "When my Henrietta was alive, we used to walk along the shore late at night, after most people were in bed. Mostly, it was her who'd notice it. Always at night, always during the biggest full moon of the year. Kinda became a game with us, you know—to spot it when no one else knew about it. She even gave it a name, since it never got close enough to see what its proper name was."

A sad smile creased his lined face. "The *Poulpes*, she called it. She was reading *Twenty Thousand Leagues Under the Sea* one year when we saw it." Declan smiled back at him. Luca had read the serialized version of the Jules Verne story to the crew a couple years ago, translating from the original French as he read. *Poulpes* was the French word for the octopuses that attacked the *Nautilus* and Captain Nemo had to fight off. A fitting name for a schooner with eight masts, he supposed.

"You've been very helpful, Mr. Lauder, and I'm much obliged to you. If there's anything I can do for you, please let me know."

Lauder's chair legs thumped as he tipped it forward onto all fours. "You're searching for that damned ship, eh?" Declan nodded. "It took someone from you too?"

"My stepbrother's fiancée," Declan replied. There wasn't much point in lying about that, at least not to the old man. Lauder nodded.

"Another thing my wife Henrietta noticed about it," he said, looking Declan in the eyes for the first time. "Every year it comes, two or three new babies get born later that year. I never would've noticed myself, but Henrietta counted the months in between and said so. Happened even in years the ship didn't take noone. Some of the babies were to folks already married, so it could be coincidence. But sometimes, a girl or two got in a family way and wouldn't say who done it to them. Every time she saw the ship, she'd shut Eva up in the house until a few days after it left. But she died in early '72, and I didn't think to lock Eva away when it came back in July."

Lauder sniffled and swiped a hand under his nose. Declan handed him the remains of his beer. Lauder nodded thanks and drained it.

This was the first time Declan had heard any connection between the schooner and bastard children. Marie had been unmarried when she'd had Elliot. Declan counted back from Elliot's birthday.

Lauder put a gnarled hand on Declan's arm and squeezed hard.

"You send my girl back to me, if you find her. Don't matter what she done or why she left. I just want her back home where she belongs."

Declan patted Lauder's hand and looked straight into his pale blue eyes. "I will, sir. I can't promise that I'll find her, but if I do, I'll send her home."

Lauder released Declan's arm and wiped his eyes. Declan shook his hand and left the old man to his memories. He still didn't understand what purpose there could be in stealing away young women like Eva Lauder or Celeste. Or whether this new information about out-of-wedlock pregnancies was connected to Elliot's mother or just a random coincidence. There was something about the pattern of the dates the schooner appeared that was tickling at the edges of his mind. He needed to check something with McKenzie before heading back to the *Black Dove* to talk it through with Elliot.

CHAPTER 15

*E*lliot leaned against the stern railing on the quarterdeck. They were staying the night in New Westminster, so there was little work to do aboard the *Black Dove* this evening. Even less to do ashore besides drink with the same men he'd been drinking with for the last three weeks.

Declan hadn't yet returned from his questioning of whoever he'd decided might have the information they were looking for. For the first time since he'd come aboard, Elliot was nearly alone on the ship. Thomas was in the galley belowdecks, sorting through the fresh produce Elliot had purchased for him.

They'd reached a detente of sorts, he and Thomas. It started one evening last week when Elliot had tossed his book aside in boredom, having read it start to finish three times. Thomas was humming to himself, cleaning up after the evening meal and starting preparations for the morning's meal. He glanced over and noticed Elliot shifting restlessly on the hard bench at the mess table. He shuffled some things around on a shelf, then plopped a bowl of potatoes on the table in front of Elliot.

"Peel," he'd ordered, sliding a paring knife, point first, across the table to Elliot. He turned back to the stove and busied himself with something on the cooktop. Elliot caught the knife by the handle before it stabbed him, stared at the potatoes for a minute, then shrugged and got to peeling. Thomas was singing to himself in Spanish and they didn't talk, but some of the hostility that had been simmering between them since Elliot came aboard eased. Elliot spent the next few nights after supper in the galley, chopping vegetables or gutting fish, whatever simple task Thomas set before him. It was a way of killing time before he had to go to Declan's cabin.

The nightmares had stopped, but other dreams had taken their place. They were still about Celeste, but in these dreams, she was happy. She still wanted Elliot to come for her, but not to save her anymore. He wasn't sure what she wanted from him now, but he still felt a force pulling him out there. Somewhere, out in the vast expanse of the Pacific, something was tugging on the edges of Elliot's mind. He felt its call in his blood and his bones, an insistent, inexorable pull, like iron filings to a magnet, that he was needed somewhere out there, wanted desperately by something.

The devilfish he'd seen when he was in the water were still out there. They stayed mostly out of sight of the crew, but Elliot knew they were under the surface, keeping pace alongside the *Black Dove* as she sailed. He wasn't sure exactly when he'd started thinking of them as creatures with sufficient sentience to purposely follow him but somehow he knew that was what they were doing. Following him—not the *Black Dove*, but Elliot himself—patiently waiting for Elliot to answer whatever was calling him.

He felt that call most when he was on deck and watching the waves slip under the hull of the *Black Dove*. Docked at the wharf here, the sensation was less, though it hadn't ceased entirely. The only time he didn't feel it at all was just as he was falling asleep next to Declan. Of course, during those moments, he was consumed with entirely different feelings.

Like the heat of Declan's back against his chest, even through the linen of Declan's nightshirt. The way Declan's hair tickled his nose and slid like silk across his forehead when he tucked his face into Declan's warm neck. How his cock nestled perfectly just under the curve of Declan's ass, as if it still belonged there.

And just like thinking of the devil making him appear, Declan's boots thumped up the steps to the quarterdeck. The smoke from his pipe curled around Elliot's head as he came up next to Elliot and leaned against the rail. "Nice evening," he commented around the pipe stem clamped between his teeth.

"Mm," Elliot agreed. The late afternoon was still warm, and the clouds were thinning in the western sky enough to let shafts of the setting sun shine on the river like ladders to the heavens.

"Saw Jo and Reg with the others at the saloon. Not up for joining them tonight?" Declan's tone was mild, but Elliot knew he didn't like Elliot to spend too much time alone. Someone was always talking to him, cajoling him to help with something, drink something, sing with them, read a bit from one of his books to them. Elliot didn't know whether that came out of an explicit order from Declan or just the crew's vague distrust of him. Either way, the attention was exhausting.

"I brought the provisions back for Thomas. Fresh asparagus, if you can believe it. There was a bumper crop this spring."

"Thomas will appreciate that," Declan said. "He makes an asparagus soup that would make angels weep." He gazed out on the water for a few moments, then tapped his pipe gently against the hull of the ship. Elliot watched the ashes drift down and float on the surface of the water until they disappeared. "Man named Charlie Lauder gave me some useful information today. Might give us some solid leads, finally."

"That's good. Tell me." Elliot tried to sound interested, although based on the look Declan tossed him, he wasn't sure how much he succeeded. The longer it was taking to find any concrete information about the schooner, combined with his growing fear that they were really on the track of something else entirely, the less Elliot was interested in continuing this search. What would happen if they just stopped looking for Celeste and he stayed aboard the *Black Dove*?

He shook those thoughts from his head as Declan related the story he'd heard from Charlie Lauder. After the vague, second-hand reports they'd heard, here was someone who had not only seen the mysterious schooner but also lost a young woman around the time it appeared. At least the Captain had been right on that front.

"We still don't know where it goes after it takes someone," Elliot said.

"No," Declan replied. "But I think I've figured out when it appears, and maybe what it's after."

Elliot shrugged. "We already know when it's appeared, don't we?" He'd made a list, based on the dates the Captain had told Declan, combined with the information they'd gathered at the towns they'd stopped at so far. He assumed Declan would add the dates Charlie Lauder had seen it to the list, but he'd pored over the list so far enough times to memorize it and he couldn't discern any pattern to it.

Declan waved the hand holding his pipe in the air. "No, I mean, I think I've found the pattern." He pulled the list from his coat pocket and stepped forward from the stern rail to spread it open on the shelf in front of the wheel. "Ken McKenzie has a set of nautical almanacs going back to 1870. Lauder says he first saw the schooner near Victoria in '65 and in Nanaimo in '69. McKenzie didn't have those editions, but he let me look at the almanacs for the early seventies."

Elliot came up to stand next to Declan, who pointed a tobacco-stained finger at the end of the list Elliot had made. Declan had added October 1865, 1869, April 1870, June 1871, and July 1872 in his careful script. In front of 1869, there was a tiny question mark, but beside the remaining entries he'd marked a pair of symbols—a small circle and a plus sign.

"What does it mean?" Elliot asked.

"Even after all these years, Charlie Lauder remembered not just the years the schooner appeared but also the months, too. Mostly, anyway. I couldn't figure at first why it would come in April of one year but July of another. But when I looked at the almanac for those years, it started to make sense. In April 1870, the moon was at perigee the same day it was full—a supermoon. Same with June 1871 and July in '72. Kenny didn't have the almanacs for 1865 or '69, but I bet there was a supermoon sometime in both years, just like in the other years."

"Full moon at perigee," Elliot repeated, thinking. "The point in the moon's orbit when it's closest to the earth?"

"Exactly," Declan said, smacking the back of his hand against Elliot's chest and grinning at him.

"But why?" Something was nibbling at the edges of Elliot's mind. Some bit of information he had, if he could just concentrate enough to remember it.

Declan shrugged. "Don't know yet. But look," he ran his finger back up to the top of the list, to September 6, 1873, the day Elliot's mother had disappeared. There was a small circle and plus sign next to that day too, and next to February 27, 1888, the last night Elliot saw Celeste.

"I knew the last full moon was a supermoon but I didn't realize until I checked the almanacs that the day your mother disappeared was too," Declan said. "And since that matches with the dates Lauder told me about, I'm betting the same has been true every time the schooner shows up."

"Which means," Elliot said slowly, but Declan didn't let him finish.

"We should be able to predict when it will appear next." He looked triumphantly at Elliot. When Elliot didn't react, Declan frowned. "What's the matter? This is a solid lead, Elliot. I don't think even Father figured that the damned thing appears on a schedule."

"No, I understand," Elliot said, trying to look more excited. Declan had figured out a pattern that had stymied the Captain for years and he'd done it all for Elliot. He should be more grateful. "Though, even if we know when it will appear next, how do we figure out where? Is there a pattern to where it goes?"

Declan tapped the stem of his empty pipe against his lips. There was a tiny bit of tobacco caught in the short beard he'd let grow. Elliot wanted to brush it away and see if his beard was as soft as it looked.

"I haven't been able to figure one out yet," Declan admitted. "I can make a guess of which months it appeared in Victoria and Nanaimo based on the charts in the almanacs for each year. We don't know of any sightings after your mother disappeared before it showed up in Nanaimo in '78 and '79, then in Victoria in '80, back to Nanaimo in '81, and then Port Angeles in '82. It seems like it only appears in one place in a particular month."

"But we don't know that for sure," Elliot argued. "It could be that it just hasn't been reported in more than one place in the same month." The sun was setting now, behind a bank of clouds at the horizon and a white fog was rolling in. Declan would suggest they go below any minute now, and then Elliot would have to choose whether to spend the evening with Declan, which would be unbearable because of all the things Elliot wanted from him yet couldn't have, or Thomas, which was only slightly less unbearable, because Thomas wasn't Declan. At least Thomas wouldn't be spending the evening with Declan, either. Small mercies, Elliot supposed.

Declan folded the list up and stuffed it back in his coat pocket. "True. And folks have argued over seeing it at all. It's almost like only certain people are able to see it." His voice trailed off and he looked toward the wharf, then swiveled and looked out along the Fraser River as if he could see where it emptied into the Pacific Ocean, then back at the wharf again, as if looking for something.

"What?" Elliot asked. "What is it?"

"What if that's it?" Declan murmured, almost to himself.

"What if what's it?"

Declan pulled the list from his pocket again and clamped his pipe stem between his teeth to free his other hand. He held the paper flat on the shelf, squinted at it in the failing light, and opened his fingers from his closed fist one at a time, mouthing words under his breath that Elliot couldn't catch. He did it a second time, then slid the fingers of the hand holding the list down to the bottom and did it a third time. Then he lifted his head and stared up the wharf toward the Fraser Saloon.

"Damn it, Declan," Elliot started. He could tell Declan had reached some sort of epiphany, but then Declan looked at him, his eyebrows drawing together.

"It's not that only certain people can see it," Declan said slowly. "Or, maybe that's true, but I don't think that's important. It's that the schooner, or whoever is on it, only comes for certain people."

Elliot nodded. "Only women, as far as we know. Mother, Celeste, Charlie Lauder's daughter, you said. Those other young women in Victoria and Nanaimo that your father found out about."

Declan sighed. "Charlie told me something else. He said every time the schooner appeared, about eight or nine months later, there'd be a bunch of new babies born." His eyes flicked down to his hands, fiddling with his pipe, tracing the intricate carvings on the meerschaum bowl. "Sometimes, a few of those babies would be born to young women who weren't married." He glanced back up at Elliot. "Like your mother. When she got pregnant with you."

CHAPTER 16

*E*lliot's face was blank, eyes staring across the water, no reaction to what Declan had just told him. A few tendrils of fog drifted across the main deck, and Declan realized that he could no longer see the buildings on shore.

"Come on," he said, tugging Elliot's arm. "Let's go below."

Elliot didn't resist when Declan steered him toward the hatch opening in the quarterdeck that led to Declan's cabin. He didn't say anything either, until after Declan pushed him into the padded leather chair in front of the desk. Declan poured three fingers of whiskey each into a pair of pewter tumblers and handed one to Elliot.

Propping himself on the edge of the desk, he nudged a knee against Elliot's leg. "Say something, man."

"No wonder Mother wanted to keep my real father's identity a secret, if he's just a common sailor who gets his jollies from raping and kidnapping any woman he can get his hands on."

Declan leaned forward and dipped his head to look into Elliot's white face. "Whoa there, let's not jump to any conclusions. We don't know your father was on that schooner and we don't know whether any of these women were raped. Or kidnapped, for that matter. They might have gone aboard voluntarily."

Elliot threw back half the contents of his tumbler and carelessly wiped a hand across his lips. "So, you're saying my mother fucked a random sailor and got knocked up, then sailed away with him eight years later after he got tired of fucking his way up and down the straits? But obviously, she wasn't enough, because then he had to come back for my fiancée. And if she went aboard voluntarily too, then maybe the thing all these women have in common is that they're all faithless whores."

He gulped down the remaining whiskey, then grabbed the bottle and sloshed another couple of inches into his tumbler, his hand shaking. Declan caught the bottle as Elliot slammed it back down on the desk, keeping it from tipping over, and moved it out of Elliot's reach.

"That's enough," he said sharply. "I am not calling your mother or Celeste a whore. Come on, Elliot, I met Celeste. I could tell she cared about you. And I never want to hear you say something like that about your mother. I was only four years old when Father married her. She was as much a mother to me as she was to you, and I loved her very much."

Elliot stared into his tumbler, and Declan's heart clenched in his chest. He'd poured all his grief in losing his stepmother into taking care of Elliot when she left and tried his damnedest to be someone Elliot could rely on. Until he'd left Elliot, too. Unwillingly, but he'd stayed away for far too long. If he had come back at his first opportunity, instead of submitting to his father's will, would Elliot have turned to Celeste? Could he have prevented any of this from happening?

He sighed and nudged Elliot with his knee again. "Look, when we find that ship, we'll figure this out. And if anyone on it really has taken any woman against her will, we'll deal with them, I promise. But nothing in the stories we've heard so far say anything about men coming off that schooner. The opposite, remember? Every story is the same—the ship appears, no one sees anyone go aboard or come ashore from it, it disappears a few days later, and there are no reports of strange men unaccounted for in the town. We're operating under the assumption that the women's disappearances are connected to the schooner, but we really don't know for sure."

And there was Sally's insistence that his father believed something not human had taken his stepmother. He sipped his own whiskey, trying to decide how to ask Elliot about the strange suspicions he was having without sounding crazy.

"Elliot, what did your mother tell you about your real father? Did she say anything about him that might help you find him, if you ever wanted to?"

Elliot snorted. His eyes were a little unfocused, thanks to the whiskey, and his lips were shiny and wet. Declan tried not to look at them. "She told me he was beautiful," he said finally, leaning his head against the padded back of the chair and staring up at the cabin's ceiling. "She said I'd grow up to be as big as him one day." Declan eyed how Elliot's long legs stretched halfway across the rug that covered the better part of his cabin's floor and how his broad shoulders filled the width of the large chair. If Elliot's father was any bigger than Elliot himself, he must be a giant.

"I asked her once where he was and why we didn't live with him. She said he lived in a faraway place that was very hard to get to but that someday, maybe he'd come for us." He ran both hands through his hair, scrubbing at his scalp. "That's why I thought she brought me down to the shore the day before she disappeared, because he'd finally come for us. But instead..." he trailed off.

Instead, a giant devilfish had nearly swept Marie out to sea and she'd disappeared before the next morning. But that was impossible. Stories of mermaids and selkies and sirens mating with humans were just that—stories. Myths and fairy tales that sailors told each other for entertainment on long voyages when the monotony of the unending sea was about to drive them mad and the light on the waves played tricks on their minds. There couldn't be any truth to tales about half-human sea creatures seeking mates along the shore.

Declan gazed at Elliot, cataloguing his very human appearance. His brown hair, the color of oak leaves in the fall; his kaleidoscopic eyes, changing from a bluish green in sunlight to amber-brown in shadow; the mole high on his left cheek. He knew Elliot was also thinking about the devilfish that drew his mother into the water that day.

"*The son is the key*," Elliot whispered, gazing back at Declan, his broad forehead creased with confusion. "If that's me, and my father is connected to all these disappearances, then what does that make me, Declan? What am I?"

Declan kicked gently at his outstretched legs. "Don't be ridiculous. You're Elliot Bishop. Whoever—or whatever—your father was, it doesn't matter as much as who you decide to be." He stood up and stretched a hand out to Elliot. "Come on, let's get some grub and make it an early night. We'll head for Nance's tomorrow and then we'll figure out how to track this schooner back to where it came from."

Elliot sighed and reached up to clasp Declan's hand. Declan tugged him to his feet, but he must have pulled harder than necessary, as Elliot stumbled against him. "No more whiskey for you tonight," he teased, gripping Elliot's biceps to set him back on his own feet.

"No more whiskey," Elliot agreed, a puff of peaty fumes fanning from his mouth against Declan's. He swayed a little when Declan let go, and draped a long arm over Declan's shoulder to steady himself. He squinted at Declan, then brought his other hand up to Declan's face. Declan froze, and Elliot brushed at Declan's chin with his hand. Elliot gave him a silly smile, showed him the bit of tobacco he'd plucked from Declan's beard on the tip of his fingers, then wiped it carelessly on his trousers.

Instead of stepping back, though, he touched Declan's face again, running the tips of his fingers lightly over Declan's beard. "Soft," he murmured in a low, lazy voice that hooked deep in Declan's belly. "I thought so."

"Elliot," Declan started, but Elliot pressed the pad of his index finger against Declan's lower lip. "Shh," he said and dragged his thumb across Declan's lower lip. He cupped Declan's jaw with his hand, then slid it to tangle in Declan's hair at the back of his neck. Declan opened his mouth to ask what Elliot was doing but before he got any words out, Elliot bent his head and put his mouth on Declan's.

His lips were soft, and Declan closed his eyes to enjoy the kiss for just a second. Just two seconds, and he'd push Elliot back and remind him that he didn't want to be doing this with Declan. But Elliot's tongue slipped in between Declan's lips and lightly traced the edges of his teeth. Declan let a soft sigh escape and opened a bit more when Elliot pushed in, sliding his tongue alongside Declan's. Elliot slid his other hand from Declan's shoulder up his neck, tilting Declan's face to a better angle, deepening the kiss and sucking Declan's tongue into his mouth. He tasted of whiskey, and Declan suddenly felt as drunk as Elliot must be.

Declan lost track of how long they stood there, kissing. Each time he pulled back, Elliot tightened his fingers in Declan's hair and pulled him closer. The slick pressure of his hot tongue undid Declan, but he finally got his arms up and pulled Elliot's from around his neck. The last thing he wanted was a repeat of the first night Elliot had slept in his cabin—a quick release followed by days weighed down under Elliot's regret. Breathing heavily, he pushed Elliot a step away with a firm hand on his chest.

Elliot reached for him, but he leaned back against the desk and shook his head. "You don't want this, Elliot. Why don't you sleep it off, and I'll join the others in town."

"No." Elliot dropped his arm to his side but didn't move away. To get to the door, Declan would have to either shove him back or squeeze past him close enough Elliot would be able to tell how the kiss had affected him. Declan sighed and gripped the edge of the desk in both hands.

"What the hell are you doing here, Elliot? The last time you started something like this, you barely spoke to me for a week. You have a fiancée, and I've got less than zero patience for a goddamn cocktease, so back the fuck off before you do something we'll both regret."

His voice had risen louder than he'd intended, and Elliot at least had the grace to look ashamed. He didn't back up, though. "I know," he said, looking down at his feet, then up at Declan. His eyes were less muddled by the whiskey, but he was still close enough Declan could smell it on his breath. "I'm sorry," he said. "I just wanted—" he trailed off and looked beseechingly at Declan.

"Just wanted what?" Declan growled. He'd be damned if he'd let Elliot's puppy-dog eyes convince him that Elliot actually wanted him this time. "Another hand job while you pretend you're still faithful to the woman you plan to marry? You're not the only one hard-up here, Elliot." He gestured rudely at the bulge in his own trousers. "The difference is, I haven't made any promises that I can't keep and I am trying my damnedest to keep my hands to myself while keeping you safe the only way I know how!"

He did push Elliot this time, with both hands, hard enough that Elliot stumbled and fell back into his chair. "Jerk off your damn self, or save it for your fiancée. I don't give a damn, but stop torturing me, for fuck's sake!" He shoved off the desk and stomped toward the cabin door, adjusting himself roughly. He needed to get out of the cabin. He'd bunk in Joey's cabin tonight, since the crew weren't likely to get back before dawn, and deal with Elliot tomorrow, after he sobered up and came to his senses.

"She's not mine anymore!" Elliot yelled back at Declan. "She's gone for good, and I don't even want her back!"

CHAPTER 17

*C*hrist. Elliot hadn't meant to blurt it out like that. Declan turned back and glared at him. "What the fuck are you talking about? You were the one who insisted she was alive and that you had to find her." He pinched the bridge of his nose, then dropped his hand and gave Elliot a hard look.

"I've had about as much as I can take, man. I've made excuses for your petty bullshit because I know you're grieving, but Elliot —" Elliot put up a hand to stop him.

"Yeah, I know. You've been a goddamn saint, Declan. But would you shut the hell up for a minute and let me say something?"

Declan's lips tightened, and a muscle jumped in his jaw. He crossed his arms over his chest and stood in front of the cabin door, legs planted wide against the slow rocking of the ship at anchor. Elliot tried to pull his thoughts together. He'd definitely drunk too much whiskey for this conversation. He was still distracted by the feel of Declan's lips against his, the taste of Declan's tongue in his mouth, and the soft bristles of Declan's beard against his skin.

He leaned forward in his chair, elbows on his knees, hands

dangling between his thighs, trying not to reach out for Declan. He stared at the rug between his feet, tracing the pattern with his eyes while he tried to decide where to start.

There was a deep sigh above his head, and Declan asked in a milder tone, "What did you mean when you said she's gone for good?"

It was as good a place as any. Without looking at him, Elliot said, "She's still out there, somewhere. At least, I think so. It's just that she's not exactly her, anymore, if you know what I mean." He looked up at Declan, who looked back at him, his expression unchanged. Of course Declan didn't know what he meant. How could he?

"I dream about her every night. Well, almost." He wasn't going to tell Declan what his other dreams were about. Not yet, anyway. He sighed. "In my dreams, she—well, she's turned into some sort of monster."

He waited for Declan to tell him he was crazy, that there's no such thing as sea monsters. That it was just a dream, and dreams don't mean anything. Declan didn't say any of those things, though. He just uncrossed his arms and retrieved his whiskey, then leaned his hip against the corner of his desk again. Not as close to Elliot as he was before, not as close as Elliot would have liked. Close enough for Elliot to smell the warm, smoky scent of the whiskey as Declan breathed out. At least he wasn't storming from the cabin.

"I'm listening," Declan prompted him.

Declan had always listened to him. That was what Elliot had always loved most about Declan. He was maddening in a dozen other ways—always acting like a big brother, always trying to protect Elliot and take care of him as if Elliot couldn't take care of himself, until Elliot wanted to push him away in frustration. Until Elliot pushed so hard that Declan really did leave him, with no warning and only a handful of sporadic letters.

But before he'd left, Declan had been the only person Elliot could talk to. He listened to Elliot's tales of boyhood adventures, the things he learned in his studies, to his plans for expanding the Bishop mercantile business as he grew older. Even to his incomplete descriptions of his dreams when Elliot could bring himself to describe them. Not that Declan didn't talk to him in return. Before he'd left the last time, Declan used to tell him tales from the shorter voyages he went on with the Captain, about antics he and the crew had gotten up to aboard ship and on shore.

But the thing about Declan was that he really listened. He reserved judgment until he heard everything, and he usually understood things that hadn't even been said. When he was listening to a person, he gave them his full attention. It was part of what made his crew so loyal. And why Elliot was hesitant to tell Declan the full truth about his dreams. He never wanted to take the risk Declan would stop listening to him. If Declan ever stopped thinking Elliot was worth listening to, there was no one else Elliot would ever be able to talk to.

"In my dreams, she's swimming in the ocean. It's still her, but she's...well, different."

"Different how?"

"Her hair and face are the same, though I don't know how she can breathe underwater. From her waist up, she's a normal woman. But then, her skin changes color and her legs separate and she grows extra limbs, just like the devilfish, and her new limbs have the same suckers underneath. I try to swim away, but she's too fast underwater, and I can't get away. She wraps her human arms around me and then she winds those tentacles around my legs and she's all over me, touching and squeezing me until I can't breathe."

Elliot's chest tightened. He tried taking a deep breath but couldn't get enough air in his lungs. Dropping his head into his hands and closing his eyes, he told the rest in a thin, shaking voice. "Then she drags me down underwater with her. I start to turn into a monster, too, and I know that's what she wants. For me to become like her and stay with her in the depths."

Elliot heard a soft thump as Declan set his tumbler on the desk. Then Declan's warm, strong hands grabbed Elliot's shoulders and hoisted him up against Declan's chest. "It's all right, Elliot. I've got you. Breathe with me, now." Declan's chest lifted and Elliot sucked in a short breath. Declan slid his hands around and pressed Elliot closer to him. "Come on now, slow, deep breaths."

Elliot tried again, inhaling with Declan, holding his breath until Declan finished inhaling and shakily exhaling along with Declan. The next breath was longer, matched closer with Declan's. So was the third. After five or six like this, the clenching grip in his chest eased and Elliot could breathe normally on his own.

When Declan patted his back and loosened his arms, Elliot tightened his and tucked his head into Declan's neck. "I feel like I'm drowning," he whispered. "I don't know who I am anymore."

Declan made a small sound, like Elliot's fear and confusion hurt him even more than it did Elliot. He wrapped one arm around Elliot's waist, pressing Elliot closer, and slid the other up and cupped the back of Elliot's neck. His large hand squeezed Elliot's neck, and Elliot let the warmth of his embrace thaw some of the cold tension he'd been keeping in his muscles. He breathed in the smoky salt of Declan's skin and closed his eyes.

"We'll figure it out, Elliot." Declan's deep voice rumbled through his skull. His lips grazed the shell of Elliot's ear and Elliot shivered. Declan tightened his arms around him, then pressed his lips to the side of Elliot's head. He pulled back and cupped Elliot's jaw, looking into his eyes. "I promise. All right?"

Elliot nodded. He took a deep breath. "In the meantime," he started. "I know I haven't given you any reason to believe me, but I meant to kiss you." He dropped his eyes to Declan's lips. He wasn't sure he could take it if Declan rejected him again, but he owed it to him to be clear about what he wanted. "I still want you. I have ever since you came back. I never stopped, I suppose. I still need to know what happened to Celeste, but I can't marry her. Not after...well, not after these dreams I've been having."

Not after being near Declan these last few weeks and remembering what he'd lost when Declan had left. He knew Declan would leave again when they found the Captain and Celeste, but if he could have Declan for a little while, he'd take whatever he could get.

"They're just dreams, Elliot. We don't know for sure what's happened to her." He didn't sound very convincing, though. Or like he was convinced himself.

Elliot shook his head, not ready to explain why he knew they weren't just dreams. "It doesn't really matter," he said with a small, sad smile. "You were right that what I feel for her isn't enough to make me a good husband to her."

Declan looked hesitant, and Elliot rushed to downplay what he'd just said. "I'm not asking for anything long-term. I know you have your own...arrangements." He wasn't sure if that was even the right word, and Declan just raised an eyebrow at him. "Just, if you wanted to," he shrugged a shoulder and flicked his eyes down to where their hips were nearly touching. He was hard enough Declan could probably feel it, even through their layers of clothing. He glanced up at Declan, who rolled his eyes.

"If I wanted to? Christ, Ellie, you're killing me here." Declan slid the hand on Elliot's jaw back around his neck and tugged on a few strands of hair. Elliot took that as an invitation and bent his head to Declan's lips.

This kiss was harder, rougher. Elliot moaned around Declan's tongue when he felt Declan's cock swell and press against his hip. He bit gently at Declan's lower lip as he pulled back from the kiss, and dragged his palms down Declan's chest, plucking at the already hard nipples under Declan's vest and shirt as he sank to his knees. He fumbled with the buttons of Declan's trousers, then wrenched them open, the last button pinging off the desk and landing somewhere behind him.

He drew Declan's thick cock out, the tip already wet. He wrapped one hand around it and slid it down to the base, then slowly back up. Declan gripped the edge of the desk, his knuckles white. "Jesus, Elliot," he said, low and rough. Elliot's lips twitched in a small smile, and he flicked his tongue out, just grazing the tip. Declan's cock jerked, and a clear stream of fluid dripped from the tip over Elliot's fingers.

Elliot bent his head and finally put his mouth around Declan's cock. Declan groaned as he slid down the shaft until it nudged the back of his throat. Elliot looked up. Declan's head was thrown back, eyes squeezed shut, a gleam of white teeth biting into his lower lip. He pulled up slowly, sucking hard as he went, and swirled the flat of his tongue around the head of Declan's cock.

He went down again, a little farther this time, the tip of his nose brushing dark ginger curls and breathing in the musky scent he remembered from the first time he did this. Declan's hand settled lightly on his head, stroking gently, but when Elliot swallowed experimentally, Declan's fingers tightened in his hair.

"Fuck," Declan swore above him, his voice rough and low.

Elliot relaxed his jaw, trying to take more, humming around Declan's thick length to encourage him deeper. He ignored the few tears sliding down his cheeks and let his mind empty as Declan thrust just the tiniest bit into his throat, until he finally ran out of air and had to pull back, hollowing his cheeks as he sucked up and off with a wet pop.

"You okay?" Declan asked, curling forward and thumbing a tear from Elliot's cheek. "Fuck, did I hurt you?"

"Shut up," Elliot rasped, his throat raw in that way he'd been missing all these years. There'd be time for that again, he hoped, but Declan's eyes were dark, pupils blown wide, and Elliot knew he was close. He ignored his own straining cock, trapped in its woolen prison, wrapped a hand firmly around the base of Declan's and found a steady rhythm between hand and mouth that drew a broken series of curses from over his head.

Everything narrowed to the hot velvet and iron weight on his tongue, battering his throat. This was what Elliot had been missing, what he'd forgotten kept him grounded. After weeks of untethered floating in nightmares and longing, he needed to feel something real, and Declan gripping his hair and pumping warm and salty into his mouth was as real as he'd ever felt in his life.

CHAPTER 18

There were fewer settlements on the western coast of Vancouver Island and even fewer reports of the schooner appearing, even given the questions they now knew to ask. A cold steady drizzle had been following them since passing through the Juan de Fuca Strait, and Declan was looking forward to a warm fire and the hot and delicious—if expensive—food he knew he could expect at Nance Carrigan's compound. He checked the *Black Dove*'s course and calculated they'd reach Nance's inlet by dinner, maybe even with enough time for a hot bath before.

Thomas came up the ladder to the quarterdeck, pausing halfway and cocked his head at Declan.

"You must have had a good night," he commented with a touch of bitterness, handing over a covered pewter mug.

Declan let the mug warm his hands, then sipped the hot black coffee. "Why do you say that?" he asked.

"You were whistling," Thomas said, as if that should mean something.

"And?"

"You always whistle the morning after."

"The fuck I do," Declan protested. How the devil had Thomas come to that conclusion? Surely that wasn't true.

"You've been whistling every morning for days now. Ask anyone," Thomas said.

"The fuck I will." Jesus Christ, did everyone know that things had changed with Elliot? Could a man not have a little privacy on his own goddamned ship?

Thomas shrugged. "Take my word for it, then. I should know." He stared straight ahead, the wind blowing his black curls back from his face. Declan felt a twinge of guilt. He'd never promised Thomas anything, and Thomas knew he wasn't the only man Declan had ever taken to bed, but he had been the one Declan came back to most often. Until now.

Without even talking about it, Declan and Elliot were keeping whatever this new thing was between them quiet—Declan, because he truly didn't want to flaunt it in Thomas's face, and Elliot, well, for obvious reasons, since every man on the ship knew he'd recently lost his fiancée. He thought they'd been behaving exactly the same in front of the crew, but he should have known. There were few secrets on a ship the size of the *Black Dove*, and Thomas knew Declan better than anyone else on it.

"Tom," Declan began softly, but Thomas waved a hand at him, then folded his sturdy forearms on the shelf. His hands and wrists were scarred with burn marks and knife cuts from half a lifetime of cooking on rolling ships with temperamental stoves. For a moment, Declan felt the ghost of those scarred hands on his body and a tinge of nostalgia for the simpler life he'd be living if he hadn't gone back to Port Townsend and Elliot hadn't come aboard.

"He's the one, then?" Thomas asked after a brief silence.

"Eh? Which one?" Declan asked, keeping his tone casual. Thomas couldn't know about the bit of Latin prophecy written on Father's chart, much less that anyone thought it was about

Elliot. Declan hadn't shown that bit of paper to anyone, not even Elliot yet.

"The one your *pendejo* of a father flogged you over when you joined him on that first Ceylon voyage," Thomas said, a touch of impatience in his tone. Declan choked on the sip of coffee he'd just taken, the hot liquid burning as it tried to go the wrong way down. He coughed a couple of times, bent over the wheel. Thomas rescued the mug from his hand and whacked him none too gently between the shoulder blades, twice.

They'd never talked about that. Declan woke up the morning after the flogging to Thomas laying warm cloths across the welts on his back, soaked in something that soothed the sting and helped the swelling. He'd caught a fever anyway, and Thomas had nursed him through it, then told him bawdy stories in a hilarious mix of Spanish and English while Declan recovered.

"You called his name a lot in your fever," he said now, not looking at Declan. "Begged him to forgive you, told him you'd come back to him."

Declan sighed. He still hadn't forgiven his father for what he'd done, but oddly, after it was over, Declan stopped giving a shit about whether anyone knew about his proclivities. He was careful, of course—he had no intention of doing prison time for committing unnatural acts, but the law at sea was the captain's word, not the sheriff's, and he was a damned good sailor. Once he took Father's punishment, most of the crew respected him, not least because he'd known half of them since he was a boy and they were all wary of Father's temper. Thomas was the first of Father's crew he'd fucked, and not the only one, and Declan took even more pleasure in committing those unnatural acts right under Father's nose.

Thomas had never told him he'd known about Elliot all along, though. If he had, well, Declan couldn't have kept Elliot off the ship for this voyage, but he might have tried tidying things up with Thomas beforehand. He didn't quite know what to say now, though. Before he could decide, Thomas handed his coffee mug back to him and said, "Used the last of the brandy in last night's turtle soup. See if you can find something to trade with Nance for a few decent bottles."

"Already on the list," Declan replied.

Thomas smacked the shelf with the palms of his hands and pushed off to return to the galley. Two steps away and with his back still to Declan, he said, "Don't fuck it up this time. With Elliot, I mean. Captain." He jogged down the steps to the main deck before Declan could say anything in reply. Thomas didn't speak to Elliot as he passed him on deck, but Declan saw them exchange brief nods just before Thomas ducked down the galley hatch. A bit of tension Declan hadn't known he'd been carrying eased. If Thomas and Elliot could get along, life aboard the *Black Dove* would be a lot easier.

"Fitzgerald! What the hell took you so long, you scurvy, swindling son of a bitch?" Nance Carrigan stood with her hands on her hips at the top of the dock, her hoarse, smoke-scarred voice carrying over the noisy flurry of three other ships unloading cargo. Declan squinted and shielded his eyes against a shaft of watery afternoon sun breaking through the clouds behind her. She was wearing men's trousers, as usual, an unbuttoned wool greatcoat that didn't hide the pair of pistols tucked into the belt slung low across her hips, and a floppy hat that dipped low over one eye, but he knew from experience that it wouldn't affect her aim with either of the pistols or the shotgun tucked in the crook of her left elbow.

"Good to see you, too, you old bitch," Declan called out to her, as he stepped off the *Black Dove* to the dock. "And you might want to change your tune with me, or I'll give your present to someone who deserves it."

Elliot stepped off behind him, followed by Joey. Elliot must have looked shocked at Declan's words because Joey murmured behind him, "Well, she is a bitch. You'll see." He ignored them both and hustled to properly greet Nance.

Declan returned the bone-crushing hug she gave him and then stepped back to gesture at Elliot. "This is my stepbrother, Elliot Bishop, Bishop Mercantile, Port Townsend. Elliot, Nance is the shrewdest trader in the Pacific Northwest and a real kitten once you get to know her. Just don't let her talk you into playing cards."

Elliot shook Nance's hand. "It's a pleasure to meet you, Mrs. Carrigan. Declan has told me a lot about you."

Nance looked him up and down for a long moment. "He has, has he?" she said, still staring at Elliot, a slight frown on her face. "Well, whatever he's told you is sure to be lies. Man can't even sail a cargo ship up here by the date he promised, you can't believe a word else he says."

Elliot glanced at Declan, then back at Nance. She still gripped his hand in hers, and Declan could see Elliot's knuckles whiten. "I'm sorry, ma'am. It's my fault we were delayed. We've been—"

"Showing Elliot the routes," Declan interrupted. "Not to mention finding new markets that you might be interested in, if you can curb that shrewish tongue of yours." This was no place to discuss their real business, surrounded by dock workers and other sailors. Nance might have useful information, but Declan wasn't trusting anyone with anything they didn't need to know.

Nance finally let go of Elliot's hand, and Declan caught his slight wince as he shook it out, then tucked it in his coat pocket. Nance's frown didn't change when she shifted her eyes to Joey's slight figure, almost hidden behind Elliot's large frame. "Joseph —" she started, then stopped short. She cleared her throat, twisted to the side, and spat a brown gob of tobacco juice into the water. "Joey. Welcome home, child."

"Thank you, ma'am," Joey said. He stood tall and looked Nance in the eye but didn't step forward to embrace her.

"I've got your old room fixed up, Jo," Nance offered. "I wager you'd like a bath before dinner?"

Joey shook his head. "I'll bunk with the crew, thanks. Don't need any special treatment."

Nance's fingers tightened on the barrel of the shotgun in her hand, and she sighed. "Suit yourself then. You know where everything is." She waved a hand at the bustle of dock workers and sailors toting cargo off the ships. "I gotta keep an eye on this lot, make sure everything brought in is accounted for properly." She lifted a chin at Declan. "Hot water and clean linen waiting in your usual room, Fitz. Tell Betsy I said set up the green room for your stepbrother. I'll see you both at dinner."

"Thanks, Nance." Declan kissed her sun-browned cheek and then looked over his shoulder at Joey with a raised eyebrow and a stern look. The kid could try a little harder, dammit. Joey stepped forward and awkwardly pecked Nance's other cheek. He cleared his throat and said with only a little hesitation, "It's good to see you, mam."

Nance smiled at him and shooed them off. Elliot had the decency to wait until Joey scampered off to the sailors' bunkhouse before saying in a voice like he'd only just made the connection, "So, Joey is Nance's son."

It wasn't exactly a question, so Declan didn't exactly answer it beyond a noncommittal grunt. They reached the wide porch that spanned the big house and mounted the steps.

"She's not what I expected," Elliot said. "Are you sure she'll help us? She doesn't exactly seem to like you." Their boots thumping on the wooden planks gave fair warning, and the double front doors opened to a small maid in a white mob cap, light brown curls tucked haphazardly under it.

"Captain Fitzgerald," the girl squealed, bobbing a slight curtsy at him. "We was expecting you days ago."

"Betsy," he smiled down at her. The top of her head barely reached his shoulder, and when she caught sight of Elliot, her eyes grew rounder as they traveled up to the top of his head. She looked at Declan and whispered behind her hand, "How much does he eat?"

"I've sworn off little girls," Elliot responded gravely, before Declan could say anything. "At least for the last few weeks, though it's been harder than I thought it would be."

Betsy stared wide-eyed at him until Elliot winked at her. She giggled, and he smiled back at her.

"My stepbrother, Mr. Bishop, Betsy. Nance said the green room for him, if you don't mind." She curtsied again and scurried away to prepare Elliot's room.

"Nance is a good egg," Declan said, answering Elliot's prior question. "And you'll see, she knows just about everything about every ship that's sailed these waters over the last quarter-century. She's not above holding a grudge, though, and she hasn't quite forgiven me for taking Joey on. Brought her a present that should help with that, though."

Assuming her lads didn't damage it unloading it from the Black Dove's hold. But that was for later. There was a hot bath waiting for him now, and Declan planned to make good use of it, and the few hours of private time with Elliot before dinner. He glanced around the foyer to verify they were alone and smacked Elliot on the ass, earning a chastising glare, but when he gestured to the huge curved staircase leading to the second floor and his bedroom, Elliot swatted him in retaliation and followed him upstairs.

CHAPTER 19

The green room was at the back of the big house, its walls papered in an elaborate pattern of broad pale-green leaves and emerald-green vines curling around small white flowers. Dark green velvet curtains enclosed the four-poster bed and hung on either side of two large windows that faced inland at rolling hills covered in red cedar, Douglas fir, and madrona trees. Opposite the windows and next to the small coal stove built into the fireplace, Elliot sunk deep into a huge copper slipper tub Betsy had filled with hot water she said was piped in from a hot spring on the island. He closed his eyes and relaxed, his muscles loosening and skin tingling in the warm water swirling around him. His legs splayed against the sides of the tub and his cock, which had been thoroughly sucked by Declan not a half hour earlier, swelled to half-hard.

He loosely grasped it with one hand, not stroking it, just holding and letting it slowly lengthen past the tips of his fingers. He ran his other hand down one thigh and back up the inside until his knuckles grazed his balls. His skin felt different under the water, smooth and velvety, the usually rough prickle of hair covering his legs soft. He spread his thighs apart as much as the tub allowed, letting the water swirl around his balls and in all his creases. He soaked until the water cooled, dozing lightly and dreaming vaguely of something warm and wet wrapped around him, suckling and kneading his cock and legs. Not Declan, but not anyone else in particular, just a slick wet pressure, flexing and sliding against his skin, exploring all his secret places.

A sharp knock at the door woke him, and he jerked upright in the tub, banging his shoulder on the curved lip and splashing a small wave of water on the floor. Betsy called through the door that dinner would be served shortly.

Trying to calm his racing heart, he pulled himself out of the water onto wobbly legs. His head ached dully, probably from hunger, since his last meal had been at dawn on the *Black Dove*. Betsy had taken his coat for brushing and laid out a new vest on the clotheshorse for him. It was made of a fine charcoal-gray wool, with a pattern of vines and leaves embroidered in bright blue thread. It was similar to the silver-threaded vest Declan had worn when he arrived in Elliot's study. Elliot slipped it on and buttoned the silver buttons, smoothing a hand over the embroidery and smiling a bit as he imagined Declan putting his matching vest on.

As he descended the curved staircase, Elliot heard piano music drifting from a room on the main floor. He turned left at the bottom of the stairs, crossed the foyer, and turned into a large library with floor-to-ceiling bookcases on three walls and a wall of windows overlooking the big lawn that stretched down to the long pier. A fire crackled in the huge marble fireplace on the north wall, and a wheeled cart filled with an excellent selection of whiskey, port, and cognac sat between the fireplace and the windows, crystal tumblers and snifters lined up in neat rows. A beautiful square grand piano was in the center of the room, angled safely away from any danger of sparks from the fireplace but close enough that the person seated at its bench would feel at least some warmth.

Elliot halted a few steps inside the library. Nance was at the piano, playing a haunting, slow piece Elliot had never heard before. The firelight gleamed on the piano's rounded corners and ornately carved legs. Nance's left hand moved up and down the lowest keys, in rumbling minor chord arpeggios, like the deep pull of a strong ocean current, underneath quiet tinkling notes from her right hand plinking like icy raindrops on a tin roof.

The lowest notes resonated deep in Elliot's chest. His pulse throbbed at the base of his throat, slowing to match the tempo of the chords. The key was discordant but not unpleasant, and something about it tugged at something in Elliot. He stood there as long as he could stand it, then took a couple of steps forward. The upper notes prickled against his skin, goosebumps rising and the hairs on the back of his neck standing on end.

A rough hand clapped him on the shoulder and he swung around, nearly colliding with Declan. "Whoa there," Declan said softly. "You all right, Elliot?"

The music stopped, but Elliot's skin still prickled. Declan was close enough that Elliot could smell the tonic he'd splashed on after shaving his beard off. His cheeks were pink and smooth, a faint dusting of freckles across his nose. Christ, he wanted Declan *again*, his cock straining in his trousers. He swallowed and tried to pull himself together before he gave them both away in front of Nance.

"Evening, gentlemen," she said, her voice dry. When he turned away from Declan to face her, Elliot thought he caught a knowing look before her face smoothed into a pleasant expression.

"Good evening to you, Mrs. Carrigan. I'm sorry for disturbing you. That was beautiful."

She smiled at him, her blue eyes crinkling at the edges. "Never been a Mrs., so you just call me Nance. And thank you. I don't generally play for people but wanted to snatch a few minutes before dinner on this old thing your stepbrother brought me."

She stood from the bench and stepped around to the side of the piano. She was wearing charcoal-gray trousers and a dove-gray jacket tailored to her womanly form, with a charcoal vest like his, also embroidered with blue thread. Elliot wondered what her source for these vests was and if he could buy some for the Mercantile. Some of the more staid gentlemen in Port Townsend would find them frivolous, but the younger crowd would snap them right up.

"What was the piece you were playing?" Elliot asked. "I've never heard anything like it." There was no sheet music on the elaborately scrolled desk above the keys that would give him a clue about the composer.

"Just a piece I've been playing around with lately, not by anyone you'd have heard of."

"Don't sell yourself short, Nance." Declan's voice rumbled, still just behind Elliot. "If you'd publish your pieces like I've suggested, then more people would know about them."

Elliot glanced at her. "You composed it?" He wasn't sure why he was surprised. There was obviously more to Nance than the shrewd, haggling trader Declan had painted her as. He wondered what else Declan knew about her that he didn't.

She shrugged. "I just play what comes to me. Don't write most of my pieces down anyway, so there ain't much to publish."

"I'd love to hear more of your music," he said to Nance. He wanted to ask her to play more now, but could hear men's voices coming from the foyer and guessed Nance's other guests would be joining them imminently. "There's something so...haunting about it."

Nance closed the piano's lid over the keys. "Mmph. Maybe. Most of my guests prefer simpler pieces, songs they can sing along or dance to. The other stuff I play when I'm alone, since most people find it too strange to listen to."

"It is strange," Elliot agreed. "But it's beautiful, too." He ran a hand through his hair, trying to think of how to explain what it made him feel. "It reminds me of something, but I can't think what. Something that I feel like I'm missing, but almost within reach, if I can figure out how to find it." He closed his eyes to keep the feel of Nance's playing in his head a little longer. When he opened them again, Nance was watching him with a thoughtful expression, and Declan had come forward to lean against the piano.

Nance gave him a small smile, then ran a caressing hand across the piano's polished rosewood surface. "Don't know how you managed to get this here in one piece on that floating tub you call a ship," she said to Declan.

Declan took a couple steps toward her, and Elliot tried not to shiver at the sudden loss of the warmth at his side. When Declan bent to kiss Nance's cheek, she rested a hand on his sleeve and squeezed.

"Thank you," she said simply.

Declan shrugged but also gave her a small smile. "I picked it up in San Francisco. It's the least I could do." He, too, lightly stroked the piano, running a hand around its curved corner.

"Nance's old piano suffered an unfortunate accident the last time I was here," he told Elliot. "Though it wasn't my fault that drunken sot came at you with a poker after he accused you of shorting him," he said, turning back to Nance. "I had to defend your honor, didn't I?"

Nance pushed Declan away with a snort. "The day I need you to fight my battles, Fitz, is the day I'll be taking a long walk off a short pier."

She shook her head as she brushed past Declan and caught Elliot's eye. He rolled his, and she smiled at him in recognition. If Elliot hadn't already cottoned on to how much Declan cared about Nance, despite their acerbic teasing, this would have clinched it. The day Elliot witnessed Declan miss an opportunity to make some sort of grand gesture to fix the problems of someone he cared deeply about, Elliot would find his own short pier to walk off.

"We'll expect a full concert after those reprobates you've allowed to stay here leave," Declan called after Nance, still examining the elaborately carved legs, bending to make sure they hadn't been damaged in the unloading.

Nance snorted. "Speaking of those reprobates, we should go into dinner with them before they come in here and drink all my best whiskey." Declan came away from the piano and offered Nance his arm. Elliot followed them through the library, across the foyer, and into the dining room.

Dinner was long and tedious. Nance presided at the head of the table, Declan at her right, and Elliot on Declan's other side. The stout man on Elliot's right, whose vest buttons strained across his stomach, introduced as Captain Ezekiel, seemed more interested in guzzling his wine and slurping his soup in a way that increasingly grated on Elliot's nerves than in making conversation.

The three men across the table got into a spirited discussion with each other and Nance about some scandal involving political figures on the British Columbian mainland whom Elliot had never heard of. Nance seemed to take sides with Captain Willoughby against Mr. Turner and Mr. Wyatt on the issue, shouting down Wyatt's and Turner's opinions on the subject and apparently competing to exacerbate Elliot's headache.

Elliot ate the food set in front of him but hardly tasted anything. He complied with Declan's unsubtle insistence that he take second helpings of the poached halibut and roast quail, but just pushed the last few bites of each around on his plate. He must have drunk more wine than he'd thought, as he stumbled against Declan when they stood to adjourn to the library. Declan shored him up with a hand under his elbow. Head spinning, Elliot barely stopped himself from pressing against Declan and whispering in his ear that they should make some excuse to retire early.

Declan raised an eyebrow at him, like he could tell what Elliot wanted. He followed Nance and the other men into the library, though, and Elliot sighed internally and joined them.

The evening was unseasonably warm, and Nance opened the library windows to let in the mild breeze. Elliot stood at one of the windows, a glass of port in his hand, and stared out at the nearly full moon shining on the water. He could faintly hear the soft murmuring of the waves lapping at the shoreline. There was no activity on the long pier at this hour, and the *Black Dove* and the other ships bobbed gently at anchor farther out in the inlet.

The tide was going out. He could tell from the subtle tug under his skin, a faint ebb of his blood that he could feel in his fingertips and wrists, the backs of his knees. It was like standing knee-deep in the ocean and feeling the undertow tug the sand from under his feet, except he was standing on a gold-and-blue Aubusson rug in a house more than a hundred yards from the shore. He wondered vaguely just when he'd realized he could tell where the tide was without looking at the water line or a tide chart.

The chatter and laughter in the library faded to the back of his attention as he watched the moonlight splinter on the rolling waves. Elliot's skin felt tight and hot, and he ached to shed the wool and linen clothes prickling against him. He turned away from the windows and set his glass down on a small side table. Declan was lounging casually on the horsehair sofa in front of the fireplace, long legs stretched out in front of him. His eyes were shining bright green in the firelight, his clean-shaven cheeks flushed pink after the wine and port, and his full red lips were clamped around the stem of his pipe. If Elliot had to look at him any longer, he'd jump him in this very room, audience be damned.

Elliot made his excuses and said good night to Nance and her guests. Away from the moonlight shining in through the library's windows, he was a little less disoriented, but he could still feel the pull of the tide, even from his upstairs room in the back of the house. It was bearable, though, especially when Declan silently opened the door and stepped inside, closing it behind him with a quiet snick.

Elliot met him at the door and dropped to his knees. He wrestled Declan's trousers open and cupped Declan's soft cock in his hands. He didn't even wait for it to harden, just kissed the tip with closed lips, then opened his mouth and slid down Declan's cock until his nose touched Declan's belly. Declan swelled immediately in his mouth, and Elliot went to work, bobbing his head and swirling his tongue in all the secret ways he'd learned to please Declan these last couple of weeks. Within minutes, Declan groaned softly and spilled into Elliot's mouth.

It wasn't enough. Elliot tugged Declan's trousers and drawers down to his ankles. "Off," he said shortly, as he stood up and started unbuttoning his own. Declan smirked at him as he bent to remove his boots and step out of his trousers, then draped his jacket and vest over the wingback chair next to the fireplace. Elliot tore his own clothes off, tossing the embroidered vest on the same chair, not caring when it slid off and crumpled into a pile on the floor. Declan had unbuttoned his shirt, and Elliot pulled it from his shoulders, over his head, and pushed Declan facedown on the bed.

"El—" Declan pushed up on his hands, but Elliot kneed up on the bed and draped himself against Declan's back, pushing Declan down on his stomach, muffling the rest of Elliot's name. Elliot slid the aching hardness of his cock against the backs of Declan's thighs, nudging just under the curve of his ass.

Declan groaned underneath him. "Elliot, wait. I want to, but it's been a while and—"

"I know," Elliot gasped in his ear. "I won't. Not that. I just need —" He couldn't wait any longer. The tide was almost at the lowest ebb and the moon nearly full, and Elliot couldn't stand the thrumming under his skin any longer. He bracketed Declan's thighs tightly between his knees, pulled his hips back and thrust forward along Declan's closed thighs, until the wet tip of his cock pushed in between Declan's ass cheeks.

"God, Declan," he moaned. "You feel so good." He pulled back and thrust again, the wet trail from his leaking cock slicking the way and making them both groan.

This was enough, for now, the slight roughness of the hair on the back of Declan's thighs against his cock, the soft skin between his cheeks as Elliot pushed through, the scent of Declan's pipe smoke and sweat around him. It grounded him, kept him together, kept him here, so that he didn't have to think about anything else. He could just be himself, with the only person who'd ever really understood him.

Elliot pushed up a little, bracing one hand on Declan's back. The skin under his hand twitched, and Elliot vaguely felt a mass of raised scars on Declan's back that he hadn't known was there. He slid his hand down Declan's back to the smooth curve of his ass. Elliot was so close now, and he'd ask Declan about the scars later. Right now, Declan was loose and pliant underneath him and making encouraging sounds, so Elliot grasped his hips in both hands and fucked Declan's thighs, faster and harder, until the unbearable pleasure crashed through him, like a tidal wave, and he came, back arched, pressed right up against Declan's hole, moaning Declan's name.

He slumped against Declan's back, then rolled off him onto his side, breathing heavily, trying to regain his senses. That sense of desperate urgency dissipated, and all he felt was peace. Declan squirmed around to face him.

"Feel better now?" His voice carried a note of amusement but his eyes were serious, like he somehow knew that Elliot had needed this more than just for the orgasm. Elliot nodded and looked away, not sure how to explain what had happened. Declan just slid a hand up his back and tucked Elliot's head into his shoulder.

"Good," he said, his voice rumbling in Elliot's ear, a firm hand stroking Elliot's back. "That's good, Elliot. You're good now. Try to get some sleep."

Elliot was quite sure he wasn't good at all. How good could he be after switching so completely from wanting to marry Celeste to needing to touch and fuck Declan all the time? But at least he felt more like himself again, almost normal for the first time today, so he'd take that for now. He closed his eyes and let himself drift off, safe in Declan's arms.

CHAPTER 20

*D*eclan stood up and stretched his back and neck, stiff after an afternoon bent over the pile of books and charts on the big table in Nance's library. He'd spent most of the past two days haggling with the other captains and Nance over the goods each ship had brought into her port, and now that business was done and Ezekiel and Willoughby had shipped out, he had time to get back to the main purpose of their visit here. Nance had a full set of the *American Nautical Almanac* from 1858 to 1888. On a hunch, he'd sent Joey to his cabin on the *Black Dove* for the tide tables for each of the towns he regularly called at.

He rubbed at his eyes, squeezed them shut, and blinked a few times to moisten the dryness caused by staring for the last few hours at stacks of paper. Betsy had lit both gas sconces installed on either side of the fireplace and the reading lamp at the big table when the sun had set an hour ago, and the soft yellow light gleamed on the sheet of notes he'd scrawled to himself.

His guess had been correct. In 1871 and '72, the full moon was at perigee in June and July, the months Charlie Lauder had told him the *Poulpes* appeared. Every appearance on his list, from

August 17, 1864, probably around when Elliot was conceived, to September 6, 1873, the day Marie Bishop disappeared, and in all the months someone had seen the ship in Nanaimo, Victoria, or Port Angeles, the moon was full and closest to the earth.

There were other months each year when the moon was near perigee, and Declan suspected they just hadn't tracked the ship to wherever it went in those months. The next supermoon was tonight, only Declan still didn't know how to predict where the *Poulpes* would appear, assuming it followed the pattern.

Declan was stretching his neck, tilting his head side to side when Nance wandered into the room, a lit cheroot in a meerschaum holder clenched between her teeth. She looked like the cat who'd eaten the canary. As well she might, considering the hard bargains she'd struck with him and the other captains. She smiled at Declan around her cheroot and peered at the books and papers strewn over the desk.

"Tracked down where your old man might be yet?" she asked. Declan had asked her when they arrived when the last time she'd heard from Father was. He hadn't stopped in at Nance's compound in November as usual, and she agreed it was worrisome not to have heard from him in so long.

"Not exactly," Declan said. He'd assured Elliot that Nance knew everything there was to know about vessels sailing in this part of the Pacific, but now that the time had come to ask her for the information he needed, he wasn't sure how to broach the subject. "You know he's been looking for his wife for some years now," he started cautiously.

Nance raised an eyebrow. "That'd be Elliot's mother, I presume?" Declan nodded. "Knew that. He asks me the same damn question every time he comes here—have I ever seen some gigantic eight-masted schooner sail up here. As if there's a shipbuilder could build such a vessel."

"So, you've never seen something like that?"

Nance snorted. "Course not. And I've seen damn near every vessel that's sailed these waters. Everyone puts in here some time or another."

Declan sighed and pinched the bridge of his nose. "Yeah. It sounds impossible, I know. I've never heard of anyone who's launched something that big, either. But, the thing is, Nance," he gazed steadily at her to catch any reaction she might have. "A bunch of folks have seen such a schooner. Not just in Port Townsend, but in Victoria, Nanaimo, even New Westminster. I never thought I'd say this, but I'm starting to believe the old man."

Nance's expression didn't change at all, which Declan supposed he should have expected. He'd certainly lost more than his fair share of poker games against the old girl. She looked back at him for a long moment, lips thinning as she inhaled, then took the cheroot holder from her lips between finger and thumb and blew a plume of smoke directly in his face.

"And what else did those folks see besides that schooner?" she asked, as Declan waved the smoke away. She raised her eyebrow at him again, clearly expecting a particular answer.

"Well," Declan began. "There's one person who saw a huge devilfish in the shallow water near the shore around the day the schooner appeared." No need to tell Nance that it was Elliot who saw the devilfish. Now, for the first time, he wondered whether he should have been asking in all the port towns along their voyage whether anyone else had seen such a thing.

Nance nodded. "Your father always asked the wrong questions," she said. "That's something I do know about."

Declan's mouth fell open. "What? You've seen it?"

She shook her head. "Nah. Never seen it. But plenty of sailors been drunk on my whiskey, and you wouldn't believe the stories they've told me. Stories about giant devilfish that live near an island out in the Pacific. Monsters bigger than the big octopuses you see round these parts. They even say they've seen ones that are half human, half devilfish."

She stuck her cheroot back between her lips and puffed on it again. "Close your mouth, Fitz, before you get flies in it."

Declan closed his mouth, since he didn't know what to say anyway. Elliot had described his dreams in which Celeste transformed into a half-octopus, but Declan had mostly chalked that up to Elliot's lifelong propensity for strange dreams. Or guilt over giving up his plans to marry her in favor of resuming a relationship with Declan. But surely these stories couldn't be true.

"Well, but…drunk sailors? I mean, we both know how much sailors love spinning a good yarn, the more so when they're drunk. You don't think they were just telling tall tales?"

Nance shrugged. "Could be. But there was a ship docked here three years ago with a naturalist on board. He was on a scientific mission, he said, to track and count all the marine species he could, specially devilfish. Man went on and on about collecting data and categorizing creatures no one has ever seen before. Stayed here couple days, then sailed west. Said he planned to cover every inch of the Pacific from here to Japan and publish his findings for the rest of the world to read."

She stopped, and Declan could hardly stand the suspense. "And? What did he find?"

She shrugged again. "More than what he bargained for, I imagine. The ship he was on came back here six months later, battered all to shit. Main mast lopped in half, sails tattered. It's a wonder they even managed to limp in here. The men were near starved, and there was less than half of them as started out. I let 'em stay until they got their strength back, then helped a few of them find work on other ships. Most of them decided they were done with sailing. Decided to go back where they were from or settle elsewhere, as loggers or whatnot."

"And the naturalist?"

"Never saw him again. The third mate who took command of

the ship on the voyage back here said the man insisted they sail to this island that wasn't on any of their charts. Said he knew how to get there and that some important new devilfish species lived there. The sailors who came back wouldn't say very much about what they saw there. Just that they found a new species for sure, but the captain, and half the crew, all died. Got the sense the rest of them fled for their lives and were lucky to get away at all."

"Christ," Declan sighed. If that was where the *Poulpes* had taken Marie and Celeste, then that's where Father would have gone and where Elliot would insist on going. He still wasn't sure how to get there. Sailing due west was the easy part, but he and Father had sailed west from Nance's dozens of times, and they'd never come across anything remotely resembling this mysterious island.

Nance watched him, still puffing on her cheroot, then heaved herself to her feet and crossed the library to the battered desk in the corner of the room. She dug around in the back of a drawer and came back with a small package in her hand. She handed it to Declan.

"The third mate gave this to me. Didn't even ask anything in trade for it; said he was just happy to get rid of it. Said they found it in the naturalist's cabin. After."

After what? Declan wondered, as he took the package. It was wrapped in a soft leather, well-tanned and flexible after having been folded and refolded over a long period of time. He turned it over in his hands, then set it on the table and unwrapped it, smoothing the leather flat and revealing an octagonal wooden box.

The walnut box was about eight inches across, with eight concentric rings on the lid made of strips of light and dark wood that formed a spiral geometric pattern. Declan tugged at the lid, but it refused to budge off the box.

Nance reached out and ran a finger along the seam of one of

the rings. "It's a puzzle box," she explained. "You rotate the rings to the right pattern, and then the lid comes off."

"What's the pattern?" Declan asked.

Nance sat back and lit a new cheroot. "Hell if I know. Never had the patience to figure it out."

Declan experimented with rotating the rings. If he kept one thumb pressed on a ring, he could use his other thumb to rotate the adjacent ring without also moving the first. He tried matching the lines of each ring to the adjacent rings, starting at the center of the lid, and fanning out into a spiral to the edge of the lid. The lid didn't open. Next, he tried a pattern of undulating half circles but that didn't open the box, either. He was just idly swiveling the rings when Elliot came into the room.

"You look like shit, boy," Nance commented mildly. "Did you sleep at all?"

Declan glanced up in time to see Elliot's guilty expression and mentally kicked himself. He'd left Elliot's room the other night after that awkward dinner and the subsequent sex so that Nance's staff wouldn't wonder why his bed hadn't been slept in. He'd expected Elliot to come to his room last night, but when he hadn't, Declan had chalked it up to Elliot being discreet with so many other guests in the big house. Declan had been so busy with business today and yesterday that he'd hardly had a minute to himself anyway.

But Nance was right. The violet shadows were back under Elliot's eyes, and his skin had the grayish tinge that usually accompanied sleepless nights filled with his nightmares. Declan should have been paying more attention to him. Elliot brushed off Nance's comments and joined them at the table.

"What's that?" he asked, gesturing at the box in Declan's hands. Declan explained how Nance had acquired it. Elliot took a few desultory tries at deciphering the puzzle, then handed it back to Declan and picked up his notes about the supermoon dates and sightings of the *Poulpes* instead. The lamp light gleamed on

Elliot's brown hair, which had grown out since they'd left Port Townsend, and he absently tucked a lock behind his ear. When Declan tore his eyes away, Nance was watching him, a small smirk on her lips and a knowing glint in her eye.

Declan rolled his eyes at her and took up the puzzle box again. The only sounds in the room for the next several minutes were Elliot turning the pages of the almanacs and the soft scraping of the rings against each other on the wooden box. There was something calming about swiveling the rings, one after another, to create new patterns. Declan methodically tried every pattern he could think of, until he finally twisted the rings into a pattern that looked vaguely like a full-blown rose.

This time, the lid came off easily, and Declan set it aside. Inside the box was a copper compass and inclining sundial. He tipped the compass from the box into his hand and showed it to Nance. Elliot was already staring at it like he'd never seen such a thing. Declan pried the gnomon upright and automatically set the angle to their current latitude, even though they were indoors with no sun to cast a shadow. There was no need to tell the time with such a rudimentary tool anyway, since either Declan's pocket watch or Nance's grandfather clock could tell him it was nearly nine in the evening.

He peered under the sundial parts at the compass needle, which wiggled aimlessly until Declan set the instrument on the table and allowed the bubbles in a pair of tiny spirit levels on two sides of the compass to settle. The needle swung slowly around the full circumference of the compass until it pointed toward Elliot, then stopped. Declan oriented the needle toward where he knew north was and it again spun around a full rotation, paused briefly as it swung past the library's windows, then pointed at Elliot again. Odd.

The *Black Dove* already had a compass mounted on the binnacle at the helm, one properly pointed to north. When Elliot reached for the compass, Declan handed it to him. Elliot took it gingerly. He had an intent look on his face, like he was listening for something.

"What is it?" Nance asked him. Elliot glanced up at her, his face pale and his eyes wide. "You feel it, don't you?"

"Feel what?" Declan asked, when Elliot just stared at her, his mouth slightly open.

"You feel it too?" Elliot asked her, ignoring Declan. She shook her head, then shrugged.

"Just a little. But it ain't pointing at me now, is it?"

Declan looked back and forth between them. "Someone tell me what the hell you're talking about," he demanded.

Elliot fumbled the compass back in the box with shaking hands, then put the lid on it, and leaned back in his chair. His forehead shined with sweat, and he looked ill. "I can't explain it," he said. "It's like it's calling to me, tugging at me to go somewhere." He looked at Declan with weary eyes. "But that's crazy. I mean, it's just a compass, right?"

Nance looked at Declan and sighed. "Ain't he supposed to be the smart one?" she asked, jerking a thumb at Elliot. "He ain't put it all together yet?"

Oh, fuck. Everything that Declan had been trying hard to delay putting together fell into place all at once. Elliot's nightmares, the circumstances of his conception, the devilfish he saw with his mother, his visions about Celeste, and his strange behavior both on the *Black Dove* and here, plus Nance's story about what that crew on the naturalist's mission saw. It all made sense now. Well, not sense, exactly, since Declan wasn't sure he'd believe in a half-devilfish, half-human creature until he saw one. Declan glanced out the library windows at the full moon rising over the inlet, its huge silver countenance shining serenely on the black water lapping at the shore. Maybe tonight would be the night he did.

Elliot shoved his chair back suddenly. "I need some air," he said and stalked from the room without another word. Declan watched him go, trying to decide whether to go after him or leave him be for a while, while Nance flipped idly through the notes Declan had made about full moons and tide times. Declan leaned forward and glanced at them.

"Shit," he said, mostly to himself, but Nance nodded.

"Better go after him," she said. "He's going to need you."

CHAPTER 21

*E*lliot walked alongside the long pier that led from Nance's front yard out into the bay. The tide was on its way out and the shore sloped gradually, its sandy beach exposed for several yards. The pier was high enough overhead that Elliot could walk at his full height underneath it at least halfway along the length of it. The rushing noise Elliot had been hearing in his own head all day eased a little. He could still sense it, but it was in sync with the sound of the waves crashing against the pilings, so he could pretend it was just normal shore sounds he was hearing. The night was quite warm for late March, and a soft breeze ruffled the loose strands of his hair.

Declan's boots crunched on the sand behind him. Elliot wasn't sure he had it in him tonight to convince Declan that he was fine, that Nance's story didn't make a sick sort of sense to him. That it hadn't confirmed to him something that he realized he'd known all along. That he was a monster and that eventually, he'd have to give up his life in Port Townsend and everything he'd ever wanted from a normal life.

Under the pier, horizontal rails spanned the side pilings every five feet or so, and Elliot stopped in front of one of these cross-braces about halfway down toward the water. He gripped the rough, splintered wood with both hands. He looked at one hand splayed on the salt-sprayed surface and brushed the fingertips of his other hand over his skin. It felt rough and splintered too, although it didn't look any different.

The water lapped at the pilings a few feet away, and the smell of damp sand and seaweed tickled his nose every time the breeze shifted. He thought about removing his clothes and wading into the water, letting it wash over him, to cool the burning ache of his skin.

Footsteps crunched along the sand behind him, and the smell of Declan's pipe smoke gave him enough warning to compose himself before Declan leaned against the rail next to him. Elliot could feel Declan's eyes on him but he just couldn't deal with the concern he knew would be there, so he kept staring out at the water. The moon was overhead, its bright light filtering through the cracks in the pier deck overhead, a misshapen reflection floating on the surface of the water past the end of the pier.

Declan sighed and bent forward to brace his elbows on the rail. "I know you're worried," he said finally, craning his neck around to see into Elliot's face. "But we don't know for sure that your mother or Celeste has turned into one of those creatures. Even if they have, it may not be permanent. Nance told me she's also heard stories of them changing back." He leaned back on one elbow and ran his other hand soothingly down Elliot's back.

The trail Declan's hand left was like a blaze of tiny fires kindled along his spine. His skin felt swollen and hot, like it was stretched over something too big to contain. The fibers of his clothes grated against his skin under Declan's hand, and he shuddered.

"Sorry," Declan murmured, pulling back.

"No," Elliot replied. "It's not you, it's just—" He pushed off the railing, stripped his coat and vest off, yanked his braces down to dangle at his waist, and shrugged out of his shirt. He was undoing the buttons of his trousers when Declan put a hand on his arm.

"Um, Elliot?" he asked, a hint of a chuckle in his voice. Elliot left his fly half undone and turned, pulling Declan toward him. He wrapped his arms around Declan's waist and shrugged Declan's unresisting arms up around his shoulders.

"Touch me," he whispered against Declan's neck. "Put your hands on me. I need you, Declan, please."

"Here?" Declan glanced up to Nance's big house, lights blazing in every front room. The pier was long and her front lawn deep, the few people moving about inside just dark shapes. No one would see them underneath the pier, but Elliot didn't care if they did.

"Please, Declan," he repeated, rubbing his bare chest against Declan's vest. Declan had left his coat in Nance's library, and Elliot reveled in the different textures dragging against his skin. The silk of Declan's vest slid easily across his chest but the raised surface of the embroidery stitches caught at his nipples, sending tiny shivers across his skin. He could feel every warp and weft thread of Declan's fine lawn shirtsleeves sliding up and down his arms. He rubbed against Declan a few more times, then fumbled the buttons of Declan's vest and shirt open and pressed against Declan's bare skin.

"Oh God," he breathed. He slid his arms under Declan's shirt and around his back. He traced each scar delicately with his fingertips until Declan twitched under his hands.

"Let's go inside," Declan whispered, warm breath tickling Elliot's ear.

"No," Elliot groaned. "I can't. I can't wait that long. Declan, please, I need you now. Need to fuck you." He pushed his hips against Declan's, slotting his hard cock against the thick length in Declan's trousers.

Declan slid his hands into Elliot's hair and cupped the back of his neck, pulling Elliot back to look at him.

"I want you to fuck me too. I can't tell you how long I've wanted that. But, come on, Elliot, wouldn't it be more comfortable inside? I want to take my time with you, not just a quick fuck against the wall like it doesn't mean anything." He pressed a soft kiss on Elliot's lips, and Elliot had to stop himself from devouring Declan's perfect mouth.

Elliot let go of Declan long enough to fumble in the pocket of his coat, then held a small bottle up. Declan stared at him, and Elliot smiled slightly. "I took it from your shaving kit. I'm not a complete innocent, Declan."

He set the bottle of sweet almond oil on the sand next to a piling and wrapped his arms around Declan's back again, tucking his head into Declan's shoulder. He couldn't explain why he needed to fuck Declan now, be inside him here, why he couldn't wait even the short distance back to the house. He whispered into Declan's neck so he wouldn't have to meet his eyes. "Out here. It's important. Please."

The urgency moved under his skin, spreading from the base of his spine along all his limbs. If he could just be inside Declan, everything would be all right. He could stay out of the water, he could stay on land. He could maybe even stay with Declan, if only he could pour everything he had into Declan, take everything he needed from him, right now. His cock stirred, swelling against the answering length of Declan's, still trapped inside Declan's trousers.

He kissed up the column of Declan's throat and felt it move as he swallowed. "Okay," Declan breathed, tilting his head as Elliot's lips reached his ear. "Whatever you need, Elliot."

Elliot trailed tiny kisses along Declan's jaw until their lips met. He kissed Declan slowly and softly, sliding his tongue in along Declan's, exploring his open mouth. He closed his teeth on Declan's bottom lip, sucking it in his own mouth, then opening again to wet, soft kisses, tongues tangling against each other. The pull of the ocean eased while Elliot kissed Declan. If only he could keep doing that forever and keep the sea from crashing over him.

Declan moaned softly against Elliot's mouth and slid his hands up and down Elliot's back. Everywhere he touched left trails of fire along Elliot's skin, contrasting with the icy burn of the ocean spray as the waves crashed against the sand in time with the thundering of his pulse.

Elliot pulled Declan's hips against his, sliding his half-exposed cock against the wool-covered length of Declan's own erection, then reluctantly pulled back from Declan's mouth. He bent his head to one nipple and teased at it with lips and teeth while pushing Declan's vest off his shoulders. Declan arched against him and let his arms dangle behind his back to slip his vest off, then lifted them to let Elliot tug his shirt over his head. Elliot tossed the bundle of cloth heedlessly upon the sand behind him, swiped his tongue over Declan's other nipple, then pulled back enough to tug Declan under the rail and turned him so they were facing the house.

Pressing between Declan's shoulder blades, Elliot pushed him against the railing, Declan's forearms bracing his body against it. He ran both hands down Declan's back, smoothing over firm muscles and taut skin. If he had time, he'd kiss each of the scars shining faintly silver in the moonlight and every other inch of Declan's body, tease and bite at his nipples until he cried out, bring him off with his mouth and only then slide into him, all relaxed and ready for Elliot.

But the tide was about to turn, and he couldn't wait much longer. His cock was aching, his skin was on fire, and his balls were throbbing with the need to be inside Declan. He pressed his chest against Declan's warm back and Declan pushed back against him, sweat making his skin slip against Elliot's chest.

He slid his hands around Declan's sides, down his belly to the waistband of his trousers. He unbuttoned Declan's fly, dragged his trousers down, and helped him pull each leg free of the cloth.

He ran his hands up the outside of Declan's legs, trailing a series of open-mouthed kisses up his left thigh, and licked a broad strip over the curve of his ass to the middle of his back. He stood all the way up and shucked the rest of his own clothes, then kicked Declan's feet wider and bent to grab the bottle of sweet almond oil. He thumbed the lid open and poured a generous amount over his index and middle fingers, rubbing the oil between fingers and thumb.

He felt Declan breathe out as he slowly inserted one finger. Declan was tight and hot, and Elliot fought the urge to slam into him with two fingers, three, his cock, his everything. He slid the finger out as the tide pulled back, then pushed it back in as a wave flowed around the pilings behind him. It was easier to keep control if he listened to the waves, pulling his finger out as the water pulled back, gliding it back in as the water rushed back in. Declan's sighs grew to moans as he took Elliot's second finger easily, and when Elliot tucked a third finger in, he dropped his head between his shoulders and pushed back against Elliot's hips.

The waves were reaching higher up the sand now, and Elliot's skin prickled every time an errant spray splashed him. He pulled his fingers free of Declan, who gave a little whine, and bent forward against Declan's back again, rubbing his nipples against Declan's sweating skin. He poured a small lake of oil into his hand and slicked his cock from root to tip. He lined up, pushed in a few inches, and closed his eyes to concentrate on the soft clench of Declan's body, opening slowly but inexorably for him.

"Oh, God," he groaned as he fought to stay in control. Declan's answering groan nearly undid him. He pulled back, squeezed his hands hard around Declan's hips, and pushed again, slowly, steadily, until his hips met the curve of Declan's ass and he was fully seated.

He gave Declan a moment to adjust to his full length inside but when Declan rocked back against him, Elliot groaned again and bent over him, resting most of his weight on Declan's back. He licked a line of sweat from Declan's neck.

"You feel so good," he whispered in Declan's ear. "I need you all the time, just like this."

"Need you too," Declan panted. "Always needed you, Ellie. Never should have left you."

Elliot pushed away the thought that Declan would surely leave once he found out the truth. He had this moment and if he could stay in control, he could stay himself and have everything he'd been wanting. When Declan rocked his hips back against Elliot again, Elliot pulled out a few inches and pushed carefully back in. It was easier this time, Declan opening to accommodate him, like he'd made room for Elliot most of his life.

He didn't need to see the waves to move inside Declan with them. He pulled back with the undertow and thrust in hard as a big wave crashed against the sand. The tide was going out but he could feel another large swell coming, rolling in from miles away and growing taller and taller, the kind of rogue wave he dimly recalled the crew of the *Black Dove* telling him could appear out of nowhere and turn everything upside down in an instant. When the cold water sluiced over him and Declan, an answering wave spread through his whole body, along all his limbs, his skin tingling, muscles expanding under the onslaught of sensation.

Elliot's cock expanded inside Declan, who was making soft, whimpering, needy sounds. He wrapped his arms around Declan's chest and leaned forward, trusting Declan to take his full weight. Cold seawater trickled down his back, and all the bones below his navel dissolved in a tidal rush of heat and pleasure. A feverish pressure spread through his pelvis and legs, straining inside his skin, pushing outwards. He gasped at the pulsing heat threatening to burst through his flesh even as Declan's heat squeezed around his cock.

The pressure and pleasure grew together, swelling his cock inside Declan, his skin aching and burning until something snapped within him and his legs split into four thick, strong limbs, a fifth growing from the base of his spine. He stretched and flexed these muscular new limbs, then balanced lightly on their boneless tips, still draped over Declan.

The cradle that used to be his pelvis spread to cover more of Declan's hot, wet body. Elliot wrapped a pair of tentacles around Declan's thighs, then coiled them around his knees and calves. He curled and uncurled the slippery undersides of his new limbs against Declan's skin, shivering at how good it felt. Every inch of his new skin was alive and independent, sliding along Declan's, gripping and tugging Declan closer and closer to him. Elliot couldn't stop it from happening any longer, no longer even wanted to. He closed his eyes, let the waves flow over and through him. He pushed as deep inside Declan as he could, and gave into the change.

CHAPTER 22

*D*eclan couldn't tell how much of the water dripping from his chest and hair was seawater or sweat, but he didn't care. He pushed back against Elliot as much as he could, crushed between Elliot's hard, muscled chest and the sturdy wooden rail he was bent over. Thank God Nance had built the pier to withstand a typhoon, since it was the only thing holding him up while the waves rammed Elliot's body against his and Elliot's cock thrust deeper inside him.

"Elliot," he moaned against his forearms, braced on the rail and supporting his head as Elliot filled him until he wasn't sure he could take any more, then expanded inside him until he knew he would have to take all of him. All of Elliot above him, moving inside him, wrapping his arms and legs around him. Declan's own cock was throbbing in time with his heartbeat, and he wanted to touch it but he didn't want this to end too soon. He braced his arms against the wooden railing as Elliot let out a long moan behind him.

The angle shifted and Elliot swelled even more inside, stroking along that spot that lit Declan's nerves like a line of gunpowder catching fire. Elliot's weight against his back also shifted, and the hard points of Elliot's hips that had been slamming into his ass dissolved into a hot, wet cradle that expanded around his own hips and slid slickly against him while Elliot kept fucking him. The hard thighs braced behind Declan's shifted, replaced by a firm, flexible squeeze wrapped around each leg.

Declan kept his eyes closed and his face tucked into his forearms, reveling in the feel of Elliot's velvet skin rubbing all over him. In the back of his mind, he knew something strange was happening, but he'd never felt so open and filled, so needed and needful all at once. Elliot made low groaning, hitching noises in his ear and Declan leveraged his arms against the railing to push back against him.

"God, Ellie, you feel so...I need you...please, Elliot, please," he panted nonsensically. He groaned like he was about to die when finally, something warm and wet wrapped around his cock. Elliot's arms were still across his chest, hands clutched just above his nipples, pressing Declan's back against Elliot's chest. Declan cracked his eyes open, blinked saltwater from his lashes, and watched a reddish brown tentacle wrap around his entire cock until only the tip of it was visible. The tentacle flexed and shifted, and a thin stream of fluid leaked from his slit, dripping down the coils of flexing muscle around his cock. Declan's body lit up, a coal fire explosion at the base of his spine, his balls tightening, licks of flame along every nerve.

He closed his eyes and in the limited space between Elliot's body and the railing, thrust forward through the wet squeeze around his cock, then back against the velvet cradle surrounding his ass. Elliot picked up the pace, slamming into Declan with low grunts, Declan's cock fucking into the tight circle of coils squeezing and flexing around it. Declan spent before Elliot did, the burning heat shuddering through his body. The tentacle around his cock stroked him through it, then uncoiled and slid away, despite Declan's small sound of protest.

Elliot's cock was still hard inside him, and Declan knew he

would be sore tomorrow but he pushed back a little against Elliot. Three more strokes, and Elliot's harsh pants in his ear raised him to half-mast again. On the last, hardest, thrust, Elliot pushed in as deep as he could, and Declan clenched down around him. Elliot's low groan sounded pained, but Declan arched back against him and reveled in the tiny jerks and twitches of Elliot's cock in his ass spreading out among all his nerve endings, like gentle waves lapping on the beach.

"Elliot," he sighed when Elliot stilled and slumped against him.

"Don't," Elliot said thickly. He peeled himself off Declan's sweating back and pressed a hand between his shoulder blades, keeping him still. "Just don't say anything. I am so...God—" he stopped and swallowed audibly. "Just don't turn around yet, all right? Please, just please, stay where you are."

Declan had no words yet in the relaxed, drifting happiness he felt, so he nodded and dropped his forehead on his arms again. Elliot pulled out carefully, Declan already feeling empty, and unwound one limb, then another, from Declan's legs. Elliot hissed a shocked breath behind him and traced his fingers lightly down the backs of Declan's legs. Declan shivered and leaned more against the railing, his rubbery legs barely holding him up. The air was cool on his exposed flesh, and goosebumps rose where the sweat was drying on his skin.

He felt rather than heard Elliot moving around behind him, collecting their clothes, dropping Declan's in a small pile next to his foot. With a small groan, he pushed up from the railing to his full height and stretched his arms overhead, fingertips brushing the underside of the pier. He leaned to one side, then the other, working the kinks out of his spine, and shrugged into his shirt. Before he'd finished doing up the buttons, Elliot said in a small voice, "All right, you can turn around now."

When Declan turned around, Elliot was standing on his own two legs, fully dressed. He'd finger-combed his wet hair off his face but wouldn't meet Declan's eyes. He looked normal, no sign of the extra limbs Declan knew he'd just had wrapped all around his body, but he also looked cold and filled with angry shame, the same way he'd looked the first time he jerked them both off in Declan's cabin and then fled without waiting to hear Declan speak. Declan would be damned if he'd let Elliot run away from him this time.

"Elliot," he said softly, taking a step forward and holding out a hand to him. "Please, Ellie, listen to me." He stumbled as he stepped forward, his legs still feeling like they wanted to float away from him, and all the remaining color left Elliot's face.

"Oh, Christ," he said brokenly. "I am so sorry, Declan. I never meant to—I thought I could keep it under control but I— "

"For fuck's sake, Elliot, will you shut the hell up and listen to me for once in your goddamn life!"

Elliot's eyes snapped to Declan's face. He shut his open mouth, lips thinned to a grim slash in his pale face. Declan ran a hand through his own damp hair and dropped it to his side. He knew if he tried to touch Elliot, he would bolt. He wasn't sure there was anything he could do to keep Elliot from bolting, but he had to try.

"You can't give a man a minute to recover after the best fuck he's ever had?" Declan tried for a little humor, but Elliot seemed like he hadn't even heard him, his eyes begging Declan to forgive him. Declan sighed.

"Elliot. I know what happened. I know what you are." Elliot squeezed his eyes shut and shook his head. Declan took another limping step forward. "It's all right, Ellie. It doesn't matter. It's you I want, you I've wanted all this time. So what if you're a," he hesitated. Was there a proper word for what Elliot was? He couldn't remember whether Nance had told him one. The proper word didn't really matter, though. Not when Elliot was barely listening to him.

"Monster," Elliot choked out.

"A little different from most men," Declan corrected him. "Not a monster, El. Don't ever think that." He tried to take another step toward Elliot. He needed to touch him, hold him close, and tell him with his hands and his lips that Declan wanted every part of him, no matter how different. But his damned legs still felt numb, and he fell to one knee in the sand, the other leg crumpled beneath him.

"Oh God," Elliot said, darting forward, stretching his hands out but not close enough to touch him. "Your legs, Declan." He turned anguished eyes up to Declan's. "I did that to you. How can you not think I'm a monster?"

Declan looked down. A series of bright red circles marched up each leg, the smallest at his ankle about the size of a shirt button. They spiraled up to mid-thigh, increasing in size, the biggest about the size of a ten-dollar coin. "Oh," he said softly. The rest of his legs were a bloodless white, and Declan felt a bit queasy looking at the marks. He looked back at Elliot's face, as pale as his legs, and tried to smile.

"I'm fine," he said, reaching for his drawers and trousers and then shaking the sand from them. His legs were tingling, like being stuck with pins and needles all over, but he could tell that wouldn't last very long. "You squeezed a little too hard, maybe, that's all." It was already easier to stand, when he got to his feet and pulled his clothes back on, tucking his shirt in and doing up the buttons.

"Elliot," he said, as he buttoned his vest and straightened his collar. He'd no idea where his necktie had slithered off to. "Elliot," he repeated, a little sharper.

Elliot looked at him, still pale and shocked-looking. Declan lifted a hand to his cheek, and Elliot flinched away. "I'm fine, Elliot," he repeated soothingly. "I know what just happened, and it's *fine*. We just need to figure out why it happened now."

Elliot shook his head, a miserable look on his face. "I can't," he whispered.

"Can't what?" Declan asked.

"Can't talk about it." Elliot shook his head again. "Can't be with you. Can't let that happen again." He covered his face with shaking hands and took a blind step backwards, away from Declan. "I thought, being with you, that I could stop it, keep it from happening. But I was wrong."

Declan's heart clenched in his chest. "Come on, man," he said lightly. "It's not like we both didn't enjoy it. I know you know that."

Elliot dropped his hands from his face and glared at Declan. His eyes shone wet in the moonlight. He gazed around him, up toward the bright blazing lights of Nance's house and out to the dark, heaving sea. He shook his head yet again, like a dog shaking water off its coat. "I can't be here," he said. "I need to be alone, Declan."

"Elliot," Declan tried again. "We just need to talk about it."

"No!" Elliot shouted. "I *can't*, Declan, don't you understand? If I stay near you, I'll just—" he turned his back on Declan and said, "Please, Declan. If you've ever cared about me, let me be. Just leave me alone, for tonight, at least."

Without waiting for a reply, Elliot stalked up the beach, his boots crunching on the sand. He reached the top of the pier and turned left, skirting the edge of Nance's front lawn and disappearing around a bend in the shoreline.

Declan watched him go, his need to run after Elliot warring with the understanding that this had been a lot for the poor man to take in one evening. He'd let Elliot have some time alone. They could talk about it in the morning.

He bent to retrieve his coat and winced a bit at the soreness in his ass. He wouldn't be able to forget this night for a long time, no matter what Elliot wanted. In the meantime, he had a few more questions for Nance. If he could figure out how to ask them without revealing everything that had just happened. He glanced once more in the direction Elliot had gone, then limped slowly up the beach to the house.

CHAPTER 23

*D*eclan and Nance were in the library when Elliot returned to the house in the wee hours, their heads bent together over a stack of books and papers, murmuring quietly to each other in front of the fire. He allowed Declan to catch sight of him as he passed the library's open door but shook his head when Declan half-rose to meet him and couldn't look at Nance at all. He went upstairs to bed but didn't bother trying to sleep. He lay down on top of the coverlet without undressing and stared sightlessly at the ceiling until dawn. He left the house again before breakfast, walking alone along the rocky shoreline away from the big house.

He tried not to think about finally fucking Declan. Because once he let himself think about the first moment when he pushed into Declan's tight heat, he'd have to think about everything that came after. He'd have to think about what happened to his body, that he'd shifted into the same creature he'd seen Celeste shift into in his dreams. He'd have to figure out why the shift happened at that moment, when every other time he'd been with Declan, he'd managed to stay himself. Why he'd thought that fucking Declan would keep him human. And how Declan had reacted to his change as if it were something he didn't mind. Maybe even enjoyed. But that was impossible.

Dried green and brown kelp that had washed up on the shore crackled under his boots as he walked. The rocky beach ended at a small pile of boulders forming the base of a short cliff. Elliot gazed miserably at the seawater swirling around rocks and boulders scattered in the water. Red and orange starfish clung to the rocks just above the sea, reminding Elliot of the red welts he'd left on Declan's legs. Declan had brushed them off as a temporary inconvenience, but he couldn't possibly be as nonchalant about Elliot's change as he'd seemed last night. A spray of salt water splashed Elliot's face, and he licked his lips. The thrumming in his blood in time with the surf had been persistent when he'd left the house and was nearly unbearable now.

On the other side of the cliff was a narrow, rocky chasm. Wisps of steam rose above the rocks and Elliot could smell sulfur underneath the briny sea spray. This must be the hot spring Betsy had mentioned when she drew his bath the first night here. The cliff sloped inland until it disappeared into the forest.

He looked back the way he'd come. He'd walked maybe a mile or so from the house, and the beach behind him was deserted. At least if he let the shift happen here, no one would see him. He folded his clothes into a small pile on a flat rock above the tide line. Naked and shivering a bit in the cool spray, he clambered carefully up and over a misshapen boulder that had a series of small step-like indentations carved into the face of the rock. Today was even warmer than yesterday—he'd never known it to be this warm at the end of March—but the ocean was still icy as it splashed over his toes.

A small waterfall cascaded down the chasm's rock face, tumbled along the rocks, and flowed down to the ocean's edge through a series of small pools. Tendrils of steam wafted from the falls and the surfaces of the higher pools. Elliot picked his way down the rocks and dipped a toe in one of the lower pools.

The water was warm where the hot spring trickled in, but as he lowered his body into the pool, a wave of icy ocean water swirled in and splashed him to mid-chest.

With the seawater swirling around him, Elliot gave in to the pressure building under his skin, let go and shifted. His legs split into two limbs each, his cock lengthened and thickened, and he had to shift position to make room for the sixth limb to grow out from the base of his spine. The skin on each new limb changed color and texture, tingling as lines of suckers emerged on the undersides and opened to the water. The oddest sensation was the bones in his pelvis dissolving as his hips spread and expanded, making room for his additional limbs.

Elliot stretched all six limbs to their full length under water. He couldn't quite bring himself to look at them yet but he felt the water flow around each tentacle and under the webbing that connected them, gasping a little as first warm, then cool, currents slid past the sensitive undersides of each tentacle and swirled around where everything met at his asshole.

Elliot leaned back, rested the back of his head on a rock ledge, and closed his eyes. He felt...good, actually. Letting go of the effort of staying human was like putting down a heavy burden he'd been carrying so long. He flexed and curled his new limbs in the water. They crept and slipped along the rocks lining the pool, taking in all the new sensations through skin that had never felt so sensitive.

"You look so peaceful, Elliot."

Declan's voice shattered Elliot's reverie and he bolted upright, forgot he didn't have two solid legs to stand on, and floundered in the pool, scraping his tender new skin on the rocks before spreading his tentacles to reach a sort of equilibrium. He curled in on himself and scrunched down as far under the water as he could.

"Go away, Declan," he growled, bracing a hand on the edge of the pool to keep from floating to the surface.

"No," Declan replied in a soft voice. "We need to talk, Elliot."

Elliot couldn't look at him. "I don't want to talk. I want to be left alone. How did you even find me, anyway?"

There was a small splash behind him as Declan slipped into the water and then a soft sigh, like the ones Declan made when Elliot kissed him. "I love this place. I come here every time I visit Nance." Warm water trickled over the boulder that partially divided the pool Declan was in from the one Elliot was in. "Plus, Betsy told me she'd seen you heading this way."

Elliot sighed. He should have known Declan would track him down. He squeezed his eyes shut tighter and tried to shift his legs back to how they were supposed to be. Nothing happened. He pushed down a small lick of panic and tried again, mashing all his limbs together as hard as he could. He wasn't sure how else to even try it. Still nothing. Declan was saying something, but Elliot ignored him, thinking back to how he'd shifted back last night and trying to figure out what he'd done then. He hadn't been underwater last night, just soaked wet from that rogue wave. What if he needed to be out of the water before he could change back? He'd have to wait until Declan left, and who knows how long that would take. What if this time he couldn't change back?

"Elliot." Declan said sharply. Goddamn it, why couldn't he leave Elliot alone?

"What?" Elliot snapped, finally looking up at Declan.

"I know what you're trying to do, Elliot, and it won't work that way," Declan said. He was naked, arms stretched across the boulder he was leaning against and looked calm, like they were talking about knot-tying on the *Black Dove*. Elliot wanted to punch him for acting like this was an everyday occurrence.

"What the hell do you know about it?" he snarled.

Declan leveled a look at him and raised an eyebrow. "More than you, evidently. At least I'm not afraid to learn about it."

Elliot stared back at him for a minute. Declan sighed, then stood and waded through the waist-deep water toward Elliot, picking his way around and over the boulders that created the natural pools. Elliot retreated to the deeper pools at the ocean's edge. The water was colder here, farther away from the hot spring's source. The tide was nearly at its lowest, so the water was still only about chest-deep on Elliot, even with all his limbs stretched to their full length. It was rougher with the ocean's waves crashing over and around the rocks.

Declan kept coming toward Elliot, his breath catching and body shivering as each cold wave splashed over him. "Elliot," he called. "Come on, man. I'm not leaving until you talk to me, so you might as well be reasonable." He opened his mouth to say something else, then misjudged a step and slipped under the next wave. Elliot took the opportunity to turn toward the ocean and really swim out into it. He pulled all six limbs in toward his center and then thrust them straight behind him. He shot forward through the water like an arrow loosed from a bow. When the momentum from his thrust slowed, he angled his way up to the surface, several yards away from the shore.

Elliot lay back and let the water cradle him, treading water effortlessly with six limbs. Declan couldn't swim, so he'd have to stay in the shallows until he gave up trying to talk to Elliot. He felt a pinprick of remorse for playing such a dirty trick on Declan, but the sooner he took the hint and went back to the house, the sooner Elliot could enjoy the hot spring pools in peace.

He couldn't see Declan, though, and after a minute or so, Elliot swam closer to the shore. There was the pile of Declan's clothes, folded neatly on a rock above one of the higher pools. He swam into the pool closest to the ocean's edge, but there was still no sign of Declan. Elliot took a deep breath and plunged under water against the hot spring's current. He slipped around and between rocks lining the chasm. There was Declan, in the next deep pool, one foot wedged between a pair of rocks, struggling to pull it free.

Elliot surfed in on a wave that battered Declan against the boulder behind him. He was twisting frantically now, hair swirling around his submerged face, eyes bulging, mouth clenched tight to keep from swallowing seawater. He must have been trying to free himself the entire time Elliot was swimming out in the ocean.

Christ, how could he have been so thoughtless and selfish? His heart pounding in his chest, Elliot raced for the rocks trapping Declan's foot. He slipped two tentacles into the gap on either side of Declan's foot, braced himself with his other limbs, and flexed the tentacles against the rocks, pushing them apart with all his might. He slid his hands down Declan's calf to his ankle and tugged Declan's foot free. Then he swam up Declan's body, wrapped his arms around Declan's waist, and thrust with his tentacles until their heads breached the surface.

Declan sucked a deep breath in and coughed a stream of water down Elliot's back. He sagged against Elliot's chest, coughing and gasping, and Elliot held him close, murmuring, "Oh God, Declan, I'm so sorry. So sorry," over and over.

Declan got his breath back, mostly, and patted Elliot's shoulder weakly. "I'm fine, Elliot. I'm okay," he said, still coughing every few breaths. "I'll be fine, just give me a minute." He rested his forehead on Elliot's shoulder, his breathing still a harsh pant next to Elliot's ear. Elliot stopped his litany of apologies out loud but kept them going in his head.

Declan had almost drowned and it was all his fault, because Elliot was too selfish and childish to just talk to him. How many times would Declan have to run after Elliot because Elliot wouldn't stop running away from him?

Declan's breathing finally eased and he tipped his head sideways to kiss Elliot's neck. "Looks like those tentacles of yours are pretty strong, eh? That's a good thing, don't you think?"

Elliot closed his eyes and squeezed Declan tighter against his chest. "Oh God, Declan," he repeated.

"Stop," Declan rasped, interrupting him. "It was an accident, Elliot. I slipped and you got me out. Quit apologizing for it." He shivered. "I'm cold, though. Could we maybe move to a warmer spot?"

Elliot let Declan go, but watched every step he took until they settled in a pool closer to the waterfall. Declan leaned back and sighed deeply. "Much better," he said, closing his eyes and lifting his face to the sun. Elliot looked him over carefully. His face was a little flushed from coughing, but he was breathing easier now. His eyelashes were wet spikes resting on his cheeks, and the sun glinted in droplets caught in the strands of his darkened wet hair. Elliot cupped his cheek and ran his thumb lightly over the faint freckles sprinkled there.

Declan smiled without opening his eyes and spread his arms out along the rocks he was leaning against. "Kiss me, Elliot," he said softly.

CHAPTER 24

*E*lliot leaned forward and touched Declan's lips with his own. Declan immediately parted his and ran the tip of his tongue along the seam of Elliot's lips. Elliot opened for Declan and then they were kissing, Elliot desperate to devour Declan. Declan gave as much as Elliot took, holding nothing back.

Elliot's hands were in Declan's hair, tugging him closer but still meeting only at their lips and tongues. Declan slid his arms around Elliot's back, then stroked slowly down, splaying his knees wide and pulling Elliot's body closer. His hands were firm as he slid them down the small of Elliot's back, tugging Elliot's lower body insistently between his knees. Elliot held his breath as Declan's hands finally slipped past the line where his ass used to be.

"You're so soft," Declan murmured against Elliot's lips. "Like velvet." His hands swept along Elliot's new limbs, squeezing small handfuls and smoothing over every inch he could reach. "Let me see, Elliot, please," Declan whispered.

Elliot flushed hot with shame and buried his face in Declan's neck. His new skin tingled with every stroke of Declan's hands, but it was another thing entirely to let Declan look at him while he was this way. As if he could read Elliot's hesitation, Declan ran one hand up Elliot's back, cupped the back of his head gently to keep it tucked against his neck, and slid the other hand underneath Elliot. He scooped Elliot's lower half up enough to get his knees under and settled him on Declan's lap.

"Christ, Declan, how can you want me like this?"

Declan dropped his hand in the center of Elliot's lap, squirmed it between two thick tentacles, and ran it firmly down the middle tentacle tucked in between them. Elliot arched against Declan's other arm holding him and moaned out loud, sudden heat pooling in his center. "Yeah," Declan murmured, a smug smile audible in his voice. "I thought that one was your cock." Elliot peeked through his own wet lashes at Declan's hand sliding up and down the tentacle. The muscle lengthened and thickened, turning a deep red, just like Elliot's cock did when Declan jacked it.

Elliot closed his eyes again and stopped thinking about anything for a minute. When Declan's hand stopped, still wrapped around the thickest part of it, Elliot was breathing heavy and so was Declan.

"How could I not want you like this?" Declan asked. He shifted position under Elliot, pressing his erection up into the webbing where Elliot's tentacles met at the center.

"It's unnatural," whispered Elliot, trying to resist the kisses Declan was trailing along his jaw. Declan pulled back a little, then burst out laughing.

"Unnatural?" he spluttered. He caught sight of Elliot's expression, which must have looked hurt, and stopped laughing. He cupped a wet hand under Elliot's jaw, forcing Elliot to look at him. "Elliot, everything we've ever done together is considered unnatural. Not to mention illegal."

Elliot had never given more than a passing thought to the sodomy laws applying to them. They were discreet, and Declan had surrounded himself with men who either shared his proclivities or didn't care about them as long as he was a decent captain.

"This is hardly the same." He shifted his gaze over Declan's shoulder to the waterfall, still having trouble looking Declan in the eyes. He gestured at his tentacles drifting lazily under the water, without looking down at them. One was twining around Declan's leg, like it had a mind of its own and was ignoring Elliot's effort to keep them contained and under control. If he couldn't shift back, how would he live the rest of his life? How long would Declan stay with something like him?

Declan was silent for a minute. "Did you know Joey was originally named Josephine?" he asked, apropos of nothing that Elliot could see. "It was Nance's mother's name, you know, and she wanted to name her only child after her mother."

Elliot shook his head. "Joey?" He didn't know why Declan was bringing Joey up now, but he'd take the change of subject over the thought of being stuck like this the rest of his life. "Why would Nance name her son after her mother?"

He tried to imagine Declan's first mate enduring the ribbing from the crew for having a woman's name. Joey was smaller than most of the other men on the ship and with his beardless baby face and yellow-blond hair, he got plenty of guff from drunk sailors in taverns. Elliot felt his brain stall.

"Wait. You mean Joey's a woman?"

"Joey is a man," Declan said firmly. "He's known he's a man since he was small."

"I don't understand."

"Joey's never felt like a woman his whole life. Caused no end of strife between him and Nance, that's for sure. When she arranged for him to go to some fancy ladies' finishing school back East, he ran away from home. I was in port when he took off and promised Nance I'd keep an eye out for the kid."

Declan shifted a bit underneath Elliot but clasped his arms tighter around Elliot's waist when Elliot tried to move off his lap.

"We'd already passed the entrance to Juan de Fuca Strait before he popped out of my hold and begged me not to take him straight back home. I would have—I got no interest in being on the wrong end of Nance's ire—but I had a rendezvous with Father to bring an opium shipment through the San Juan Islands, and the weather had already made us late for it. Lucky for me it was my ship he snuck aboard and not someone else's, as he turned out to be one of my best men. Promoted him to first mate within the year and never had a better one."

Declan shook his head, smiling slightly. "Caused quite a stir explaining things to Nance when we came back around, though. She nearly shot my own manhood off and threatened to never do business with me or Father again."

Elliot couldn't see what Josephine or Joey or even Nance had to do with him. "Why are you telling me this?"

"I shouldn't be," Declan admitted. "It's not my secret to tell, and I'll thank you not to mention that I did to Joey, nor treat him any different now that you know. It took Nance longer than it should have to come around. She's mellowed a bit in the last year, and they're finally starting to rebuild their relationship."

When Elliot still looked blankly at Declan, he sighed. "I'm telling you because what makes Joey a man is knowing deep down that he is one. Whatever he has under his drawers is his business and that of anyone he trusts to get close enough."

Declan stroked both hands along Elliot's side and caressed the skin from his waist to where his tentacles began. "It's the same for you, Elliot. You're not less of a man because you're occasionally shaped differently."

Elliot snorted without any mirth behind it. "You're not seriously comparing swapping a dress for a pair of trousers and living as a man to what's happened to me," he said. He couldn't keep a note of bitterness from his voice. "At least Joey still has the two legs she was born with."

"He," Declan corrected, a steel note in his voice, the same tone

Elliot had started thinking of as his captain's voice, when he was displeased by something one of his crew had done. "And no, I'm not saying that what's happening to you is the same as what Joey's gone through. Which you are never to bring up to him, Elliot, and I mean that." He held Elliot's gaze with a stern look, until Elliot nodded and dropped his eyes to his lap. He'd seen how Declan and the rest of the crew interacted with Joey on this voyage and if they could treat him like just another man on the ship, Elliot could too.

Declan's hands resumed their stroking, bracketing Elliot's ribcage and sweeping wide arcs from his shoulder to his waist. "I'm just saying that you're still all the things you are—successful merchant, barely passable sailor." His eyes were glinting bright green in the sunlight when Elliot looked back up at him. "Annoying stepbrother who used to drive me crazy with all your questions when you were a boy." He waggled his eyebrows suggestively. "Who grew up to be the best cocksucker I've ever known."

Elliot rolled his eyes at Declan's attempt to lighten his spirits. He was definitely not the same man. Looking down at the tentacles where his legs used to be, he was barely more than half a man right now.

But Declan leaned forward and kissed Elliot softly. His hands caressed Elliot's skin while his tongue moved in Elliot's mouth, the wide sweeps across Elliot's ribs and flank matched with gentle strokes against his tongue, small circles with Declan's fingertips echoed by tiny nips at Elliot's lips. "Everything that makes you *you* is still the same," Declan murmured as he kissed along Elliot's jaw. He slid both hands between Elliot's tentacles and ran them up and down Elliot's cock until he shivered. "You've just got some new parts to enjoy, that's all."

Every place Declan touched felt lit from within. Tiny sparks danced along Elliot's veins and he shifted under Declan's hands, aching for more of his touch. He hadn't quite believed that

Declan really knew what happened last night and he'd never imagined that Declan would still want him once he knew what Elliot really was. But there was no mistaking the acquisitive explorations of Declan's fingers or the insistence of the hard length Elliot was sitting on.

The same urgent need he'd felt last night washed over Elliot with the next wave. He rutted into Declan's fist and squirmed against the hard length pressing up underneath him. He kissed Declan back, hard, and gasped into his open mouth as Declan squeezed and stroked him. It felt amazing, but it wasn't enough. He needed to be inside Declan, moving in him where the dark heat gripped him tight, pushing and thrusting until he couldn't get any closer. If Declan really was willing, Elliot wasn't going to stop himself from taking anything he could get from him.

CHAPTER 25

*D*eclan kissed Elliot until his resistance melted into lustful desperation. He pulled back far enough to see Elliot's face and smiled at him.

"Can we shift position a little bit, El? You're crushing my legs here."

Elliot slid off Declan's lap and floated on his back in the middle of the pool. With the tentacles spread out under the clear water, flashing pink and red, Declan could finally see the whole of Elliot's new form. "That's it," he encouraged. "Show me, Elliot, I want to see all of you."

Elliot blushed and tipped his face up, closing his eyes against the sun. He didn't stop Declan from looking at him, though, and Declan started at the bronze column of Elliot's throat, his pulse jumping in the small hollow there. His broad shoulders, flexing as Elliot's arms moved just under the water's surface, keeping his chest afloat. His chest was the same, sleekly muscled, his nipples sharp points poking just above the waterline. His torso still tapered down to a slim waist, a drop of water sparkling in the shallow cup of his navel. The pale skin over his firm abs darkened to a reddish brown and spread into five thickly muscled new limbs that shifted and writhed around Declan's human legs. A sixth appendage, shorter than the others, peeked in and out between the front pair of tentacles.

Declan ignored this version of Elliot's cock for the moment and ran his hands over the velvety softness of each tentacle from the firm width at Elliot's waist down to each delicate, slim tip. The smooth texture changed under his stroking hand, prickling into tiny ridges and whorls the color of new red bricks, like the goosebumps Elliot got sometimes when Declan stroked his human skin.

When he reached the tip of one tentacle, he gently turned it over and ran his fingertips along the two rows of white suction cups marching up the pale pink underside. The suckers were rubbery and firm, the tiny cups at the tip cool even in the hot spring but warmer as he trailed them up closer to Elliot's center. He pressed a fingertip into the middle of one sucker and inhaled sharply when the cup tightened against his finger, like a warm, sucking mouth.

Elliot shivered, and Declan saw his skin shift and prickle in waves up each tentacle to the thick web of flesh where they all met just below his navel. Declan glanced up, and Elliot was looking down his body at Declan, a slightly drunk look on his face. "You're so beautiful like this," Declan told him.

Elliot blushed again but didn't look away from him this time. Declan stretched his legs out, planted his feet wide apart on the rocks lining the bottom of the pool, and slid both hands up the underside of two tentacles. Elliot swished his arms under water enough to float closer, and Declan brushed the backs of his hands along the underside where the tentacles met until his fingers met around Elliot's cock.

With Elliot straddled over Declan's lap like this, Declan's own cock leaped to attention, nudging against the firm, webbed skin. Declan explored all the secret spots under Elliot's web with one hand while he slowly jacked Elliot's cock with the other. Elliot arched his back, still floating on the surface of the pool, arms stretched wide, mouth open and eyes closed. His tentacles spread wide too, wrapping around Declan's back and legs, pulling himself closer and opening more for him.

Elliot's cock filled in Declan's hand, and a slick wetness, entirely separate from the water they were floating in, coated Declan's hand when he brushed his palm over the blunt tip. Declan brushed his hand over the tip again to gather more of that slick and rubbed it along the shaft of Elliot's cock. That would make things easier, since the oil Declan had brought was in the pocket of his coat, on some dry rock above him.

He wasn't sure how close to low tide it was by now, but Elliot was writhing in his lap, flexing his tentacles around Declan and thrusting his cock into Declan's hand. The sounds he was making were making Declan hotter too, all rough moans and bitten-off curses. It was probably close enough to the right time.

He pulled the hand that had been exploring under Elliot's web free, trailing his fingertips against the suckers on the underside of the tentacle closest to Elliot's cock. Elliot whined in protest, and Declan shushed him as he slid that hand from Elliot's navel up his chest. He crooked his fingers in a "come here" gesture. Elliot grabbed his hand with both his own, and Declan tugged Elliot until they were chest to chest. Elliot wrapped his arms around Declan's shoulders, and Declan slid his arm around Elliot's waist.

"It's time, Elliot," he whispered, still stroking Elliot's cock and loving the feel of it sliding wetly against his own.

"Time?" Elliot asked dazedly. He thrust into Declan's fist, and Declan groaned at the feel of another spurt of slick fluid from the tip of his cock. "Declan," Elliot moaned, his hot breath tickling Declan's ear. "I need, please, Declan, need you, need so much..."

"I know, Ellie," Declan groaned, stroking Elliot's cock faster. "You know what to do, Elliot, take what you need from me." He was pretty sure Elliot's brain hadn't made the connections he needed it to, but figured Elliot's new instincts would take over when the time was right.

He was right. Elliot thrust once more into Declan's hand, then pulled back just enough to worm two tentacles under Declan's legs. Declan lifted his ass enough so Elliot's cock slid under his balls and nudged against his hole. Declan leaned his shoulders back against a smooth rock on the edge of the pool and pushed his hips forward and up, wrapping his legs around Elliot's waist.

The tip slipped in easily. Declan had done what he could to get himself ready before coming to find Elliot. Even so, the hot burn as Elliot shoved farther into him was almost too much for Declan to take. He put a hand on Elliot's chest and pushed against him a little. Elliot hovered above him, water dripping from his hair onto Declan's chest, and some of the dazed look in his eyes cleared.

"Don't want to hurt you," he whispered, even as two tentacles squeezed tighter around Declan's legs.

"I know," Declan said. He ran his hand up Elliot's sweating chest and rubbed his thumb against his lower lip. "I'm fine, just need a minute, that's all." He took a couple of deep breaths, willing his body to relax as much as possible with Elliot stretching him open and filling him up. Elliot squeezed his eyes closed and clenched his jaw, and Declan knew he was fighting his instincts, trying to be still and give Declan time to adjust.

Declan pulled his knees closer to his chest, and the change in angle made all the difference. He groaned as Elliot's cock brushed against the spot inside that made stars burst behind his eyes. Elliot groaned too, a hot wet moan that fired up every want Declan had ever had and made him want to do anything, absolutely anything, to make Elliot make that sound again.

Declan hooked an arm around Elliot's neck and pulled Elliot closer, tucking his face into the join at Elliot's neck and shoulder. Elliot planted his elbows on either side of Declan's shoulders and pushed into him for what felt like forever. Declan hitched his legs higher around Elliot's waist, his calves and the insides of his thighs gliding over Elliot's wet, velvety skin. Elliot pulled back fractionally and thrust back in.

Elliot's cock swelled inside him, stretching him, and twisted, brushing against that spot again and again, until Declan was breathless with the bright-hot feeling. Instead of pumping in and out, Elliot pulsed within him, expanding and contracting, twisting and writhing. Elliot's other tentacles flexed and squeezed against Declan's thighs and hips in the same undulating motion, like the relentless waves crashing against the rocks at the ocean's edge.

Declan's own cock was squeezed between them, the soft give of the velvet web below Elliot's navel surrounding it and lying heavy against Declan's hips. Declan rocked his hips up slightly to slide his cock along that slippery skin. The friction was so good, it loosened something Declan had been holding tight since Elliot first entered him. Elliot's cock expanded again, and Declan shut his eyes, let himself be opened and cradled and filled. He wrapped his other arm around Elliot's lower back and rubbed his cock up and down against Elliot in time with the steady pace at which Elliot was fucking him, until he felt Elliot push impossibly farther in, go still for a moment, then shudder in the circle of Declan's arms as he pulsed hotly inside him. Declan thrust up against Elliot's body once, twice more and groaned as the world went white and yellow behind his closed eyes.

When Declan came back to himself, Elliot was lying heavy on top of him, his forehead resting on Declan's chest. He was breathing hard, but his tentacles had relaxed their grip on Declan's legs. Declan pushed a little and Elliot rolled off him, sprawling all his limbs in the water and resting his head against the edge of the pool. Declan stretched his legs out in front of them, wiggling his toes to get the feeling back in them. He rolled slightly to face Elliot, draping an elbow on the boulder behind him and resting his chin on his forearm.

Elliot looked even more debauched than Declan felt. His hair was a disheveled mess of wet spikes, and his cheeks were still flushed pink. A bite mark at the spot where his neck and shoulder met was blooming into a dark bruise. Declan vaguely recalled setting his teeth there when Elliot first flexed inside him and stretched his hole more than he'd thought possible.

Elliot's arms were splayed across the rocks, looking as boneless as his lower limbs. Declan picked one of his hands up, kissed the center of the palm and the inside of his wrist, then let it drop back in the water. Elliot rolled his head against the rock and looked at Declan. His eyes were heavy-lidded but clear, and the strain at the corners of his eyes was gone. He looked more peaceful than Declan had seen him in months.

Declan traced a fingertip under the water at the line where Elliot's human skin changed into the reddish brown of his octopus skin. "Try it now," he said softly, still enjoying how the soft smoothness above Elliot's navel shifted to the wet velvet below it. He'd loved the feel of that slippery skin against his cock. Still, they needed to get back to the house before someone came looking for them and caught sight of Elliot like this.

"Try what?" Elliot asked, his voice low and wrecked.

"Shifting back. It should work now."

Elliot pushed himself upright, losing some of the happy relaxation in his expression. Water sloshed over the boulder Declan was leaning against, splashing all over his face. Sputtering, Declan sat upright too.

Elliot's mouth was opening and closing, as if he had so many questions, he didn't know what to ask first. Declan thumbed a few drops of water off his cheekbone and cupped Elliot's jaw briefly.

"What's the tide doing now?" he asked.

Elliot's eyes flicked to the open ocean and his gaze unfocused, like he was listening to something only he could hear.

"It's turned," he said. "It's past the lowest point and is now coming in."

Declan nodded. "And you've gotten off," he said, flicking his eyes from Elliot's face to his lap and back, "gotten what you needed at the low tide point. You should be able to shift back now."

Elliot looked stunned. "Is that how it works? How do you even know that?"

Declan shrugged. "Give it a try." When Elliot just looked at him, blushing a little, Declan smiled and stood up. "I'll just get out and get dressed."

He kept his back to the pool as he picked his way over to where he'd left his clothes. The sun was high overhead but the air was cooler than the water and he shivered a little as he toweled off and dressed, resisting the temptation to watch Elliot shift back. After a few moments, Elliot said in a low voice, "You can turn around now."

He looked smaller, more like the boy Declan used to comfort after his nightmares, hunched into himself and shivering even in the warm water. Declan knew they'd have to talk about it eventually, but for now, he could help Elliot keep a bit of dignity. "Where did you leave your clothes?" he asked. A little practicality now, that was the trick.

"Up there," Elliot gestured at the rock ledge above his head. Declan fetched Elliot's clothes and propped himself up against a tall dry boulder while Elliot dressed himself.

"Can I see your legs?" Elliot asked, head down as he buttoned his trousers.

Declan sighed. The last thing they needed was more of Elliot's guilt eating away at him. But maybe if he saw that Declan was fine, he'd be able to let it go sooner. Silently, Declan unbuttoned his trousers and slipped them down to his knees.

Elliot crouched before him, tracing the red circular welts with furrowed eyes. "Go on," Declan said with a small smile. "Touch them. I'm not that breakable, Elliot."

Elliot ran his fingertips lightly over Declan's legs. Declan shivered and Elliot pulled back sharply, his eyes lifting to look miserably up at Declan. "I'm fine," Declan said gently. "Just tickled, is all."

Elliot smiled tentatively back and put both hands on Declan's legs, sweeping up the outside of his thighs. When he reached Declan's hips, Declan was hard again, his cock straining toward Elliot's mouth, right in front of him.

"You see?" Declan said. "I still want you."

Elliot's mouth curved up in that wicked smile Declan had missed seeing on his face. He put his tongue out and licked the tip of Declan's cock.

"We should get back," Declan groaned, but he didn't stop Elliot from taking him fully into his mouth and sucking him until he spent a second time, fists clenched in Elliot's wet hair.

CHAPTER 26

*W*hen they got back to the big house, Declan showed Elliot the research he and Nance had done. How they'd concluded that salt water brought about the change, at least during a supermoon. How Declan figured out that it somehow involved the tides, though Elliot pointed out that the tide hadn't been at its lowest point when he'd shifted in the pool, before Declan arrived. Declan countered that Elliot hadn't been able to shift back until after the tide turned. Neither mentioned in front of Nance what else they'd done before Elliot was able to shift back.

Elliot still couldn't believe how easily Declan had accepted what happened under Nance's pier and in the hot spring. And not just accepted it, but wanted it. Wanted Elliot even after he'd changed. How Declan taken his tentacled cock inside him as if it were the same as when Elliot had pushed inside him last night before the change. How he'd touched Elliot's new limbs with gentle fingers and wondering eyes, no disgust or fear of what Elliot had shifted into.

They'd kept up appearances during the next few days for the

sake of Nance's servants, and Elliot had stayed out of the water despite the lure of the evening low tide, but that didn't mean he wanted Declan any less. After another interminable dinner, he'd dragged Declan upstairs and fucked him until they were both too wrung out to do anything besides crash dead asleep, tangled up with each other in the sheets.

In the morning, Elliot woke to the sound of bells and Declan jerking upright in bed next to him.

"Shit," Declan muttered as he threw the covers off and scrambled out of bed.

"What?" The sun hadn't even risen yet, and only a sliver of pale gray was visible in the gap between the curtains they hadn't drawn all the way closed last night. "What's the matter?"

"Father's arrived," Declan said, as he tossed the pile of clothes strewn around the bed. "Trousers," Declan muttered from somewhere at the foot of the bed. "Goddamn trousers, where the fuck did they go?"

"Your father? How do you know?" Elliot watched the firm pale muscles of Declan's ass and thighs shift as he stood up, a bundle of white cloth in his arm. Elliot stretched an arm across the bed toward Declan. "Don't put that on. Come back to bed, it's too early for anyone to be arriving here."

The bells rang again, two short clangs followed by four long peals. Declan gestured in the general direction of the long pier. "That's Nance's warning system. Lookouts ring the bells when a ship enters the inlet. There's a pattern for each ship that calls regularly here, and that," he stabbed a finger as the sound of the last peal faded, "is the pattern for the *Argonauta*."

He yanked his drawers over his hips and tied the drawstring with quick fingers. Elliot pushed himself up on an elbow. "Okay. So? If the Captain's ship has only just entered the inlet, it'll be another hour or so before he's docked and made it up to the house. And Nance'll probably greet him, won't she, the way she met us when we arrived? It's not like he's going to come bursting into your room with no warning."

Declan stilled briefly mid-stride toward the wingback chair next to the window, where Elliot had apparently flung his trousers last night when he'd stripped them off Declan. He huffed a strangled noise and then snagged the trousers and sat on the far side of the bed to put them on.

"Yeah, well, I'm taking no chance of that happening again."

Elliot scrambled out of the bedclothes twisted around him. "Wait, again? What do you mean by 'again'?"

Declan snapped the wrinkles from his trousers and bent forward to get one foot in. "Nothing," he muttered.

Elliot knee-walked to the side of the bed Declan was sitting on. The freckles sprinkled across Declan's shoulders faded into white stripes of scars that began at his shoulder blades and criss-crossed down his back to his waist. The only thing Elliot knew that could leave scars like that was a cat o' nine tails. The same type of whip Elliot knew the Captain had on his ship. Jesus Christ. Elliot traced light fingers over the scars and Declan bent forward, away from Elliot's hand. He jammed his other leg into his trousers and pulled them up over his hips as he stood.

"Did he catch you once? With Thomas?" Now that Declan was his again, Elliot could let go of his jealousy of Thomas, though he didn't really want to know any details about them.

"No," Declan scoffed. He buttoned his fly, then cursed under his breath and unbuttoned it again, craning his head around, looking for his shirt and avoiding Elliot's eyes. "The bells will have awakened everyone, and Betsy'll be along soon with water and coal. I need to get back to my room."

Elliot grabbed his hand before he spun away. "Betsy just leaves the water and coal outside the door and hasn't come in unannounced once since we arrived." He tightened his grip when Declan tried to pull away, a cold realization washing over him. "Oh, Christ. Did he catch us?"

"What? No." Declan jerked his hand from Elliot's and crossed the room with three quick strides, picking up a shirt—Elliot wasn't sure whose it was—and throwing it over his head. He stabbed his arms into the sleeves and yanked the shirt down, stuffing it into his waistband. He kept his back to Elliot and he was normally an excellent liar, but something about the catch in his voice clued Elliot in.

"He did, didn't he?" Elliot remembered finally convincing Declan to let him touch him in all the places he'd been wanting to touch him—since forever, it had seemed then. Reveling in his newfound power to reduce his more experienced stepbrother to a quivering mess and not paying a damned bit of attention to whether anyone in the house heard them.

"Declan. He found out about us?" That year he'd turned seventeen, Elliot had spent nearly every night in Declan's room, ostensibly because of his nightmares but really as part of the long campaign he'd waged to seduce Declan. The Captain must have come to Declan's room one night or early morning, maybe to discuss an impending voyage. When Elliot recalled some of the things he'd done to Declan or begged Declan to do to him in the late nights and early hours of those mornings, he felt a stab of horror on the old man's behalf.

Declan's shoulders slumped. "Fine. Yes, he did. Two nights before I left the last time. Okay? Happy you know that now?" He resumed tucking his shirt in and re-buttoned his trousers.

"That's why you left," Elliot breathed, everything slotting into place now. "You didn't even leave, he *took* you. You'd never left me without saying goodbye before. You wouldn't have done that if you'd had a choice about it. And then he punished you, because of me." He scrambled off the bed and started searching for his own clothes. "Fucking bastard. I'll kill him."

"Elliot." Declan sounded more tired than anything else, but Elliot wasn't about to listen to him defend the man. He stumbled into his own trousers and found the other shirt—this one was originally Declan's, he thought—and pulled it over his own head.

"Come on, Elliot," Declan said. "It's old news. He was just doing what he thought was right."

"Right? How was kidnapping you and taking you away from me right? How was *hurting* you right?"

"Jesus, Elliot, he didn't kidnap me. We'd already been talking about me joining him on one of the Far East voyages soon." Declan shrugged awkwardly. "Look at it from his perspective, hey? You were seventeen, Elliot, and under his care. And I'm your stepbrother. I was supposed to take care of you while he was away. I wasn't supposed to corrupt you into unnatural acts like that."

Elliot could tell from the way Declan said it that line was a direct quote from the Captain. Well, the joke was on him, because it wasn't Declan who'd corrupted Elliot. Declan had resisted him far longer than Elliot had hoped. They'd only had a few months of doing any kind of "unnatural" acts before the Captain had taken Declan away.

"No." Elliot whirled around and jabbed a finger at Declan. "You do not defend the man for what he did to you. He hurt you because of me. And I'm going to hurt him twice as much for what he's done to you."

"The fuck you are, Elliot," Declan snapped. "I don't need you to fight my battles for me. It's done, it was years ago, and he and I are fine now. I'm not having you reopen something we put behind us a long time ago."

"Well, good for you for putting that behind you. But I didn't get to do that, did I? He took you away from me and you never even told me why. If I had known, I would have—" Elliot covered his face with his hands. Christ, if he had known that Declan hadn't willingly left him, hadn't abandoned him, hadn't regretted what they'd done together, he would have answered Declan's letters. He would have kept their relationship alive instead of freezing Declan out and forcing him to turn to Thomas and whoever else Declan had turned to instead of Elliot.

Declan took a few steps toward Elliot. "Well, I'm back now, Elliot. So, it's all in the past, all right? There's no need to dredge it all up again with him. Just let it alone and everything will work itself out, I promise."

Elliot turned his back on Declan and stared into the cold fireplace. Declan's words flowed over him like a gentle wave, deceptively calm. It was the undertow of his next realization that pulled everything out from under him. If the Captain hadn't taken Declan away, if Elliot hadn't thought that Declan didn't want him anymore, Elliot would never have asked Celeste to marry him. And if he hadn't asked her to marry him, Celeste wouldn't have been caught up in this curse that first stalked his mother, then took Celeste, then turned him into a half-devilfish monster that couldn't even shift back to fully human without fucking Declan raw. He hadn't missed the stiff way Declan had limped back from the hot springs yesterday, or his wince just now when he perched on the bed's edge to put his trousers on. He wondered bitterly what the Captain would think about his unnatural nature now.

Declan came up behind him and wrapped his arms around Elliot's waist. "Look. I know you're angry. But let it go, please, Elliot. I told you, it's old news. Father knows about me and as long as I don't rub it in his face, he mostly leaves me alone." He kissed Elliot's neck, then rested his chin on Elliot's shoulder. "He won't be happy about us, but you're no longer his ward, and he can't control what we do anymore. Just try and keep a civil tongue with him while he's here, all right? For me?"

Elliot wrapped his own arms around Declan's and dropped his head back against Declan's shoulder. He let Declan pepper his neck and collarbone with kisses, but he wasn't agreeing to anything. He'd bide his time, though. It was surely no coincidence that the Captain was here just after the supermoon and

Declan's and Elliot's discoveries about what happened to his mother and Celeste. The Captain had been on this trail far longer than they had and if he was here at the same time they were here, then he had to know at least as much about it as they did, maybe more.

Elliot would find out what the Captain knew. And then he'd decide what to do about him.

CHAPTER 27

*D*eclan stood at the shore end of the long pier, watching the *Argonauta*'s crew tie up and disembark. She was floating high in the water, so she couldn't be bringing much cargo in for trading. Her mainsail was set, but tattered, and barely hanging on at the clews. Rigging lines hung loosely against the shrouds. The red paint on her hull was faded and peeling, and her sides were pockmarked with an irregular pattern of shallow, splintered holes.

She could have been battered in a storm, but that wouldn't explain the holes, or at least not all the holes he could see. They looked like something had eaten away at the wood. Declan was used to the constant maintenance a wooden ship needed to guard against teredo worms burrowing into the hull, but these marks were above the water line. He couldn't think of anything that would damage a ship like this, especially at sea.

The temperature had dropped after the last few unseasonably warm days, and the brisk wind that had blown the *Argonauta* in this morning was more typical for early April. Elliot was probably lingering over eggs and sausage in Nance's breakfast room, hot coffee at hand. Declan had bolted a cup of coffee but abandoned his breakfast when he caught sight of the *Argonauta* tying up at the end of the pier. Nance had tactfully stayed at the house, too, so Declan could speak privately to his father.

Declan made it through the hand-shaking and back-slapping from the crew as they jostled around him. His father's first mate and bosun looked half-starved, their shore clothes hanging off their gangling frames. The crew members Declan didn't recognize didn't stop to introduce themselves, making a beeline for the bunkhouse and the hot meal Nance had waiting for them.

His father was always the last to disembark the ship when he pulled into port. When he finally appeared at the top of the gangway, Declan hardly recognized him. He seemed smaller, his greatcoat flapping around his knees and its turned-up collar obscuring most of his face. The sleeves bunched around his wrists where his hands were stuffed into his pockets.

Declan waited as he made his slow way up the pier. His head was down, and he seemed distracted, apparently not even recognizing Declan as he made to pass him.

"Father." Declan said, a little sharply.

His father stopped short, blinked a few times at him, and then something in his face cleared. He smiled at Declan, that rare lopsided smile barely visible behind his thick mustache and bushy beard, stretched his arms wide, and enfolded Declan in a crushing bear hug.

His father felt thinner under the bulky coat, but his arms still had the wiry strength of a man half his age. Declan caught the combination of cigar smoke and sun-warmed wool he always associated with his father, but it was overlaid with old sweat, unwashed linen, and a strange coppery note Declan couldn't identify.

The Captain drew back enough to cup a hand under Declan's jaw and gaze into his face. His eyes crinkled under bushy eyebrows, and the lines in his weathered cheeks deepened. "It's good to see you, boy," he said gruffly. He patted Declan's cheek, then let go, and brushed past him.

"Father," Declan said again, but the Captain shrugged him off. Declan grabbed his arm. "Wait a minute, damn it."

The Captain swung around. "What?" he demanded. Declan stared at him.

"What do you mean, what? I haven't heard from you in months. You missed our usual rendezvous and left no word other than that map and cryptic note. I've been sailing up and down the goddamn west coast looking for you for months. And you sail into port here today with your ship all beat to hell, and all you have to say to me is 'good to see you, boy?'"

Not to mention everything else that had happened since the last time Declan had seen his father.

"What do you want from me, Declan?"

"An explanation, for one thing. Where the fuck have you been?"

His father sighed impatiently. "I finally found the blasted thing. She slipped away in a storm, and I need a few repairs before I can get back out there. But this time, I've got a bead on where she's heading and I'm going to catch up to her." He patted Declan absently on the hand clutching his arm. "Just need to pick something up Nance is keeping safe for me."

Declan matched strides with his father up the lawn to the front door of the big house.

"You figured out the pattern of the supermoons, too, then?" Declan asked. "Charlie Lauder told me what he told you in New Westminster."

"You been tracking me, son?" He flashed Declan that crooked smile again. "Should have known you'd catch up to me sooner or later."

Declan smiled back. "Well, it cost me a pretty penny when I had to tell Ah Ling his next opium shipment from you would be delayed. Had to scrounge up double the shit Wong Chin produces to cover the deal. So yeah, I've been trying to catch up with you. Ling might deal with someone else next time if we can't get him his usual."

The Captain grunted noncommittally, and Declan sighed internally. For all the years his father had been looking for the ship that took Marie, he'd never let the search interfere with business. Which meant he must be close to finding the damn thing.

"So, you know where it's going next? That's the part we haven't figured out yet."

"We?" The Captain shot him a sideways look. They were trudging up the lawn, approaching the house, and his father would find out in a few minutes anyway. Declan took a deep breath.

"Elliot and I. I picked him up in Port Townsend last month."

The Captain stopped walking and swung around to face Declan. "Why the fuck would you do that? After everything I've done to keep that boy safe, you brought him here? On the trail of this thing?" His eyes flashed at Declan. "Damn it, Declan, I thought I could depend upon you to protect him!"

Declan clenched his fists to keep from striking his father. "I have kept him safe! For fuck's sake, Father, you were the one who sent me back to him! And he was fine, when I first saw him. He was about to get married, you know. To the Reverend Brady's daughter."

The Captain crossed his arms over his chest, his brows furrowed in thought but his eyes still cold. "I remember her. Nice girl. Bit odd, as I recall."

Declan shrugged, remembering Celeste's bright expression the day she introduced him to the octopus she'd named Eleanor and her strange behavior the night they'd played Charades with her in the parlor. Odd or not, she was important to Elliot, not to mention part of whatever was happening to him now.

He glared at his father and continued. "The night before the wedding, she disappeared. And when Elliot found out that Pat Lennan saw the same goddamn schooner off Union Wharf, do you think he was willing to just sit at home and wait for her to come back? Of course I tried to convince him to do that. But no, he insisted on tearing after it, chasing it down wherever the trail led him, just like you did when Marie disappeared. How exactly would you have suggested I stop him?"

He took a deep breath to calm down, conscious that their shouting was likely to draw the attention of everyone inside the house. He lowered his voice a little but couldn't keep the bitterness out of it. "For all that you're not blood kin, the two of you are exactly alike sometimes." Always chasing after something—or someone—else, with little regard for their own safety, or for what it was like to travel along on an obsessive fool's errand.

The Captain sank into one of the wicker chairs on the front porch, elbows on his knees, head cradled in his hands. "I didn't know," he whispered, almost to himself.

Declan scrubbed both hands over his face and through his hair. He could use another cup of coffee. Or a stiff drink. Dealing with his father was enough to drive even a temperance activist to the bottle. "How could you not have known? You've been chasing it for fifteen damn years and you knew it had come to Port Townsend once before."

"Twice," the Captain muttered, his voice muffled by his hands.

"What?"

He lifted his head. His eyes were bloodshot, though no tears shone on his cheeks. "The schooner has been to Port Townsend at least twice before that I know of. Sally told me after Marie disappeared. The first time was in 1864. In August."

Declan had already figured out there was a supermoon that month. Eight and a half months before Elliot was born. How much did the Captain know about why the schooner collected all these women? Did he know about the devilfish hybrids? Could he have any idea that Elliot was now one of them? How long could Declan keep that information from him? And what the fuck would he do when he found out?

"When it took Marie and you left us, you told me to take care of Elliot. And even though I was only twelve years old, I did. I was there for him when no one else was, and still you never told me it could come back."

Until he took Declan away from Elliot for long enough that Elliot turned to someone else to care for him. Though that was as much Declan's fault as the Captain's. If Declan had gone back to Elliot sooner, he might never have agreed to marry Celeste. But then the ship might have come for Elliot himself instead of Celeste, so there was little point in bemoaning the things he couldn't change now.

The front door opened behind them, and Elliot's broad figure filled the doorway. Declan looked over the Captain's shoulder and shook his head slightly to signify they'd be inside in a few minutes. Elliot nodded back and disappeared into the house interior.

The Captain rubbed a thumb across his forehead, just above his eyebrow, then looked up at Declan. His knuckles were gnarled from his years at sea, and he suddenly looked older than Declan had ever seen him.

"I'm sorry, son. I should have told you more. But I'm so close to it now. And when I find the damned thing, I'll force them to tell me where they took Marie. Elliot's girl is probably there too. We can go after them together, the three of us." He gave Declan a tired smile. "Maybe finally find you a nice girl too, to settle down with. Then things can finally get back to normal."

Declan sighed. He doubted that things would ever get back to normal, at least not the normal his father meant. He couldn't even fathom how to explain Elliot's shifting, much less exactly how Elliot shifted back. Or that he didn't even care what Elliot shifted into, now that he finally had him back in his bed. After what had happened between them these last two days, Declan had foolishly believed they could concentrate on each other for a little while. Next month was another supermoon, the last one for this year. Declan had thought he could be selfish for once in his goddamn life and have Elliot to himself, at least until the full moon passed. Then they could talk about what to do about Celeste. And maybe by then, Elliot would decide to stay with him and give her up for good.

But if his father was right—if he knew where the schooner was going next—Elliot would surely want to track it down. And if it could lead them to wherever it had taken Celeste, he might well stay with her, since she was now more like him than Declan. How could Declan stand in the way of Elliot learning more about his new form from someone who shared it?

Declan dropped a hand on his father's knobby shoulder as he crossed to the front door. "Come inside, Father. We'll figure it out." Whether they told the Captain about Elliot's shifting or kept that to themselves, it was long past time for the Captain to share all the information he'd gathered with them.

His father nodded, then pushed himself up from the chair and followed Declan into the house.

CHAPTER 28

*E*lliot tried to ignore the raised voices on Nance's porch. He'd never heard Declan and the Captain argue like this before. Declan had always wanted to be just like his father, had always obeyed him without question. It was Elliot who'd always clashed with the man, the Captain's rare stints at home filled with Elliot chafing against his dictatorial demands, and the Captain's shouting recriminations, usually followed by Elliot's sullen silences until the Captain sailed off again.

The only time Declan ever stood up to his father was on Elliot's behalf, until the Captain had shanghaied Declan onto his ship without even letting him say goodbye, letting Elliot think Declan had abandoned them just when Elliot had finally seduced him.

Elliot stared at the stacks of books and papers on the library table in front of him. After all these years of bitter frustration about the Captain abandoning them for his obsessive search, here Elliot was, on the same damn path, searching for a woman who he wasn't even sure he wanted to find anymore. He needed to know more about what he was now, but he needed Declan too, maybe more than ever.

Since he'd shifted the first time, Elliot's dreams about Celeste had changed again. Last night, instead of her calling to him and Elliot resisting her call out of fear, he'd called out to her. He didn't remember many of the dream's details, but he could feel a sense of connection and reassurance from her. Like he was one thread in a web of interconnected minds, on his own independent trajectory, but part of a cohesive whole, one that Celeste was part of too.

Wherever she was, she was happy and safe. He woke with the phantom feel of her kiss on his cheek and a still-present faint connection to her in his mind.

If Celeste no longer needed him to rescue her, then maybe Elliot could give up the search for the schooner. Stay with Declan, here maybe, or even back in Port Townsend. And yet, a part of Elliot still needed to know why it took the women it had taken, what the connection was between the two women in his life it had taken and the half-devilfish creature he'd twice now shifted into. If there was any way to keep from shifting into it again, any way to stay fully human.

The sound of the front door slamming echoed faintly, and Elliot tracked two pairs of boots crossing the foyer toward the library, muffled here and there as they passed through the carpeted areas of the hall. Elliot stood as Declan entered the library, his father just behind him.

"Elliot."

Elliot straightened his spine and crossed his arms behind him, resting his hands at the small of his back. "Captain."

"It's been a long time."

"Yes, sir."

The Captain eyed him, coming close enough that Elliot could see he'd grown several inches taller than his stepfather. "You look well."

"Thank you, sir." He couldn't say the same thing about the

Captain, who looked grizzled and exhausted. He was much thinner than the stocky, barrel-chested man Elliot remembered.

The Captain's gaze didn't waver from Elliot's as he said, "I'm sorry about your fiancée."

Elliot swallowed. "Thank you, sir," he repeated. He couldn't think what else to say.

The Captain took another step toward him, hesitating in a way Elliot had never seen in him, then strode around Nance's big library table and embraced Elliot. He let go before Elliot could react, and seated himself in the chair opposite Elliot without saying anything else. Elliot took his seat as well, a little shocked at the Captain's uncharacteristic display of affection.

Declan went back to the doorway to call for Betsy to bring some breakfast. He brought his father a cup of coffee from the service on the sideboard and motioned to Elliot's cup. Elliot shook his head, not needing anything else to ramp up the anxiety he was already feeling. Declan poured himself a fresh cup and sat down at Elliot's left.

Elliot folded his hands atop the short pile of naval almanacs and tide tables in front of him. Where to start? *Hello, Captain, we think my mother and fiancée were taken to a place where people turn into half-devilfish, half-human hybrids and it looks like I'm one of them too, without even having been to that place. You didn't happen to notice my mother had tentacles when you married her, did you? Oh, and by the way, your son seems to like my tentacles, so whatever you thought taking him away from me would accomplish, it doesn't seem to have worked the way you expected, eh?*

Declan cleared his throat and then broke the tense silence. "Tell us what you know, Father. Where is the ship going next?"

The Captain looked like he was about to object but then sighed and shook his head. "Here," he said, his voice gruff in the quiet room.

Declan leaned forward. "Here?" he repeated. "Are you sure?

Nance said it's never been here before. All the other places we've heard reports of it, it's been spotted there more than once."

The Captain shrugged. "There's something here they're looking for. Something new."

Elliot exchanged glances with Declan. Could he be what they were looking for? As far as they knew, the ship had only taken women so far. But if he was one of them now, would they be looking for him?

The Captain took a piece of paper from his vest pocket and slid it across the table toward Elliot and Declan. It was another copy of the map Declan had brought to Port Townsend, this one intact and with more Latin writing on the corner that had been torn away on the copy Declan had. The two pages had similar phrases, written in the same barely legible scrawl.

"It's a prophecy," the Captain said. "Supposedly about a promised one."

"Come again?" Declan asked.

The Captain waved his hand impatiently. "A son. Long expected, who finally arrives, when conditions are right. An heir."

"*Filius est clavis*," Elliot murmured. "The son is the key."

The Captain nodded, and Declan leaned forward. "That's what was written on the map you left for me." He glanced at Elliot, then back at his father. "Who is this promised son?"

The Captain shrugged. "Who knows?" he said, but he looked cagey and wouldn't meet either Declan's or Elliot's eyes. "Does it matter?"

Elliot glanced at Declan, whose face was set in the carefully blank expression he used when listening to the grievances of his crew. If the prophecy referred to him, then of course it bloody well mattered.

"How do you know it's a prophecy?" Declan asked.

The Captain still wouldn't meet their eyes. "Met the man who wrote it down. A naturalist by the name of Josiah Elkins, who claimed he'd been on the schooner I've been searching for. He drew the map."

"You think this Josiah Elkins is the same naturalist Nance told us about?" Declan asked Elliot.

"Probably. It would be a pretty big coincidence if there were two naturalists searching for the same remote spot in the Pacific." He was about to say more when Betsy came into the room with a covered tray.

The Captain and Declan switched to small talk about changes the Captain had made to crew rosters on the *Argonauta* while Betsy bustled around the table, shaking out the Captain's napkin, uncovering several dishes on the tray, fetching more coffee. Elliot shook his head when she offered him some, simultaneously impatient for her to leave and wishing she would linger so he could put off the rest of the conversation they were having.

"Can you translate the Latin, Elliot?" The Captain asked around a mouthful of sausage and eggs, when Betsy finally left the room, taking Elliot's dishes with her. He jabbed his fork at the prophecy. "I got some of it, but the rest is beyond me."

Elliot scanned the paper again. "I can try. Whoever wrote it had a rather precarious grasp of the language. The verb inflections are all over the place." He gestured to Declan to pass him a clean sheet of paper and a pen. Declan plucked a copy of Riddle's Latin-English dictionary from Nance's library and set it next to Elliot's elbow. It was an older edition than the one Elliot had at home but it would have to do.

"It's mostly just a series of cryptic phrases," he said, after scanning the paper. His rational mind resisted the notion of prophecies or premonitions about some vague chosen son. He was a businessman, not the subject of some sea monster's oracle. At least he had been. And Declan said he was still the same man, albeit with new parts now.

"A lot of stuff about the tides going in and out, waves overwhelming from the depths." Also being carried away by desire and giving into passion, but Elliot wasn't about to explain that to his stepfather. He risked a quick glance at Declan, who was gazing at him with a slight smile playing about his lips, as if he knew what Elliot was leaving out. Elliot tried not to blush as he flipped back and forth between pages.

"What about this?" The Captain pointed at a line on the prophecy. Elliot leaned forward to see which one he meant. *Lustrum est iacturam vitae.*

"That could mean a number of things. There are several definitions for *lustrum*." He flipped through the dictionary until he found the right page. "One meaning is a den, which colloquially, it could refer to a den of iniquity, like a brothel. But it also could mean a haven for animals, like a den in the wilderness."

"So, it could refer to the place that Elkins was searching for. The place where the devilfish he was looking for live?" Declan asked.

"That's possible," Elliot said. Or the brothel reference could be related to the other words about passion and giving into desire.

"And *iacturam vitae*?" Declan demanded. "Didn't you tell me before we left Port Townsend that it means a sacrifice? Sacrificing something by throwing it overboard?"

The Captain's eyes narrowed and Elliot glared at Declan.

"And I also told you that it was an idiom. A figurative phrase, an expression, not necessarily to be taken literally."

The Captain and Declan crossed their arms over their chest in identical skeptical postures, and Elliot sighed. The Captain had never showed much affection when Elliot was growing up, but he knew his stepfather cared about him. He wasn't sure how much of the combined weight of their protectiveness he could stand. He ran a hand through his hair and continued.

"Here's something else. The Romans used to perform a sacrificial purification ceremony every five years, after taking a census. The word *lustrum* eventually came to refer to both the ceremony and the five-year period."

The Captain was running his index finger along the second to last phrase—*iacturam vitae pro redemptionis*. "Sacrifice for redemption," he translated, looking at Elliot for confirmation. Elliot nodded.

Declan grabbed the list of dates and locations where the *Poulpes* had appeared and pointed at the little marks he'd made for the supermoons. "By my count, the schooner appears for five years in a row, then it takes a break or goes somewhere else, or whatever, before it's spotted in the Pacific Northwest again. So, a five-year period fits. But a sacrificial ceremony?" Declan passed a hand over his eyes. "Jesus, Elliot."

There was a long silence and then Declan slapped both hands on the table and stood up. "So, what we know is that there's a huge ship out there that shows up in certain port towns during full moons close to perigee, over a five-year period, kidnaps young women sometimes and sometimes just knocks them up, that it's looking for something new this time, some promised son or whatnot, for some kind of sacrifice, and you," he gestured to the Captain, "think it's coming here next."

"How do you know it's coming here?" Elliot asked the Captain, staving off the obvious question about who it was coming for here.

"There's a Haida village up in the Queen Charlotte Islands that has something of a truce with whoever sails on that schooner. They trade with them sometimes, and none of their women have ever disappeared. It took me years to earn enough of their trust to even confirm they knew what I was looking for, and they wouldn't tell me very much. But somehow, they figured out that it's headed here next."

For Elliot. The Captain didn't say so, and he still seemed to be holding something back, but Elliot couldn't help but assume that was it. Since the ship had taken his mother and Celeste, and since Elliot had already shifted into a devilfish hybrid twice now, it was hardly a leap to assume the ship was coming here for him. Even so, he'd have a word with Nance about making sure the girls in her service stayed as far away from the water as possible. Just like he would, at least until the next supermoon passed.

"We don't really know for sure what it wants," Elliot said. Celeste was still alive; he was almost sure of that. His mother, he was less sure of. He'd dreamed enough of her in the years since she disappeared and in his dreams, she'd always seemed to be alive and happy, but he'd always chalked that up to wishful fantasies of a lonely boy who'd lost his mother too young.

"Well, whatever the hell it wants, it's not getting you. Not as long as I'm around. I'm not losing—" Declan stopped and swallowed. "I'm not letting that damn thing take Elliot." He glanced at his father, then turned sideways to face Elliot. "So it can come here or it can sail off into hell, for all I care, but it's not leaving here with you."

Elliot gazed back at him, tracing his eyes over the firm line of Declan's mouth, his eyebrows drawn together sternly, and remembered how soft and vulnerable that face looked when Elliot moved inside him.

He wanted to touch Declan now, kiss him to reassure him that it wasn't Celeste he wanted anymore, but him. If Declan was willing to be with him even when he was part devilfish, then part of Elliot wanted to find some remote, hidden place and do just that. Maybe he could even get used to his new shape, if he had some time to figure out when and why he shifted into it.

He held himself in check, though, and not only because the Captain was watching them. Declan's right hand clenched into a fist, as if he too were trying not to reach out to Elliot. Instead, he turned on his heel abruptly and headed for the hall.

"The next supermoon isn't until April twenty-sixth," he tossed over his shoulder. "We have plenty of time to figure out what to do about it." His boots echoed along the uncarpeted portions of the hall, and then the front door slammed.

CHAPTER 29

A week later and they still hadn't decided what the hell to do about the schooner, the search, or the prophecy. The night of the new moon, Declan gave up trying to sleep after an hour of restless tossing and walked down to the shore underneath the long pier. The cool, damp breeze was refreshing after the watchful, oppressive atmosphere in the house.

He and Elliot had tacitly agreed to sleep apart since Father had arrived, and the deprivation was surely contributing to his sour mood. From a handful of reproachful looks he'd gotten, Declan suspected Father knew he'd taken up again with Elliot anyway, but they all carefully avoided talking about Elliot's nightmares, the last time they were all in Port Townsend together, or anything else that might touch too close on how Declan really felt about Elliot.

They'd stolen a few moments together here and there, but hurried kisses and rushed hand jobs weren't enough for Declan and he was damned tired of sneaking around like he had something to be ashamed of. They couldn't even meet at the hot spring, since Father liked to bathe there in the cool mornings and Elliot was far too afraid of shifting to get near any water deeper than a washbasin, even though there was still another two weeks until the next supermoon.

The lamps along the pier above him glimmered faintly on the black water, the only small sources of light on this dark evening. A thick fog had rolled in before sunset and the stars winked in and out behind dark clouds. The three of them stayed up past ten o'clock, going over for the dozenth time all the information they had about the devilfish hybrids, the eight-masted schooner, and where it or the devilfish den might be. Father had been pressing them for days to head out and track the *Poulpes* down before it reached Nance's inlet. Declan was all for leaving the damned thing alone and dealing with it when it came to them, assuming it even did.

Elliot didn't say much and avoided direct answers whenever Father or Declan asked him what he wanted to do. He didn't seem anxious to go after Celeste but wouldn't commit to staying put either. All this afternoon, Declan had caught him looking out the front windows every few minutes with that distant gaze, as if waiting for someone or something.

At the water's edge, Declan squatted on his heels among the rocks, a piling supporting the pier at his back. The beach dropped off precipitously here and swirled around the rocks tumbled around the pilings. He reached absently behind him for a handful of pebbles, rolled a few around in his palm. The small egg shapes scraped faintly against each other, and he tossed them one by one into the black water.

He could hardly blame Father for wanting to go after the *Poulpes*. After all these years of searching for the ship that took his wife, it must be agonizing to be so close to finally finding it and yet not underway after it. But what did Elliot want? He'd told Declan he would give Celeste up. But that was before he'd shifted. If the schooner was sailing around the Northwest, impregnating women with children who turned out to be like Elliot, then wouldn't Elliot want to be with his own kind?

When the next wave washed over the rocks, he dipped his hand in the water and brushed it across the tops of the kelp strands clinging to the rocks, trying to imagine what it was like to change the way Elliot had. He wiggled his fingers in the cold water, bits of eelgrass wrapping around his wrist the way Elliot's tentacles had wrapped around his legs. The lapping waves eddied around the rocks, and he let the whiskey he'd drunk after dinner and the hash he'd smoked to try to ease himself to sleep lull his senses into a numb calm.

The next wave washed over the rock Declan was perched on, wetting the tips of his boots and the hem of his overcoat. As the tide pulled back, a large piece of bull kelp wrapped itself around his wrist. A second wave, even stronger, washed in, wetting both arms, another long piece of kelp winding around his other arm. When the wave receded, the kelp went with it, tugging at Declan. He pulled against the undertow, but the kelp strands tightened more and pulled back. As the long brown strips snaked slowly up to his elbows, Declan realized it wasn't kelp at all. Two brown flat tentacles exerted a gentle but inexorable pull until Declan tumbled from the rock into the water.

More tentacles wrapped around Declan's legs and waist, pulling him beneath the surface. He twisted against them, catching sips of air as his head bobbed above the waterline. The numbness crept from his fingers and toes up his arms and legs. It wasn't just the frigid water numbing him. Something about the tentacles wrapped around him stilled his body and shut down his mind like a deep hit of opium. Even as Declan worried what Elliot would do if he failed to free himself and return to the house, his body relaxed against the tentacles holding him and his mind drifted to oblivion.

∿

When he woke, it was in little fits and starts, and Declan couldn't place himself. He was lying on a soft bed, under crisp linen sheets, and naked. His head throbbed dully—the aftermath of whatever he'd been drugged with, he supposed. He was in a narrow bunk built against the wall of a small cabin, a single porthole showing water as far as he could see, under heavy gray skies and a pouring rain. Aboard a ship, then. The bunk hardly rocked at all, so she must be a large one with a wide, stable hull. Or else they were in calm waters.

He turned over, intending to get up and find out where he was, but his head ached so much, and it seemed like an insurmountable effort. He vaguely registered a small brazier on a table near the head of his bunk, smoke wafting through its pierced holes. The sickly sweet smell of opium filled the cabin. Declan tried turning his head away and holding his breath, but to no avail, and he sunk down into a fitful doze.

He couldn't keep track of how many days passed while he drifted in and out of disturbing dreams. In most of them, Elliot was just out of Declan's reach and no matter how he struggled to touch him, his hands closed on empty air, Elliot slipping away from him, like a current taking him out to sea. A tangle of octopuses surrounded the Elliot in Declan's dreams, their colorful mantles and tentacles flashing in a murky haze but vanishing every time he looked directly at them. Twice he woke fully in the middle of the night and saw a large gold eye watching him through the porthole. The strange horizontal pupils narrowed as if assessing whether he was worth eating. A few times, Declan dreamed of a woman who resembled Celeste, amber eyes large in a pale face, dark hair unbound and drifting around him. She stroked his cheek and her mouth moved, but he couldn't make out what she was saying.

In between dreams, gentle hands fed Declan bits of soft food and tipped a bowl of water to his lips. He swallowed obediently, too drugged to feed himself or hold a cup. The same hands occasionally sponged his body clean and rolled him from one side of the narrow bunk to the other to change the sheets he was lying on. The hands were capable and cool against his flushed skin, and when their owner declined to answer the questions Declan couldn't quite articulate, he gave up and just let them take care of him.

Finally, a shaft of sunlight woke Declan fully for the first time since he'd fallen into the water. The sky visible through the cabin's porthole was a clear bright blue. Declan's head was mostly clear, too, though a slight headache thrummed behind his right eye. There was a bowl of broth on the table next to the bunk, chunks of fish floating amid strands of seaweed. He picked up a bone spoon resting next to the bowl and spooned it up ravenously. A short stack of pillowy flatbreads sat on a plate, and he used the bread to sop up the last of the broth.

He stood up on shaky legs and surveyed the cabin. It was smaller than his cabin on the *Black Dove* and sparsely furnished. Someone had washed his clothes and folded them into a neat pile on a shelf at the end of the bunk. He pulled them on quickly, yanked his boots on, and tried the knob of the cabin door. It turned easily in his hand, and he looked out into an empty passageway with a half dozen or so closed doors on either side. Stepping softly to make minimal noise, he left the cabin and pulled the door almost closed behind him.

He hadn't brought any weapons on his walk to the shore, but if whoever had taken him wanted to hurt him, they'd already had plenty of opportunities to do so. Still, it was past time to find out where the hell he was and who had taken him. He turned left, on a hunch that a hatch to the main deck was likely aft, and strode quickly along a passage lit by a pair of tubes running parallel along the ceiling overhead. The tubes were made of some sort of translucent material and encased a milky, glowing substance. The ship barely rocked under his feet, and he couldn't hear any sounds of water lapping against the hull. There was a low hissing sound instead, barely audible, and a faint shudder under his feet that gradually increased as he headed astern.

Before he discovered the source of that, he reached a ladder leading up to a windowed deckhouse. He crept silently up and peered through the windows of the deckhouse door before exiting onto the main deck. The deck amidships was empty, though he could see figures fore and aft, hauling lines, holystoning the deck, carrying out the routine work of sailing. He hesitated at calling attention to himself, even though his presence on this ship was surely no secret. The ship was far bigger than any vessel he'd seen or been aboard. The deck stretched as far forward and astern as he could see, and her width was at least twice that of the *Black Dove*.

Four masts marched along the deck to the bow and four more aft of the deckhouse. Fore and aft rigged sails, all of them, on rings to haul the sails up the masts. A schooner, then, built on the design of Pacific coast shipbuilders, and a large one. Son of a bitch, this must be the *Poulpes*, the schooner they'd been looking for.

He squared his shoulders and stepped away from the deckhouse toward the starboard railing. The sails of all eight masts were unfurled and belling in the stiff breeze, and the schooner was flying over the waves. Wherever they were headed, they were sailing at a good clip. Declan gripped the rail and leaned over the metal hull, gazing across the water, then forward and astern. The sky overhead was still clear blue but a bank of white fog was rolling swiftly toward the ship. He glanced over his shoulder toward the port side and saw more fog, a circle of it slowly tightening around the ship like a noose.

No land visible, and no telling how long Declan had been aboard. He couldn't see the sun behind the blank wall of clouds stretching from horizon to horizon, but he guessed the schooner was heading west. What about Elliot? Was he still back at Nance's? Declan hadn't checked the other cabins he'd passed to see if Elliot lay drugged in one of them, but he'd have to have been out walking along the shore like Declan for the ship to have caught him too. And since Elliot had been avoiding the shoreline ever since they came back from the hot spring, likely he was still back at Nance's.

Safe, at least, but surely wondering where the hell Declan was. Declan wasn't sure how many days had passed while he lay drugged and dreaming belowdecks, but the moon shining through the porthole last night had been more than half full. So, ten days, perhaps. Declan clenched the rail with both hands and dropped his head, knocking his forehead against the hard steel. Christ almighty, he'd just gotten Elliot back. How would Elliot know that he was on the *Poulpes* now? They'd never heard of the damned thing appearing anywhere during a new moon.

He lifted his head and gazed astern in the vain hope he would see the *Black Dove* or the *Argonauta* chasing after him, but the fog was too dense. He could only pray that Elliot didn't believe Declan had left him voluntarily.

If he were a praying man, which he wasn't. Mooning about amidships wasn't going to reunite him with Elliot any sooner, so Declan might as well try to find out where the hell he was being taken. He pushed off the rail and headed toward the helm to confront whoever was skippering this godforsaken tub.

CHAPTER 30

*E*lliot was reading in the library, waiting for the rest of the house to finish breakfast, when Joey told him Declan was missing.

"What the hell do you mean, missing?"

Joey shrugged. "We were supposed to meet at breakfast. To talk about our usual trip up to the Queen Charlotte Islands." He cast a sidelong look at Elliot. "Wasn't sure whether we was going to make that trip this year, what with whatever you and the Captain's father been planning." He paused, but Elliot didn't offer an explanation. With a small snort, Joey continued.

"When he didn't show, I sent Betsy to knock on his door. His bed hadn't been slept in." Another sidelong glance, like Joey knew there might be another reason Declan hadn't slept in his own bed. Elliot kept his face blank.

"And?"

"And Captain Fitz don't miss breakfast." Joey shrugged again. "Man does like his sausages." His lips twitched, and Elliot suppressed a sudden urge to snicker. He rolled his eyes instead, and Joey let a full smile crease his face. Elliot looked away to hide any tinge of pink on his cheeks.

He left the library, and Joey followed him down to the pier. Nance was standing at the shore end, barely visible amidst the frenzied activity of four ships loading and unloading their respective cargoes. A couple of Nance's longshoremen shouldered past him, ready to help unload cargo and hustle it to the various warehouses Nance used to store goods while traders and ships' supercargoes bickered over prices. Elliot had planned to ask if she'd seen Declan today, but her attention was divided between a ship's master Elliot didn't recognize and Carlos, her head stevedore, who was gesturing broadly and relaying instructions to his crew in a mix of gutter Spanish, French patois, and English curses.

He scanned the organized chaos of the pier, searching for Declan. The *Black Dove* was still floating out at anchor in the inlet and Declan surely wouldn't have left on another vessel.

"Maybe he's at the hot spring," Elliot suggested, though if that were the case, he highly doubted that Joey would be bothering him. Joey was already shaking his head.

"You think I haven't already searched for him?" He gestured around him. "I know this part of the island better than anyone and I'm telling you, Captain Fitz is missing. Ain't no way he left voluntarily without no word to me or Reggie."

Elliot knew that. He knew how dedicated Declan was to his crew. How he considered them his family, maybe even more so than Elliot himself, and how he always knew what his crew were up to. It stood to reason that his crew would be as aware of Declan's whereabouts as Declan was of his men.

"Mr. Bishop?" Joey said. "There's something else."

Elliot sighed. Of course there was. "What?"

"Luca says he saw a ship late last night. He was outside after midnight, taking a piss. Saw a huge schooner, he says, with eight masts. Seamus and Reg told him he'd drunk too much and was seeing things, but he insisted. Biggest schooner he ever saw, and definitely eight masts."

"And it was gone by morning and no one else saw it?" Elliot asked, already expecting Joey's nod in answer. A wave of cold anger washed slowly over him. He felt like he was standing apart from himself as he surveyed the inlet with its bustling activity and the forest of rigging floating along the pier and at anchor. His stepfather had warned them the schooner was on its way here, but they had all thought they had more time.

The moon was new last night, but low tide had been shortly after midnight, and Elliot had awoken with the sense that something was waiting for him just off shore. He'd ignored it as long as he could, then distracted himself by jerking off to the memory of Declan bent over the rail under the pier. He'd come just as he recalled the first time he'd shifted while inside Declan, throwing an arm over his face and biting the inside of his upper arm to stifle his moans while he stroked himself through the aftershocks. He'd desperately wanted to sneak into Declan's room, but he'd cleaned himself up instead, and read by the light of a single lamp until dawn.

If he had gone to Declan, could he have stopped him from being taken by the ship? What the hell was Declan doing out along the shore last night anyway? Yesterday, Elliot hadn't decided whether he wanted to confront the damn thing or leave well enough alone. But if it had taken Declan, he was going after it. And whoever was on it, or whatever, they were going to pay.

"How long until the *Black Dove* can be ready to sail?"

"Couple hours," Joey replied promptly. "Thomas is sorting the provisions. She'll be a little shaky to handle with no ballast, but she'll be fast."

"Good." Elliot clenched a fist against his leg. "I'll inform the senior Captain Fitzgerald, and we'll leave as soon as we're packed."

He turned to go back to the house, but Joey's quiet, firm voice stopped him. "No, sir." Elliot swung around and stared at him.

"No? No what?"

"The crew won't sail under him." He dropped his eyes under Elliot's stare but continued, his voice low but unwavering. "Half the crew left his service for good reasons, sir, and the rest of us— well, we've heard enough stories that we ain't willing to find out for ourselves how much of them is true."

Elliot thought of the white scars on Declan's back. Of course Declan's crew wouldn't want to serve under the man who'd done that to his own son. But what other options did they have?

"I can't captain the *Black Dove*," Elliot said. "I've no master's papers, for one, and I'm hardly capable of steering her out of Nance's inlet, much less out on the open ocean. And I've no idea where the schooner went from here." Which wasn't exactly true. He'd been feeling a pull westward for several days now and had ignored it while Declan and the Captain debated where the devil-fish den might be. And since they hadn't told Declan's crew anything about their search when they left Port Townsend, how would he explain why the *Poulpes* took Declan or that the Captain was the one who would know where to look for him.

Come to think of it, Joey was much less surprised by the notion that Declan had disappeared onto a schooner bigger than any known vessel than Elliot would have expected. And he seemed to have taken it for granted that Elliot would want to sail after it immediately. "Declan's father may be able to track the schooner," he said, testing the waters.

"Because it's the same ship as stole his wife," Joey said, matter-of-factly. "Same one as took your fiancée."

Elliot stared at him. "You knew about that?"

Joey shrugged. "Reggie served with the captain's father. So did Thomas. It weren't a secret what he's been obsessed with all these years. Our captain don't talk about it, but we've all served with him long enough to know this ain't been the typical voyage."

Elliot snorted, acknowledging the point. "Fine. Still, the senior Captain Fitzgerald is our best shot at following the damned thing."

Joey looked Elliot in the eyes. "I doubt that." Before Elliot could ask him what he meant, he added, "But this crew takes orders only from our captain." He cocked his head at Elliot. "He trusts you, though." He thought a minute, then nodded. "If you think we need his father, he can come along, but anything he has to say goes through you. I can talk the crew into that."

Elliot gazed out across the inlet. His stepfather sure as hell wouldn't stay behind while the *Poulpes* was out there somewhere. And neither would the crew of the *Black Dove*, if Declan was in danger. The *Argonauta* was beached on the northern bank of the inlet, listing away from the water as a handful of men swarmed over her, scraping and sanding her hull. She was barely seaworthy yet, even after a week of repairs, and Elliot knew none of the men on the *Argonauta's* crew. He knew Declan's crew, though, after these weeks of sailing with them. He trusted Joey and Reginald and the others, as much as he trusted anyone other than Declan. He even trusted Thomas, at least when it came to Declan's safety. He nodded to Joey.

"All right." He didn't know how he would convince his stepfather of this plan, but the most important thing was getting after Declan as soon as possible. "We'll sail in two hours." Joey sketched a faint salute and turned toward the end of the pier.

"Aye, aye, sir."

Convincing the Captain to leave the *Argonauta* and her crew behind and sail on the *Black Dove* was easier than Elliot expected. He scowled when Elliot told him of the crew's conditions but then just gave a short nod and went to pack. He joined Elliot on the quarterdeck and gave the commands for getting the *Black Dove* underway in a low voice. Elliot felt a little silly repeating them verbatim like a trained parrot, but the few times he delayed, Joey and Reginald just stood still, waiting for his orders, as if the Captain wasn't even there. Joey relayed the orders to Reginald, who repeated them to the deck crew anyway, so it didn't take long before it became just the normal rhythm of the ship.

Once they were out on the open ocean, the Captain showed Elliot how to set a course west-southwest. From Declan's room, Elliot had grabbed the compass from Mr. Elkins's puzzle box, and brought it aboard. He took it from his coat pocket now and held it in his left hand, his right hand resting on the ship's wheel, keeping her steady. The needle wasn't pointing at him this time, but along the heading they were sailing. The same feeling he'd had while holding the compass in Nance's library tugged at him, pulling him forward. With every league that passed, the feeling grew stronger. He was getting closer—to Declan, he hoped, but also to whatever was waiting for him at the devilfish den.

The days bled into each other. Elliot hardly slept, since when anyone else held the compass, it merely pointed at him. The Captain kept close by but said little. He seemed to be watching Elliot more often than not, his eyes hooded by his bushy eyebrows, his unkempt mustache and beard hiding his mouth. Elliot couldn't remember the last time he'd been alone with the man, or if they'd ever had anything to talk about. He didn't know whether his stepfather guessed how Elliot really felt about Declan, but he no longer cared what he thought about their relationship. Elliot would find Declan, get him back on this ship where he belonged, and then figure out how they could have a life together. The devilfish and their prophecy could go to hell. Without him.

Nearly two weeks after they'd left Nance's inlet, Elliot woke to the thump of scurrying boots and muffled shouts overhead. The dawn light streamed through the windows in Declan's cabin. He'd stumbled in here long after midnight at Joey's urging, who pointed out that he'd be no good to Declan if he was exhausted when they got there. He swung his legs over the side of the bed and stood, waiting for the brief lightheadedness from lack of sleep to subside.

He splashed some water on his face but couldn't shake the sense that something was missing. Something other than the constant aching lack whenever he thought about Declan. Declan was fine, he told himself, like he'd been telling himself every few minutes for the last two weeks. In the short snatches of sleep he'd gotten, he'd seen glimpses of Declan, pale and with his eyes closed, but no obvious signs of injury. Sleeping, Elliot fervently hoped, not dead. If the *Poulpes* had gone to the trouble of sailing to Nance's inlet and taken Declan, Elliot had to believe they wouldn't have harmed him.

As he pulled his clothes on, Elliot finally put his finger on what was missing. The sensation that had been tugging him forward, guiding them to the devilfish den, was gone. In its place was a lighter feeling, calming the edge of anxiety he'd been living on since he'd left Port Townsend. The same feeling he used to get when he would come up the path to the Bishop house and see the lamps lit in the windows of his study and smoke curling from the chimneys. Like he was nearly home at the end of a long, hard day.

He closed his eyes and stretched his senses forward. There it was, just a few leagues ahead, the place his mother had been taken, the place Celeste had shown him in his dreams. The place Declan surely had to be. He wondered how the Captain felt about finally reaching the place he'd been seeking for fifteen years.

"Elliot!" The Captain thumped a fist against the cabin door as he passed, then stomped up the ladder to the deck. Elliot sighed and pulled his coat on. There was no point in trying to avoid his fate any longer.

Elliot trudged up to the quarterdeck and joined the Captain at the helm. A barren, rocky atoll winked in and out of view in the drifting fog off the port bow. The Captain opened a telescope and gazed at the island through the eyepiece for a long, silent moment. He handed it to Elliot. "There," he said unnecessarily.

CHAPTER 31

*D*eclan strode along the deck of the huge schooner, weaving around covered hatches and past another deckhouse, toward the enclosed structure on the poop deck that must be the wheelhouse. He took the steps to the poop deck two at a time and grasped the doorknob, which failed to turn in his hand. Locked.

He knocked on the windowed door and when no answer was immediately forthcoming, cupped his hand around his face and peered in the window. The interior was lit with a diffuse white light from tubes similar to those that lit the passageway belowdecks. He could make out three figures inside, one dwarfed behind the huge ship's wheel, its spokes longer than the helmsman's arm span. A second figure stood behind the helmsman's left shoulder, and a third was seated at a long table at the rear of the wheelhouse.

Declan banged on the door again. "Hey!" The helmsman ignored Declan, eyes forward as if looking straight through him. The person standing behind the helmsman glanced at Declan but otherwise ignored him too. The figure behind the table leaned sideways as if to get a better look at Declan around the wheel spokes. A long braid slipped from behind a shoulder, swinging heavily toward the floor, and Declan squinted through the glass. A woman, her full bosom visible under an unbuttoned coat and a second thick braid tossed behind her other shoulder. Now that he looked at the other figures, Declan realized all three were women.

The woman behind the table righted herself and pushed her chair back. Declan lowered his arm, expecting her to come to the door to speak to him, but she just lifted her booted feet, crossed them at the ankles, and rested them atop the table. She leaned back in her chair and crossed her arms behind her head. A slight smile played around her lips, as if she were taking pleasure in this conscious rudeness.

The helmsman—helmswoman, he guessed—turned the wheel a quarter turn, and the tall woman next to her pointed at something just over Declan's shoulder. He turned around. The ring of fog had closed in tightly, and he and the wheelhouse were the only things in its center. For now, anyway, because more wisps of fog were creeping toward him, and it would only be moments before the fog engulfed the whole ship. Already, Declan couldn't see anything past the eighth mast in front of the poop deck. He glanced over his shoulder at the women in the wheelhouse. They seemed unfazed by the total lack of visibility, and the full set of sails snapping overhead were still carrying the ship forward at the same brisk clip.

The woman at the wheel made small course corrections. She'd have a compass, Declan presumed, which would keep her in the general direction they were heading, but she seemed to be relying more on the woman next to her, nodding each time the other woman pointed or gestured, and easing the wheel to starboard or port in response. The woman seated at the table— the schooner's captain, he presumed—paid little attention to their actions. Either she was better than Declan at hiding the fear any skipper would have in sailing through such fog or she trusted her crew more than seemed prudent. At least they were out on the open ocean. Colliding with another vessel also hampered by the lack of visibility would really cap the week Declan had had.

He turned to press his back against the sturdy frame of the wheelhouse and closed his eyes. Since he couldn't see anything and he couldn't help sail the ship, there was nothing to do but listen. If there was another ship out here, maybe he'd hear it first and could give some warning. The sails snapped and flapped overhead in the wind, the rope lines creaked against the pull of the sails, and the wind whined past his ears. There was a faint rumbling, hissing sound coming from belowdecks that Declan couldn't place, the same sound he'd heard as he'd explored the passageway from his cabin.

It took Declan a few moments to realize what he wasn't hearing. There was no sound of human voices. No orders relayed from the captain to first mate to bosun to deck crew. No sailors boasting about their talents or bellyaching about their tasks. No conversation, no shouting, not even any grunting or whistling. How the hell were the sailors communicating aboard this ship?

A fresh breeze sprang up, warmer than the cold wind that had been blowing so far, and Declan opened his eyes. While he'd been listening with his eyes closed, the fog had dispersed and the clouds were thinning. A shaft of sunlight burst from behind a cloud, shredding the cloud into thin strips as he watched, and the air was suddenly several degrees warmer.

Just off the port bow was a large atoll he'd never seen before, and the schooner was heading straight for it. As they approached, Declan could make out a long ridge stretching northwest for a couple of miles. Cave-like indentations pocked the base of the ridge. Bits of scrubby brush clung to its sides amid moving white dots, probably the heads of nesting seabirds. The top of the ridge leveled off to a flat plain that ran the length of the island until a tall peak jutted sharply up at the north end, its summit obscured by circling cormorants. The island looked desolate and forbidding, the sort of place only desperate sailors would try landing at.

The women in the wheelhouse looked excited to see it, though. The way Declan felt when he sailed into Port Townsend, or Nance's inlet, which felt more like home these last few years. The schooner tacked to sail along the eastern edge of the island, then heeled around to approach from the north. They carried forward leeward toward the island's tallest peak at the north end. Declan braced for a collision on the rocks at its base before the fore, main, and mizzen sails reefed and the schooner slowed.

As the ship approached the island, Declan could make out a crack in the mountain just wide enough for the ship to slip in. A pair of deckhands reefed the sails on the rest of the masts sequentially, and the schooner glided smoothly through the crack into a tall cavern.

Women on the port and starboard sides forward of the mainmast tossed lines over the gunwales, and the door to the wheelhouse opened behind him, the captain briefly filling the doorway. Declan opened his mouth to speak to her, but she brushed silently past him, just an impatient snap of her fingers and a cock of her head indicating that he should follow her. He hesitated for a second but then trailed after her. Might as well find out wherever the fuck they'd taken him.

He followed the woman down a gangplank to a wide stone ledge hugging the narrow wall of the cavern. Behind him, a deep groaning sound came from the stern of the ship. Like metal scraping against metal, then suddenly garbled as if muffled underwater. A wave washed over the gangplank just as Declan stepped from it onto the stone ledge, and the ship rocked as if it had just lost a huge load of cargo. Declan craned around the stern to see behind the ship. The light in the cavern was dim, but he thought he saw a purplish hump break the surface of the water, then disappear before he could see what it was. The coils of a pair of tentacles were unmistakable, undulating in the water astern of the ship. They were far larger than Elliot's had been, and thicker, with suckers the size of dinner plates. They disappeared, too, though the tip of one wiggled above the water's surface, almost as if it were waving at him.

A hard hand grasped Declan's upper arm, and the captain yanked him forward with a low grunt. She was shorter than Declan, but not much, and did not look friendly.

"Where are we?" he demanded, not really expecting an answer. "Who the fuck are you and what do you want with me?"

She didn't say anything, just yanked him forward again. Her hand was like iron around his bicep, and he stumbled forward a few steps as she pulled at him. She gave him a hard look, then let go and walked ahead of him along the stone ledge. He risked a glance back at the schooner and saw one of the other women from the wheelhouse standing at the top of the gangplank, arms crossed over her chest, staring down at him with an equally unfriendly expression. No getting back aboard then to find his way back to Elliot. Not that he'd be able to commandeer her on his own. It wasn't like he had anything to offer her current crew to take orders from him. Better to go along and try to figure out where the fuck he was before trying to figure out how to get away.

The schooner fit perfectly tucked inside the cavern, or maybe she'd been built to fit inside the cavern. The stone ledge wasn't wide enough for two to walk side by side, so Declan followed the woman, her thick braids swinging behind her back. They passed alongside the schooner, its massive shape floating easily in the water. Forward of her bow, the cavern opened up into a wide, bright room. Sunlight poured from an opening in the rock ceiling, and a wide stone beach sloped gently to the far wall of the cavern. Even as he was hustled past, Declan saw a group of women along the water's edge, dragging lines down to the ship, getting ready to pull her up the beach.

The stone path curved along the cavern wall, then through an arch into a tunnel that must lead farther under the island. A channel of blue-green seawater gurgled along the center of the tunnel, a dry path on either side, hugging the tunnel walls. Declan followed the woman along the right-hand path. He had to quicken his pace to keep up with her. There wasn't much to see along the way. The tunnel ceiling arched overhead a bit higher than Declan could reach with his arms stretched above his head. Short stalactites clung to the ceiling, but the walls were a smooth pink sandstone. The path he was treading was the same sandstone, but pitted and pockmarked in a honeycomb pattern. The same tubes of milky-white substance as had been on the schooner ran along the walls and filled the tunnel with enough diffuse light to see where they were going, but the tunnel was dimmer than the sunlit-filled cavern behind him.

The water in the channel rippled as they trotted along, like something—or several things—were swimming along just underneath the surface, keeping pace with them. Declan wondered just how many half-devilfish creatures like Elliot there might be in the world. Did they all live here? Was the woman he followed one of them? She looked as human as Declan, but then, so did Elliot most of the time.

"Don't suppose you'd tell me where the hell you're taking me?" he said, mostly to hear himself speak. His voice echoed weirdly against the tunnel walls. "I mean, not that I don't appreciate the hospitality," he went on, trying to get a sense of how long the tunnel was by the lag between his words and the echoes and where the echoes came from. "It's just that I'd like to know who to thank for it." The woman ahead ignored him, just as she had while on the schooner. "Or maybe you could tell me where you got that opium you drugged me with," he ventured, "because that was some high-quality dope. I've contacts in Chinatowns up and down the coast who'd pay a pretty penny to get ahold of that."

This caused the woman to toss a glance over her shoulder at

him. There might have been a glimmer of interest in her eyes, but she shook her head and faced forward again, quickening her pace even more. So, she understood English at least, even if she wouldn't speak to him.

They turned right into another arched tunnel with more tunnels and several small caves branching off it. Declan had already lost track of how to get back to the schooner. He wasn't sure how long they walked, Declan filling the silence with inane chatter, still trying to monitor the echoes, before passing into a room even larger than the first cavern. More tubes of white light along the walls and ceiling, brighter here and illuminating the cavern almost as much as sunlight. A large pool dominated the middle of the room with a handful of women standing around it, gesturing over it, murmuring to each other in small groups. More women gathered in other small groups sprinkled around the room, some lounging together in smaller pools, chatting quietly, others perched on ledges next to the pools or sitting cross-legged on dry ground.

Every pair of hands was busy with some kind of work, sewing together strips of seaweed, carving pieces of bone or coral, or folding and rolling flexible pieces of a transparent material into shapes Declan couldn't discern the purpose of. A few women glanced at Declan as he crossed the room, then nudged their companions until everyone not focused on the center pool was staring at him. It took him a moment to realize there wasn't a single man in the room.

The woman he'd been following marched straight to the central pool and stopped before a woman who was bent over it. She straightened and turned around. Declan's mouth fell open as he recognized Elliot's fiancée, Celeste.

CHAPTER 32

*D*eclan stared at Celeste. She looked much the same as she had the evening he'd spent with her before she'd disappeared. Her black hair was down, falling gently over her shoulders, and she wore a golden-brown sleeveless robe of a shiny, clinging material, but her amber eyes gazed at him with the same intelligence and mischief as when she'd shown him her pet octopus.

"So, you are alive." Elliot had been so certain that she was, even though Declan had never quite known whether to credit that to truth or just wishful thinking.

She smiled. "Of course. I didn't think I'd see you again, though. That is, until..."

"Until that ship kidnapped me, just like it did you?" Declan kept his voice mild and his body easy. None of the women had weapons he could see, but he was outnumbered by far, and not a few of them looked plenty capable of holding their own in a fight.

Celeste shook her head. "I wasn't kidnapped. I told you I needed to go down to the shore that night, but neither of you would let a woman make her own decisions about how to spend an evening."

Declan raised an eyebrow. "If being with the man you'd agreed to marry was so unbearable, there were surely kinder ways to break your engagement."

She had the decency to blush at that, at least. "I couldn't explain it then. I hardly knew what was happening to me. All I knew was that I had to go down there. And then, once I understood why, it seemed like it would be better for Elliot if I just left so he could move on and find someone else. I didn't know, then, that he was one of us."

"And me?" Declan asked. "I'm not one of you."

"You're not, but you're a means to an end."

"And the end is Elliot? Why not just take him, then? Why take me?"

She shook her head. "We don't go on land, nor do we force anyone to come with us. He has to decide to come to us himself."

"You forced me. Something dragged me into the water, and then your women drugged me and brought me here."

Celeste shrugged. "I meant we don't force anyone who can hear the call. We know that Elliot's heard it and we know he's still resisting it. But Elliot is special, and we need him. He just needs a little more persuasion than most of us, it seems."

"Well, I'm no maiden in need of rescuing, and Elliot's had a lot of years to get used to me taking off without him. He gave up searching for you, you know, and he was going to marry you. He's not going to be coming for me."

Celeste turned and bent over the pool behind her. The surface of the water shimmered with bioluminescence in a rainbow of colors. Tiny pinpoints of light winked here and there as they moved across the surface. There were several masses of light clustered together in irregular shapes, other smaller collections that marched and undulated and crept across the pool. On the far side of the pool, a series of glimmering white dots traced outlines that looked vaguely familiar. The kaleidoscopic effect was dizzying and Declan blinked, focusing and refocusing his eyes, trying to make sense of it. Celeste seemed to find what she was looking for and turned back to him.

"Oh, he'll come for you. He's on his way now." She pointed at a little cluster of blue lights, winking and blinking as it slowly drifted toward the center of the pool, just under the surface. The pool must function as a map. He recognized the white outlines tracing the coast of Alaska and northwest British Columbia. A tiny outline of Vancouver Island glimmered faintly near the far edge of the pool. Celeste gestured at the blue cluster.

"I knew he would. I could tell there was something between you two when we met in Port Townsend."

"I've no idea what you mean," Declan said automatically.

"Oh please. There's no point in denying it. Not to me, anyway. You forget that I know him too, perhaps better in some ways than you do." She smiled at him. "He used to talk about you all the time, did you know? Not so much the last year or two, but when we first started walking out together. We'd stroll along the shore and he'd tell me about the letters you wrote, about your travels, and the places you'd been to. The places he wanted to go to with you someday." She glanced up at him. "He never told me outright, but anyone with eyes could see what you mean to him."

Celeste didn't sound shocked or disgusted by her fiancé's feelings for another man. She sounded sympathetic, even, and her eyes were kind when she looked at Declan. "He missed you very much."

Which didn't make Declan feel any better about the five years he'd stayed away from Elliot. If he'd gone back to Port Townsend sooner, could this whole mess have been avoided? Elliot might not have proposed to Celeste, and she could have found someone else, perhaps. Or she could have still ended up here, but Elliot wouldn't have insisted on sailing after her. But Elliot might have shifted anyway, Declan thought, remembering why he and Celeste were even having this conversation.

"So, you're using his feelings for me to manipulate him into coming here? A place you know he doesn't want to be, and for what? Some prophecy about a promised son? What do you think he'll do when he gets here? You think he'll stay with you based on some cryptic Latin mumbo-jumbo?" Declan wasn't sure that Elliot wouldn't, truthfully, but the more he could find out about the devilfish's plans for Elliot, the better chance Declan had of figuring out what to do when Elliot arrived.

Celeste rolled her eyes. "That wasn't my idea. I thought it was silly, planting notions of a fake prophecy up and down the coasts. I mean, who believes in prophecies of any kind these days? Plus, it turns out that Elkins's Latin was abysmal, and it's hard to imagine anyone crediting it as meaning anything." She shrugged. "But that was before I came here, and before we knew about Elliot."

Declan stared at her. "Wait, there's no prophecy? It's fake?"

"It's true that we have trouble drawing male octopians to us. Humans are obsessed with myths and legends—sailors more so than most—so we thought it might draw any sons of the women who stay behind to us, without revealing our true nature to too many people." Celeste sighed. "Mostly, it's brought quite the wrong sort of attention to us so far. Still, Elkins served his use, in the end."

She smiled at Declan in a predatory way, similar to how Thomas looked at a small shark Luca caught once, when he was considering all the ways he could cut the thing up and use it.

"What is this place, anyway?" Declan asked, changing the subject for the moment. "I've never seen an island with a cave structure like this before."

Just like the morning she'd introduced him to Eleanor, Celeste seemed happy to have a captive audience to explain things to.

"The caves span the entire island, which sits atop a hydrothermal vent. The vent keeps the water in the tunnels and around the island at an optimal temperature for us. It's larger than it looks from the outside. I haven't even explored all of them yet."

"How many of you," he paused, wondering if she'd find the word "devilfish" to be offensive, "live here?"

"Octopians?" She'd said that word before but shrugged when Declan must have looked confused. "My name for us. We're not exactly *homo sapiens* anymore but we're not true cephalopods either. I'm not sure where Ernst Haeckel would place us on his tree of life, but we need a proper name for what we are, don't you think?"

Declan vaguely remembered Celeste explaining how the German naturalist classified all life forms into kingdoms, groups, and families, and showing him how octopuses were related to snails and humans related to chimpanzees.

"All right. How many octopians live here, then?"

She cocked her head at him, looking curious. "How many do you think? Can you tell?"

"How the hell would I be able to tell?" Declan paused. "Is that why no one on the schooner spoke to each other? Can you read minds?" That would explain that faraway look Elliot sometimes got, like he was listening to something no one else could hear.

Celeste raised an eyebrow, looking impressed. "Not precisely. But we can sense each other. Anyone who shares our blood is part of our collective consciousness. Proximity strengthens it, of course, but just like you always know what your arms or legs are doing without thinking about them, we're all more or less aware of how each of us moves through the world. You don't tell your legs to move when you start walking, right? But your legs know that you want your body to end up over there," she gestured across the room, "and they carry you there."

That explained how the octopian women sailed that massive

ship with no audible orders from her captain. Declan could think of some narrow escapes that the *Black Dove* could have avoided if there'd been less of a delay between him thinking of an order and relaying it through Joey and Reginald to the deck crew. But there were plenty of other thoughts Declan had had that he wouldn't want anyone to know about.

"So, you can control others of your kind?" Declan asked, for the first time hoping Elliot wasn't on his way here. Elliot had been horrified enough when he shifted, especially when it happened without his wanting. He'd already been taken from his home and normal life by visions of Celeste drawing him forward. If by coming here, Celeste would be able to take over his body, Declan would rather he stay far away, even if that meant they never saw each other again.

"Not control, no," Celeste protested, although he could tell she wasn't being completely forthcoming. "It's more that we understand how each of us fits into a greater whole and we act in furtherance of what's best for us all. But to answer your original question, there are a few hundred of us living here now. That will change soon, we hope." She glanced sideways at him again, a look he couldn't decipher in her eyes.

"And you all…" his voice trailed off, not sure how to ask. "Um, shift? Sometimes? Like Elliot?"

"No," she answered. "Some of us can shift back and forth at will, though that takes quite a bit of practice. Some can only shift at the right time. Some are born in one form or the other and stay that way. Then there are those who have enough of our blood to serve our purpose in the human world, but never shift."

"Elliot won't be serving your purpose, whatever the fuck that is."

Celeste shrugged. "It's his choice, of course. But no one who's heard the call has resisted us for very long."

Declan snorted. "Since the only way you could get him here

was by kidnapping me, you might reconsider whether you're calling the right man."

Celeste smiled again at him, this time the way he recalled her smiling at her pet octopus, Eleanor. Like a specimen she found intriguing and delightful, one she liked enough to give a name to, but was still willing to cage away from its natural habitat. Something necessary for the work she was doing, but ultimately replaceable once she got what she needed.

"There is something about you. Something unexpected." She took a few steps closer to Declan. She didn't touch him, but walked around him, looking intently at him. He kept an eye on her as she circled him but stayed loose, ready to defend himself, still conscious of the dozens of eyes pretending not to stare at him. "You're taking all this very well, considering."

Declan shrugged. "There are more things in heaven and earth, et cetera. Live and let live is my motto."

Celeste smiled slightly at him. "Still. You're not reacting the way sailors normally do on the occasions they've stumbled upon us."

Sailors these women have killed, Declan suspected, recalling Nance's story about the ship Elkins sailed on. Still, some of them had escaped. None of the octopian women had done anything threatening to him so far, so Declan would simply wait and be prepared for whenever Elliot arrived.

As if reading his thoughts, Celeste gestured to another wide, arched tunnel on the other end of the cavern. "Come. You must be hungry, and it will be a day or two before Elliot arrives."

With no other options before him for the moment, Declan followed her. The tunnel she led him down had small caves branching off like little rooms on a central hallway. About halfway down the tunnel, Celeste turned into a room slightly larger than the rest.

"This is yours?" Declan asked, standing awkwardly in the doorway as Celeste moved deeper inside. She tapped on a tube that ran along the room's perimeter, and the same milky-white phosphorescence that lit the tunnels brightened the space. Water flowed from the tunnel's channel into a pool in the center of the room, and the cave's walls were carved into approximations of furniture—a pair of chairs shaped into the wall on the left, a bench of sorts across from the cave entrance with deep shelves laddering up the wall over the bench, and a platform that served as a bed tucked around a curve shielding it from the open doorway.

"There's less of a concept of 'mine' versus 'yours' here. Everything is ours. For now, this can be yours."

"While I'm your prisoner, you mean."

Celeste gestured for him to come in to the room and take a seat. He waited until she curled up in one of the carved-out chair shapes, then settled into the other one. The stone was warmer than he'd expected, hard but smooth, and he found that if he angled so he faced Celeste at about forty-five degrees, the wall comfortably supported his back and a little shelf carved into the back of the cave functioned as an armrest.

Celeste smiled sweetly at him. "Not a prisoner. A guest. Though we'd appreciate it if you didn't wander around alone. You may have heard what we do to sailors who come here uninvited."

There was a tray resting on a ledge within Declan's reach.

"Eat," she said.

Declan ate. Resisting the urge to cram as much food into his mouth as possible, he took a few small bites to give his empty stomach time to adjust to his first real meal in days. A few pieces of a fish he didn't recognize, raw, but soaked in a flavorful brine, a salad of various seaweeds, something spongy and bland that was a refreshing contrast to the strong flavors of the rest of the food.

When he finished, Celeste led Declan to the platform on the other side of the room. She pushed him gently until he sat down on a soft, firm mat that cushioned the stone, then rearranged a stack of small pillows at one end of the bunk.

"Rest," she said softly. "We'll talk later."

Declan opened his mouth to protest, then gave in, lying down and letting her pull a thin sheet over him. A wave of exhaustion rushed over him, and he was asleep before his head hit the pillows.

CHAPTER 33

*A*s the *Black Dove* gradually drew closer to the island, Elliot caught sight of Reginald and Joey exchanging glances. He couldn't blame them for doubting how Elliot could be sure that this, of all the rocks in the wide Pacific, was the place they'd been seeking. The eastern side was a series of sheer cliffs with no obvious place to land. The compass shifted south-southwest and, after consulting with the Captain, Elliot steered a wide course to come around the southern tip.

On the western coast, the ocean had carved out a deep overhang that looked possibly high enough to fit the *Black Dove* if they could get close enough to land. A herd of elephant seals lounged on a narrow strip of beach. They jostled for space just above the waterline, basking half in the sun outside the overhang and half under its shade. Joey ordered a series of depth soundings.

"That must be the entrance." The Captain gestured to a point past the beach with the molting seals, where the water disappeared into a deep cavern at the back of the overhang. "Under there, see?"

"Yes," Elliot replied. "Best to wait for the tide to ebb some, though."

The Captain grunted, scanning the overhang through his scope, searching for the entrance. "How long?"

Elliot watched a wave as it rushed into the cavern, swirled against the pocked rocky walls, then slid back out. He tracked the next few waves and compared the swell and ebb of each wave with his internal sense of where the tide was. When the Captain dropped the scope from his eye and looked at him, he shrugged.

"A couple of hours." The tide would be at its lowest just before four bells.

The Captain looked at his watch, then collapsed the scope, and tucked both items back in their respective pockets. "Fetch me when it's time. We'll need the small boat." Elliot nodded, and the Captain disappeared below deck.

The next two hours were excruciating. Elliot watched the waves flow in and out of the cavern and counted each minute as the tide drew back. For variety, he counted and recounted the elephant seals lounging on the beach, then made up a little game where he tried to predict when each would roll over or shift position. The sun beat down on his uncovered head, and he tried not to think of how long it had been since he'd seen Declan.

When it was time, he sent for the Captain. Luca held the small boat steady as Elliot climbed over the *Black Dove's* rail into it. The Captain tossed a copper spear with a wicked barb on the end into the bottom of the boat and settled on the stern thwart, facing Elliot. The crew lowered the boat to the water, and Elliot took up the oars.

Maneuvering the small boat by himself was harder than he'd expected. He pointed the bow toward the cavern, dipped the oars in the water, and pulled the oar handles toward his chest. The boat zigzagged away from the *Black Dove* as he figured out how hard to pull with one oar or the other to steer toward the island. The Captain neither corrected his course nor chastised him for his clumsiness but just stared straight ahead at the cavern's mouth. Elliot focused on the tide, letting the gentle swells carry them toward the island and pulling with the oars to keep the tide from drawing them back.

They made steady, if slow, progress and Elliot held his breath as they eased past the seals lounging on the beach. One especially large seal lifted its head, staring at Elliot with its liquid black eyes. It snorted a short, harsh bark, then yawned hugely, its bright pink tongue glistening wetly in the sun. It swiveled its head to follow their progress past the beach, then turned on its side and closed its eyes again, unthreatened by their presence.

They passed under the overhang, the air cooler in its shade, but the water splashing on his hands and forearms warm. Warmer by far than the Pacific ought to be, nearly as warm as the hot spring near Nance's compound. He kept rowing, checking over his shoulder every few strokes, steering clumsily toward a small arch at the far back wall of the cavern.

The arch led to a narrow tunnel hardly bigger than the boat, and the Captain motioned for Elliot to keep going, then hunkered lower in his seat, elbows braced on his spread knees, hands dangling between them. He gripped the spear in his right hand, knuckles white, the barbed tip pointing between Elliot's legs, a little lower than his crotch. The bow scraped against the cavern wall as Elliot overshot the entrance to the tunnel, and Elliot used the starboard oar to push off, then pulled the port oar into the boat to avoid scraping it on the other side of the narrow passage.

Elliot and the Captain ducked their heads as the boat slid into the tunnel. It was so narrow Elliot could almost reach each side with his arms stretched out. The boat stalled in the middle of the tunnel, white light from the sun shining in at the end they came in from, faint blue and green lights twinkling at the other end. The slick, black tunnel walls closed in, and water dripped from the ceiling into his hair and eyes, the entire weight of the island pressing down on them.

Elliot fumbled with the oars and nearly lost one over the side of the boat. The tunnel was too narrow to use both to row them through, but using one just pushed the boat against the opposite wall, scraping the boat's side and Elliot's head against it.

"Here," grunted the Captain, as he angled the spear up between Elliot's legs. Elliot jerked back to avoid being impaled on the damned thing. "Relax," the Captain said, jabbing the butt end into the ceiling. "This ain't for you." Gripping the spear with both hands, he used it as a lever to propel the boat forward a few feet. Elliot leaned back out of the way as he did it again and again, poling them along the tunnel like some inverse Venetian gondolier.

Finally, they slid out of the tunnel into a huge cathedral-like cavern. Elliot stared, trying to decide what to take in first. The boat bobbed in blue water, gentle waves rippling toward a series of terraced pools surrounded by labyrinthine dry paths. The ceiling was higher at one end, which Elliot realized must be under the spire at the northern tip of the island. Sunlight filtered down in weak shafts from openings in the rock, but most of the light in the cavern came from milky-white lines running along the cavern walls and the edges of the paths. It was beautiful, a glowing, pulsing, calm oasis. All of Elliot's fear and anxiety drained away.

Until a half dozen heads popped above the surface of the water, surrounding the boat, their eyes fixed on Elliot and the Captain, black horizontal pupils in amber irises, water dripping from dark wet hair over pale shoulders.

"I've come for my wife," the Captain growled, half-standing in the middle of the boat behind Elliot.

The women in the water tightened their circle around the boat.

The boat rocked as the Captain shifted position. Elliot saw the tip of the copper spear come into his peripheral vision, but before the Captain could do anything with it, something on his other side heaved and the boat tipped over, dumping him and the Captain into the water.

Water rushed into Elliot's mouth and up his nose as he sank, and he tensed his muscles to keep from shifting. More tentacled limbs than he could count thrashed around him in the churning water, flashing reds and pinks and mother-of-pearl. The Captain kicked his legs and flailed his arms and lost his grip on the copper spear, which arrowed down, point first, landing in a bed of kelp on the floor of the cavern pool. Something shoved the shadow of the overturned boat out of reach.

Elliot sank further, his skin pressing against the inside of his heavy, wet clothes, his boots weighing him down. He held himself as still as possible, afraid that if he kicked his legs too much, they'd unfurl into tentacles and he'd be trapped inside his shifted form. Above him, two of the devilfish women caught the Captain, subdued him easily, and dragged him away. Two more grabbed Elliot, winding their tentacles around his arms, legs, and torso, bearing him to the surface.

When his face broke the surface, Elliot coughed and spit out water. He struggled against the limbs restraining him, until the two around his middle squeezed him hard enough to grind his ribs together. He stopped struggling, and the crushing hold eased. The tentacles holding him shifted to suspend him in the water, head and shoulders above the surface, as if tied to an odd, flexible, malleable chair.

His wet hair was plastered to his face, obscuring his vision, and as soon as he wished he had a hand free so he could brush it out of his eyes, a slim tentacle did it for him. It gently plucked the wet strands off his forehead, smoothed them back, and tucked them behind his ears, then patted his cheek. It even squeezed him lightly with a couple of suction cups, as if in affection, then draped itself across his collarbone.

He couldn't see the Captain or the heads of the devilfish women holding him, but there was a woman perched on a rocky ledge that ringed the pool he was floating in. She looked barely a day older than the last time he'd seen her. She was surrounded by a dozen women in a loose semicircle, sitting or standing on a series of terraced ledges stair-stepping up from the pool to the wall of the cavern. The women ranged in age from late teens to mid-thirties, maybe, but Elliot only had eyes for the woman in the center of the group. Her dark hair drifted softly around her face, and she was looking straight at him with the fond expression she'd worn when she tucked him into bed the last night he'd seen her.

"Mama? Is it really you?"

Marie Bishop smiled sweetly at him.

"Of course, my darling boy. We've been expecting you for some time now."

Elliot twisted in the grip of the tentacles holding him upright, looking around and over his shoulders for the Captain. After all these years of searching, he must be ecstatic to have finally found her. There was no sign of him, though. The devilfish women must have taken him somewhere else, assuming they hadn't drowned him for threatening them with that copper spear.

His mother was still seated on the ledge, watching him, her bare toes peeking from the hem of her gown. He stared at her, a hundred questions swirling through his mind and no idea where to start. He coughed more seawater up, then croaked out the first word that was beating around his brain. "Why?"

His mother cocked her head. "Which why?"

Elliot shivered, even though the water was warm. Which why, indeed? Why had she left him? Why had she stayed away? Why had she taken his fiancée?

She gave him a sympathetic smile.

"It's a lot to take in at once, I know. Let's go someplace more comfortable to talk."

The devilfish women holding him swam to the nearest edge and boosted him up until he could scramble to his hands and knees on a hard ledge, shallow divots pocked in a honeycomb pattern. His mother wound her way down to the level just above him, her gown swishing softly around human legs. She gestured to a path that led to another arched entrance to another tunnel. Elliot got shakily to his feet and followed her.

CHAPTER 34

*E*lliot's boots squelched on the path, leaving damp prints behind him. Water dripped in cold trickles down the back of his neck and off his clothes. Next to him, his mother moved silently on the path, her bare legs flashing through the opening of her robe as she walked.

She tucked her hand into the crook of his elbow and Elliot flinched, trying to pull his arm free. She tightened her grip, keeping close to his side, apparently indifferent to how his drenched clothes were dampening hers.

As they walked along, Elliot sensed other minds surrounding him. Not louder, precisely, but closer and more present in his mind than the way he'd first sensed Celeste. He couldn't distinguish more than a few individuals from a collective, cacophonous whole. He could pick out Celeste, her calm presence like a cool hand on fevered skin, an odd comfort in this strange place. There was an even stronger personality, distinct from the rest, but he couldn't quite put his finger on it.

He glanced sideways at his mother, who was watching him with a slight smile on her lips. The sense of others in his mind receded to a faint hum.

"It takes time to learn how to distinguish individuals," she offered. "The more of us you meet in person, the easier it is to recognize particular thought patterns."

They turned into yet another tunnel that sloped gently down, into the interior of the island, Elliot supposed.

"Why did you leave me?" He hadn't meant to start with such a childish question, but it just came out. His throat still burned from inhaling salt water, which was surely what explained the plaintive crack in his voice.

His mother stopped and turned to face him. "Oh, my darling boy, I never wanted to leave you." She lifted a hand and placed it against Elliot's cheek. He closed his eyes and leaned into the soft warmth of it.

"I stayed as long as I could, dear one. But I had responsibilities here too, and you were old enough to live without me for a time."

Elliot opened his eyes and stared at her. "Mama, I was eight years old! You left without a word. The Captain's spent all these years looking for you, and you've been alive and here this whole time? How could you do that to us?"

She gazed back at him and sighed. "I know, darling. I'd hoped that the Captain would eventually give up searching for me. I see now that was a foolish oversight. I'd forgotten how stubborn the man is." She caressed his cheek once more, then pulled her hand back. "But it was simply too difficult to resist the call. I know you understand what that's like."

Elliot remembered the desperate pull of the tide the first time he shifted. How he needed to be close to the water and how much he tried to stave the shift off by fucking Declan under the pier. He tried not to think about his mother desperately fucking his stepfather the same way, but images of their twining, writhing bodies filled his mind.

"Mama, please," Elliot groaned, turning his face away and trying to clear his thoughts.

His mother smiled slightly. "Yes, well, perhaps I did leave you too long among humans with their Puritan notions of sex and fidelity." She raised an eyebrow at him. "Though it seems you've found an outlet I hadn't expected from a proper Port Townsend gentleman."

Elliot blushed hotly at the notion of his mother reading his thoughts about Declan, but she just laughed lightly and patted his cheek again. "No need to be embarrassed, son. We've all done what we've had to to get through the supermoons." She tucked her arm back under Elliot's elbow.

"Do you remember when you were small and I told you what a special little boy you were?"

"You said that someday you would tell me who my real father was." Elliot remembered how his mother's eyes had shone when she described how beautiful and strong his father was and that someday, Elliot would know him the way she had. She tugged him down the tunnel's passage into an immense cavern. The ceiling opened above it to a pale blue sky. Gentle ripples in the seawater glimmered in the soft light.

Dozens of women were in the cavern, lounging on the sandy beach that sloped into the water on one side of the cavern, swimming lazily in the water, or frolicking in the shallows together, splashing each other and giggling. When he entered the cavern with his mother, a wave of mingled curiosity and hostility flowed into his mind, prickling the back of his neck. Two women who'd been sorting through a large pile of yellow and green seaweed stood and took a few steps toward him. His mother shook her head slightly, and they stopped. And just like that, every woman returned to what she'd been doing before noticing him. The curiosity was still there but the hostility was dimmer, like the whole room had decided they could wait and see what Elliot would do.

His mother reached into a deep recess in the cavern wall and tugged out a folded mass of brownish fabric. She shook out the folds into a simple robe like hers and handed it to Elliot. "Why don't you get out of those wet clothes?"

Elliot fingered the robe's material to avoid looking at her. The last time he'd been unclothed before his mother was after his bath the evening before she left. When he was eight years old. She raised an eyebrow at him, looking disconcertingly like Declan for a minute, wordlessly chastising him for his prudery, then turned her back to him. He turned his back to her and the other women in the cavern and quickly stripped out of his wet clothes and waterlogged boots.

The robe was made of long strips of gold, brown, and yellow shades of kelp sewn together in a subtle chevron pattern. The armholes were a little tight, and the robe stopped at mid-calf on him, but it draped like cool silk against his bare skin. It was big enough that the fronts overlapped to cover him completely and a pair of ties were attached at the back, which he tied in a firm knot just above his navel.

When he turned around, decent and less damp, if not exactly comfortable, Celeste was standing next to his mother. She smiled and came toward him with open arms. Elliot folded her into his arms, and she tucked her head under his chin against his chest.

"You're all right?" he murmured into her hair. It smelled faintly of sea salt and was soft against his lips. He kissed the top of her head before she pulled back and gazed into his face.

"Of course," she replied. "You've known that for a while now."

He cupped her cheek and smiled at her, then stepped back. "I'm glad." He took a deep breath. "Now tell me where the Captain and Declan are."

His mother waved a hand. "They're fine. They're unimportant, though. You're what's important, Elliot. We've been waiting so long for you to come into who you really are."

"And what's that?" Elliot demanded, suddenly tired of her cryptic secrets. His whole life had turned out to be a lie. His devoted mother, who abandoned him to live in a remote lair with God knows how many other unnatural creatures like her, who'd neglected to explain that he would one day turn into a monstrous half-octopus *thing*, who'd married Declan's father to hide her shame but had left him too, left him with an obsession to find her that had permeated every corner of his life. Who'd sent a ship to steal his fiancée from him and damned Declan to continually pick up the pieces of the messes she had made.

As Elliot stood there, anger and frustration filling him, the water washed up and over his feet and ankles. The undertow sucked at the sand beneath his bare feet. His mother and Celeste were now knee-deep in the water, their robes swirling around their legs. As he watched, his mother's legs split into four tentacles, firmly clenched to keep her upright a few moments, and then she gracefully sank down and let the shift finish under the water. The seaweed strips of her gown floated around her tentacles, and she leaned back on her elbows in the water.

Elliot glanced up at the sky. "But it's not a full moon yet." The water was lapping up to his knees now, and Elliot's legs were tingling like they had just before his first shift. The need to let go and change was less desperate this time, the blood throbbing in his veins bearable for now.

"It takes practice," Celeste said. "Some of us never gain the ability to shift when the full moon's not closest to perigee. But your mother has taught many of us how to shift back and forth at will." As if to demonstrate, Celeste's legs also split, though she sank beneath the water before he caught much more than a glimpse of her tentacles.

"I'm sure you'll be able to, as well. You're very like her, you know."

"Can we stop it, then? During the supermoon?" Because if he could stop it from happening, then maybe he could go home. And spend the rest of his life trying to stay away from the sea.

Celeste shook her head. "None of us can stop the change during the supermoon. It won't happen out of the water, but it's deeply unpleasant to stay on land."

"Come into the water, son, and I'll teach you." Elliot's mother beckoned to him, the water cradling her as she leaned back, the tip of one tentacle lazily wiggling just above the surface. Elliot took a few hesitant steps forward, his mind flooding with a yearning to be part of the collective, to be together as one body with many limbs. That strong presence was back in his mind, a dark sentience rising from the deep and pulling him toward it. It was a few moments before he realized something was literally rising from the deep, waves rippling in from far across the wide sea.

Elliot stared over his mother's shoulder. A deep thrumming resonated through the water and in Elliot's body. He could feel his blood stirring in response, his pulse throbbing in the same cycle, ebbing and flowing in tune with his mother, with Celeste, with all the women in the cavern. The barely audible sound echoed off the cavern walls and rolled through the water, slow waves washing over the sand and his skin as he waded closer to its source.

A huge shape swelled from the water, the mantle of a giant octopus, far bigger than any he'd seen before. Its skin was a riot of deep purples and pinks, changing color as it undulated closer to him. His mother and Celeste swam toward it, one on either side of it, and stroked their hands over its mantle and web. The beast rolled lazily over and spread its tentacles wide, like a cat stretching its exposed belly for petting. A giant yellow eye, the size of a dinner plate, opened and closed as the women rubbed themselves all over the creature.

Elliot drifted closer. He wanted to touch it, put his hands on that shimmering skin and see if it felt as soft and velvety as it looked. He remembered how fascinated Declan had been by his own tentacles and realized his cock was hard. The octopus draped a heavy tentacle, thick as a tree trunk, over his mother's and Celeste's shoulders, and reached another out toward him.

"Is this?" he breathed as he reached slowly forward and grazed the tip of a tentacle with his fingers.

"Your real father," his mother confirmed softly, "the origin of the blood we all share."

The tentacle twined around Elliot's hand, delicate and gentle, and a wave of erotic warmth flowed through his nerves from his fingertips to his groin as the suckers gently pulsed against his skin. He glanced at Celeste, and she smiled at him, her cheeks pink and eyes bright. Her dark hair curled damply against her neck, and he almost wanted to kiss her.

She moved toward him, and he might have kissed her if he hadn't felt the desire to do so ratchet up too far, too fast. It wasn't his own desire but that of the collective consciousness in his mind, the sense of someone other than him stoking the feelings he had for Celeste into something different, more urgent. He pulled back and glared at his mother.

"Stop that. However you're doing that, get out of my head."

The giant octopus's tentacle gripped his arm hard enough to cut off the blood flow for a few moments, then let go as his mother smiled at him. "You can't blame me for a little match-making, darling. Don't most mothers look forward to grand-children?"

Elliot kicked backwards, out of reach of the giant octopus. The waves of lust still washed over him, but he kept his fists clenched against his side and his eyes off Celeste. He stared at his mother. "What are you talking about?"

His mother's body undulated against the huge octopus's side, her tentacles winding around his. "You're the first male octopian, Elliot. We're still not sure why, or why you, but we're all looking forward to seeing what your children will be like."

"Children?" Elliot echoed, his mind still sluggish. "Jesus Christ, you mean you want us to…" He trailed off and thought of Declan. "Oh, my God." He realized his mouth was open as he stared at Celeste in horror, then closed it and sat heavily down on the sandy slope at the water's edge. He braced his elbows on his knees and dropped his head into his hands.

Celeste floated next to him and put a gentle hand on his arm. "The moon isn't quite full yet, so we don't have to do anything right now. I know this is a lot to take in, Elliot, but I promise, everything will be all right."

Elliot put his hand atop hers for a moment, then gently lifted it off and pushed himself to his feet.

"You don't understand. I'm not here to stay. I only came for Declan." He splashed clumsily up the beach and out of the water. His legs felt rubbery, like they were half-shifted and could barely hold his weight. And tearing himself farther from his mother and the pull of the giant octopus hurt, the thrumming call reverberating in the cavern pounding in his blood. But not as much as the thought of giving Declan up.

"And how is that going to work, Elliot?" His mother called, still in the water, wrapped in a pair of giant tentacles.

"How is what going to work?" He tried to keep any thoughts of Declan out of his mind so she couldn't see him there.

"The full moon is at perigee at midnight tonight. You won't be able to resist the change, and the rut will come on stronger than you've ever experienced. You need to be here, among your own kind. And we need you. Like any species, we want to breed the best offspring and you, Elliot, you are our future. You'll help us make a whole new generation of octopians."

"No." Elliot shook his head. "Not me. I don't want that."

"Don't want what? A home? A family? Isn't that why you were going to marry Celeste?"

Elliot looked at her. "I have a home," he said quietly. "And a family." With Declan, on the *Black Dove*, or wherever Declan was willing to settle down with him.

His mother sighed. "You are what you are, Elliot. You can't change that."

"Maybe not," Elliot said. "But I don't have to make more of whatever I am. I can't do that. I won't do it."

CHAPTER 35

*I*n the room Celeste had left him in, Declan woke with a start. The lack of natural light in these underground caverns had thrown off his sense of whether it was day or night outside, but he thought it had been a few days since he'd arrived on the *Poulpes*. He'd spent the first day exploring every inch of the room Celeste had put him in, even dipping into the pool in the middle, holding his breath and keeping one hand on the side wall of it while exploring as far as he could before his breath ran out. The room's pool was connected to the channel in the tunnel outside. The dry tunnels and chambers he'd seen seemed to be mirrored in waterways and pools throughout the subterranean island. He'd even ventured from his room and explored as much of the tunnels as he dared, keeping to the shadows along the walls and staying out of sight as much as possible.

Despite Celeste's vague threat, no one interfered with his explorations. He figured they knew he was poking around because he always had the sense that someone or something was watching him from the water, confirmed occasionally by a flash of tentacle just out of sight now and then, but no one came to stop him.

No one came to speak to him, either, not even Celeste. Food appeared at regular intervals just inside his chamber and since it was generally laced with opium—to keep him quiet and pliant, he supposed—he ate sparingly.

He'd mapped out a general sense of the tunnels in his head by now and had found three or four that he was almost certain led outside to the colder waters of the Pacific Ocean. But there was little point in reaching the exit of this labyrinth without a ship he could use to sail away from this place.

Perhaps that was why Celeste and the octopian women didn't stop him from his explorations. Declan's presence here was mere bait to draw Elliot, and they knew Declan wouldn't try leaving until Elliot arrived. Assuming Celeste hadn't been lying when she'd said he was on his way here. He was pretty certain she wasn't lying, though. All the inhabitants of this island seemed to be holding a collective breath, waiting for Elliot.

Whatever woke Declan today, he had the sense that something was finally happening. The waters in the pool in his chamber rippled, and when Declan crossed to where the pool emptied into the channel outside, the waters churned as if several creatures were swimming through it in a great swarm. He walked softly along the tunnel's dry path, in the direction everything seemed to be headed, farther into the depths of the island than he'd yet explored.

The cavern at the end of the tunnel was the largest he'd seen yet, lit by more of the glowing white bioluminescence that lit the rest of the island's living areas. The walls of the cavern rose far overhead, and there was a huge opening in the ceiling.

Declan pressed his back against the wall outside the cavern, out of sight for the moment. He heard voices in conversation echoing faintly around the cavern. Celeste's voice and another feminine voice he vaguely recognized but couldn't place. He couldn't make out the words, but there was another voice in there too. Elliot's voice, deep and lowered in stubborn argument.

Declan let the back of his head fall against the tunnel wall and closed his eyes briefly in gratitude that Elliot was here and at least unharmed enough to be arguing with them.

Before he could decide whether revealing himself would make Elliot's situation better or worse, a large shadow filled the doorway, blocking the light streaming through the cavern's open ceiling. He almost didn't recognize the tall figure as it rushed past the doorway, the hem of a brownish-green robe flapping at bare heels. Declan took four long strides after him and stretched forward to grab at the nearest long—also bare—arm. Elliot spun around, his other arm drawn back for a punch, but Declan grabbed his wrist before he could. He let go of Elliot's arm and clapped a hand over Elliot's mouth.

The arm Declan had hold of dropped like a limp noodle, and Elliot's eyes widened. Declan pursed his lips together in a silent shush and Elliot nodded, so Declan took his hand from Elliot's mouth.

Elliot grabbed him into a bone-crushing embrace. "You're alive," he whispered almost soundlessly against Declan's ear.

"Of course, I'm alive," Declan whispered back. He squeezed Elliot just as hard, then thrust him at arm's length to get a better look at him. "Came to rescue me, Ellie?"

Elliot snorted, then rubbed the back of his hand across his eyes and blinked hard several times. "I suppose I had to, since you got yourself kidnapped. What the hell were you thinking, Declan?"

"Just testing your navigation skills," Declan joked feebly. He cupped Elliot's jaw and ran his thumb across his cheekbone. "You hurt?" he murmured, running his other hand down Elliot's arm and eyeing the rest of him for any visible injury. Elliot had lost his clothes somewhere and had the same kind of silky robe wrapped around him that Celeste had worn, but seemed otherwise unharmed.

Elliot shook his head. "We need to find the Captain and leave here," he said in an urgent low tone. "Now."

"Father brought you here? But his ship was nowhere near ready to sail when—"

Elliot shook his head and looked a little nervous. "We didn't sail here in the *Argonauta*. We, um, came in the *Black Dove*."

Declan stared at him. "And how did you get Joey and Reginald to agree to that?" He shook his head before Elliot could answer. "You know what? Never mind that for now. Let's find Father and get the hell out of here."

Declan turned to lead Elliot down the tunnel he'd just come from when a sudden commotion erupted in the cavern behind them. Elliot's head snapped around to see what caused it, and Declan tugged at Elliot's arm. Whatever was happening in the cavern would be an excellent distraction for their escape. And Elliot followed behind him for a few steps, but then stumbled to a halt and fell to his knees. Declan raced back to him and bent to brace a shoulder underneath him.

"Come on, El, let's go," he urged. Elliot swayed against him, his head cocked, listening for something Declan couldn't hear. A strange look flickered over his face.

"No," he whispered. "He can't. They won't let him." He pushed himself to his feet and raced back to the cavern.

"Son of a bitch," Declan muttered, then sprinted after him. When he stumbled inside, falling against Elliot's suddenly immobilized broad back, he saw his father, clothes disheveled, face red with rage, splashing straight into the water, brandishing a copper harpoon in his hand and stabbing it in the water.

An unearthly collection of screams rent the air in the cavern, and the water was suddenly a maelstrom of flashing tentacles and churning whitecaps. Several devilfish women launched themselves toward his father and pulled him under the surface. A black cloud swirled through the water, obscuring everything from Declan's view.

Declan held his breath as the water slowly calmed, the black cloud gradually dissipating, and a cascade of large ripples rolled away from the spot he'd last seen his father, toward the far side of the cavern. A set of smaller ripples marched toward the beach, and then two devilfish women surfaced, the Captain's body between them. They dragged him into the shallows and dropped him at Marie's feet.

He coughed out a stream of water, and Declan moved from behind Elliot to go to him. Elliot caught his arm, though, and held him back. The copper harpoon washed up a few feet from the devilfish women, apparently forgotten in the melee, and Elliot cast his eyes from Declan to it and back.

Declan gave a tiny nod. If either of them moved for it now, the devilfish women would get there first. But if they could be distracted, maybe he or Elliot could grab it. Declan had no beef with Celeste or Marie, as long as they let him leave here with Elliot. His father could stay here if he wanted, or the devilfish women could keep him prisoner if they preferred—damn the man for charging in like that. But with the hostility directed at him and Elliot, the only other men in a goddamn underground island full of half-octopus women, Declan would feel better with a weapon in his hand. Remembering the strength of Elliot's tentacles, Declan wasn't looking forward to tangling with these women.

"Is he all right?" Elliot called to his mother. He held his hands up in a non-threatening gesture as he took a couple of careful steps toward his mother and Declan's father.

"Stabbed by this damn fool here, but he'll be fine," Marie snapped. She knelt next to the Captain, and he raised a trembling hand to touch her face.

"I meant the Captain," Elliot said.

"I know who you meant," Marie said, as Declan's father shuddered through another set of wracking coughs. "Jack," she said, brushing wet hair back from his face. "What possessed you to do that, you foolish man?"

Declan's father traced his fingers over Marie's face. "I found you," he murmured, his voice thick. "After all this time, I found you. I knew I would someday."

"You found me," Marie agreed calmly. She bent forward and kissed his forehead. When she sat back up, a slim pair of tentacles wrapped around his neck and slowly squeezed.

"I never stopped loving you," he gasped, as his face purpled, eyes bulging and rolling in their sockets.

"I know you didn't, dear one," she replied, stroking his face gently. His legs kicked feebly until Marie wrapped another pair of tentacles around them, and they stilled.

"Mother! Stop!" Elliot shouted, rushing toward her, arms outstretched to pull her off. Declan rushed forward too, only to be pushed back by a sudden wall of women between him and Elliot, Marie and his father. It was already too late. His father's eyes rolled toward Declan as his struggles weakened and stalled, his limbs falling slack when Marie unwound her tentacles from him and flipped his body out of the water and onto the sandy beach. Declan pushed past the women in his way and dropped to his knees next to his father.

"Believe me," Marie said calmly as Declan felt for a pulse under the Captain's swollen jaw. "It's a kindness. I did love him once, you know."

"A kindness?" There had been a number of times Declan had wished his father dead, but he'd never meant it. Certainly not at the hands of his stepmother. Jesus. Her eyes glittered at him as she folded her arms over her bosom, her tentacles neatly tucked underneath her.

"He was going to die from the poison in the ink," she explained. "It just would have taken longer and been much more unpleasant for him."

"We're leaving," Elliot said, his voice flat, with none of the longing or affection that had always been there when he'd talked about his mother. His face was white and his eyes cold. "I won't be what you want." He had the copper harpoon in his hand. He must have scooped it up while Declan's stepmother was strangling his father.

"Try to stop us," he said, then gestured at himself and Declan with the harpoon, its wicked barb glinting in the cavern's soft light, "and I'll kill you myself."

He pivoted on his heel and left the cavern without another word. Marie gazed at Declan for a long moment while he looked back at her.

"The ink isn't the only fluid that's poisonous to humans," Marie said, as Declan turned to follow Elliot. "An octopian's secretions," she paused delicately, "take a toll on humans who have sex with one of us."

Declan stared at her until it dawned on him what she was talking about. She nodded.

"Some last longer than others." She glanced at the Captain's body. "Your father lasted longer than most. I should have left him after Elliot was born, but, as I said, I loved him." She stretched her tentacles to their full length, tucked her robe around them fussily, then held Declan's gaze as the cloth hid her shift back to her human legs.

"It's why we're selective about who we take. Those who can hear the call usually have enough of our blood that they can survive the first shift, but full humans who mate with one of us tend to sicken. The longer an octopian woman and human man stay together, the harder it is for him to resist her, yet I've never heard of it ending well. For him, anyway."

Declan wondered if that was what happened to the sailors on the ship that had brought the compass to Nance. Marie and her devilfish women had fucked them to death? Or some of them, anyway, and the others had fled before meeting the same fate?

Nance had told Declan that the one who gave her the compass had refused to tell her how his fellow crew members had died.

Marie got to her feet and advanced on Declan. He stood his ground next to his father's body, until she stopped only a few inches in front of him. She smiled at him, like she could read his thoughts. "And why should we not defend ourselves against men who intrude on our home and have only one thing in mind?" She patted Declan's cheek, her damp palm leaving a salty film he itched to wipe off. He wouldn't give her the satisfaction, though, and she stepped over his father's body and turned her back on him.

He hesitated to just abandon his father's body here, but he also wasn't sure he could carry it all the way out to the *Black Dove*, even with Elliot's help. Marie was rummaging at a low shelf carved into the wall of the cavern. When she turned to face him, she had a knife in one hand. She drew it along the inside of her other wrist, cutting deeply into her skin.

"What the fuck?"

She waved him off with the hand that held the knife before putting the knife on the shelf and pressing a small bottle to catch the blood flowing from her arm. She flexed her hand open and closed until the bottle filled, then set it down and clumsily tried to wrap a strip of seaweed around her arm.

Declan stepped around his father's body and came toward her. He took her cut arm and finished wrapping it. Despite everything, she'd been the only mother he'd ever known, and he owed her something for raising him while his father was at sea. The seaweed clung to the cut, staunching the blood flow, and Marie nodded her thanks. She capped the bottle firmly with a cork, then handed it to him. He took it and turned the bottle over in his hands.

"What the hell am I supposed to do with this?"

"Find some way to mix it into your blood," she said. "A little at a time, at the new moon."

Declan stared at her, and she shrugged. "Or don't, since the sooner the hold you have on my son's affections ends, the sooner he'll come back here, where he belongs. I don't know if or how long it will work for you, but it seemed to help your father. For a while, at least."

She turned away from him, cleaned the knife off, and tucked it somewhere in the back of the shelf where she'd found the bottle. Declan just stood there for a minute, his mind overloaded with all that had happened in the last half hour. His stepmother wasn't seriously telling him to inject himself with her blood as calmly as she would advise him to take a patent medicine for the measles so he could keep having sex with her son, while Declan's father lay dead only a few feet away.

How could she possibly know about him and Elliot anyway? Declan hardly wanted to ask her, but then Marie lifted an eyebrow with a tiny smirk at him.

"I know far more about my son than you do, my boy, and I see the way you look at him. You are not as hard to read as you think you are."

Declan decided not to dwell on what, exactly, she thought she knew about him and Elliot or ask her any more questions on this subject. Marie glanced at his father's body, then at the door. "Go on now. I won't stop you, but the farther you get from me, the less my persuasive my protection will be to others who are not as forgiving of sailors in our home."

Declan pocketed the small bottle and sent a silent goodbye to his father without looking again at his sprawled body and swollen face, and turned to leave.

"You know that Elliot belongs with us, though," Marie called after him. "The more you hang on to him, the more it will hurt him when he has to let you go. And one way or another, he will have to let you go."

Declan paused, his back to her, then shook his head without answering and left the chamber. He wished he'd caught up with

Elliot and gotten him out of this place before this little family reunion. As painful as her absence had been, Elliot would have been better off with his mother as a childhood memory. But if Elliot was willing to give up whatever plans his mother had for him, then Declan would be there with him. He touched the bottle in his pocket. For however long he had with Elliot.

CHAPTER 36

*E*lliot was halfway down the tunnel before he realized Declan wasn't behind him. When he turned around, Declan was hustling through the cavern's archway, his face pale. He was the most beautiful sight Elliot had ever seen. He wanted to grab Declan and kiss him until neither of them could stand. But more octopians were coming in answer to his mother's call to dispose of the Captain's body, and the last thing Elliot wanted was to be caught here with Declan and the copper harpoon. He could leave it here, but something about it made him want to keep it. At least it was something he could use to defend himself.

He tightened his grip on the harpoon and motioned for Declan to catch up. Declan thankfully didn't ask him what had happened with his mother and Celeste. They ran pell-mell down the tunnels until they reached the opening to the cavern he'd come through with the Captain. Declan halted at the end of the tunnel's dry path. The small boat Elliot had rowed in with the Captain had drifted almost to the tunnel's opening, and Declan stretched his arm out, fingers just barely missing the bow's point.

"No time," Elliot whispered to him. "The others can swim much faster than we can row."

"And? How else are we supposed to get out of here?" Declan snapped in a low voice, gesturing at the expanse of black water between them and the low tunnel Elliot had rowed through with the Captain. "It's not like I have gills or fins here, Elliot."

But Elliot did. Or, if not gills and fins, at least the capability to swim faster than they could row, assuming he could shift this time. The supermoon was at midnight, and the tide was going out now. He could feel it tugging at his blood, under his skin. He'd shifted the night before the supermoon last month, when they were staying with Nance, and again the next day. Could he do it again here? If he did, would he be able to shift back without fucking Declan?

He watched the muscles in Declan's arms and back stretch as Declan reached again for the boat. He couldn't imagine ever passing up the opportunity to fuck Declan, any way or any time he could. But if he left the cavern in his devilfish form, there would be no way of keeping his secret between him and Declan. The rest of the *Black Dove*'s crew were just outside. How would he explain himself to them?

The sense of someone—or several someones—following them increased. They were searching the tunnels for Declan, whose father had tried to harm the giant octopus, and some of them were looking for Elliot himself. His mother might be willing to let him go without fulfilling his destiny, but not all the devilfish women were.

Elliot shrugged out of his robe, tossed it to Declan, and slipped into the water. He ducked under the surface briefly, then popped his head up and slicked back his hair with his hands. Declan, crouched on the path still trying to reach the boat, squinted at Elliot.

"Really? Now?"

Elliot shrugged as much as he could while treading water. "Who was it that said 'time and tide wait for no man'?"

Declan snorted. "Fuck if I know. As long as you can pull us

out of here before your mother comes to fetch her baby boy and locks him up in the nursery."

Elliot threw Declan a dirty look. "She's not who we have to worry about." He swam the short distance to the boat, grabbed on to the starboard gunwale, and kicked strongly with his legs to push the boat closer to Declan. The oars were lost who the hell knew where, so if this didn't work, they'd have to paddle themselves out with their arms. He hung on while Declan settled himself on the stern thwart, facing forward, then drew himself, hand over hand, along the boat until he was even with Declan. A coil of rope lay in the bottom of the boat, and Declan grabbed it and heaved it over the side.

Elliot slipped his arm through the coil. He rested his forehead on the gunwale and closed his eyes. He breathed in and out, slowing his breaths to match the tide. The warm water swirled around his dangling legs, and he let the motion of the water roll through him, slowing his heartbeat, building toward the change.

Declan's warm hand covered one of Elliot's clutching the gunwale, and Elliot turned his hand over and grasped back. The same sexual energy he'd felt in the cavern with the giant octopus flowed through him, but this time, he focused on the hard strength in Declan's grip, the way the calluses on his fingers felt when Declan stroked his cock. He closed his eyes and squeezed Declan's hand as he shifted, then stretched all six lower limbs to their full extension and lifted his head to look up at Declan.

"All right then, Elliot?" Declan asked. He glanced quickly over his shoulder, then ahead to the mouth of the entrance to the front cave. "Ready to go home?"

"God, yes." Elliot draped the rope attached to the bow of the small boat over his right shoulder, letting it play out to its full length as he swam in front of the boat. "Hang on."

Without checking to see whether Declan was ready, Elliot took a deep breath, submerged, and gathered his tentacles in close. He thrust powerfully back, shooting forward through the dark water. The rope slithered over his shoulder until he swam out the slack, then went taut and jerked the boat forward.

Elliot flexed and thrust his limbs behind him, shooting forward, towing the boat at a much faster clip than they could have rowed. Small fish darted out of his way, but he paid little attention to the underwater scenery as he swam faster and faster through the cavern toward the low arch of the entrance. He still had to surface to breathe air occasionally, but he was amazed at how long he could swim under water between breaths.

As he neared the entrance, he hoped Declan had the sense to duck his head and keep his arms inside the boat. Even at low tide, the maximum clearance would be barely enough for a man of Declan's height. Elliot slowed a bit as he swam toward the bright shaft of blue light on the far end of the tunnel entrance and let the ebbing tide help draw the boat through. The taut rope over his shoulder shuddered as the port side scraped along the tunnel's side wall.

Elliot finally glided free of the tunnel's entrance into the pale blue waters surrounding the island and surfaced, taking a deep breath of air. Treading water to keep his head above the surface was much easier with his powerful tentacles, and he swiveled around to check on Declan. One long pull, hand over hand, on the towline, and the boat slid from the tunnel with a wrenching scrape. Declan sat up straight in the boat, craning his neck to catch sight of Elliot.

Elliot ducked under and flicked his limbs to swim back to the boat, coiling the rope as he went. He surfaced starboard-side as Declan was leaning over the port gunwale, pursed his lips, and shot a mouthful of seawater at the back of Declan's head. Declan whipped around and glared at him, running a hand across the back of his neck and wiping the droplets on his trouser leg.

"For fuck's sake, Elliot," Declan muttered. "I couldn't see you anywhere. Are you trying to put me in an early grave?"

Elliot grinned at him. They were out. The oppressive

cacophony of thoughts in his head was calmer, more distant. He could still sense his mother and Celeste, but their presence was faint now, indistinct.

"Are we good?" Declan asked. He plucked a wet strand of Elliot's hair off his forehead, smoothed it back, and tucked it behind Elliot's ear. Elliot smiled at him.

"We're good. They won't leave their home just for us." The most he felt from his mother was a kind of expectant patience, like she would wait as long as it took to see him again. She could wait until this island crumbled into the sea, as far as Elliot was concerned.

"Good." Declan slapped both hands on his thighs. "Okay, then." He shaded his eyes from the sun with one hand and waved the other at something over Elliot's shoulder.

"Although," Elliot started, glancing behind him. The *Black Dove*'s second small gig was scudding toward them, Reginald handling the oars with far more agility than Elliot had managed. And the rest of the crew were lined up along the rail, waiting for their captain to confirm that everything was all right.

Except that everything wasn't all right. Not for Elliot, at least. He'd channeled the sexual energy his mother had warned him about into the swim to get out of the octopians' den, but the adrenaline from that was fading now, and that desperate need he remembered from last month's full moon was building under his skin. It helped that he wasn't trying to resist the shift this time, and the warm seawater caressed his skin as it swirled around and between his tentacles. But when Declan dropped a hand on the top of his head and stroked his hair in a way he probably meant to be reassuring, it was all Elliot could do not to pull him from the boat and take him then and there, in front of the entire damned crew.

"Declan, um…" Elliot murmured. He rested his hot face against the cool side of the boat.

"I know, Elliot." Declan replied. "Hang on a bit longer, all right? I'll handle them."

Elliot let go of the boat and closed his eyes so he wouldn't see how Joey and Reginald, these men who were important to Declan, who Elliot now considered friends, reacted to their first glimpse of him in this form. He let himself float just under the surface of the water and if a tentacle or two flicked into view, well fuck it. He might as well get their disgust out in the open.

"Goddamnit, Reg!" Joey sounded truly shocked, which was a pity. Elliot sighed and didn't bother opening his eyes. "Do you have to be right about every fucking thing? I can't afford to keep betting against you."

"No one forced you to, boy." Reginald sounded more smug than anything else. "Ain't my fault you chose to bet against a man who's seen more things on and under the sea than you have anywheres in your young life." He hocked and spat, a familiar sound from the never-ending plug of chewing tobacco permanently lodged in the bosun's cheek. "'Sides, you think I could make this shit up? Boy has tentacles under there. Like a goddamn devilfish, but he still look like a man up top. Not many's seen somethin' that odd and don't remember it the rest of his cursed days."

And yet, Reginald's tone was matter-of-fact, like he was discussing a never-before-seen fish they'd caught, or the topography of a new island they were sailing past. Not like he thought Elliot was evil or monstrous.

"They're kinda pretty, ain't they? The tentacles, I mean." This was Joey, who sounded less outraged now and more curious. "That one there is the same pink as the roses my mam grows in her garden." Elliot pulled all his tentacles under the surface, out of sight. Comparing his tentacles to Nance's roses was really the last straw, even if the comparison was more or less favorable.

"Knew a whore once who had legs that same pink color,"

Reginald replied. "Dead of the pox next time I come through town, she was."

"If you lazy scabrous bastards are done gawking and gossiping, you might give a report on the state of my ship, for fuck's sake." Declan interrupted mildly, like it was a normal scenario for his crew to be commenting on Elliot's body. Elliot sank beneath the surface so he couldn't hear any more of their chatter. By the time he resurfaced, Reginald was rowing the gig back to the *Black Dove*. He caught sight of Joey peering over his shoulder. Joey gave a little wave, and Elliot waved the tip of a tentacle back, which caused a broad grin to split across Joey's sunburned face. Maybe things would be all right between him and the crew after all.

Declan was leaning back on his hands, braced on the thwart he was sitting on, face upturned to the sun. "There's a cove just past there," he said, gesturing at the end of the overhang that concealed the entrance to the octopians' den. "Out of sight of the ship, but only about a mile south. How quickly do you think you could get us there?"

Elliot didn't bother answering. He just grabbed the towline, dove underwater, and zoomed forward, tugging Declan in the boat behind him.

CHAPTER 37

The cove was a natural pool tucked at the base of a cliff near the southwestern edge of the island. The cliff rose steeply up to the island's flat plateau, and a ring of half-submerged boulders partially enclosed the cove. The boulders protected the cove from large breaking waves and made a secluded lagoon shielded from the *Black Dove*'s view. A series of terraced ledges sloped from the cliff's base into the water like a grand staircase with wide stone steps.

Declan sat on one of the lower steps, bare legs dangling in the water. He'd stripped his clothes off and left them folded in the boat, which was tied loosely to one of the boulders protecting the cove. The water gently lapped against his waist. He tipped his head up and in the slanting rays of the setting sun, his eyes were greener than ever.

"It's beautiful here," he murmured, leaning back on his elbows. "You sure you don't want to stay?"

Elliot swam a little closer and put a hand on Declan's knee. "Not if I can't have you here with me. And after today, I doubt Mother will want you around very much."

"Mmm. Probably not," Declan agreed. He closed his eyes for a minute, then opened them. Fine droplets of water dripped from his slicked-back hair down his forehead and glistened in his eyelashes. "I'm sorry, Elliot."

Elliot blinked at him. "What are you sorry for? I'm the one who should be apologizing to you." He took his hand from Declan's knee, despite wanting to slide it up the length of Declan's thigh. It didn't seem right to just lunge into fucking Declan after everything that had happened in the caves. "It's my fault," he said quietly. "What happened to your father, I mean. I'm so sorry, Declan. I should have..." he trailed off, not sure there was anything he could have done to save the Captain, but feeling like he'd failed the man, and Declan, too.

Declan sighed and looked over Elliot's shoulder out at the horizon. His lips tightened and his jaw clenched, but when he looked back at Elliot, his eyes were clear, no tears clouding the bright green. "It wasn't your fault, Elliot. Stubborn bastard never gave up on finding your mother, and at least he got to see her again."

Declan looked around them, taking in the clear blue water, the rough pink sandstone cliff, and then glanced at Elliot's tentacles floating in the water. "Anyway, I know you didn't want this to happen to you. And finding out your mother is still alive and the leader of a group of..."

"Half-human, half-octopus hybrids descended from an octopus bigger than your ship who seem to mainly want me for stud services to breed more hybrids like me?" Elliot offered, not quite able to look Declan in the eye.

Declan slid down another step and moved closer to Elliot. "Yeah. That," he said. "You sure you wouldn't rather stay? It's not every man who gets to bed a whole harem of women these days. There's a lot you and those gals can get up to, with all your extra limbs and everything."

Elliot looked up at Declan, whose pensive expression had

been replaced with a most lascivious smirk on his face. Elliot snorted. "What, are you jealous?"

Declan winked at him. "Maybe a little." He curled a hand around Elliot's waist and stroked where Elliot's lower back spread into the web connecting his tentacles. "If you'd rather not stay here with your people, though, I'll try to be satisfied with just you."

Elliot surged up over the ledge next to Declan. He propped himself on one arm and cupped Declan's jaw, turning Declan's face toward his.

"You're my family," he murmured. "Your crew are my people. And your ship is your home. Wherever your home is, that's where I want to be." He glanced down at his waist where the skin spread and expanded and disappeared under the water's surface. "Once I get my legs back, I mean."

"About that," Declan said. He rolled onto his side and slid his other arm up Elliot's ribs and across his back. He pulled Elliot closer, until their noses bumped together and Elliot could feel Declan's breath on his cheeks. "Think I remember how to help you with that."

He touched his lips softly to Elliot's, then shoved Elliot onto his back and rolled on top of him. Every cell in Elliot's lower body lit up. Declan squirmed over him, settling his already hard cock into the firm skin under Elliot's web. Elliot spread out underneath him, splayed his upper arms out on the sun-warmed steps, and stretched his lower limbs out under the water.

He resisted the temptation to wrap everything around Declan for just a minute, glorying in the weight pressing down on him, the feel of Declan's warm skin sliding up and down his. Declan rubbed against him a couple more times, then braced his forearms on either side of Elliot's head.

"You won't hold back this time, right?" he asked, rubbing his nose against Elliot's. "Take what you need. I want everything."

Elliot slid both hands up Declan's back, skating over his scars.

"I don't want to hurt you," he murmured, tracing his fingers over the raised and puckered skin.

"You won't," Declan promised. "I trust you." He flicked his tongue at Elliot's lips, then slid it inside, licking into Elliot's mouth. They kissed deeply until Elliot ran out of breath, then Declan trailed a series of wet kisses to Elliot's ear and whispered, "But if you wanted to hurt me a little, I'd probably like it."

Elliot's cock stiffened. He wasn't sure how much longer he could hold out. The longer he waited to be inside Declan, the more he could feel the blood singing in his veins. He let one tentacle wrap around each of Declan's legs and slid them up his calves. The hair on Declan's legs tickled against his suckers, and Declan squirmed a bit when they reached the sensitive smooth skin behind his knees. He gripped tighter, sucking and kneading every inch of Declan's legs as if he were kissing him from heel to knee.

Declan breathed into Elliot's ear, and Elliot shivered. He kissed a line down Elliot's neck, squirmed lower down Elliot's body, and kissed over his collarbone and down the center line between Elliot's pecs. Declan drew his knees up, straddling Elliot's waist and rubbing his cock over the line where Elliot's human skin met his slippery web.

"God," he murmured. "You feel so good. I could do this forever." He slid even lower, almost to where Elliot's web tapered off between two tentacles, and fastened his mouth on Elliot's nipple.

Elliot arched underneath him, and Declan's cock slid underneath the web, bobbing up and tapping the suckers on his sensitive underside. Elliot groaned. He slid the tentacles wrapped around Declan's legs higher and used their strong grip on Declan's thighs to hitch his center closer to Declan's cock. His own cock pressed against Declan's belly, throbbing desperately, but he wanted to prolong this as much as possible.

Elliot contracted around Declan's cock, enfolding it, wet

suckers gripping and squeezing gently. Declan groaned around Elliot's nipple and thrust against him.

He scraped his teeth gently over Elliot's nipple, then sucked it into his mouth and let go. Still rocking into Elliot's tightness, he shifted and took Elliot's other nipple in his mouth. Elliot closed his eyes against the pleasure rippling along his skin. Another nip of Declan's teeth, then Declan sucked deeply and let go. He lifted his head and looked into Elliot's face.

"I want to be inside you," he whispered, his warm breath ghosting over Elliot's stiffened nipple. He pushed against Elliot's center, cock nudging his entrance. "If I belong to you, then you belong to me as well."

Elliot nodded. "Yes," he said hoarsely. "God, yes." He wrapped his arms around Declan and tightened the grip of the tentacles wrapped around Declan's legs. "Let me just—" he flexed his free limbs and slid their bodies down another step into the water, chest deep.

The warm water lapped deliciously against his oversensitive skin, but Declan got a mouthful of salt water, which he spit at Elliot in retaliation. He tucked his head into Elliot's neck and nipped at his skin. "The next time we're doing this, it's going to be in a bed, inside. Preferably in front of a fire."

Elliot chuckled. "Fine," he said, tilting his head to encourage Declan to kiss that particular spot behind his ear. "Seems like you're the one who's gone soft with fine living."

Declan thrust his hips against Elliot. "Nothing soft about me," he murmured. "Which you'll see as soon as you let me in."

Elliot's chuckle trailed to a groan as Declan fastened his teeth on Elliot's earlobe and tugged gently. He squeezed tighter around Declan's cock, his suckers drawing it closer to his entrance. "Please," he murmured, turning his head to seek Declan's mouth.

Declan kissed him, tongue lazily exploring Elliot's mouth as his hand drifted down Elliot's waist, squeezed the top of a tentacle, and slid under his web. His fingers drew delicately along

Elliot's suckers, resisting their tug, circling one, then another, and another, slipping in between them, gathering the slick now pouring from Elliot's skin, coating his hand.

Elliot closed his eyes as Declan's fingers reached his hole and traced softly around it. His whole lower body felt like it was expanding, the gentle waves in the cove pushing Declan closer to him, his hole softening and widening, ready to encompass Declan, draw him inside, and hold him forever.

Declan pushed one finger in, slowly dragged it out, and immediately pushed a second in alongside the first. "Oh," Elliot breathed. He'd no idea this would feel so good.

"Need a little help here, Ellie," Declan murmured. He was sliding three fingers now, in and out of Elliot's hole, and Elliot, lost in the wash of pleasure flowing over him, had relaxed his hold on Declan. He was still resting against Elliot's chest, but he'd slipped down a little, his legs treading water between Elliot's drifting limbs.

"Oh. Right." Elliot opened his eyes, heavy-lidded, to Declan's green ones, crinkled at the edges, laughing indulgently at him. He tightened the tentacles around Declan's legs and boosted him up, closer to Elliot's center, Declan's cock nudging against his underside. Elliot took a deep breath, stretched his web as wide as he could, tugged Declan even closer, then wrapped the edges of his web around Declan's hips.

He brought a free tentacle up the back of Declan's thigh and traced its tip along the crack of Declan's ass. Declan's eyes darkened, his pupils expanding and swallowing the green, his lids slipping closed as Elliot gently probed at Declan's hole, then opening again as he slowly drew his fingers out of Elliot's. He rubbed his cock under Elliot's web, coating it with slick, then guided it to Elliot's hole with one hand, the other moving to cup Elliot's jaw.

"I want to look at you," he said softly. He pushed in slowly, so slowly, and Elliot sighed deeply as he concentrated on opening up. He drew Declan's hips even closer as Declan pushed in, inch by inch. Declan's eyelids fluttered but he kept them open, gazing into Elliot's eyes. It was almost too much, the feeling of expanding to take Declan in, enfolding him and surrounding him. His own cock was leaking and aching, and he couldn't hold back any longer.

He pushed a tentacle a few inches into Declan just as Declan pushed his cock into Elliot. Pulled back as Declan pulled back, then pushed in again, matching him stroke for stroke. Declan was impossibly tight and so hot, but he groaned as Elliot worked his way inside and clenched against him when Elliot pulled back.

When Declan finally seated himself fully inside Elliot, he paused and stroked a thumb over Elliot's cheek. "I love you," he said, so quiet Elliot could barely hear him. "I love everything about you. You've always been mine, and I'll never be anything else but yours. No matter what, it's you and me, together."

Elliot pushed a little deeper into Declan, then swelled his cock, stretching Declan from the inside. "You and me," he agreed, a little breathless with the need to thrust into Declan and let Declan pound into him. "Always."

Declan smiled at him, a heartbreakingly sweet lift of his soft lips, then slid his hand down and gripped Elliot's shoulder. His other hand wrapped around Elliot's waist and then he drew back several inches and thrust back in, hard. Elliot stiffened the limbs suspending them in the water so Declan would have some leverage and then matched Declan's pace with his own tentacle, hammering in and out of Declan.

He knew he'd found Declan's sweet spot when Declan whined suddenly in his throat and stuttered against Elliot. He dragged his tentacle mercilessly over and over that spot and Declan let loose a series of muttered curses, taking a few beats to find his rhythm again.

Elliot let the cove's waves gently buffet them against the side of the pool as the pleasure washed over him. He knew Declan was close and he plumped his tentacle up a little more, stroking over that spot faster and faster, until Declan plunged into him, stalled, and came, shuddering in Elliot's arms, head tucked into Elliot's neck, his cock pulsing inside him.

Elliot's own cock was dripping against Declan's belly. Declan stroked it as he pulled out of Elliot, and Elliot groaned. He slid further down into the water and let Declan straddle him, then pulled the tentacle from Declan's ass and pushed slowly into where Declan was already open and waiting for him. Declan rocked down against him, and then Elliot could no longer hold back. He pulled out halfway, then surged forward, expanding his cock as he thrust, pushing Declan to open up around him, take all of him.

Declan fell forward against his chest, and Elliot wrapped his arms around him. He slid his hands down Declan's back and thighs, hitching his knees higher to spread him open even more. Declan squirmed against him, and Elliot knew he'd found his sweet spot again when Declan tucked his head into Elliot's neck and groaned so long and deep it rattled Elliot's bones. He pulsed his cock against that spot until Declan shuddered and went boneless in Elliot's arms.

Two more deep pulses and Elliot let go, all sensation rushing down his limbs, through his cock, unloading inside Declan in a burst of light and color behind his eyelids. He stilled, letting Declan's tight grip milk the last drops from him and reveling at how every inch of his skin rippled and buzzed with sensation.

They stayed joined for a few moments, breathing heavy against each other. Declan's skin cooled and prickled into goose-bumps again and he shivered. "Fire, man. Inside, in a bed. Next time."

Elliot pulled his softened cock out, and Declan winced. "Next time," he said. "Promise." He let Declan clamber over his body and gave him an extra boost out of the pool. Then he hauled himself up onto the ledge and closed his eyes as his tentacles shifted back to human legs. He still didn't like watching the change and he appreciated that Declan didn't linger to watch either.

When it was finished, he opened his eyes to Declan, fully dressed, standing over him with the seaweed robe his mother had given him draped over an arm. At least it was dry and would cover him until he could dress in the spare clothes he had on the *Black Dove*.

"Come on, Ellie, my boy. Time to go home."

He smiled up at Declan and reached for the robe. Home. Wherever Declan was, that would be home enough for Elliot.

Declan and Elliot's adventures continue in Sea Change, book 2 of the Octopian Shifters series.

AUTHOR'S NOTE

Port Townsend, Washington is a delightful town that was a major economic port on the West Coast during the late nineteenth century. I wrote much of this story while visiting the town and used some of its well-preserved Victorian buildings and atmosphere for inspiration. I've also name-dropped a few prominent Port Townsend or Washington State historical figures, but to my knowledge, none ever saw or knew of any half-human, half-octopus creatures stealing young women from Pacific Northwest coastal towns to increase their population and further their mysterious plans.

The Hall brothers really were ship-builders on Puget Sound, although their foray into building five-masted schooners happened somewhat later than I suggested in Chapter Seven. The largest Pacific Coast schooner built during the age of sail had seven masts and none ever had eight, so the octopians' schooner is a figment of my imagination. The one seven-masted schooner ever built, the *Thomas W. Lawson*, is loosely the inspiration for the octopians' ship.

More information about the sleek and fast fleet of sailing ships that plied the commercial trade on the West Coast is available in Jim Gibbs' excellent book, *Windjammers of the Pacific Rim*. I also toured historic tall ships at Port Townsend's Northwest Marine Center and San Francisco's Maritime Museum. Any errors about ship design or sailing are the fault of this mostly landlubbing author.

And speaking of errors—yes, an octopus has eight arms and zero tentacles (squid have eight arms and two tentacles). But since my devilfish hybrids have human arms too, describing which arms wrapped around which other limbs got confusing. Not to mention that I started writing this story mostly as an excuse to write some tentacle sex and I simply refuse to apologize for finding octopuses sexier than squid. Creative license trumps scientific accuracy, so let's just roll with it, shall we?

This story would not have been written, much less finished, without Carrie and the other women of my Port Townsend writers' retreat gang. Dan and Deb provided plot advice and graciously allowed me to use their eldest's son's name. Gillian, Louis, and JoLinda encouraged me to finish, even after I told them what the story was about. And everything in this story, and my life, works better thanks to the constant support and love of my wife, Emily. My princess, always and forever.

Thanks for reading, friends! If you enjoyed this story, please leave a review!

Join Anna Kensing's Eight Arms Reading Room for community discussions of this book and other queer romance books, exclusive bonus content, and more.

ABOUT THE AUTHOR

Anna Kensing writes steamy contemporary and paranormal historical romances that flirt with taboo. Her characters are often weird, mostly queer, and always get their happily-ever-after. Eventually. She's obsessed with octopuses and the tv show *Supernatural*, listens to classical flute duets and heavy metal music while writing, and loves her scotch and Irish whiskies. When she's not thinking about writing, she's usually thinking about her next tattoo.

Sign up for her newsletter at annakensing.com.

Join Anna Kensing's Eight Arms Reading Room for community discussions of her books and other queer romance books, exclusive bonus content, and more.

ALSO BY ANNA KENSING

Will Do Series

Love doesn't wait for permission

His Dad Will Do

Revenge-banging a cheating ex-boyfriend's dad.

His father is my Daddy now.

My Dead Wife's Ex Will Do

Fifteen years ago, Jason fell into bed with his wife's ex on the night of her funeral. He's avoided Victor ever since.

Now their daughter's destination wedding has them trapped in paradise. Victor is done waiting. Jason is terrified wanting him will cost everything.

But Victor might be worth burning it all down.

This Ride Will Do

I'm tied up in his trunk, headed off the map, and in way over my head. That's what I get for thinking this ride will do...

❧

Hard Chrome

A second chance, small town romance with an age gap between a hot-tempered mechanic and a cool-as-a-cucumber lawyer, competence kink (on both sides), a 1955 Ford Thunderbird in need of restoration, meddling best friends (and former best friends), a cat named Simone and a dog named Giles, at least three hundred houseplants, and car sex.

❧

Octopian Shifters Series

A high seas adventure where Victorian propriety dissolves into a tidal rush of passion at the mercy of the moon and tides. Queer historical paranormal romance—with tentacles!

Devilfish

Sea Change

Tidal Rush